Other Books by Rae D. Magdon

Fur and Fangs

Tengoku

Death Wears Yellow Garters

Amendyr Series
The Second Sister
Wolf's Eyes
The Witch's Daughter
The Mirror's Gaze

And with Michelle Magly

Dark Horizons Series
Dark Horizons
Starless Nights

Lucky 7

Lucky 7

Rae D. Magdon

Desert Palm Press

Lucky 7

By Rae D. Magdon

ISBN (trade): 9781942976769
ISBN (epub): 9781942976776
ISBN (pdf): 9781942976783

Desert Palm Press
1961 Main Street, Suite 220
Watsonville, California 95076
www.desertpalmpress.com

Editor: Cal **Faolan**
Cover Design: Rachel George

Printed in the United States of America
First Edition January 2018

Acknowledgments:

I would like to thank Jocelyne, Mikayla, Shan, Amanda, Selena, Joe, Alejandra, Train, and Anna for reading this manuscript in advance as sensitivity readers, and in some cases, offering Spanish translations. Lucky 7 is a story about what makes us human, and humanity itself is big, beautiful, and diverse. Your perspectives, corrections, and advice were invaluable to achieving the vision I had for this novel. Some of you made a few pointed comments where it counted, and some of you wrote entire essays, but in no way, shape, or form could I have done this without you.

I must also thank my editor, Cal Faolan. You are my best friend, and the godparent of this book. Parts of this story feel like they're as much yours as mine. It has the stamp of your heart all over it, and by that I mean it's funny, clever, emotional, and beautiful (because goodness knows I can't take credit for all that on my own). You are one of the most fantastic editors I have ever worked with, and one of the most fantastic people I know.

part one — elena

.

Monday, 06-07-65 21:53:00

I SLIP INTO THE dimly lit bar, closing the door behind me to shut out the howling wind. I'd been ready for snow in St. Petersburg, but the chill outside is worse than I'd expected—the kind of cold that burrows bone-deep in a matter of seconds and lingers long afterward. My limbs ache with it, and I can't feel my feet inside my boots.

My lungs burn with my first breath of warm air. A cloud of stale cigar smoke clogs my throat, and I muffle a cough with my scarf. The less attention I draw to myself, the better. Corps like Axys Generations have eyes everywhere, even in the underworld.

Once I stop choking, I kick the snow from my boots. Other people haven't been so polite. Chunks of dirty ice are scattered across the floor, crushed by dozens of boot prints. It's a tacit warning to outsiders: *Don't come here.* A year ago, I wouldn't have.

I try to stay invisible as I pick my way through the tables, but I still feel naked. Vulnerable. I always do in meatspace, without my cloaking programs or my shield. The pistol at my hip is cheap, and I'm a barely passable shot. All my money's in the jack behind my ear, and for now, I'm all tapped out.

Most of the bar's patrons are bundled up, their bulky coats concealing custom mods and weapons. They're either old or old before their time, professionals who've seen some serious shit. If they notice me, they don't react. Everyone here knows the freelancer's code: mind your own fucking business.

When I arrive at the dark corner where Jento told me to wait, someone is already sitting there. That someone is a woman, although she's so tall it takes a second for me to tell. Her dark brown skin looks almost blue beneath the flickering lights. Her face is striking—square jaw, high cheekbones, blunt nose. Her tight cornrows barely peek out from under her hood. Possibly the only thing soft about her is her lips. They're full and round, but when she sees me, they tighten into a thin line.

As I get closer, I notice a scar running beneath the woman's chin. It

1

slices across the front and wraps all the way around her throat. The fact that she survived an attack like that tells me a lot about what kind of person she is. I shudder. She's got plenty of stud swagger, but the sex appeal is spoiled because she looks too fucking dangerous. A little danger is sexy. She looks like death decided it wanted a body one day.

The woman settles back in her seat. While I've been gawking, she's been sizing me up. The silence makes my skin crawl, so I blurt out the first thing I can think of. "Are you the handler Jento told me—"

She shakes her head. My jaw snaps shut.

"Sit."

It's an order. Her low voice makes my heart thud. My thighs twitch with the urge to run. Instead, I sit.

"I didn't know what to expect when Jento told me he was sending someone, but you aren't it," the handler says after a while. She leans forward, bracing her arms on the table.

"You aren't what I was expecting either," I say before I can stop myself. My mouth usually drives the shuttle when I'm scared.

The handler's expression doesn't change. "What were you expecting?"

"An actual name, maybe?" Jento had warned me about this contact beforehand, but he hadn't given a name. According to him, she's dangerous, ruthless, and impossible to kill. That's why I'm here looking for her. I need a little immortality myself.

"Were you expecting someone beyond human?" she asks.

"I don't care who or what you are as long as you're interested in credits."

"I don't have much use for credits." The handler leans back in her chair, resting her hands in her lap. I wonder how many guns are strapped to the lower half of her body beneath the table. Or maybe something fancier. Some of the best handlers have so many mods they're almost cyborgs, and she looks experienced. One of the first things you learn in this business is how to separate the pros from the rookies at a glance. Unfortunately, pros come at a price.

"I can offer you twenty for protection. I need to disappear."

"Twenty thousand? If you were offering twenty million, maybe. Otherwise, don't waste my time."

My heart sinks. "Give me a few days. I can try and get more. My last op went bad and the rest of my crew died."

She doesn't seem impressed. "Your fault?"

Logically, I know the clusterfuck that killed the rest of the crew wasn't on me, but the churning of my gut and the pressure squeezing my chest say otherwise. "Our client lied about the op. I jacked out right before the hotel blew up."

It all comes rushing back again in a blur. Mumbai. Screams, sirens, a building consumed by flames. Shattered glass, the lurching sensation of a fall. Smoke everywhere. That smell stays for days—in your throat, in your hair, on your clothes. The hazy grey cigar clouds around the other tables don't help my nerves. The handler's still waiting.

"Everyone else was dead and I knew I'd be next. Jento told me you'd be interested."

"Jento told you wrong." She stands up, barely sparing me a glance. "I have my own shit to take care of."

I leap out of my chair, my hand shooting out to clutch her sleeve without my permission. "If I don't do something, AxysGen's gonna kill me!"

The handler jerks her arm free, but doesn't head for the door. Her dark brown eyes narrow to cold slits. She looks like she's staring at me through the scope of a pulse rifle. All she says is, "Axys Generations?" Suddenly, I have her undivided attention.

"My crew's last op." It takes a conscious effort to keep my voice steady. Thinking about what happened still makes my pulse race sickeningly fast. "Someone hired us to break into a local AxysGen facility and swipe a databox. 'All low security,' he said. 'No need to decrypt it, just walk out with the whole thing.' I had to jack in and redirect the security feeds while our cloak and our grunt walked through the front door. Fucking idiot."

"You, or your fixer?"

Me, I don't say aloud. My gut had told me the op was sketchy back then. I hadn't listened.

The handler folds her arms across her chest, fingers drumming above her elbows. "Let me guess. Their intranet system was bugged. Another jacker tried to melt you. Your grunt got smeared. Your cloak got stabbed in the back. Someone tricked your wrench and rigged the building you were working out of to explode."

It's true. Every word. "How did you know?"

"I know my business, and I've had run-ins with Axys Generations before. The straight crews they hire to prevent freelancers from stealing their products are top notch. So, how'd you get out in time?"

I almost hadn't, but she doesn't have to know that. "I know my business, too. I'm fast. Faster than any corp jacker. And...I trawled a bit of AxysGen's source code and used it to modify my programs. Their security systems let me jack in like a regular cog."

Usually people flip their shit when I tell them about my secret sauce, but the handler just looks skeptical. "Really."

"Yeah. It saved my ass in there, and it's kept me a step ahead so far."

There's an uncomfortable pause. "I've changed my mind," the handler says at last. "You ride with my crew, I'll help you out. Is your gear still good?"

I'm suspicious of the handler's sudden change of heart, but a new crew means a new chance. Alone, I won't survive the month. With an experienced team watching my back, I might get to keep breathing. "I'm running the latest version of Dendryte Silver and a Retinal Visual Interface System." I decide not to add that my VIS-R is a few months out of date. When you're short on credits, you have to make hard choices about which hardware to upgrade. "Point me at an entry port, and I'll get you where you want to go."

"Then we're in business." The handler heads toward the door with brisk strides. I trot to keep up, nearly slipping on the wet floor. Those long legs of hers are going to be a pain, I can already tell.

"Wait." I hurry to catch up. "At least give me a name first. If I'm working for you, I need something to call you. Here, I'll go first: Elena Nevares."

She stops with her hand on the door. "Jento didn't tell you who you were dealing with, did he?"

I shrug. There's a reason the Spanish term for fixer is *cabrón*—literally, asshole. Need some quick money? Go visit the local asshole. Every crew relies on fixers to connect with paying clients, some more than others. Every crew also wishes they didn't have to. "You know fixers. They always keep the important details back until you pay them. You can't trust them half the time."

"Much less than half. Here's what he didn't tell you. They call me the Wolf of the Kremlin. Stupid name, but reputation gets you hired."

I shiver. I know that name. Everyone in the business does. I also know the Wolf of the Kremlin is supposed to be dead.

"If you think it's so stupid, tell me your real name."

Her eyes dig into me like teeth and refuse to let go. "For now, you can call me Sasha."

Tuesday, 06-08-65 00:23:03

"SO WHERE ARE WE headed?"

Sasha doesn't spare me a glance from the pilot's seat of the shuttle—a Series 3 Eagle, couple of years old but armed like a gunship and built like a flying tank. Her gaze stays locked on the terrain ahead as she jerks up on the controls. The shuttle's propulsion system flares, vaulting us over a mound of snow. We land hard, stopping a few inches above the icy ground as the hoverguard kicks in.

"Away from St. Petersburg."

"Can you be more specific?" In the few hours since we've left the city, Sasha has gone from terrifying me to pissing me off. Her answers aren't really answers. I get why she likes Siberia: it's the only thing colder than her.

"No."

"At least tell me how much longer it's going to be?"

Sasha doesn't answer me directly. Instead, she sighs deeply and speaks to the shuttle's dashboard. "Val, what's our ETA?"

A warm female voice answers from the Eagle's speakers. "Your destination is four hundred and seventeen kilometers away. Estimated time of arrival, twenty-one minutes."

I look at Sasha in surprise. "Your shuttle has an AI?"

"Yeah," Sasha says, without looking at me. "Custom-coded. We call her Val."

"Val," I repeat to myself.

Some professional jackers use AIs to enhance their programs, but I'm not a fan. Normal programs complete the function they were designed for, exactly the way they're told to. But AIs? They learn. They modify their own coding to be more efficient, but they don't have emotions or morals or common sense to keep them in check. I've heard stories of AI-enhanced targeting systems unable to discriminate between friendly jackers and enemies because of self-modifications gone wrong, and AI-enhanced shields getting so overprotective that they stop other programs from running. I decided early on never to trust something that thinks for itself, if I can't see where it keeps its brain.

"Is that a nickname you gave it, or what? I haven't heard of an AI series named Val before."

"I said she was custom coded," Sasha repeats, obviously irritated. "You think I'd trust some corp model to help pilot my bird?"

I hold up both hands in a gesture of acceptance. "Hey, I don't blame you. I don't use AIs either." Sasha gives me a sidelong look, and my face heats up. "Not because I'm a rookie or anything. My programs are top of the line. I just don't always trust AIs."

Sasha's silence is an obvious question...or maybe I'm too nervous to shut up.

"With standard software, you know everything about the tool you're using," I explain. "They do exactly what they're supposed to do and nothing extra. When I'm running ops, I like to know exactly what result I'm gonna get every time I run a program. Too many unknowns can get you killed."

That answer seems to satisfy Sasha. Her shoulders relax, and she pulls her hood off before focusing back on the empty tundra. Her face is annoyingly attractive; some people pay money for a jawline that fine. Pity it's attached to someone so obnoxious. As I follow that jawline, I notice a port glinting behind her ear. That's not unusual. Plenty of handlers have basic jacking skills. *But if she's any good, why use me? Just for the code I trawled, or something else?*

I look away from her and out the window, watching streaks of white whip by. The landscape is the definition of monotonous until Sasha sends us flying from another snowdrift. "*Dios,* I literally just said I didn't want to get killed! You didn't even turn the stabilizers on."

"Actually, I did."

"Then you're just a terrible driver. Maybe you *should* use that AI of yours."

Sasha finally looks at me. That blank stare of hers is almost worse than anger. "I'm surprised no one in that bar pulled a gun on you, the way you run your mouth."

"Jackers have to be impulsive. Comes with the job. When you're plugged in, it's move or die."

Sasha resumes staring at the endless stretch of white, but her gaze seems more distant than that. "You aren't the first jacker I've met who describes it that way. She said it was physical, like running or dancing. Hard to believe when I watched her sit there and stare at the screen."

6

"Who's 'she?' Your crew's previous jacker?"

Sasha doesn't answer. Her silence makes me itchy, but I get the feeling that if I ask again, it won't end well. I circle back to my first question. "At least tell me where we're going. Some kind of safe house?"

"No." The Eagle vaults over another frost heave, soaring like its namesake before its skimmers stop us inches short of the ice. "Here's the deal, Nevares. I might be dead to most people, but AxysGen has a hit out on me too. If we want to live, we need to erase ourselves from their databases. For that, we need my crew."

At first, I think she's joking, but Sasha doesn't seem like the joking type. Snooping around in AxysGen's localized security systems is one thing. Modifying their core databases is different. Impossible is a generous word for it. Crazy is a better one.

"Pinche loca."

Sasha gives me the side-eye. "You better be talking about yourself, Nevares. This is your only option."

She's not wrong. My current situation is already bleak. I tried going off the grid in Mexico, but AxysGen was banging down my door within forty-eight hours. They'll keep sending people as long as I'm in their system, and I can't keep running forever.

"Guess I'm in. So, why's your crew out in the middle of Siberia?"

"Not my whole crew. Just two." Sasha eases up on the propulsion, bringing us into a glide. A dark shape looms beyond the next snowy hill, growing larger and larger. "We're here. You have any mods aside from your implant?"

I rub nervously behind my ear where my jack is. I can do wireless with my hand too—all jackers with professional gear Bronze and better can—but there's a delay: a tenth of a second. In cyberspace, that counts. "Never needed them."

"Weapons?"

"Only this." I unclip my pistol from my hip, an S3 Hurricane without any extras.

"That won't work. Unfasten your harness and check the back."

The Eagle chooses that moment to jolt. I give Sasha an exasperated look. "You want me to undo my harness? With the way you handle your bird, you'll be doing AxysGen's job for them."

Sasha's fingers clench tight around the wheel. "We're about to walk into a serious firefight. If you don't upgrade, crashing will be the least of your worries."

"Fine." I unbuckle my harness and slide out of my seat. I have to clutch the headrest as the Eagle rocks around me, but I clamber into the back of the shuttle without cracking my skull. Benches line both sides of the shuttle's rear, wide enough to seat at least four more people, but it's the back wall that grabs my attention. An entire armory is bolted to the top half: full automatics, pulse rifles, and short-range pistols. I'm not a gun girl, but it's pretty impressive shit.

"¡Qué chingados! You're prepared for a war."

"Only if we're lucky. Pick something out."

I guide myself to the wall of guns with one hand on the bench. I need something lightweight, but with enough firepower to pierce shields and stop an oncoming enemy with a few shots. A medium-sized pistol catches my eye almost immediately. From my limited knowledge, it looks like what I want. LightningBolt v.6 is stamped across the grip in blocky golden lettering.

"Perfect." I test the grip in my hand, aiming at the wall. "It'd be nice to fire a few rounds so I can get a feel for the recoil, but looking at it..."

Sasha glances back to see what I've picked. "Good choice. That should keep you breathing a little longer."

I head back to the copilot's seat, pistol in hand. "Only a little longer?"

"As long as you're riding with my crew, Nevares, we'll keep you alive. Can't make any promises after that."

"Fine with me. Once I'm off AxysGen's shit list, I'm going straight back to Mexico."

"Home?"

I'm surprised Sasha even cares enough to ask. "Was. I have two kid brothers. Jacobo and Mateo. They need to eat and study for their APS, and the freelance jobs that pay are international."

Sasha doesn't look surprised, and she shouldn't be. It's an average story. You're either born into a corp dynasty family, ace the Aptitude and Proficiency Survey, or work as a cog in the corp machine. Even the cogs are lucky, though, because most people don't have jobs at all. The PBIs—partial basic incomes, or peebees—the corps give out to keep the unwashed masses from revolting is hardly enough to keep food on the table—and everyone knows they could take it away with a snap of their fingers the moment anyone dares to ask for more. It's a rigged system, but saying that too loudly could mean the difference between eating table scraps and starving to death.

Outside the window, the dark blotch in the distance resolves itself into a large square building, maybe three stories. Black columns of smoke rise above a large sign: *Axys Generations Research & Biomedical Processing Facility.*

"That it up ahead?"

"Yes," says Sasha.

"Give me the rundown. Who are we after? What type of security are we up against? How do we get inside?"

"Doc and Rock, I don't know, and buckle up."

"What?"

Val's pleasant voice fills the shuttle again before Sasha can answer. "Collision will occur in approximately fifteen seconds. Please fasten your harness and brace for impact."

Her placid tone is the opposite of calming. I fasten my harness just in time to see a large grey wall hurtling toward us. Sasha fires the front guns, and the wall explodes in fire and rubble. Chunks of concrete and steel rain down on top of the Eagle as we lurch through the opening. The shuttle shakes hard, red lights flashing from its dashboard, and sirens start to shriek outside.

I panic. My eyes are open, but I don't see the Eagle anymore. I'm back at the hotel in Mumbai, choking on smoke, fighting to get free of it, falling...

A hand reaches over to hit my chest release. It's Sasha, sitting calmly in her own seat, like the shuttle isn't tilted sideways and half-buried in a pile of rubble.

Once I can breathe, I glare at her. *"¡Hija de la chingada!* Seriously, what the fuck?"

"We had the heat shields up." Sasha presses a button on the dashboard, and the red lights stop flashing. Another button releases the seals on the doors. As I haul myself out, water spatters onto my face from above.

"You set off the sprinkler system. We're gonna die of hypothermia if we get out of here."

"Be quiet and follow me." Sasha climbs out behind me, strapping her pulse rifle across her back. "We don't have much time."

"But—"

"For fuck's sake, just do what she says," says someone who definitely isn't Sasha.

I whirl around. A short white kid is standing a few feet away from the wreck, glaring at Sasha impatiently through the glowing orange stripe of a VIS-R. I activate my own, and it adjusts the lighting so I can get a better look. Her stringy brown hair is matted down by the water raining down from the ceiling and she's dressed in clothes big enough to swallow her. She looks the same age as Jacobo, maybe eleven or twelve.

"Come on," the girl insists. "Rock's not gonna last much longer."

"What were you thinking, Doc?" Sasha's tone is hot with anger as she talks to the kid, but there's actual concern on her face instead of icy blankness. I know that look. This kid is hers somehow—her responsibility. "I told you to stick to surveillance and wait for me to find us a jacker."

"He's on borrowed time already," the kid—Doc, I guess—protests. "And you were taking forever."

"We'll find him," Sasha says, switching from anger to determination. "Go get the rest of your gear from the back."

Doc runs for the Eagle and rips open the nearest door.

I stare at Sasha in disbelief. "She's like twelve years old! What's a kid doing on your crew?"

"She's here because she's the best medical officer I've ever had. And she's probably a better shot than you, Nevares."

"It's not about that."

Doc runs back with a pistol in her hand. "Unless you two wanna stick around and wait for the guards, we need to move."

Tuesday, 06-08-65 00:54:34

WE MOVE, BUT NOT fast enough. A group of guards collides with us as we run through the first doorway. I aim my new pistol at one of them, but I'm unfamiliar with the location of the safety, and when I try to fire the gun just clicks. My reaction times are lightning fast on the extranet, but not so much in meatspace.

While I fumble, Sasha dispatches him with her pulse rifle. The guard's groan crackles through his helmet speakers as he slumps to the floor with a smoking hole in his chest. The other two guards raise their weapons, and I freeze. I've got nothing: no cloak, no shield, no protection.

"Duck!"

Sasha drags me to the ground. Something flies over my head from behind, glowing blue dots about the size of a thumbnail that stick to the guards' armor. They drop their guns, tearing at the tiny orbs with their gloves. I cover my head with my arms and close my eyes, unwilling to watch what happens next.

Boom!

An explosion shakes the hallway, followed by a series of gut-churning splats. My body seizes up, and I have to push back against an instinctive tide of fear. Ugh. I hate biogrenades. It's lucky I'm not on this weird kid's bad side.

Sasha slaps the middle of my back, urging me to move. "Get up, Nevares. We can't stay here."

I wrench my eyes open. The walls in front of me are smeared with red. I try to avoid staring at the chunks on the floor, but I can't ignore them completely. The back of my throat twitches in disgust as I turn away from the three corpses—if the two exploded bodies can even be called corpses.

Sasha brushes straight past me. "Leave the grenades to Cherry next time, okay, Doc? I don't want you blowing up Nevares."

Doc ignores her. The kid's on a mission, no detours allowed. "I tracked Rock to the west side of this floor before you got here. He can't wait much longer."

Concern flashes across Sasha's face. She speeds up, leaving me to stumble after her. Doc is surprisingly fast on her feet, moving with the speed of desperation. We turn down another hallway, following the flashing red lights. The sirens wail louder as we stop at the next corner.

"Get ready," Sasha orders, keeping her back to the wall. "Nevares, stay in cover when you're not shooting, and try to keep out of Doc's way."

Sasha doesn't need to tell me twice. Doc still has a belt full of biogrenades, and the look in her eyes is terrifying. This time, we hear the crackling of comm units before we reach the next hallway, and we get the jump on the guards instead of the other way around. Sasha leaps around the corner, taking out the first one with a chest shot before the others even realize they're under attack. One aims at her, but she dodges, knocking his arm aside and rolling under. She rams her shoulder into his stomach, sending him off balance. Before he can recover, she fires her rifle straight into his helmet.

A third guard takes aim, and this time I finally remember how a trigger works. I extend my arm and squeeze. The guard jolts with the force of the round, crumpling to the floor. Either his armor's crap, or my LightningBolt packs a wallop.

"Glad to see you don't always freeze up in meatspace." Sasha steps over the bodies at her feet, avoiding the blood on the floor. I try not to breathe in too deep as I follow her, but a tinge of copper has joined the smell of recycled air.

"Yeah, well..."

Sasha turns. "Doc? Wait, Doc!"

I catch a glimpse of Doc near the end of the hall. A door slides open, and she sprints ahead without waiting for us. Sasha takes off after her, and I bring up the rear...again.

I flick off my pistol's safety, but there's no need. The only guard in the room is already flat on his back with his helmet off. Doc is kneeling over him, holding a stunner under his chin. "Tell me where my brother is, or I'll fry your fucking brain until it leaks out your ears."

Everything clicks. No wonder Doc wants to find Rock so bad. They're siblings. *Dios*, Doc and Rock. Bet that got them teased in school.

The guard's eyes roll back and forth in his head, searching for an escape. There is none. Sasha deliberately turns to watch the door. I'll definitely be asking her some questions about this later. What guardian lets a kid do this kind of work? I risk my life daily to keep my *hermanitos* out of it. I try to step between Doc and the guard, but he cracks before I can intervene.

"Down the hall and to your right. Room 307. He's—*ahh!*"

There's a sickening crunch, but at least it isn't the sound of a body frying. Doc hops back to her feet, but the guard stays sprawled on the floor, a river of red pouring down his face. "I only broke his nose," Doc says when she notices me staring. She nudges his head with her foot so the blood spills onto the floor instead of pooling in his mouth. "He'll wake up. Probably."

The three of us head for the large steel door at the end of the hall. It's heavily reinforced. At a glance, I doubt anything short of a bomb can crack it—but there's also a glowing orange access port beside the frame. I square my shoulders. This is something I can handle. "I'll jack in and get the door open."

Doc doesn't hear me. She slams both hands into the door, resting her forehead against the metal. "Rock! Rock, are you in there? It's me, open the door!"

Sasha lowers her rifle and puts a hand on Doc's shoulder. "We don't know what they've done to him, Doc. Let our jacker go in. It's why I brought her."

Doc's fists clench, but she steps away and nods. She remains silent, trembling with anger and impatience. That's probably the best 'go ahead' I'm going to get. There's no access cable, so wireless will have to do. I touch my finger to the port.

network: ag 61049 . 991147
Connection established
welcome: user escudoespiga

My eyes snap open. I'm standing in a dim grey hallway, not unlike the corridors of the research facility. I let out a breath. Luckily, my brain's decided to interpret the building's intranet security system in a familiar way. There are no doors or windows, only smooth walls. The sirens are absent, and no one else is nearby.

I head down the hall, searching for an entrance. At first there's nothing distinctive, only grey, grey, and more grey. I select the scanning program on my VIS-R's toolbar by looking at its icon, a blue square with concentric white circles in the shape of a bullseye. I've got room for eight programs on my main dash, plus several others downloaded, but I keep the ones I use most often the most accessible. When I activate the scanner, a blue crosshatch pattern appears on the grey walls, and a door melts out of the sameness, just as huge and intimidating as the one I left behind in the physical world.

Facilísimo.

I curl my right hand into a fist and select another program: a silver circle with nine dark grey studs. A solid grip presses into my palm as a shield extends across my forearm. I aim the vertical rows of spikes on its surface at the door. Most jackers rely on their shield programs for protection, but I've turned mine into a battering ram.

Elbow-first, I throw my entire weight at the door. Red light pours through the cracks spiderwebbing across its surface, and then, after a moment of stillness, the dull metal shatters completely. I dig my feet in, ducking behind my shield. When I look up, there's a diamond-shaped hole in the middle of the door, and the light has turned from red to green.

logging off network
disconnection complete

I slam back into my body. Even though I'm used to it, the return to meatspace is always jarring. I pull my hand away from the port, shaking the tingle from my arm. "Open sesame."

"Move!" Doc shoves past me and into the room without a second glance.

"You're welcome," I mutter.

Sasha heads in after Doc, but pauses to give me a look. She doesn't smile or nod, but I can tell I've gained at least a sliver of her approval.

Tuesday, 06-08-65 00:58:13

I GRIP MY PISTOL tight as I enter the room. No, not a room—a cell. The weak light from the open door is enough to flood the small space. Most of it is filled with a huge, shadowy shape, and it takes me several seconds to realize that the dark mass is moving. I step back.

"Rock?" Doc is standing beside the trembling mountain, pressing her hands against its sides. "Rock, it's me. You have to get up."

I stare at the mass in shock. The mountain is actually a man's shoulders, and the movement is his breathing. He's slumped over on the floor, but he has to be two and a half meters tall. His clothes are in tatters, and so are patches of his bruised skin. I'm pretty sure I can see cables twisting through some of the ripped flesh. Two yellow lights shine from his face, and I realize they're his eyes. This giant has been modded to hell and back. I can't tell how much of him is still human.

My first thought is that AxysGen must've done this. Only they could be that fucked up, stealing some kid's brother and turning him into a cyborg. But Doc doesn't seem intimidated or even surprised by his appearance. She keeps on examining him.

"Rock, can you hear me?"

The mound of muscle twitches, but doesn't speak. His eyes flicker in and out of focus. Doc picks up one of his enormous hands and spreads his fingers, choosing one and pressing down on the nail bed. When he doesn't respond, she lets out a choked sob of frustration, looking back at the two of us. "This is bad, Sasha. He's not reacting to pain stimuli and he's hardly conscious. We have to get him out of here."

"If you've got ideas, tell me." Sasha's words are terse, but her stony expression has some softness as she glances between Doc and the giant. "He's too heavy to move, even with all three of us working together."

"NervPacs?" I suggest. "We've got some of those, right? Maybe if we put one on, he'll come to."

"No." Doc moves protectively in front of him, but her slender body barely covers a sliver of his bulk. "He's got built-in mods to repair his

15

body. If we flood him with a NervPac, it could be too much."

Sasha crouches, touching Doc's shoulder and fixing the kid with a sympathetic stare. "If this was another patient with Rock's mods, would you say the same thing? Or would you take the risk to get them out of here?"

Doc's face is tortured. She bites her lip, brushing off Sasha's hand and turning to stare at Rock. His slow breathing continues, but aside from his glowing eyes, he doesn't seem alert enough to notice us. Eventually, Doc nods. "Fine, but I'm doing it. And I'm lowering the dose."

"Try and get him moving in under five," Sasha says.

Doc reaches into a pocket in her fatigues and withdraws a circular silver patch. She rips the seal open, tilts Rock's head to the side, and slaps the NervPac over his jugular. His body twitches as soon as it makes contact. Doc remains completely calm. Her mouth forms numbers, counting down the seconds as Rock's muscles start to spasm. As soon as she hits ten, she rips the patch off.

Rock bolts upright, filling the entire cell. I barely manage to scramble back through the door before he comes bursting out, taking a good chunk of the wall with him. Rubble and dust sprinkle the ground at his feet, but he doesn't seem to notice. He whips around in a frantic circle. Though his eyes are no longer yellow, they're wide with terror.

"Rock!"

Rock stiffens at first, then a smile spreads across his face. His huge shoulders slump with relief as he sinks to his knees.

Doc rushes him, flinging her arms around his neck. "Are you okay?"

Rock doesn't answer with words. He merely shakes his head yes, even though it's obviously a lie. His mods are already starting to close the holes in his body, but there's bruising and dried blood all over his skin. He puts his giant hand on top of Doc's head until she stops squeezing him. Once Doc steps back, Rock seems to notice she isn't alone. His eyes rest briefly on Sasha before he fixes me with a curious look. I shudder. It's not aggressive, but definitely wary.

"Glad to have you back, Rock," Sasha says with a curt nod. Rock nods in return. Without the glow of his darkvision mods, his eyes are a piercing blue like his sister's.

Sasha makes the briefest introductions possible. "Rock, Elena Nevares. New jacker. Nevares, this is Doc and her brother Rock. My M.O. and my grunt."

Rock nods again. I'm not sure whether he can't speak, or he just

16

doesn't want to. He stands up, and then he and Doc head for the door, her at a run, him at a slow lumber.

"Do we have a weapon for him?" I ask Sasha as we follow them.

Sasha snorts. "You kidding me? Rock *is* a weapon."

I'm treated to a demonstration as soon as we leave the room. Another group of guards is waiting for us in the hall, weapons drawn. I reach for my LightningBolt, but I don't need it. Before they can fire, Rock charges. One swing of his fist sends the first guard flying. A jab of his elbow knocks two others into a tangle on the ground. The movement is so quick that I barely catch it. Rock's as fast as he is huge.

A fourth guard manages to get off a shot, but the pulse bounces harmlessly off Rock's chest. He doesn't even flinch as he hauls the man over his head and brings him crashing to the floor. All that's left is a red puddle in a big dent.

"No mames." I shake my head in disbelief, but there isn't time to stare. Sasha, Doc, and Rock are already heading back toward the shuttle. The sirens are still wailing, but there's no more trouble between us and the crash site. I cup my hand over my eyes, blocking the flurries of snow that blow in through the open wall. What I see isn't good. The Eagle's nose is still jammed into a pile of rubble, tilting the whole shuttle forward.

"How do we get out of here?" I ask.

Sasha takes in the damage. "It's just a few dents. She should still fly once we pull her out."

"Pull her out? The ship's half-buried!"

"Not a problem," Doc says. "Rock, give us a lift?"

Rock considers the Eagle for several moments before bracing his feet apart and hunching forward to slide his hands under the metal frame. My eyes widen. Lifting a man is one thing. Moving a Series 3 Eagle is completely different.

"He's not actually gonna," I mutter in disbelief.

Doc grins. "Watch."

Rock's arms bunch, flexing with effort. I hear the whir of pistons, and steam seeps from between his joints. Slowly, the Eagle begins to move, rubble from the broken wall sloughing off its sides. Once the shuttle is free, Rock turns it around until its nose points out at the wasteland. Carefully, he lowers it back to the ground, rolling his giant shoulders as he releases the weight.

I stare at him, stunned. Sasha nudges my arm. "Move your ass, Nevares. We don't want any more Axys people to find us."

That breaks my trance. I climb into the shuttle and grab a seat. Sasha heads for the pilot's chair, crossing her arms when she sees it isn't vacant. "You trying to be funny, Doc?"

"Nope." Doc activates the dashboard, and the Eagle's floor vibrates as the engine roars to life. "Making sure there won't be any more accidents. I'm not letting my brother die in a shuttle crash after busting him out of here."

"The crash was to get through the wall," Sasha says. "What part of that don't you and Nevares get?"

Doc gives Sasha a pleading look. "Come on, boss. My brother, my op."

I'm both impressed and upset. Doc seems highly competent, but she's still a kid. She shouldn't know how to pilot combat shuttles out of secret corp biomedical research facilities. The fact that Sasha lets her makes my stomach simmer with anger.

"Fine," Sasha says, climbing into the back. "Get us out of here."

"You got it, boss."

The Eagle protests at first, but after a shuddering hesitation, it creeps forward. We launch into the air, shooting through the hole and out into the snow. I don't relax my muscles until the factory has become a dark blur on the horizon. A hundred questions buzz in my brain, but for the moment, I'm grateful to be alive.

Tuesday, 06-08-65 7:02:25

"NEVARES?"

MY NAME FLOATS toward me from very far away. I can't tell who's calling, but I don't care enough to find out. Wherever I am is warm and comfortable, and my sore body protests at the prospect of moving. I keep my eyes shut, ignoring the noise.

"Nevares." This time, the voice is insistent. Familiar. As my foggy mind tries to place it, someone shakes my shoulder. "Unless you want to freeze out here, you'd better get up."

I recognize the voice. The events of the past few hours come flooding back. I open my eyes and realize I've fallen asleep on Sasha's shoulder. *Mierda.* I just hope I didn't drool. I pull away, yawning into my hand to play it off.

"Where are we?" I look around, but the back of the Eagle doesn't have any windows. All I can see through the front windshield is a faint glow.

Val's pleasantly neutral voice answers my question. "Now arriving at the Hole. Begin descent in six hundred meters."

"The Hole?" I repeat, looking at Sasha. "Why do you call it that."

Sasha shrugs. "Because it's underground. Why else?"

The shuttle slows to a stop, and its engines switch off. Sasha unfastens her safety harness, but because of her height, she has to duck to keep from hitting the ceiling when she stands. Rock has it even worse. He has to fold himself up to avoid bumping his head. For once, I'm happy to be short.

Sasha opens the side doors. The shuttle has taken shelter in a dimly lit garage. Loud gusts of wind blow somewhere outside, and the air is frigid enough to show the silvery mist of my breath. I unfasten my belt and clamber to my feet, holding the wall until my numb legs regain feeling.

"How long have I been out?"

Sasha answers me for once. "A couple hours."

I grimace. *Was I sleeping on her the whole time?* "Sorry."

19

Sasha ignores me and climbs out of the Eagle, turning back to extend her hand. I stare at it in surprise. So far, she hasn't been what I'd call chivalrous. Before I can accept the offer, Rock's bulk fills most of the exit. Sasha guides him down instead, and as he drops to the ground, I notice he's shaking. Whatever AxysGen did to him, it's bad.

"Is he going to be okay?" I ask, hopping down after him.

Sasha sighs. "You never stop with the questions, do you?"

"Considering I almost died today, I think I'm entitled to some answers."

Sasha ignores me, circling around the Eagle. "Doc? Rock doesn't look too good. Better get him to the med bay."

Doc hurries over. "On it. Come on, Rock," she says, grabbing hold of his elbow and guiding him away from the Eagle. Rock obeys, allowing her to lead him onto a wide metal platform. "Val, can you get the lift?"

"Yes, Doc," Val says, from speakers I assume are somewhere in the garage. "Initiating descent." The platform begins to move, descending into darkness.

I think about following, but Sasha's still standing nearby. She's half in and half out of the Eagle, rummaging through a storage bin bolted to the floor just under the armory.

"Want me to put my pistol back?" I ask, walking over to stand at her shoulder.

Sasha shakes her head. "No. You'll need it to defend yourself...from me, if you don't stop with the interrogation."

"It's not an interrogation."

"Could have fooled me."

My jaw clenches. I'm not the type to make friends with coworkers—or at all. Watching my old crewmates die was horrible, but they were business partners—acquaintances. I don't need Sasha to be my friend, but we have to get along, because her dislike could be very hazardous to my health. More fights are coming, and I need her to watch my back.

"I'm not trying to piss you off, okay? I just want to know what we're getting into. Tell me what we need to do and how you plan on keeping me alive while we're doing it, and I'll step back."

I wait for Sasha to lash out at me again, but she doesn't. She takes a seat on the raised shuttle platform, feet dangling off the edge. Her legs are so long that her boots nearly brush the floor. "We need to finish getting my old crew back together. What's left of it, anyway. I've got my grunt and my medical officer, so that's a start. I still need my cloak and my wrench."

"I still can't believe Doc is your MO."

"Yeah. So?"

I exhale in frustration and disbelief. "She hasn't even hit puberty yet. What makes you think it's okay to take a fucking kid on ops?"

"I don't make her go," Sasha says, her brow furrowed with annoyance. "She wants to, and she's more than 'a fucking kid'. She's the best medic I've ever had."

I'm still angry, but I sense this conversation isn't going anywhere. For now, at least, Doc isn't getting shot at. And I get why Sasha's pissed. If I was a handler, I wouldn't want some idiot coming in and telling me how to run my crew. *Next time we go out, though, I'm not letting that kid risk her neck.*

"Anyway, two more pickups?" I ask, trying to defuse the situation. "Not so bad."

"You say that, but you haven't met Cherry yet. I don't know what she's gotten into, but it definitely involves explosives."

"She your wrench?"

"Among other things," Sasha says. "You can bother her once we get her. She likes intrusive personal questions."

"Come on. Asking how we're going to get AxysGen off our backs hardly qualifies as intrusive or personal. I'd classify it as vital information." Sasha doesn't disagree. I decide to count that as progress. "What about your cloak?"

Sasha actually smiles a little. "Rami. Master of disguise. They can paint their face to look like anyone, and that's just the tip of the iceberg."

"They?"

Sasha nods. "'They' out of disguise. Otherwise, it's whatever the situation calls for."

"Okay." I hop onto the platform beside Sasha, sitting an arm's length away from where she's brooding. "What about your jacker? You've got me for now, but didn't you have one on your old crew? We're one of the most essential ingredients."

Sasha's eyes lock onto mine with a frozen stare. "Remind me how your crew died, Nevares."

That's the last thing I want to talk about, and she has to know that.

When I don't answer, Sasha turns away, fixing her gaze on the far wall. "Then you tell me. What do you think happened to my last jacker?"

Suddenly, everything makes sense: Sasha's protectiveness toward her crew, her moodiness, her hatred of AxysGen. Of course she wants revenge. I'm not the crewbonding type, but she obviously is. In her eyes, AxysGen has cost her a family member.

"I understand." I scoot a little closer. "If a corp killed one of my brothers—"

Sasha hops off the platform, taking several steps away. The echo of her boots sounds unnaturally loud on the concrete floor as she turns her back on me. "I'm done with twenty questions. Go down into the Hole, get some food, and grab a bunk. We're riding out tomorrow to pick up the rest of my crew, and it's not going to be any easier than busting Rock out."

I climb down and head for the lift where Doc and Rock disappeared. The light next to the keypad is green, and when I press the down arrow, I'm lowered into a bunker beneath the garage. I stare up at Sasha's back until her boots disappear, then her torso, then her head, replaying the conversation in my head. Talk about hidden landmines. With everything else going on recently, I've forgotten something: I'm *really* bad at being part of a crew. My rocky relationships with all my previous ones are evidence of that.

The platform arrives in a spacious, well-lit room. It's warm and insulated, so I shrug out of my coat. Obviously, Sasha has invested in a good heating system. There's a table with chairs, a kitchen area in the corner, a large couch, and what looks like an entertainment system mounted on one wall. The decor's modest, but the Hole is definitely cozy.

"Hey, Nevares. What took you?" Doc emerges from the only doorway, looking slightly less scrawny without her brother beside her.

"You can call me Elena, *chiquita.* How's Rock?"

Doc smiles. Her pale face has a little more color. "Better. It takes more than a few weeks of torture to take him out. His mods heal him up pretty well, and I can handle the rest."

My eyes widen. "A few weeks? They had him that long?"

"Yeah." Doc's smile fades almost as quickly as it appeared. "He was bait. AxysGen knew Sasha wouldn't be able to resist. She'd go on a suicide run if it meant keeping the rest of us alive. Plus she'll do anything she can to hurt them. Kill Sasha's crew and murder her fiancée, see if you don't rise to the top of her shit list."

"Wait. You mean your last jacker was…" Doc nods. I close my eyes and roll them backward. *As if she didn't already hate me.* "Guess I really put my foot in it. But if Sasha's out for revenge, what was she doing in

St. Petersburg?"

Doc looks at me like it should be obvious. "What do you think? She needs you. There's no way we can do this without a jacker. Rescuing Rock would have been impossible if you hadn't broken the security on that door, and Cherry and Rami are gonna be even harder." Her smile returns, and she suddenly seems her age again. "Thanks, by the way. Rock might not be alive without you. If you ever get shot, poisoned, stabbed, melted brain, anything like that, I've got your back."

"I'm more worried about you. You seem talented, kid, but aren't you a little young for this?"

Doc's expression immediately sours "Aren't you a little ugly for this?"

"Ha fucking ha. I'm serious, *chiquita*. I have brothers your age. They're smart—smarter than me—and they can handle themselves. But I don't want people shooting at them. I do this job so they don't have to."

"You mean you don't even want to do it?" Doc seems to forget she's supposed to be mad at me. "Being a jacker is supposed to be fun."

"Sure, it's fun hacking the security simulations in Darkspace, but this isn't a game to level up your skills. I like a challenge. What I don't like is people trying to kill me. I'm surprised you do."

"Don't worry about me getting killed. I've been doing this a while." Doc turns back toward the door. My unwanted concern is apparently forgiven. "Come on. We can sit with Rock for a while. That is, if you want to."

I glance toward the lift. "Sure, but Sasha's still up there. Maybe you should check on her."

Doc laughs. "You're sweet as fucking pie, aren't you? Boss will be fine. She'll come down before the temperature gets too bad. She's not stupid enough to freeze to death."

Not stupid enough, I think, *but maybe stubborn enough.*

Doc leads me out of the living room and through the only remaining door. Beyond is a hallway, and Doc points out each room as we pass by. "Bunks, bathroom—there's more than one shower, so go in whenever. Storage, armory, uh...more storage. And the med bay."

"Just more storage, huh?"

Doc avoids my eyes. She's already heading through the medbay door. The room beyond is small, but all the stainless-steel surfaces are spotless. Doc obviously keeps this place clean, which bodes well for me if I ever end up on her table. Rock is lying on a cot against one wall. His giant limbs almost don't fit, but he seems to be sleeping peacefully. The torn patches of skin on his body have been repaired with shiny red skin, and his eyes are closed.

"So, big guy's gonna be okay?" I ask Doc.

"Yeah." She lets out a long breath. "I'm just glad I got there in time. He wouldn't have lasted much longer."

"How did AxysGen get ahold of him anyway?"

Doc pulls over a chair, sitting in reverse with her arms folded across the back. "After our last op went bad, we had to scatter. There was no word from Sasha, Rami, or Cherry. I didn't even know they were alive until Sasha contacted me a few days ago. Anyway, Rock and me ran. AxysGen caught up with us..." Her expression reads guilt, an emotion I'm all too familiar with. "He gave me time to get away."

I look at Rock's slumbering form. "That's what older siblings do, *chiquita*. Don't feel bad about it. I bet he doesn't."

Doc gives me a weak smile. "Yeah?"

"You can ask him when he wakes up. He'll say the same thing." I pull up a chair beside Doc's. If sitting with her for a while will cheer her up, I'm happy to do it. She and Rock are better company than Sasha, at any rate.

Wednesday, 06-09-65 16:25:30

"AND HERE I THOUGHT the cold was bad," I mutter, tripping over another root. I'm outfitted with sturdy hiking boots and breathable clothes, but I can't find even footing, and my skin is sticky with sweat. The temperature by itself isn't so terrible, but the humidity is unbearable. It's even worse than home.

The bug shield clipped to my belt is all but useless. I have to stop every few seconds to swat at the mosquitos hovering around my face. I might not have believed it yesterday, but today I'd trade the Amazon rainforest for the Siberian tundra in a heartbeat.

If Sasha notices me struggling, she doesn't comment. Her eyes remain fixed straight ahead. Beside her, Rock seems almost peaceful as he lumbers along with Doc on his shoulders. It's good to see him up and moving. I hadn't been sure he'd be able to come with us, but he's doing better than I am. His pace never falters, while I have to trot every couple of steps to keep up.

"What is it with your crewmembers and remote locations?" I ask Sasha. "First Siberia, now this. What's next? The Sahara? Everest? Antarctica?"

"I'll tell you when you need to know." Sasha seems calm, but I've been watching her the past few days. Her jaw is clenched, and she can't quite hide the worry in her eyes. All her energy is focused on making sure her crew is safe. It's definitely not what I expected. The Wolf of the Kremlin isn't a cunning, bloodthirsty beast. She's a fierce mother protecting her pack.

I remain silent as long as I can bear, but the buzzing of mosquitos and the burbling of water and the howls and shrieks of God-knows-what in the trees threatens to drive me out of my fucking mind. I need to talk to someone, whether Sasha likes it or not. Since she's focused on the op, and Rock isn't much of a conversationalist, I settle on Doc.

"Tell me about Cherry, *chiquita*. How'd she get snatched by Axys?"

"I'm not sure she was," Doc says. "We got separated when Axys..." Sasha gives a brief shake of her head, and Doc corrects herself. "This is one of her old hiding places, like the Hole back in Siberia. She's got them everywhere, all set to blow if someone puts a foot wrong."

Of course she does. Explosives are the last thing me and my messed-up brain need. It's already taken way too many trips back to Mumbai recently. "If you haven't heard from her, how do you know your girl's here? Do you know if she's even alive?"

"Because I know my crew, Nevares," Sasha says. "This was Cherry's best bunker. If she isn't here, she's dead."

"Or worse," Doc mumbles under her breath.

An almost proud smile crosses Sasha's face. "Cherry isn't the type to go quietly, Doc. She would have gone up in a huge explosion, along with several hundred AxysGen mercs. That kind of disaster usually makes the news."

The group falls silent again, but this time, it's mercifully brief. Before my brain starts eating itself, Rock comes to a stop. I almost run into him, which turns out to be a good thing. Two feet away, the edge of the world drops off into nothing. The jungle stretches all the way to the edge of a massive cliff, concealing what has to be at least a forty-meter fall.

I step back, swaying with vertigo, but then one of Rock's giant hands presses down on my shoulder, steadying me. He smiles, and I smile back. He looks much less intimidating without his skin peeled away to reveal all the cables inside him.

"Thanks, Rock." I risk another glance at the cliff. It's a straight shot down, no bridges, ladders, or steps. "What now?"

Sasha runs her hand along a twisted tree trunk, searching its contours for something. After a moment, she pulls away a piece of the bark to reveal a glowing orange port. I start to offer my services, but Sasha just touches her hand to the light, opening the tree wirelessly. Five packs are stashed inside the hollow trunk, with empty space for a sixth. Sasha looks visibly relieved, and I can guess why: the missing pack must belong to Cherry.

"All right!" Doc says. "Pass me my harness, Rock. It's time for a climb."

Rock pulls out the biggest pack and the kid-sized one next to it. I examine the remaining four. One is large, although not as huge as Rock's, and the remaining two are a medium and a small. I reach for the smallest pack.

"Don't!"

I draw my hand back, meeting Sasha's intense stare. To my shock, there's a flash of anger in those cold, dark eyes, and the scar that slashes across her throat quivers as she swallows hard. Five packs. One missing. One each for Rock and Doc. The remaining large pack is probably Sasha's. That leaves two more: a medium for their cloak, a small for the dead jacker. I hold up my hands. Better to get this out in the open.

"I'm not trying to take something that doesn't belong to me, okay? But I need gear that fits. Can't help that I'm short."

After a long, tense second, Sasha gives me a stiff nod. She reaches into the trunk and hauls the small pack out, tossing it into my arms.

"*Gracias.*"

"Don't thank me. Just don't fuck up." Sasha opens her pack and starts unbuckling a simple black harness. "The two of us are doing a spider climb. If you go, so do I."

"What's a spider climb?"

As usual, Sasha doesn't answer. She takes over the job of putting on my harness, checking the buckles and straps with confident fingers. Her touch is all business, but I hold my breath. She has strong hands, with several thin scars across the backs.

Nope. Not going there. Wrong place, time, and person to get all *cachonda* over.

I'm actually disappointed when Sasha finishes securing everything. It's fucked up, checking out dangerous handlers with dead fiancées in the middle of the jungle when a corp is trying to murder us. My brain knows it, but my body hasn't gotten the memo. Like my thighs need to get any stickier in this heat.

"You're done." Before I can shake off my haze, Sasha turns away. "Rock, you got those anchors set?"

Rock nods. He's already clipped and knotted the climbing rope to a sturdy-looking crag at the edge of the cliff. He tosses the other end of the rope to Sasha, who catches it and loops it in on itself.

"Over here, Nevares."

Qué chingados. She's sexy giving orders, too.

Sasha threads the rope through the clip at my waist, skimming the edge of my stomach. "You're up first."

"Me? Nuh-uh. Don't like heights. Jumping out the window of a burning building does that to you."

"You won't be jumping, and you won't be alone. We'll be climbing together to balance each other's weight." Sasha attaches her belt clip to the same rope. "Rock's strong enough to take care of himself and Doc, but we need to do this in tandem. It's the quickest way."

It takes Sasha less than a minute to explain the procedure. I try to listen, but the only thought going through my head is *Shit, shit, shit.* For once, I don't ask questions.

The spider climb is exactly as terrifying as it sounds. Sasha checks our harnesses one more time, then helps me over the edge of the cliff. It's much cooler past the trees, but that's not a comfort. Feeling the breeze reminds me that I'm dangling above empty air. My stomach sloshes, and I have to swallow my heart back down.

I try to remember Sasha's explanation. *Belay, weight, anchor point...Fuck, I've got no clue what I'm doing.* I resist the urge to look down, but looking up isn't any better. The blue sky above me heaves like the upside-down waves of an ocean. My limbs shake in my harness and I might be going crazy, but I think I can taste smoke in my mouth.

Sasha drops beside me, feeding the rope through her belt. "You're fine," she says with a small, forced smile. "Keep breathing and let me stay a few feet below you."

A laugh cracks in my throat, and the taste of smoke fades. "I've finally figured out how to get a smile from you. I have to put myself in life-threatening situations."

"You're not going to die. Look at Rock." Sasha nods at where Rock is climbing hand-over-fist down another rope. He doesn't even seem to be paying attention to his harness. Doc is sitting securely on his shoulders.

Shit. If a twelve-year-old can do this, so can I.

"Three, two, one." I clench my chattering teeth and drop. My body seizes up, but I come to a stop, swaying softly. Okay. Still panicking a little, but I don't think I'll ruin my pants.

Sasha's voice floats over to me. Maybe she senses that talking helps. "Good news is, we won't have to climb back up. Three, two, one, weight." She plunges down, and I try to ignore the tug of the rope. "Cherry's got a spare shuttle tucked away. We can fly out of the jungle in style."

"Thank God. Three, two, one." I feed the rope through my clip, coming to a stop over Sasha's head. It's easier the second time. The sky stays in one place. "Couldn't we have called ahead? Maybe she'd have met us on *top* of the terrifying cliff."

"Not sure that would have worked. Three, two, one, weight."

I brace for the jolt. I'm getting better at anticipating Sasha's movements.

"Well, after AxysGen tried to kill us, our crew didn't split on the best of terms. There...were some issues."

"Like what?"

The sound of boots hitting rock gives me the courage to look down. Sasha's standing on a narrow but blessedly flat ledge. I slide the last few yards, sagging as my feet hit solid ground. It's only when my head stops spinning that I notice we're not alone.

"Like me," says the woman who's apparently been waiting for us. She's almost a match for Sasha in height—fuck, what *is* it with all the tall people in this crew?—with a striking face and bronze skin. Her hair is flaming red and her eyes burn hot. Her arms are folded over her chest, and clutched tight in her hand is a remote with a big button in the middle. She taps the tip of her thumbnail beside it, glaring at Sasha.

"You have thirty seconds, *jefa*. Convince me not to blow you off the face of planet Earth."

Wednesday, 06-09-65 18:03:14

MY EYES CAN'T DECIDE where to look. They only rest on the detonator for a moment before darting to where Cherry's finger taps dangerously close to the button. Cold sweat runs down my spine, and my vertigo returns with a vengeance. Somehow, though, I don't miss the fact that Cherry's nails are immaculately polished in a red as bright as her namesake.

While I fight to keep myself together, Sasha holds up her hands in surrender. "What exactly do you want me to tell you? I know you're upset about Rami—"

"Upset is a fucking understatement," Cherry snarls. "Rami was part of our crew. You *abandoned* them to go after Megan, when you knew she was probably dead."

Sasha's face falters. I've never seen this expression on her, but I know what it is: guilt. "We didn't know for sure about Megan. Rami was hurt but moving, and you know as well as I do that they had to get far away from me. I did the best I could in the situation."

As I listen to the two of them argue, something in my brain breaks. I've suddenly had enough of being afraid. A weird wave of calm washes over me, and I notice that Cherry's lips are perfectly outlined. The pencil and gloss match her nail polish, with neither a chip nor smudge in sight. I have no idea why my fear-drunk mind has fixed on such insignificant details, but I can't help it. I laugh.

"*¡No mames!* Face and nails on point in the middle of the fucking jungle? Marry me or something."

Cherry's perfectly threaded eyebrows rise higher on her forehead. "*Lo siento, chaparrita.* I'm taken, assuming Rami's still alive and this *ladilla* hasn't ballsed everything up." She looks pointedly at Sasha when she says that. Even though it's not an insult I'm familiar with, I get the drift from her tone.

I know an opening when I see one. I need to keep Cherry talking, get her invested in me. Maybe then she'll be less likely to blow us all up. "*¿Está pesada, si?*"

31

Cherry stops tapping her finger next to the giant red button. "Annoying is a fucking understatement." She uncrosses her arms, towering over me as she begins a thorough inspection. "You're the new jacker, right? Shit, you look like a rookie."

My face heats up. Cherry's examination reminds me of Sasha back in St. Petersburg, trying to look beneath my skin. "Kind of an asshole thing to say, isn't it?"

Cherry ignores me, speaking to Sasha. "Where'd you find this one, *jefa*? You been making her promises you can't keep, too?"

"I didn't promise Rami anything, Cherry," Sasha says. "They made their choice. They told me to go back and see if Megan was alive."

"Rami thinks they need to be a goddamn hero. Did you really expect them to ask you to stay instead of going in to look for Megan's body?"

The scar along Sasha's throat twitches. "No. Would you?"

"No. Fuck." Cherry sighs and drops the remote, stomping on it with her heel. I start to dive, but Cherry stops me. "Don't. It was fake."

My legs wobble with fear and relief. I lean on Sasha's elbow for support without even thinking, but Sasha doesn't seem to care. "Then what, Cherry?" Her voice is quiet, but the breeze carries her soft words a long distance. Or maybe she just seems distant. "You trying to teach me some kind of lesson? Make me feel guilty? Because I don't need help for that."

Cherry chews on that for a moment, then turns to me and sticks out her hand. "Cherry Vidal. Engineer, explosives expert, Sasha's wrench."

Sasha gives her a searching look. "Not my ex-wrench?"

"That depends," Cherry says, holding the eye contact. "You going to find Rami?"

"Of course." Sasha seems almost defensive, as if she's hurt that Cherry would even ask.

I edge myself between them. "Elena Nevares. You're right, I'm a jacker."

"A jacker, yeah," Cherry says, relaxing slightly. "But maybe not such a rookie after all."

"What makes you say that?"

"You're running with Sasha. Some skill can be assumed." Cherry looks back at Sasha. "Rami was last seen in Paris. Once we pick them up, what are we doing about AxysGen?"

"We're going to delete ourselves from their database," Sasha says.

"So, are you in or not?"

"Yes. Am I the first one you came for, or...?"

Sasha's lips twitch into the briefest of smiles. "Look up."

Cherry tilts her head back. Rock and Doc are hanging a few yards overhead, waving down with identical grins. She waves back, then gestures at the other side of the ledge. A reinforced steel door is set into the rock, one I didn't notice before.

I groan in frustration. "You mean I could've gone inside this whole time instead of standing out here and listening to you two bitch at each other?"

Cherry shrugs. "You never asked to come in."

"Sorry your fake detonator grabbed most of my attention," I mutter. "I'll look for a door first next time."

Sasha gives me a look as if to say, *Really?* I ignore her and go through the door.

There's a network of tunnels inside the cliff—smooth stone underfoot, overhead lighting too. It's also blessedly cool, without the added fear of falling. I want to soak it all into my skin and let the layers of sweat evaporate.

"I try to keep up with the place," Cherry says when she notices me looking around. "It's a hole in the wall, but it's *my* hole in the wall."

"I thought it was rigged to explode. Why bother if you're gonna blow it up later?"

"That's what I told her," Doc says. She and Rock have joined us inside, although she's back on her own feet. The tunnel is barely tall enough for Rock to stand up straight.

Cherry ruffles the hair on top of Doc's head. "And I explain that I can't find anything when she leaves her crap lying around."

"Hey, don't give me that sappy shit," Doc grumbles. "I'm mad at you, Cherry. You're mad at Sasha for leaving Rami to try and save Megan, but you didn't look for me and Rock after things went south. Check a dictionary under hypocritical."

Cherry gives a small sigh. "I was gonna track both of you down after I found Rami."

I bite back more questions. This is exactly why I don't crewbond. Family dynamics can get pretty fucked up.

There's a door around the next corner. Cherry presses her hand to the glowing orange scanner pad next to it. "Control room. We can take what we need and head to the shuttle bay."

"There's a shuttle bay here, too?" I ask. "Any terminals?"

"Only intranet ports," Cherry says, glancing at me sidelong, "and you'd be dealing with *catira's* personalized code."

"What? Who's Blondie?"

"Megan. They told you about Megan, right?"

The hallway holds its breath.

"Yeah, they did."

"Well, her shit's locked down tight. It won't be useful to you. Is it important?"

I get what Cherry really wants to know. Some jackers get a little too hooked on the virtual world. It can mess you up, make you dependent for a fix if you're not careful. Meatspace sucks, and the extranet is this vast floating ocean of freedom. The temptation's been there for me sometimes, but...brothers. Obligations. I limit myself.

"No, just been a few days since I checked in. I have spyders and a few bitminers running for extra credits."

"You all do," Cherry says. "This way."

I follow her into the control room. It's not as big as the Hole, but big enough. There's a fridge in the corner, a few cots pressed against the walls, and a glowing terminal that still looks active. Sasha, Cherry, Doc, and Rock begin taking the place apart bit by bit. They silently work to dismantle the furniture and gear as a team, not even pausing to divvy up the jobs. Everyone already knows what to do.

"Nevares."

I turn around. Sasha's brown eyes are fixed on me, boring into my head. The shudder that zips down my spine isn't from the cold air. "Yeah?"

"I need this wiped." She nods at Megan's terminal. It's nothing special. Haptic interface, port, medium-sized screen—pretty typical setup. I snort when I see the manufacturer, though: Axys Generations.

"Sure thing." I gesture at the terminal. "You need it wiped fast, right?"

"Yes."

"And you don't care how I do it?"

"No."

"Great." I look around the room until I spot a short piece of piping. There's five square feet of mess around it, but it's a neat, contained mess. It looks like Cherry was in the middle of deconstructing an engine of some kind before we barged in on her. I walk over and grab the pipe. When I look at Sasha for permission, she shrugs.

I pop the body of the terminal open and remove the hard drive, setting it on the floor before swinging the pipe down with all my strength. The drive crumples. I swing again—one, two, three times—until it's only bits of wire and shards of metal. No way AxysGen can pull anything off this thing, no matter how good they are.

"Rock might've been better at this," I pant, hefting the pipe back onto my shoulder.

"He's busy," Sasha says. She doesn't seem fazed by the fact that I smashed a hard drive in front of her.

"Doing what?" I turn to see Rock removing a large section of solid wall using only his fists. Dust and rock crumble on top of his head, but he doesn't seem to mind. "Ah. So when Cherry said 'grab what we need'..."

"She means we're tearing this place down."

"So you're not gonna blow it up?" I ask hopefully.

Sasha snorts. "An explosion. In a rainforest. With lots of trees. Sounds like a great idea, Nevares."

"Then why rig the base in the first place?"

"Because sometimes a forest fire is the least worst option."

"I'm good with calling that Plan B. But why bother destroying this place? Do you really think AxysGen will find us all the way out here?"

RRROOOM.

A loud rumble shakes the control room. Only Sasha's hand on my shoulder keeps me from losing my footing. *"¿Qué chingados?"* I gasp.

"The answer to your question. You just had to ask, didn't you?"

Wednesday, 06-09-65 18:50:54

ANOTHER RUMBLE ROCKS THE control room and a shower of dust shakes free from the ceiling, getting in my mouth as I curse. "Goddamn shitting *fuck*."

"This way." Sasha grabs my arm, hauling me back through the doors. We burst out of the control room, the others right on our heels. Sasha's long legs carry her swiftly down the tunnel, but I scramble to keep up. Running is rarely part of a jacker's job, and I've been doing way more of it lately than I want to.

Sasha skids to a stop and slams the pressure pad on another set of doors, which whoosh open to reveal a cavernous chamber. A shuttle's parked there, smaller than the Eagle, but big enough to hold all of us. I sprint for it, throwing both arms over my head as more rock dust rains from above.

Cherry hauls open the side doors, and I hop on one of the benches, fumbling with my harness. Doc takes the pilot's seat, with Rock right beside her. That leaves Sasha to climb in last. To my surprise, she sits next to me.

"Fasten your seatbelts," Doc shouts over her shoulder. "This is gonna be a bumpy ride." The engines roar to life and the smell of burning plasma fills my nose. With a loud whir, the shuttle lifts off the ground, its nose pointing up toward the ceiling. The very solid ceiling.

"Please tell me there's a hole," I mutter, digging my nails into my palms.

Sasha looks at me. "There's a hole."

"That's what she said," Cherry snickers.

The roof of the shuttle bay whines open. Bright sunlight streams in, blinding even through the shuttle's tinted windows. I barely have time to brace myself before the bird launches, throwing me back in my seat.

We streak out of the cave, soaring into the open air. After a few watery blinks, I can see smudges through the windows. Cliffs. Trees. More trees. Other shuttles converging on us. Shit. They're jet black, with bright red logos printed on the side: *AG*. The rattle of mounted guns and the shriek of firing missiles rings out, but nothing hits us as Doc banks away from the cliff.

"Nice flying, kid!" Cherry whoops. "Rami would be proud."

Doc's giggle is maniacal. "Yeah! Come get some!" She swerves, sending the closest AxysGen shuttle spinning into a tree. The trunk catches fire, going up in a blossoming tower of red. My chest contracts painfully. I do *not* like fire. I'm getting sucked into the dark pit of fear inside me, while everything outside begins to blur.

"This is bad," Sasha says. I struggle to focus on her voice, using it to anchor myself in the present. "There are..." She glances out the window. "One, two, three, four gunships on our tail. And we need to get to the Eagle. We can't outrun them in this bird."

I've managed to stave off a flashback, but my belly is a swirling pit. It's probably my imagination, but I'm sure I can smell smoke seeping in around the shuttle's doors. "I think I'm gonna be sick."

Cherry pulls something from one of her pockets: another remote. "Hold onto your ass, Nevares. Things are about to get bumpier."

I don't glance back at the flames behind us, but I catch their reflection in the windshield. My heart does a sickening flip inside my chest. I really, *really* don't like fire, especially when I'm stuck in a harness and can't do anything to get away. "...Is there a Plan C, maybe?"

"'Fraid not, *chaparrita*," Cherry says.

"Then blow the fucking thing already!" Doc yells.

I close my eyes as Cherry pushes the button.

The world explodes. Light flashes through my eyelids like they aren't even shut. Sharp pain lances my eardrums, then everything goes fuzzy. I can feel the pressure of hot air pushing against the shuttle's tail, carrying us forward even faster. My thoughts are stuck on a desperate loop. *Stop stop stop STOP stop STOPstopstop.*

It doesn't stop. The roar of the blast fades quickly, but its absence echoes in my head long after. I can't breathe around the burn in my lungs and my breath feels unnaturally hot, bouncing off my knees to hit my buried face. I've curled into a ball in the middle of my seat, knees to chest, and I can't let go of my legs.

Finally, I hear something else, a familiar voice shouting from the pilot's seat. "Cherry," Doc hollers, "that was awesome!"

I open my eyes, peeking out from over my knees. We're soaring over a winding blue river, heading upstream. Breathing still hurts, especially since the harness left painful stripes on my chest from curling up, but I gradually remember how to do it. My sigh of relief becomes hyperventilation, interspersed with awkward, gasping laughter.

Apparently, it's contagious. Doc, Rock, and Cherry all start to crack up, until they realize I'm not laughing for the same reason. Sasha shushes them, then places a hand on my shoulder. The touch feels alien. I'm aware of it, I can see it with my eyes, but it's like she's touching someone else's body instead of mine.

"You okay, Nevares?"

I nod weakly. *Pull it together, idiot. You can't let her think you're too fucked up to be part of her crew.* "Yeah. Okay."

Sasha doesn't look like she believes me, but she doesn't push. "That was a risk, Cherry. We could have gotten caught in the blast."

"Nah," Cherry says. "I'd never blow you up for real, boss. Sorry, Nevares," she adds, in a more sympathetic tone. "Don't like things that go boom, huh?"

I shake my head. "Not a fan," I croak.

"Mind if I ask why?"

Yeah, I mind, but I don't blame her for asking. If someone on my crew had a freak-out, I'd want to know what was up. Crewmembers have to depend on each other to stay safe. If I want Sasha's people to have my back, I need to prove I'm capable of watching theirs.

"AxysGen has it in for me," I say, struggling to sound casual. "Think they're trying to give me tinnitus."

"Girl, get you some noise-cancelling mods," Cherry says. "Take it from an explosives expert. You don't wanna go deaf in your twenties." I suspect that's not the real reason for the suggestion, but I appreciate the attempt to be candid. "Seriously, though, why's AxysGen coming for you?"

"They wiped my old crew. There's safety in numbers, so here I am."

"But why, though?" Doc says. "They're a huge corp. You're just one jacker."

That's actually an excellent question. It's true that I've used some of AxysGen's private code to modify my programs, so I can move through their systems more easily, but their reaction still strikes me as overkill. I'm pretty much a nobody. "Don't know." I hope she and Cherry will drop the subject.

Surprisingly, it's Sasha who comes to my rescue with a well-timed interruption. "Pull over, Doc. The Eagle's three hundred meters northwest."

"I remember where it is," Doc protests, but she pulls the shuttle in for a landing. We touch down right before the plasma engines stutter out, and its bones groan with metallic exhaustion as it settles down onto the forest floor. I unfasten my harness and hop out, taking a moment to reassure myself that my feet are firmly on the ground. The non-shaking, non-collapsing ground.

The Eagle's right where we left it, hidden from aerial surveillance beneath some low branches. Sasha exits behind me, heading straight for it. "Next destination is Paris," she says to the crew. "No stop-overs. As long as AxysGen knows which continent we're on, they're a threat."

"They're always a threat," Cherry says. "Ask Doc to look at your ears, Elena. We need your help to find Rami."

"Why? You and Sasha talk like you already know where they are."

"It's not about where they are." Cherry hops into the Eagle and heads for the weapons rack, selecting a heavy-duty shotgun from the wall and slinging it over her shoulder like she's done it a thousand times. "It's about who they are."

Thursday, 06-10-65 09:24:32

"COME ON, SASHA."

"NO, Nevares."

"Please?"

"No."

"We're in Paris. We *have* to visit the Eiffel Tower!"

"It's not even the original Eiffel Tower," Sasha says, continuing down the crowded street. "They rebuilt it twice. You'd be visiting a copy."

"You just have to make everything depressing, don't you?"

The smell of the waterfront hangs in the air, wet and slightly metallic. Beyond the cobbled path, tour boats drift down the wide, lazy river that cuts through the city. Across the way are several restaurants, all with adorable tables for two beneath colorful umbrellas. Rami has the right idea, hiding out in a place like this. Paris beats the Siberian tundra and the Amazon rainforest any day.

Sasha doesn't seem to appreciate the atmosphere. She's hyper-focused, outstripping me again with her long strides. As I hustle to catch up, I have to duck out of the way as a man in a business suit passes by. He barely spares me a glance. To him, I'm just part of the scenery.

The exchange isn't surprising. We're in corp territory, the rich part of the city where only people with money go. There are a few cogs, people in customer service and other worker bees who do the few jobs that haven't yet been automated out of existence, but like me, they're barely noticeable. Even though their numbers decrease with every passing year, they're the lucky ones. Undesirables—people who don't serve on a corp's board and aren't cogs in their machine—live in the outer rings of most cities. That's where I lived before I joined up with my first crew, where my brothers still live.

"Just avoid eye contact," Sasha mutters, slowing down so I can catch up. "Even if we don't fit in, they don't want to see us."

I roll my eyes. She's telling me rules I learned a long time ago. The Parisian waterfront disappears around us. As the smell of the Seine

41

fades, the restaurants and boutiques become shiny skyscrapers with mirrored windows. People in business suits scurry around, all with somewhere important to go. They don't notice the two of us—or, at least, they pretend not to.

Sasha stops in front of a large silver building. When she looks up, so do I. The giant red and black logo above the front entrance makes it obvious where we are: *AG*. Axys Generations. One of their few locations open to the public, the ground floor hosts a massive showroom for their domestic mechs and other hardware.

I give Sasha a skeptical look. "Rami's in here?"

"Right in the belly of the beast. Where better to keep tabs on the people trying to kill us?"

Sasha heads into the building. I hesitate, then follow through the large revolving doors. AxysGen's ground floor is as busy as the street outside. It's pretty much a street in itself, full of bustling people, small side shops, and scrolling neon billboards with numbers and ticker symbols on them. Tinted lights flash from all directions, competing for my attention. Aside from the mission, though, I'm mostly focused on the smell of the nearby food court. I haven't eaten since the Hole.

"Can we maybe grab a—"

"No," Sasha says.

"I didn't ask the question yet."

"Still no. Look."

Sasha points up. Hanging above everything else is a huge billboard, projecting the face of a smiling white woman in 3D. Looking at her is unsettling. Her perfectly styled dark hair, perfectly straight teeth, and piercing blue eyes (undoubtedly with perfect vision) are eerie.

"Welcome, visitors! I'm Veronica Cross, Chief Executive Officer of Axys Generations: the world leader in extranet search and advertising, robotics, and virtual intelligence technology. We hope you enjoy your visit, and please, stop by the nearest kiosk or terminal for more information."

The prerecorded speech ends, but I keep staring. I already know what Veronica Cross looks like, but for some reason I can't look away. She's on the extranet, signs, product boxes, but somehow it's especially unsettling seeing her blown-up smile thirty meters above me. "Creepy, huh?"

Sasha doesn't look at me. She's still watching the billboard. "Definitely."

Veronica starts her speech again. *"Welcome, visitors! I'm Veronica*

Cross"

I turn away. I don't want to hear that voice anymore. "Where next?"

Sasha leads me to the far corner of the lobby, where a row of guest terminals is waiting. Several people are already at the stations, some using haptic interfaces, others jacked in behind the ear. The people using the interfaces move, but the jackers don't. They sit slumped in their chairs, breathing slow, staring at the wall with empty eyes that only occasionally blink.

My port itches. It's been days since I jacked in. I have spyders to check on, research to do, messages to send.

"I need you to find Rami," Sasha says.

I snort. "What, at a regular terminal?"

"Don't think you can handle it?"

The challenge in Sasha's eyes makes me bristle, which is probably her intention. "Sure, I can handle it, but you're underestimating how dangerous it is. This is a public terminal. I can break the kiddie settings, but as soon as I jack in, I'll be vulnerable...in there and out here."

"That's why I'm here. To watch your back in meatspace. So?"

"Unplug me as soon as possible if anything looks weird, okay? I recover fast after a hard cut, and a few seconds could save my ass."

Sasha nods. "Rami's not a jacker, but their cloaking programs are top quality. Megan helped with the coding, so seeing through them won't be easy."

"Can you give me anything else? A DNA signature, or at least their gear specs? I'm diving in blind here."

"Hmm." Sasha sits at one of the terminals. "Give me the specs on your gear."

"Dendryte Silver, serial code...hmm...2460169. That's one of my recent numbers."

Sasha activates the terminal's haptic interface. "I'm forwarding you a DNA scan, vitals, and the specs on Rami's gear. That good enough?"

I smirk. "I'll make it work."

Sasha stands up and offers me the terminal. I sit and unhook the cable, twisting the narrow silver thread between my fingers. Sasha's still so close I can feel the warmth of her arm bleeding into mine through the sleeve of her leather jacket. "Okay, Nevares," she says, narrowing her eyes at me. "Show me what you've got."

I blink, tearing my gaze away. Jacket or not, she's still got a distracting physique underneath. I refocus on my mission, plugging the cable into the jack behind my right ear.

network: ag 48856 . 23522
connection established
welcome: user escudoespiga

I'm standing in a room that's almost identical to the showroom lobby. The same shops are there, the same scrolling ticker symbols, even the smiling billboard of Veronica Cross. The virtual crowd's smaller, but still sizable. Most avatars are dressed in business suits and blazers like the ones in meatspace, but a few are more unique: cat ears and angel wings and tropical-fish-colored hairstyles.

No one notices when I slide into the flow of the crowd. I pull up my toolbar and check my messages. I scroll past the ones from Jacobo and Miguel and open the most recent one from Sasha. There's a download attached—Rami's DNA, vitals, and gear specs. I upload the data to my scanning program, and then run it. Its range should be wide enough to cover the whole building, even the upper floors. My surroundings shift again. About half the avatars change shape and color as their add-on decorations disappear. All the extraneous information vanishes, leaving me with the basics. I scan the crowd as subtly as I can, waiting for a match.

No luck. All the avatars around me are grey. Rami could be anyone, anywhere, and my more powerful scanner settings are useless if I don't know where to point them. I could try a spyder, but those are better at trawling and sorting through code. Plus, someone might notice. Spyders are invisible to most defense matrices, but not to people or other jackers. I need to think outside the box. If I can't find Rami, maybe I can attract them to me?

I pretend to read AxysGen's stock prices while I open my inventory interface. The familiar window pops up, showing me a closet full of clothes for my avatar. I usually present on the extranet the same way I do in reality—female, brown skin, wide hips. I change my hair, nose, and lips sometimes, but that's about it. During most ops, my avatar isn't visible at all. Looking like someone else is a cloak's job. Here and in meatspace, jackers prefer to be invisible.

I dig through my closet, searching for something that might catch Rami's attention. *No, no, no...yes.* When I withdraw from the menu, my avatar's head has turned into an enormous red cherry with a lit fuse on top. If that doesn't get Rami's attention, nothing will. An unfamiliar serial number messages me immediately. Dendryte Bronze, v3.4, which matches the specs Sasha gave me. After scanning for suspicious attachments, I download it. *'Meet me under the billboard.'*

I head toward Veronica Cross's giant face. Several avatars are lingering there, but an old white man with a bad toupee lights up my scanner like a Christmas tree. Got them. I head over, switching my avatar's head back to normal.

"You're not subtle, sweetie," the man says when I arrive.

"Did I need to be?"

The man's eyes slide to the left, and I tense when I see what he sees. Several avatars in black suits are closing in around us. They aren't actual people—their metallic skin and glowing eyes give them away. *Mierda.* Defense programs. Maybe I should have tried something subtler after all.

I activate my shielding program just in time to deflect the blue stun beams that burst from the nearest defense program's eyes. They bounce off my shield, glancing up toward the ceiling, but I know there'll be more. I step in front of the man with the toupee. "Get behind me!"

"No, jack out," he whispers. "I'll find you in meatspace."

"¡Hijo de la chingada! Fine."

I swing my shield around, blocking more beams—red this time. This just gets better and better. These security programs have Puls.wavs. The only thing worse than stunning a jacker and preventing them from logging out is shooting them with a Puls.wav. One hit and your brain is melted forever. As soon as the man in the toupee disappears, I jack out too.

logging off network
disconnection complete

Thursday, 06-10-65 09:56:53

I JERK BACK INTO my body, breathing heavily. Someone has my shoulder in a painful grip, and it takes me a moment to realize it's Sasha. She stares down at me, muttering urgently, "What's going on? Where's Rami?"

I start to answer, but someone else speaks first. "Here, cupcake." Instead of a balding *gringo*, a young woman is heading toward us at a fast clip, high heels clicking on the marble floor. She has long black hair and smooth brown skin, with golden contours on her high cheekbones. Her lips are painted a deep shade of maroon.

"Rami." Sasha lets go of me, leaning in for a hug.

"Reunions later," Rami says. "Run now!"

I shake the blood back into my tingling limbs and hop out of the chair. More men in suits are approaching through the crowd, real ones this time, although they're trying to avoid attention.

"This is your fault, isn't it, Nevares?" Sasha groans, glaring at me.

"You said find Rami. I found Rami. The rest was your job."

"I thought finding them without alerting security was implied."

Rami pushes Sasha toward the exit. "Come on, you can flirt with the new girl later."

I hurry after the two of them, brushing past several startled-looking people in business suits.

"Cherry's outside, right?" Rami asks.

I check over my shoulder. The security guards have started jogging, so I pick up the pace too. "Sasha, is she?"

"She'd better be." Sasha comes to a hard stop, and I almost bump into her. There's no clear shot to the exit. More guards in suits have converged on the doors, forming a line to block us.

The surrounding crowd finally starts to notice. Several people murmur in confusion while others duck behind the kiosks, fear on their faces.

"What now?" I hiss.

Rami doesn't seem upset. They smile and start counting off.

"Three, two…"

When Rami hits "one," a loud boom shakes the foundations of the building. Several people scream. Most of the security guards whirl around, aiming their rifles at the doorway, which has become a smoking crater. The once-silvery metal walls are now black and smoldering, with twisted support beams jutting out.

I freeze up. The smell of smoke is in my nose, my throat, the rapidly tightening cavity of my chest. My ribs are getting smaller and smaller while my heart thumps harder and faster.

"Run!"

Sasha grabs my elbow, hauling me forward hard enough to jerk my shoulder in its socket. That snaps me out of it. We make a break for it, hoping that the guards are still distracted enough by the wreckage not to notice the three of us escaping. We sprint through the cloud of dust and rubble, coughing and sputtering—or at least, I'm coughing and sputtering. Sasha never seems to tire.

Clear of the blast zone, my watery eyes pick up a welcome sight. Cherry is parked at the curb, perched atop a sleek black hoverbike in glide mode. A smile spreads all the way across her face when she sees Rami. "Babe!" she shouts, waving one arm in a beckoning motion.

"You blew up the front door," Rami yells back, taking the steps two at a time.

"Because I love you," Cherry hollers. "Even though you left me in Brazil!"

"How do you run so fast in heels?" I gasp as I stagger down the front steps. I don't know how Sasha finds all these magical bitches who can run ops in perfect makeup and designer shoes, but if I wasn't terrified of dying, I'd be jealous. Anything to keep my mind off…this.

Rami climbs onto the front of Cherry's hoverbike. "I'd never leave you for long," they say, exchanging the helmet Cherry is offering them for a kiss.

"I know." Cherry wraps her arms around Rami's waist, and Rami revs the engine, speeding off down the street.

That leaves me and Sasha. "Come on," she barks, hopping onto a second hoverbike parked right behind Cherry's. Sasha guns the engine, and I have just enough time to clamber on and fling my arms around her waist before we zoom off.

We pull out into the road, weaving between parked cars. Drivers stick their heads out of car windows, gawking at the smoldering remains of AxysGen's front door. It's a wreck, but the building's still standing, and I don't see any mangled bodies. Cherry must have placed everything perfectly and timed it to the millisecond.

It's cold comfort to my racing heart. These rescue missions just keep getting worse and worse. The plasma belching from the hoverbike mixes with the scent of the explosion, and I gag on the sour air. *Get me out of here,* I think, and fortunately, Sasha's on the same page. She peels off down the street, and I bury my face into the back of her leather jacket to block out the stench I can practically smell with my eyes.

"Heads up, Nevares. We're being followed."

Despite my reservations, I tear myself away from the safety of Sasha's back and look back over my shoulder, shaking my head to see through the whipping locks of my hair. Several more hoverbikes have pulled out onto the street behind us. Their engines roar dangerously as they snake through the maze of parked cars, trying to catch up.

"Reach in my pocket," Sasha yells.

Before I can, she lurches over the curb and up onto the sidewalk, nearly mowing down several pedestrians. On the opposite side of the street, Rami and Cherry have found a safer path. Cherry lets go of Rami's waist, pumping her fist in the air. Clearly, she's having the time of her life.

"Reach in my pocket!" Sasha shouts again.

This time, I manage it. When I pull my hand out, I'm holding a fistful of small blue orbs. *Mierda.* Biogrenades. She really wants me to throw them? One of the AxysGen hoverbikes puts on a burst of speed, drawing close enough for me to see the red lettering on its side. The man riding it points a rifle directly at me.

My entire body breaks out in sweat, and the biogrenades nearly slip out of my hands. If I throw them, it'll mean another explosion. Just the thought has me shaking like crazy. But it's throw or get shot. I toss the biogrenades in a panic, praying I won't accidentally hit any pedestrians. *Shit shit shit. This will be all my fault, just like before.*

Luckily, the biogrenades hit their intended target. The tiny blue spheres stick to the man's chest, and he veers off course while trying to rip them off. A moment later, his bike explodes in a ball of flame.

"Nice one, Nevares!" Cherry cheers from across the street.

I don't answer. I can't answer. My stomach lurches with fear and guilt, and I almost lose my lunch as Sasha veers around a sharp corner, gunning through an alleyway that *definitely* isn't wide enough to drive down. I'm pretty sure I'm going to puke if we don't pull over soon, but the third security guard is still following us, and he's gaining rapidly. In desperation, I shove my hand back into Sasha's pocket. No biogrenades left, although I'm not sure I could make myself throw them again.

We burst out of the alley and onto the waterfront, snaking through groups of startled tourists. Pigeons squawk, people shriek, and I almost get a face full of parasol as a woman walking her poodle dives for safety. I wrap my arms around Sasha's waist, squeezing her as tight as possible.

Around the side of Sasha's flapping jacket, I make out where we're going, a bicycle path that leads over the river. The miniature bridge is splitting in two, rising on either side to let a ferry full of shocked boaters pass through. Several gasp and point as they realize what's about to happen.

"What the fuck, Sasha?" I scream into the wind. "This is a *hover*bike, not a *flying* bike. You're gonna get us killed!"

Sasha slams on the gas. "Hold on!" She speeds across the bridge, sailing off the edge and over the water.

For one fantastic, sickening moment, I feel like I'm flying. Then the hoverbike slams down on the other side of the bridge, shock absorbers shuddering and squealing. Only my desperate grip on Sasha keeps me from flying off as we hit the pavement. We speed off down the street, leaving the AxysGen motorcycle far behind. After a few more swooping turns, Sasha brings the bike to a halt. I have to blink several times before the world stops spinning.

"Hey..."

I open my eyes to see Sasha's face—or, rather, three of Sasha's faces—floating in front of me.

"Nevares, you with me?"

"Yeah," I mumble. "I'm fine."

I bend over the side of the bike, throwing up all over the sidewalk. By the time my stomach stops heaving, another hoverbike has pulled up beside ours.

"No fair," Cherry says over the purr of the idling engine. "I wanted to jump a bridge."

"It wasn't a real bridge," Rami points out. "Just a bicycle bridge."

"I still wanted to jump it," Cherry says "Now, *mi vida, mi amor, mi tesoro*, would you like to explain why you left me, your wife, in *motherfucking Brazil* without even trying to look for me?"

I continue to retch, but my stomach's already unloaded all its contents.

"I was trying to protect you, to protect all of us," Rami protests, sounding hurt. "I thought I could—"

"You were thinking long term," Sasha says. "I get it."

"*I* don't," Cherry snaps.

"Enough. Rami couldn't just hole up with you in your bunker and wait for AxysGen to show up."

"Why not?"

I straighten with a groan. I've gone from panic to numbness. The arguing is making my head hurt, and I can't take much more. *"¡Cállate el pinche hocico!* Take me somewhere *not* in the middle of the street. Somewhere we're not gonna get shot, either," I say in a trembling voice.

"Oh my god." From the look on Rami's face and the wary glance they cast at the puddle of vomit on the sidewalk, they're just realizing what happened. "Sweetie, are you okay? Sasha, what did you do to this poor girl?"

Sasha seems to notice how messed up I am. "Nevares—Elena? You okay?"

It takes moment to process the fact that Sasha said my first name, and another to realize she's pushing my hair back from my face, staring at me with something that looks almost like concern.

"Yeah." I wipe my mouth on the back of my sleeve. "I'm okay. And I never, ever wanna do that again."

"Come on, sweetie," Rami says. "Let's head back to the hotel. You could probably use some mouthwash."

I swallow around the raw burn in my throat. Rami's not wrong.

Thursday, 06-10-65 13:42:29

I SWISH THE TOOTHPASTE around in my mouth and spit, staring at the white foam as it circles the drain. I've brushed my teeth four times in the hotel bathroom, but even though the taste is long gone, the sharp smell of vomit is still trapped in my nose.

The more I think about our escape from AxysGen, the angrier I feel. Sure, the hoverbikes were cool, in theory. The explosion was cool—or I would have thought so once, before the incident at the hotel. Even jumping the bridge had been cool.

But, I can't forget the terrified people leaping to avoid our hoverbike and the biogrenades. I didn't hit anyone innocent—this time. And what about the guy I blew up? Corps are evil, no question, but he was probably just a cog trying to earn a paycheck. Before I started jacking, I would've done any kind of shitty corp job to keep my *hermanitos* fed.

Don't be stupid, I tell my reflection. *It was him or you.* It's true, but that doesn't make me feel better. I could justify it in Siberia, sort of, because the guards we killed were holding Rock hostage. He was badly injured, and if we hadn't freed him, he might have died in that cell. But the lady walking her poodle? She was an innocent bystander.

"What the hell were you thinking, Sasha?" I murmur into the mirror. My reflection doesn't give answers. I need to go to the source for those.

I rinse the sink out and return to the hotel room. We booked three: one for Rock and Doc, one for Cherry and Rami (who, from the PDA I witnessed during their arrival in the lobby, are probably making up for lost time), and one for me and Sasha. She's my absolute last choice for a bunkmate, but I can't split up a married couple or siblings.

Sasha lounges on the bed, staring at the ceiling with her hands behind her head. Her body is relaxed, but her dark brown eyes are wide open. She almost looks like she's in a trance.

I clear my throat.

"What?" Sasha asks without moving an inch.

"Bathroom's free if you want it." I cross the room to pull back the curtains, resting my forehead against the window. Cold from the glass seeps in through my pores as I stare down at the street. The yellow lights are fuzzy, almost like fireflies.

"Leave them shut," Sasha says. "We don't want anyone seeing in."

I keep my face against the window. "On the seventeenth floor?"

"One of the largest corps in the world wants to kill us, in case you hadn't noticed. I don't think a window will stop them."

I turn around. "Oh, I noticed. I also noticed we could have killed a bunch of innocent people today. What the fuck, Sasha? I signed up to erase myself from AxysGen's database, not blow up old ladies walking their dogs. There's a big fucking difference."

Sasha sits up without using her arms. For a split second, I forget I'm angry. It's impossible not to notice the way her muscles move beneath her compression shirt. The white material's so thin I can see her dark skin through it, the line that bisects her stomach, the half-hard peaks of her breasts.

"You didn't blow her up, did you?"

Oh, right. I'm supposed to be pissed at her. "Yeah, this time. But what about next time? I'm all for sticking it to the corps, but I draw the line at killing civilians. And honestly? The fact that you're okay with that risk bothers me."

"It bothers you?" Sasha narrows her eyes. "Well, I'm sorry it *bothers* you, Nevares, but this is life or death."

"Yeah, it is, and our lives aren't the only ones that matter. Your empathy only goes as far as your crew, huh? Risk your life for four people and the rest of the world can go fuck itself?"

Sasha abandons the bed and stalks toward me. She towers over me, cold brown eyes glaring down into mine. "You don't know what you're talking about. Drop this before you say something you'll regret."

I glare right back up at her. I don't care if she's my handler. I don't care how sexy she is. I don't care if I could probably reach her stupid mouth with mine if I grab her neck and stand on my toes. Sasha was reckless before, and she's being a *pendeja* now. My conscience has standards even if my *concha* doesn't.

"What I'm regretting is saying yes to your crackpot plan. Tell me you'll be more careful, or I'm out. I'll take my chances on my own."

Surprise flickers in Sasha's eyes, and then a hint of fear. Doc was absolutely right back at the Hole. Sasha and the crew need me as much as I need them. I've got leverage here.

Sasha remains silent for a long moment, her whole body a rippling mass of tension. It feels like steam's pouring off her skin and clinging to mine. At last, her shoulders lower an inch and she backs off. "Fine. We try to keep our hands clean. But I have to know you're ready to do what it takes to survive, Nevares. I don't need someone on my crew who hesitates."

"I can handle it. If someone's shooting at me, I'll shoot back. But if there's someone innocent in the way, I'm out."

Sasha turns away, pulls the curtains shut, and throws herself back on the bed without another word.

I take the hint and head over to the hotel's complimentary terminal. It's not much, but it has a jacking port, and that's all I need. I drop into the chair and plug in.

network: ag 48851 . 23528
connection established
welcome: user escudoespiga

My body relaxes as soon as I hit the extranet. It's been forever since I plugged in without worrying about something or someone melting my brain. I take a moment to savor the freedom of floating in a world of code before focusing on my messages. I open the ones from my *hermanitos* first. They're short but increasingly worried, the last one especially:

"elena where are you. abuela keeps asking n i dont know wat to say. please tell me ur safe. i dont trust the news. jacobo."

My throat stops up. Logically, I know there hasn't been time for me to answer their messages, but I still feel guilty. My brothers always count on me to provide for them, to do right by them, and I've been doing a shit job lately. I never seem to make enough credits to buy them the things they deserve, and I never seem to have enough time to give them the love the deserve either.

I dictate a response as fast as I can think it: *"cant tell you where but im safe. with a new crew. not safe to come home, but i miss you and ill see you soon."* After a brief hesitation, I add, *"tell abuela i got to visit the eiffel tower. beautiful."* Sasha won't like me giving away our location, but AxysGen definitely knows we're in Paris already. *"heres some credits. love you."* I attach the last of what I have in my shell account and send the message off.

After that's done and I've managed to silence the nagging voice in my brain telling me I'm the world's shittiest sister, I throw on a cloak and tab out of the menu, heading for the extranet. At first I float in dark, empty space, but as my thoughts branch out, silver filigree appears in the air around me. It crawls in every direction, shining like tinsel. I remember the wonder I felt the first time I saw it—a never-ending net that stretches over the horizon, a million little nodes along its strands.

"Wolf+Kremlin," I say.

Several of the nodes brighten, swelling like dewdrops until they're almost as big as I am. They play raw news footage—a burning building, not singed like AxysGen's Paris headquarters, but demolished to rubble. Fire crews attempt to put out the blaze, but it keeps smoldering. I tab away quickly. Fire is the last thing I want to see.

I look at the next node, news footage dated three months ago. A reporter's face appears in the corner of the screen, a thin, heavily made-up *gringa* with platinum hair. "A highly dangerous crew of mercenaries attempted a violent attack on Axys Generations' London headquarters today—"

I snort. This looks like more than 'attempted'.

"...Sasha Young, also known as the Wolf of the Kremlin. Investigating authorities believe she was caught in the blast she initiated..."

I cut off the feed. I already know the rest of the world thinks Sasha died along with Megan, even if some top-level suits at AxysGen know better. That reminds me. I pull up my menu again, selecting one of my spyders. In addition to extracting information from other people's intranet servers, they also do deep extranet searches.

"All right, little buddy," I whisper into my hand. "Keywords: Megan, Sasha+Young, Wolf+Kremlin, jacker, handler, AyxsGen, Axys+Generations." The spyder's delicate legs tickle my palm as I set it on the nearest silver tendril. It scurries off, disappearing from sight.

Once it's gone, I drag a savefile from my inventory. The world of black and silver fades until I'm surrounded by the sound of the ocean and the warmth of the sun on my skin. The air smells like fresh salt. I'm on the deck of a private yacht, sprawled on a lounge chair. A gorgeous woman is sitting beside me: dark curly hair, brown skin, washboard abs, and kissable lips.

Maybe a little too kissable. I make her lips thinner, her hair longer, her hips and breasts bigger. When I'm still not satisfied, I lighten up her skin too. She's not really my type, but my presets are uncomfortably familiar, and I don't want to think too much about why.

I moan as the woman's hand runs up along my stomach, unfastening the strings of my swimsuit. Maybe it's rude to play a porn VR while Sasha's so close to my body in meatspace, but I honestly have no fucks left to give. I almost died twice today. I deserve a little stress relief.

Friday, 06-11-65 02:43:45

I REST MY CHEEK against the cool metal of the Eagle's belly, hovering somewhere between awake and asleep. I'm exhausted, or at least my brain is. Staying slumped in the hotel chair for a couple hours doesn't count as sleep, especially since Sasha shook me awake and shepherded me back to the Eagle in the middle of the night.

She's sitting next to me, careful to keep space between our thighs. Rock and Doc are side by side on the opposite bench. Rami and Cherry are in the pilot and copilot's seat, although I think Cherry's snoring. I'm tempted to join her. It's a struggle to keep my eyes open.

Doc's in the opposite frame of mind. The kid is twitchy, both knees jiggling, taking up more space on the bench than she needs. The motion's strong enough for me to feel despite the vibration of the engines. "How'd you become a jacker, Elena?"

I yawn. "Luck. Me and my kid brothers were stuck in the outer rings of Mexico City. No family left except a sick *abuela*. Taking care of them full time meant I failed my APS. An ex-corp jacker was working for this fixer I knew, Jento. He felt bad for me, I guess, and gave me a key to Darkspace. You know, the deep web where jackers learn the trade. I was self-taught from there." I sit up a little straighter. "Someday, I'll pass a key along to some other kid. What about you, *chiquita*? You're around that age. You're what, eleven?"

"Thirteen," Doc says, clearly annoyed.

"Yeah, you look...never mind."

Doc snorts. "That's right, never mind. But yeah, I took my APS. Aced 'em. One year of a corp scholarship, then I started to feel gross about it. So I left."

I wake up a bit more, surprised. "You know how many kids would kill for one of those slots, right? I mean literally kill someone. Straight up murder them."

"Didn't feel like being a marketing tool," Doc says. "They used me in promotional vids. 'See? If this poor girl from the slums can do it, so can your kid! Look at her and ignore all the corp dynasty kids who got spoon-fed the answers in advance.' They're selling fake hope to keep the starving masses complacent, pretending it's all randomized."

"What about your family? They could have used the credits on top of their peebees."

Doc slugs Rock's enormous arm. "Don't have one except for him. When I left, they tried to come after me. They didn't want their 'investment' to get away. So Rock suggested I make myself a bodyguard."

"Wait, *you* modded him? I thought AxysGen did him like that, or maybe some back-alley surgeon." I study Rock with new eyes, trying to process it. From what I saw in Siberia, he's more machine than man under the skin. He must have had a shit-ton of surgeries—probably painful ones.

"His idea," Doc says warily. "He wanted to protect me."

"So you turned him into a cyborg?" I look at Rock. "And you were...okay with that?"

Rock nods. He puts one of his massive hands on top of Doc's head in what's clearly a gesture of affection. His palm nearly swallows her whole skull.

"See?" Doc says. "Patient consent."

"And you're the reason he doesn't talk?"

Doc's face clouds with anger. "No. He just doesn't. And he's fine the way he is," she says, an edge of protectiveness in her tone.

"Says the girl who modded him to hell and back."

"Cool it," Cherry says from the passenger's seat. Our argument must have woken her up. "No one thinks there's anything wrong with Rock. Right, Elena?"

It's clearly a warning. "Yeah, there's nothing wrong with him."

"Damn right," Doc grumbles, but her eyes flick down toward her lap. I wonder if she feels guilty under it all. I would if I had turned my big brother into a cyborg, no matter who was after us. It's really fucked up, and it tracks with what Sasha claims—Doc isn't an ordinary kid. No ordinary kid could make Rock, or *would* make Rock. Hell, no ordinary adult would either.

"Doc didn't have much choice, sweetie," Rami says from the pilot's seat. "It's what the corps do. Claiming the peebees are all they can afford to give while they live in their mansions, 'uplifting' a few undesirables with the APS and random shows of philanthropy. They go through the motions just often enough for people to forget they should be angry. And if somebody disagrees or tries to buck the system, they shut them up. Permanently."

I know. Everyone in this shuttle knows. Injustice can be staring you right in the face, but if there's a sliver of a chance to rise to the top, to beat the system, a lot of people will ignore it. It's not their fault for hoping. We all want to believe we'll win the lottery, so we all end up screwed.

"Prepare for arrival at the Hole. Begin descent in six hundred meters," Val announces, interrupting my thoughts.

When I glance through the viewscreen, the endless white tundra doesn't have any distinguishing features. Then the Eagle glides to a stop, perching above a snowdrift. The ground beneath us opens, allowing Rami to park the shuttle. "Nice job, Val," they say, giving the dashboard an affectionate pat.

I narrow my eyes at Rami. "You like AIs?"

Rami smiles back at me. "I like this one."

"Ever use 'em for ops?"

"Sometimes. Why, do you prefer VIs?"

"Yeah. I like knowing exactly what my programs will do. Plus the idea of a fully-realized AI creeps me out more than a little."

Suddenly, I've got the whole shuttle's attention. Cherry stops in the middle of unbuckling her harness. Doc sucks in a quick breath. Rock tilts his head. Most unsettling of all, Sasha's hard brown eyes fix straight on me, dark and inscrutable and decidedly unfriendly.

"What?" I say, slightly defensive. "Corps make 98 percent of the AIs on the market, right? Do you want *them* in charge of designing one that's basically a human made of code?"

Cherry laughs, and it's only a little bit forced. "You've got a point, *chaparrita*. Corps aren't exactly beacons of morality."

The rest of the crew chuckles along, but Sasha's stare is unwavering. "Don't you think it depends on the creator?"

I resist the temptation to squirm. "I guess so. It's all hypothetical, though. No one's managed to create a FRAI yet." In an effort to avoid Sasha's eyes, I look at the ceiling where the rear speakers are. "Hey, Val, what do you think? Can a good creator make a good FRAI?"

"Yes," Val answers. "According to an analysis of peer reviewed studies by known experts in the field, the general consensus is that the creation of a fully-realized artificial intelligence with appropriate moral parameters is theoretically possible."

"Well, Val has spoken. Let's hope she's right, for the sake of the future." I unbuckle my harness and stand up. "So, we going in or what?"

The Hole looks the same as we left it, an empty garage with a few dark puddles on the concrete floor. I jump out of the shuttle as soon as the doors open. The shuttle bay is heated, but the air following us in is freezing. I wrap my arms around myself, shuddering as the others climb out.

"Get some rest," Sasha says to the crew. "We'll finalize the details for our next job first thing in the morning."

I force my teeth stop chattering. "Job? I thought protecting ourselves from AxysGen was our job."

"That's the job I'm talking about, Nevares." Sasha heads for the bunker, taking long strides that make it clear she doesn't want company.

There's a tap on my shoulder. "Don't mind her," Rami says. They've taken off their wig from earlier, revealing a short black pixie cut underneath. Though they're wearing makeup again, it's much lighter and more natural-looking than the maroon lipstick. "Sasha gets tense during times like this."

"I hope she has a damn good plan, because otherwise we're screwed."

Cherry approaches from my other side, her red bob bouncing. I have to crane my neck a little to meet her eyes. "Don't worry. Sasha knows her shit, and so do the rest of us." She claps a hand on my opposite shoulder, making it clear that she means me too.

"Thanks."

We head down into the bunker together. Compared to the wind outside, the air in here feels like a warm blanket. The place smells like CO_2 scrubbers and disinfectant, but it's not unpleasant. The Hole feels exactly like what it is—a safe space sealed away from the world.

"So, I heard Doc's story. Why are you two in this?" I ask Cherry and Rami. "Credits? Family?"

"I played it straight for a while," Cherry says. "Passed my APS with high scores, got shipped off to engineering school. Then I realized I hated it. Or maybe my coworkers hated me. My teammates and I... we didn't get along. After that, it was whatever freelance shit I could find until I met Sasha."

Rami glances at me when Cherry hesitates, but they don't have to worry. I'm nosey, sure, but I don't pester people for bad memories. "What about you, Rami?" I ask them.

"I was a corp kid. I tried to be what my family wanted, but one day, I just...couldn't anymore. I wanted to be someone, *anyone* else. So, I kind of became everyone else. You know what I mean?"

"Yeah, I get it," I say, even though I really don't. As much as I hate corp kids, I'd send my brothers off to live that life in a hot second. Anything to keep them warm and fed. I can't wrap my mind around how Rami could give that up.

We arrive at the bunks. Inside the room is a metal sink and a mirror, two dressers, and six thin cots, maybe big enough to hold two people if they spoon the whole night. Aside from the three of us, the room's empty. Sasha's nowhere to be seen.

I take the same cot Doc gave me last time, glancing warily at the door. "Sasha's not gonna come in here and start freaking out because I took Megan's old bunk or something, right?"

"Nah," Cherry says, flopping on the bunk across from me.

Rami heads over to the sink to wash their face. "She means Megan usually shared Sasha's bunk."

I strip off my shirt, tossing it somewhere beyond the foot of my cot. I'd keep it on for extra warmth, but it still reeks of diesel and vomit. I need to pester someone for a change of clothes soon. "So, what's Sasha's story? I mean, I can see how the whole dead-fiancée thing would mess you up."

"That's not really a bedtime story," Cherry says.

"And we're not the ones who should tell it." Rami finishes removing their makeup and heads over to one of the dressers. "Here, sweetie," they say, tossing a bundle at my chest. "Thought you might like a fresh nightshirt. The shower's down the hall if you want it."

I snuggle into the clean shirt. Comfortably large, but very soft. "Nah, I showered back at the hotel. Just needed something clean to wear." I yawn, wiggling under the covers. They're a little scratchy, but heavy enough to offer some comforting weight. "Hey..."

"Hey, what?" Rami asks, sitting beside Cherry.

"Can you give me an outline, at least? I'm not trying to stick my nose in Sasha's business, but if there's any landmines I should avoid..."

"I feel you," Cherry says. "The short version is, Sasha and Megan were APS kids who met at school. Megan was...uh, how do I say this without sounding like an asshole?"

"I think it's fair to say she could be self-centered sometimes," Rami says, at the very same moment that Cherry decides on, "Kind of a brat."

"She was brilliant, but sometimes her work took precedence over everything else," Rami continues.

Cherry sighs. "Right. She left Sasha for a while after they quit school. Ditched her to work on some crackpot projects. That's when Sasha and I met." A sly grin spreads across her face. "She was definitely a ladykiller then, until Megan came back. Had a new girl every week."

I raise my eyebrows. "Really?"

"You really surprised?" Cherry chuckles. "You've seen her. Boss-lady can get it."

That's absolutely true, although I've never seen Sasha turn on any kind of charm. The girls she seduced must have been looking for hookups that didn't involve much talking. It's uncomfortably obvious to me that, in years past, I might have been one of those girls. But, Rami and Cherry don't need to know that. "But Megan came back, right?"

"Yes, she came back," Rami says. "We were all on Sasha's crew by then. The one-night stands stopped immediately. Sasha...when she makes you part of her family, there's no one more devoted. That goes for all of us."

That tracks with what I've observed. Sasha might be an asshole, but she's a protective asshole.

"It's true," Cherry insists, perhaps interpreting my silence as skepticism. "Sasha would take a bullet for any of us, no hesitation."

"I know she seems cold," Rami says, "but try and trust her. She *always* has a plan, and she'll do...whatever it takes to keep us safe."

"Hey, I believe it." I flop back on my bunk, folding my hands under my head. "She definitely knows her shit. But she's just one handler. We're one crew. A whole corp is trying to kill us. Kind of unfair when you think about the odds."

"Aren't the odds of most ops unfair?" Cherry points out. "Bad odds didn't stop you from becoming a jacker and joining a crew, did it, *chaparrita*?"

"Guess you have a point. But hey, if we have to die, no more explosions. That's not how I wanna go."

"No fun at all," Cherry grumbles. Rami shushes her.

"Get some sleep, Elena. And welcome to the crew."

Even though I'm not the crewbonding type, Rami and Cherry's friendliness is a nice change. Sasha's made it clear she doesn't like me, but everyone else seems to think I'm okay. I'll take 'okay' from these people, at least until we're done working together. I settle under the covers and roll onto my side, curling my knees up to my chest.

I close my eyes, but sleep doesn't come. First Doc and Rock make a minor commotion finding their bunks, and after that, the loudness of my thoughts keeps me awake. I only drift off after hours of tossing and turning, trying not to imagine the smell of smoke. Sasha never joins us.

Friday, 06-11-65 11:32:45

WHEN I WAKE UP the next morning, I'm just as exhausted as I was before I went to sleep. A layer of sweat drips from my skin, and the sheets are twisted around my legs. My limbs feel weighed down, heavy, a contrast to the strange floating sensation in my chest. Or maybe not so strange. I've been riding the nightmare for months now.

I kick the covers off and look around the room. None of the nearby bunks are occupied, and all the sheets are stripped. All that's left in the room is Cherry and Rami's makeup cases, sitting side by side beneath the mirror. I sigh, which turns into a jaw-cracking yawn. Running from AxysGen hasn't really given me time to keep up with my beauty routine.

I grab some spare shorts and a tank top from the dresser before swinging by the mirror. After borrowing one of Rami's eye pencils and smudging some of Cherry's lipstick on with my finger, I feel more like myself. Rami doesn't have the right colors for contouring, but I bet they have more shades somewhere for their disguises. They'd probably let me borrow some if I asked. But first, I *really* need to pee.

My timing is awful, because I find the bathroom right as Sasha's leaving. When my eyes zero in on the short white towel wrapped around her body, I freeze in place. *Dios.* This *chula* isn't just a trial against my willpower. She makes my fucking bones ache with want. It's not fair that she's this tall, this toned, this good at claiming every inch of space around her.

Droplets of water cling to Sasha's smooth skin, and her cornrows are freshly oiled. Her shoulders are squared, her brow furrowed in annoyance or perhaps frustration. Yeah, frustrated. That's how Sasha looks. She's frustrated, and that's frustrating for me too, because it makes her look hotter. My shorts soak through in less than a second.

"Sorry," I blurt out. "Need to pee."

If Sasha's embarrassed about being caught in a towel, she doesn't show it. Her eyes are as cold as ever. "You asking for permission, Nevares?"

"Yeah, right." It's not my wittiest comeback, so I scoot past her and into the bathroom. There are several toilets as well as some shower stalls, and the warm air still holds traces of steam and citrus soap—Sasha's soap. That thought leads to other, less innocent thoughts. Sasha's soap, Sasha in the shower, joining Sasha in the shower. I shake myself. Just because I'm attracted to an asshole doesn't mean I need to do anything about it. There's also the fact that Sasha hates me. My chances of a 'yes' are somewhere between *cero y nada*.

After visiting one of the stalls, I head to the sink. "Who the fuck does she think she is anyway? 'You asking for permission, Nevares?'" I say mockingly, as though repeating it in a dumb voice will make it any less sexy. "What kind of line is—*¡chingada madre!*" I yank my hands back, hissing in pain. The water's gone scalding while I wasn't paying attention. I turn off the faucet and shake my hands dry. "Thinks because she's buff and has that damn jawline, she can march around acting like—whoa."

For the second time, I nearly run straight into someone else. A shirtless, barrel-chested someone. At first all I can see is a solid wall of muscle covered in a few curly blond hairs, but then I crane my neck back to see Rock peering down at me. He pats me gently on the arm and walks on by, taking up the entire bathroom doorway with his bulk.

I shake my head in disbelief. And I thought my old crew was quirky. Compared to them, Sasha's people are just plain weird. But as long as they're the right kind of weird to keep me alive, I guess it doesn't matter.

"I think Rock likes you," a low voice says. Doc's lurking nearby, staring at me with laughing eyes.

"Not my type, kid. I like pretty boys with long eyelashes and girls who look like they could step on my windpipe with their jackboot and make me thank them for it." That second category is my favorite, and it's my bad luck that Sasha falls right into it.

Doc's nose scrunches up in disgust. "Ew, I didn't mean in a sex way. He's not into any of that, plus he's my *brother*. Are all adults like this, or just you?"

I lean one shoulder against the wall and fold my arms. "Shouldn't you know? I'm not the only adult you've met."

Doc rolls her eyes. "These 'adults' are statistical outliers. Any data I gather from them is useless."

"So, that mean I'm not a statistical outlier? Thanks, I guess."

"This conversation is over," Rami says, gliding in from the next room. Today they're in slightly more masculine clothes as well as makeup, with a pencil-thin mustache above their lip and a classic smoky eye.

"Thanks, Mom," Doc grumbles.

"And you." Rami aims an accusatory glare at me. "No talking about eyelashes and jackboots with the resident minor."

I stick my lip out. "She started it. Besides, the kid slices and dices people in her spare time. I doubt sex is going to faze her."

"I've got ears," Doc says, more amused than upset.

Rami boxes said ears lightly in both hands. "Quiet, you...now get. Meeting's in ten. *Don't* be late."

Doc scurries over to the table near the 'kitchen' section of the bunker. "Don't worry," Rami says once she's out of earshot. "She wasn't trying to set you up with Rock. He just doesn't warm up to people quickly...which makes sense, since most of the people he meets try to shoot him."

"At least someone on this team likes me."

"I like you," Rami says. "Doc likes you because you saved Rock. Cherry likes you because you found me."

"Fine, you made your point. We all know who doesn't like me."

"You mean Sasha," Cherry says, striding out of the bunkroom to join us. She slings an arm around Rami's shoulders, leaning down to kiss the top of their head. "Is she being a dick? Because I'll kick her ass for you."

"How'd you know?" I ask.

Cherry smirks. "You have the Sasha look on your face."

"The Sasha look?"

"Like you turned your milkshake upside down in your lap to cool off."

"I do *not* have a Sasha look," I protest while Rami snorts out a laugh.

"Yes, you do," Cherry says. "Anyway, be patient with her. She's...not herself. Things have been different since our last op went wrong."

That causes a flicker of curiosity. "You mean she's not always like this?"

We're interrupted by the sound of boots on the floor. Sasha steps out of the bunk as well, wearing a sleeveless grey shirt and black fatigues. I pretend my shudder is from a stray lock of hair escaping my bun to tickle my neck.

"Meeting, now," Sasha says, jerking her head toward the table and chairs. The others wander over, with Doc already seated and Rock emerging from the bathroom. Thanks to his size, the towel draped across his shoulders looks more like a washcloth.

When we arrive at the table, Sasha claims one of the chairs while Doc kneels on another. Cherry sits on Rami's lap despite having four inches on them, and Rock leans against the wall. There's one chair left, but I hesitate to take it, since it's next to Sasha's. I brace my arms against the back and lean over it instead.

"If we want to stay alive," Sasha says without preamble, "we need to wipe ourselves from AxysGen's database of undesirables. It won't be easy, and we'll have to be *subtle*." Her eyes fall directly on me as she says that, and my skin heats up. "Megan wrote a program called Poison Fruit that can change the information in a database, then alters any other databases or backups that communicate with it so there are no discrepancies. Think you can use something like that, Nevares?"

"Alter the database? Sure. But a central database like that is gonna be a nightmare to get into. Decoys, booby traps, automatic Puls.wavs, not to mention corp jackers patrolling AxysGen's intranet systems. And that's not even touching what we'll have to go through in meatspace to gain access."

"I didn't ask if it would be hard," Sasha says. "I asked if you could do it. You have those programs you modified with AxysGen's code, right?"

"Well, yeah."

Sasha doesn't wait for me to go on. "Which brings us to step two. In order to stay gone after we wipe the database, we need to retrieve... something I lost. Something AxysGen stole from me."

I don't miss the hesitation. "What something?"

"A brainbox. I lost it during our last op." It's obvious Sasha doesn't mean our last op, but her last op with her old crew. With Megan.

I narrow my eyes at her. "That's it? Really? Sorry, but I'm gonna need a little more info before I risk my neck."

"My brainbox has all kinds of important data on it. If AxysGen manages to decrypt it, we're through. And it has some time I'm missing. My memories have been...choppy...since they took it."

I'm surprised. Sasha doesn't seem like the type of person to record her memories. Or maybe she is. I barely know her, other than the fact that she loves her crew, dislikes me, and hates AxysGen. "*Dios.* How do you lose something that literally sits inside your skull?"

"Putting that aside," Cherry says, "getting your box back won't be easy. Do you even know where it is, *jefa*?"

"Definitely somewhere under really tight security," Rami says. "If it hasn't been destroyed."

"It hasn't," Sasha says with certainty. "AxysGen wouldn't waste a resource like that. We have methods of pinging its location, but that might alert whoever has it. We'll wait until after we wipe the database. Otherwise, AxysGen could move it before we get there, or set up a trap for us." She looks at the rest of the crew. "I know I'm asking a lot, but I need you with me on this, okay? Remember who you're doing this for."

The room goes silent. Even though it isn't a real explanation, and the way she phrased it is strangely vague, I'm almost convinced for a moment purely by Sasha's sincerity. When I glance at the rest of the crew, there's fear, worry, and concern on their faces, but absolutely no doubt.

"I'm with you, Sasha," Rami says, placing their hands flat on the table. "One hundred percent."

Cherry exhales upward through her bright red bangs. "Shit. Me too."

"I think you're crazy," Doc says, but when Rock gives her a pleading look, she sighs. "Us too."

Sasha turns to me. "Nevares?"

"Doc's right. This is crazy." But I know I'll go along with it anyway. Even if Sasha's brainbox recovery heist doesn't work, wiping AxysGen's database is a good idea. A close to impossible idea, but a good one. It'll increase my chances for survival exponentially if I'm not on their private hitlist. If I have to, I can bail before Sasha and her crew go to retrieve the brainbox. "I'm in for step one. No promises for step two yet, at least not until you give me a better explanation."

"Fair enough," Sasha says, "although I'll remind you that *you* were the one who came to me begging for protection in St. Petersburg."

"That was before you tried to jump the Seine on a hoverbike and made me puke in a sketchy Parisian alley."

Sasha snorts, and I stare at her in shock. I'm not sure I trust my ears, but that *almost* sounded like laughter. "Gear up," she says, getting out of her chair. "You too, Nevares. We leave in thirty."

"Thirty? Don't we need to plan more?"

"It's a couple hours to Tokyo. We can strategize on the way."

I smile. Tokyo. *Abuela's* going to enjoy hearing about that.

Friday, 06-11-65 16:04:43

I TUG AT THE shoulder of my blazer, annoyed with how the seam digs into the soft flesh of my underarm. Rami's clothes make a good disguise, but they've got a couple inches on me, and I'm fuller than they are in some important places. The business attire fits, but barely. It's an effort to keep from making impolite adjustments.

Rami, on the other hand, pulls the corp look off seamlessly. They're wearing a hijab this time, as well as a sharp hound's-tooth women's suit. A pair of square-rimmed glasses are perched on their nose, and their lips are painted one of the rare shades of bright pink that's still neutral enough to be business-appropriate.

We weave through the throng of people, heading for the silver tubes that will carry us to AxysGen's upper floors. "If anyone tries to speak to you, let me do the talking," Rami mutters from the corner of their mouth. "Just give them a white people smile."

"The close-lipped 'I acknowledged you, now please go away' *gringo* smile?"

"Exactly."

"What about the elevators? We need IDs."

"I've got you covered." Rami produces a shiny red button that reads "AG" and pins it to my lapel. "Coded DNA and fingerprints should match yours. Welcome to AxysGen, new employee Esperanza Alvarez."

"That'll work. And who are you?"

"Laila Ahmad."

"This is your favorite part, isn't it? Dressing up and picking a new name?"

They grin. "Absolutely. Best job in the world."

We follow the sluggish river of people onto the elevator. No matter how much the corps stress productivity and efficiency, there's no changing human nature. It still takes everyone forever to file in, and the enclosed space reeks of cologne and perfume.

The elevator doors close, and the lift soars up through its silver tube. It stops on the first floor, then the second, and I twist to avoid being jostled by the people exiting and entering. Finally, we reach the third floor. I squeeze out of the sardine can, stepping into a large, segregated office area.

Glowing terminals stretch as far as I can see. Hundreds of pale faces, all slack and lifeless, are bathed in the light shining from the screens. I shudder. I know I look the same when I'm jacked in, but the sight of so many organized rows of people doing it at once is downright eerie.

Rami touches my elbow, guiding me down the rows until we find two empty terminals. They sit in one chair and I take the other. No one around seems to notice us. I guess assigned seating isn't a thing.

"Before you plug in, there's one more thing we need to do," Rami says.

My heartbeat thuds faster. Now that I'm actually here, I'm increasingly aware of how dangerous this op is. Once I jack in, I might not jack out again. "What?"

"This." Rami passes me a tiny black box. It's small enough to fit in my palm, with a red button on one side.

"A databox?" I run my thumb over the button, and two sides of the cube open up. There's a port on one end, shaped exactly like the one behind my ear. On the other is a thin silver cable. "What's on it?"

"A copy of Val. Hear me out," Rami adds when I open my mouth to object. "I know you aren't fond of AIs, and I understand why, but Val is really useful. I've taken her on missions myself, and she's gotten me and the rest of the crew out of more sticky situations than I can count."

"You mean she's programmed to run ops too? Not just pilot the shuttle?"

Rami checks once more to make sure that no one's listening. "Running ops is Val's primary function, and she's darn good at it. She's the reason I managed to stay hidden under AxysGen's nose for over a month. The best cloak in the world couldn't have done it without her help."

I grimace. Using an AI when I'm used to regular programs has bad idea written all over it, even though I'm inclined to trust Rami. On the other hand, I'm sitting in the middle of enemy territory, about to infiltrate a security system that will melt my brain inside my skull if I put even one toe out of line.

"Over a month, huh?"

Rami nods. "Val knows AxysGen's security inside and out. You'll see."

"Fine," I grumble. I'm already in for this op, and I'll need all the help I can get. I attach the silver cable extending from the terminal to the black box, then insert the box's cable behind my ear.

network: ag 35689 . 13969
Connection established
welcome: user escudoespiga

AxysGen's employee intranet system is the same as it was months ago: a bunch of pulsing crimson cables and glowing gridwork that stretches high above my head. I try not to let the tall red tower and the empty black backdrop put me on edge. I've been here before, I've done this before... and I almost died.

Almost, I tell myself. The key word is 'almost.'

I activate my toolbar and pull out my shield, bracing it on my arm with the forward spikes extended. I feel at least a hundred percent safer. My shield's saved my life so many times I've stopped counting.

Next, I start my doppelganger. Another version of myself pops up, a decoy made of light that looks exactly like me. Ideally, it's meant to confuse automatic targeting programs. With a flesh-and-blood jacker, though, I've only got a fifty-fifty shot of pulling off the ruse; less if their scanning programs are stronger than my disguise.

After activating the doppel, I put on my cloaking program. I can't pull off complicated disguises in meatspace, but here, I'm in my element. A shroud of blue code envelops me, running over my body. To AxysGen's intranet system, my twin and I should look like harmless interoffice e-mails.

Last, I check the final slot in my inventory. The icon for the Poison Fruit program is cheesy-looking, a bright red apple with a dripping green skull on its shiny skin. But if it works as well as Sasha says it does, it's some serious shit.

I check my toolbar one more time. Shield, scanner, doppel, cloak, stuns, Poison Fruit. And there's also one more thing, a final icon I haven't installed myself. It's a small black square with a red circle in the middle, one that looks identical to the box Rami gave me. It's time to see what Val can do.

When I activate the program, a female avatar appears beside me and the doppel. She's Black, thin, beautiful with medium-dark skin that has pink jewel tones for highlights. Her hair is long and wavy, and wearing a grey business suit, the type that looks sleek and expensive, with a purple shirt underneath.

"Hello, Elena," she says in a melodious voice, gazing at me with dark, expressive eyes. "As you know, my name is V.41, but you may call me Val. I am a multi-functional, fully realized artificial intelligence program designed to assist you."

My jaw drops. "Did you just say 'fully-realized AI?'"

"Yes." A small smirk spreads across Val's face, one that makes her avatar look surprisingly realistic. "As I recall, you did concede the point that a FRAI created by an independent programmer and offered the opportunity to develop proper moral parameters might not be a threat to the world."

I roll my eyes. "Ah, I get it. You're fucking with me. Did Sasha tell you to say that? No, she's too preoccupied with the stick up her ass. Was it Rami? *Mierda,* I'm gonna kill her."

"I would not recommend that course of action, Elena," Val says.

"Fine, whatever. If you're a FRAI, then tell me who made you."

Val doesn't seem bothered by my skepticism. "I was created by Megan Delaney, and my primary function is to assist the Lucky Seven. This priority was given to me by my creator. Now, how may I assist you?"

I don't answer her question. Instead, I activate my scanning program on its highest setting. The readings don't make any sense. I've gone up against other jackers using AIs, and even a few specialized AI security programs. But Val is different. There isn't even a category for her in my database. Shit, this is getting weird. Scary weird.

"So, Val, Megan, uh, created you?" If my predecessor actually coded the first legitimate FRAI, she must have been a fucking savant.

"Yes," Val says.

"You mean some crazy genius jacker on a crew of misfits managed to do what a bunch of corps with all the resources in the world haven't been able to figure out yet?"

"Yes."

I laugh in disbelief. "Well, shit."

"Your doubts are understandable. Humans are often confused and afraid when they encounter the unfamiliar."

"I'm not afraid," I snap, but if I'm being honest, that's a lie. I still don't believe Val is actually a FRAI, but doubts are starting to creep into my mind. What little my scanners can read of her code make it clear she isn't like anything I've ever seen. "You mentioned the Lucky Seven. Who are they?"

"The Lucky Seven are a team of operatives led by Sasha Young. Current members are: Sasha Young, Rami Hajjar, Cherry Vidal, Doris Wilson, Ralph Wilson, and myself."

I snort. With names like Doris and Ralph, it's no wonder they choose to go by Doc and Rock instead.

"Past members are: Megan Delaney. Would you like me to add you to the roster of current members, Elena?"

I do a quick cost-benefit analysis. On the off-chance Val is a legit FRAI, and her primary function is really to assist the crew, it could be to my benefit. "Sure. Why the hell not?"

"Adding you to the roster of current members. Welcome to the Lucky Seven, Elena Nevares. What are our mission parameters?"

Right. The mission. I try to refocus, but my brain's a mess of confusion. I'd expected surprises during this op, but meeting a self-proclaimed FRAI is the absolute last thing I'd imagined. I consider my options. I can't sit here forever waiting for a corp jacker to stumble across me. Jacking out is a no, not before I wipe the database. It's forward or nothing.

"Okay. We need to get through AxysGen's intranet defense system to their central database node and erase ourselves from Santa's naughty list. Got it?"

Val nods. "Mission parameters accepted. Working together, I estimate our probability of success at sixty-four percent."

"Only sixty-four percent?"

"Correct. Acting alone, I estimate your probability of success at twelve percent."

I scoff. "Seriously?"

"Analyzed comparatively, twelve percent is a high probability. Most human jackers would have lower chances of success...without my assistance, of course."

"Great," I grumble. "A FRAI *and* a smartass. Just what I wanted in a partner."

Val smirks again. "I will make note of that in your file."

"One more question. How do I know you're telling the truth about any of this?"

The smirk on Val's face vanishes, replaced by a look of sincerity. "The ethical and moral parameters that guide my behavior were modeled after user Sasha Young. I have spent many hours observing her behavior and analyzing her brain activity to facilitate this goal."

"That's not exactly reassuring," I say, remembering the way Sasha almost mowed down the pedestrians in Paris.

"Sasha would assist you in this situation. Therefore, I will assist you."

"Fine," I sigh. "I'll take all the help I can get in here, I guess."

"That is a logical choice, considering your probability of success without me."

I roll my eyes. "With all those hours of human observation, did you ever learn that sometimes it's better not to know things?"

"Acquiring knowledge of human behavior is another of my primary functions," Val says. "I look forward to learning more by observing you, as well as improving my learning algorithms. Allow me to help us begin." She waves her hand, and the world in front of us tilts. The large crossbeam tower turns sideways, becoming a glowing red hallway.

I swallow. This op just keeps getting weirder.

Friday, 06-11-65 16:23:22

I'M NOT SURE HOW to walk with Val at first. Going in front puts me right in the line of fire. Hanging back gives Val control of where we're going and what we're doing, and I don't trust my new 'partner' enough for that. Eventually I make my doppel lead the way and fall back behind, keeping Val in the corner of my eye.

A short distance down the hallway, we encounter our first roadblock: a wall of scrolling blue code. I smirk. It'll get harder from here, but at least the beginning's easy. I lift my shield, bracing my arm in front of me, and charge. My shoulder jolts with the force of the collision, but my shield is stronger than the forcefield. The code shatters like glass, flying apart around me.

"I could have rerouted the code to flow in a different direction, or we could have passed through with your cloaking programs," Val says.

I roll my shoulders. "But that wouldn't have been nearly as satisfying."

"An interesting decision. I will remember it."

"Why do I feel like you're judging me?"

"I was not judging you. I am simply observing. Observation is—"

"One of your primary functions. Yeah, yeah."

I step through the human-shaped hole I've made. It's a little ragged-looking, but my shield is coded with automatic alarm-dampeners. My entrance shouldn't have been detected.

Past the wall, I proceed more cautiously. The hallway branches off in five different directions, which becomes ten, which becomes one hundred, forming a huge web. I open my inventory and withdraw some spyders to find the right way.

"Please, allow me to help."

I glance over at Val. If she's sticking around, I might as well make use of her. "Okay, give it a shot. But don't trigger any alarms."

Val gives me a look. "Most humans would likely be offended by that comment. It implies a lack of confidence in the recipient's abilities."

"You really are just like a wordier version of Sasha, aren't you?"

79

Val seems to recognize that as a rhetorical question. Rather than respond, she places her hand against the wall. Streams of golden code travel from her fingertips, branching out in every direction like little beams of sunlight. They race back after a few seconds, disappearing into her palm.

"Holy shit," I blurt out. I've never seen anybody do something like that, not even as a proof of concept. The fact that Val might be a FRAI suddenly seems a little less crazy. No matter how much experience I have and how good my programs are, I'm just a visitor here, speaking a foreign language. Val seems totally at home, like she's made of the same fabric as the world around us.

"This way." Val motions toward one of the paths on our right.

I chew my lower lip. This is the tipping point whether I'm going to listen to Val or not. Eventually, I decide to go with it, not because I trust Val, but because I trust Rami. They promised she would help me, and I can't think of a reason for them to lie. Still, they're definitely getting an earful if we make it out of this alive. We run into our first trap a short distance down the passageway. It's invisible, but my scanner picks it up anyway: several square-shaped slivers in the ceiling.

"Okay, get ready to run." I suck in a breath and sprint down the hall.

The moment I step past the first sliver, sharp blades of code swipe down from the ceiling. They fall one after another, a hair's breadth behind me, but I stay a step ahead. I've never been more grateful for upgrading to Dendryte Silver. It cost me a year's freelance pay and at least half my soul, but it's clearly worth it. If I was still running Bronze, I wouldn't have been able to make it.

I stop at the end of the gauntlet, turning in time to watch my Doppel avoid the last blade. As my heart rate slows, I see that Val isn't running. She walks calmly through the row of guillotines, allowing them to pass right through her.

"Seriously?" I groan, equal parts annoyed and astonished. Chalk up another point in the 'maybe she actually is a FRAI' column.

Val reaches the end of the hallway, looking calm and collected while I struggle to get my breath under control. "I have no biological components for the blades to injure. My intelligence exists in a different form."

"Good for you, I guess. Come on, *Elena Dos*." I stalk down the hallway, sending my doppel ahead. Val is really starting to get on my nerves, almost as much as Sasha does.

"Elena, are you sure you're ready to proceed? Your vitals just spiked."

"I'm ready." I know exactly why my vitals spiked and I definitely don't want to talk about it. "And stop monitoring me like that. It's creepy."

"Very well. I will route the data to your personal file without analyzing it."

"Still creepy."

We arrive at the next obstacle: an enormous sea of messages all swarming together. It's like watching a school of fish swimming this way and that, moving in beautiful currents so they don't collide with each other. I stare for a second, entranced, until Val clears her throat.

"Your cloaking programs should be suitable here, Elena."

"Okay." I double-check to make sure my cloak is active—professionals never assume—then slide into the ocean of data.

When I touch them, the currents change. The messages flow around me and my doppel, leaving a small gap where we can move. I join one of the streams that seems to be heading toward the opposite shore.

It takes a while to navigate across the vast chasm of data, but I arrive safely. I haul myself out of the intranet ocean, and Val does the same alongside my doppel. The path branches out again on the other shore, and Val gestures left. "This way."

The hallway beyond is quiet. My scanner doesn't pick up any traps, but the stillness doesn't feel right. Neither does the sharp bend ahead. I creep forward cautiously, preparing to use my stuns just in case.

That proves to be smart. Two guardog.exe programs round the corner from the opposite direction, and their glowing yellow eyes fix right on me before they raise their heads, howling out a distress signal. I don't hesitate. Moving lightning-quick, I load a stun into my shield and then lift it, firing a blue beam from its center.

My stun hits one of the dogs as it leaps for me. It freezes in midair, locked in strands of red code. The other dog goes for my doppel, but it never connects. Val sends a smaller pulse of red shooting from her hand, and the second program falls apart, dissolving until there's nothing left.

I look at Val, impressed and also intimidated. "I'm not saying I believe you're a FRAI," I grumble, "but if you are, I'm starting to see why Megan made you."

Val looks pleased. "She considered me useful, yes. Let's proceed."

We round the corner, coming face to face with another, smaller version of the blue wall from earlier. It's shaped more like a bubble, and inside is a golden stream of code stretching up through the ceiling and down into the floor.

"This is our destination," Val says. "AxysGen's database of undesirables. Please allow me to lower the shields this time instead of shattering them. Your alarm dampeners are well designed, but AxysGen's security matrix is extremely sensitive."

I cross my arms over my chest. "Fine."

Val steps forward, placing both hands inside the blue bubble and pulling its surface apart. Soon the hole is large enough for a person to pass through. I step inside as Val holds it open, reaching out to touch the golden pillar of light.

A large window pops up, scrolling through names so fast I can't make sense of them. I run a filtering program, forcing the data to slow down, then remove one of my spyders from my toolbar.

"Sasha+Young," I whisper into my cupped hand.

The spyder dives into the golden code and returns a few seconds later. The screen comes to a stop, and I look up to see a giant version of Sasha's face peering down at me. She looks younger, softer. The scar on her throat is noticeably absent.

Before I delete the profile, I can't help but study it. There's surprisingly little information:

Gender: Female;
Age: 34;
Aliases: Wolf, Wolf of the Kremlin;
POB: United States, Naturalized Russian;
Wanted For: corporate espionage, grand larceny, stock manipulation, murder,
   property damage, vandalism.
Status: Deceased.

That doesn't make sense. Sure, the world at large thinks Sasha's dead, but if AxysGen does too, why are they trying so hard to kill her? Besides, tons of AxysGen employees have seen her in the past week alone—in Siberia, Brazil, and especially Paris. Someone must have reported in to say her death was faked and correct the database. I erase the information, but not before clicking into the 'listed associates' portion of Sasha's profile.

Next up is Cherry.

Name: Cherry Vidal (formerly Alejandro Vidal)
Gender: Female (transitioned from male)
Age: 29
Aliases: Cherry Bomb, Alejandro
POB: Venezuela
Spouse: Rami Hajjar
Wanted For: corporate espionage, grand larceny, stock manipulation, murder,
arson, property damage.
Status: At Large.

I blink, then take particular delight in erasing Cherry's deadname from the profile. Bureaucracy is such bullshit. Rami's profile is similar to Cherry's, except their place of birth is listed as Palestine and their gender is listed incorrectly as male. I delete that one as well, then Doc's and Rock's, although his does contain an interesting detail.

"Only twenty-one? Damn. He has so many mods it's hard to tell his age."

"Are you almost finished?" Val asks. "The longer we stay here, the greater risk we run of being discovered."

I pull up my own profile, curious to see what AxysGen has on me.

Name: Elena Nevares
Gender: Female
Age: 27
Aliases: escudoespiga (Darkspace username)
POB: Mexico
Wanted For: corporate espionage, grand larceny, property damage.
Status: At Large.

The picture is a less than flattering one from my 'bisexual bob' phase. I erase it from existence, promising to never cut my hair that short again. I get ready to exit the datastream, then remember there's one more profile to delete. I go back to Sasha's profile, then select Megan Delaney. The woman staring at me looks young. Happy. She's white, with long blonde hair and bright green eyes. I stare at her for a moment, unsure why I feel compelled to memorize this woman's face.

Name: Megan Delaney
Gender: Female
Age: 28
Aliases: None
POB: Ireland
Wanted For: corporate espionage, grand larceny, stock manipulation, murder,
    property damage.
Status: Deceased.

The red lettering of 'Deceased' blinks at me until I delete the profile.

"Elena, hurry!" Val shouts.

I break away from the database. A figure is heading toward us, surrounded by glowing red armor and carrying an assault rifle. The stylized letters 'AG' are printed on his chest.

"Mierda!"

It's a corp jacker, probably alerted by the guardog.exe programs from before. We didn't cut off their sirens soon enough.

I bolt for the hole Val is holding open, but remember I haven't finished. I turn back and tap the Poison Fruit icon, and what looks like a green apple glittering with code appears in my hand. Without hesitating, I chuck the apple into the golden column of light. It flashes a toxic green with a glowing red skull in the middle, and then fades back to neutral gold.

The jacker's almost on top of us. I climb through the hole and activate my shield, but he's focused on my doppel. He fires a red pulse that hits it instead, shattering it into bits of swirling blue. My heart clenches. This guy is using red. That means Puls.wavs instead of stuns. If I get hit, my brain is soup.

Before I can even raise my shield, another red beam fires—not from the jacker, but from somewhere on my left. It streaks toward him, hitting right in the chest. He freezes, then crumples to the ground

I try to move my legs, but they won't respond. I can only turn my head. Val is standing beside me, one hand extended. There are no remnants of light or code around it, but I know she fired that shot. A chill races down my spine. Whatever she is, she's capable of killing someone...and she did, to save my life. Which means that, in a way, I killed someone.

This isn't the first time I've seen an enemy jacker go down. My memories of Mumbai are hazy, but I do remember that I killed at least two people during my escape by reflecting a Puls.wav with my shield. Guess that tally is higher now, counting the guard in Siberia, and...this. Val might have fired the Puls.wav, which is terrifying on its own, but I share responsibility. That's why I don't carry my own Puls.wavs. I'll do just about anything to find another way.

"Remain calm, Elena," Val says from beside me. "Your vitals have spiked."

I flinch, taking a step back from her. "Stay the hell away from me."

Val's expression becomes sad, a surprisingly realistic facsimile of human regret. "I see you are upset, and I understand why. However, I determined using a Puls.wav to be the best course of action in order to ensure your safety."

"I didn't *ask* you to ensure my safety!" I snap, but I feel shitty immediately afterward. Val did just save my life. I suppose I should be appreciative, although it's hard to summon any gratitude from within myself.

"Ensuring the safety of the Lucky 7 is my primary function," Val says. "However, I am sorry to have caused you distress. And I am sorry I could not find a less violent alternative with the same probability of success."

I don't know whether I believe her, but there isn't time to think about it. My thoughts and emotions have both reached their limit, and it's all I can do to process what Val says next: "I have altered the signal from the Puls.wav. During initial inspection, the jacker's death should be attributed to an equipment malfunction."

I exhale shakily. I didn't even think about that part. Killing one of AxysGen's jackers will draw unwanted attention—which means Rami is in danger. I force my feet to move. "Let's get out of here, like right now."

logging off network
disconnection complete

Rae D. Magdon

Friday, 06-11-65 16:23:22

I SLAM BACK INTO my own skin, trembling and soaked with sweat. While my brain reconnects with my body, a hand brushes back my hair, unplugging the silver cable from behind my ear. "Esperanza. Esperanza, are you all right?"

It's Rami. I sigh with relief. "It's done, but Val melted a corp jacker," I mutter. "We don't want to be around when they figure out it wasn't an accident. Also, *why didn't you tell me you had a fucking FRAI?*"

"I'll explain later." Rami helps me to my feet. When their hand clasps around mine, I feel something hard in my palm—Val's databox. I shove the cube inside my blazer. The only thing worse than getting caught in the heart of an AxysGen office would be getting caught with a FRAI, and I'm almost convinced that's what Val is, no matter how unlikely it seems.

"This way," Rami murmurs. They walk down the row of terminals with a smile, fingertips braced beneath my elbow for support. I struggle to keep my legs from wobbling. Hard cuts can make rookies dizzy, but that's not why my head's spinning.

Val killed someone for me. Maybe someone with a family. Killing the jacker didn't have to happen. If I'd had more time...if I'd gotten off a stun so Val didn't have to save my stupid ass.

Rami drags me into the elevator. Once the doors shut, they murmur in my ear: "Keep it together, sweetie. You can do this. All we need to do is walk out the front door."

The front door. I focus on that as the floors fly by. Get to the front door and walk out. That's all. We reach the lobby, and Rami lets go of my arm. I follow them out of the elevator, staring straight ahead at the back of their hijab. I don't want to make eye contact with anyone else. Some irrational part of me is terrified they'll know by looking—see the guilt on my face or something. But no one notices me. I blend right in until we arrive at the front entrance.

I make a beeline for freedom, but Rami stops me. "No. Wait." Four security guards in black suits and red visors are standing near the doors.

They're scanning everyone who walks in or out, stopping people at random to question them. Sweat breaks out on my forehead. AxysGen must have heard about the jacker and decided to beef up security. I look at Rami in a panic, but their face is calm, reassuring.

"You said it's done, right?"

I nod.

"Then there's no data left," they say cheerfully, like we're talking about work. "All scrubbed, nothing to worry about. I think the two of us should reward ourselves with an early lunch."

They're right about our DNA profiles, but everything that could go wrong still flashes through my head as they lead me to the door. Cold sweat runs down the middle of my back as one of the guards locks eyes with me. His face is neutral, impossible to read. Almost reminds me of someone.

He holds up a hand to stop us. "Name?"

My mind goes blank. For the first time in my fucking life, I can't remember how words work. "Uh..."

"Esperanza, what's going on?" Rami's tone is impatient, and their brow is creased with annoyance.

The guard's gaze flicks over to them. "Possible security breach, ma'am. Name?"

"Laila Ahmad. What security breach? You mean this isn't a drill?"

"I'm not at liberty to say."

Rami huffs in annoyance. "Well, I'm not missing my lunch meeting over a drill. I have seven hundred million credits riding on this deal! My boss—"

The guard's face becomes emptier, if that's even possible. "Ma'am, please remain calm. This will only take a moment." He scans us with his visor, and I get the sense he's going as quickly as possible so he can send us on our way.

"You're both clear. Have a pleasant day."

Rami turns their nose up in the air. "Hmph. I'll be registering a complaint with your supervisor. These kinds of delays are unacceptable." They storm through the doors, pulling me along behind them.

We don't talk until we're three blocks away from the AxysGen building. I break down first, sagging against one of the lampposts and hanging my head. My adrenaline high has worn off, leaving me shaky and exhausted.

"Elena, sweetie, it's okay." Rami runs their hand up and down my back. "You did it. The op was a success. We're wiped from AxysGen's database."

I can't answer at first. My chest heaves a few times, but my eyes stay dry. I don't know whether I'm numb or overwhelmed, and it scares me. "A FRAI. You have an actual fucking FRAI," I say, with increasing speed and desperation. "And she killed someone. For me! Fucking shit."

"I know it's hard, Elena, but you and Val did what you had to do. This isn't your fault."

I turn away from the lamppost, shaking with quiet anger. Most of that anger is directed inward—*all sorts of ways you could've put food on the table for your brothers, and you chose the job that puts you with a murderous FRAI*—but Rami's words are like a slap in the face. "You sent me in there blind. Maybe if I'd been prepared...If I'd known...why do none of you *tell* me anything?"

"About Val being a FRAI, you mean? Would you have believed us if we'd told you?"

I bite my lip, fighting against the tight coil in my chest. No, I wouldn't have believed them. I needed to see Val in action to buy it. And it's not my fault Val killed that guy, even though it still feels like it. She made the choice, and from a logical standpoint, it was probably the right one. Maybe that's what's so fucked up about it. "Fuck. You're right. And you were right about Val. She saved my ass in there."

"Try and keep it together thirty more seconds, sweetie. The Eagle's coming in hot." Rami looks past me to the street, where a shuttle is descending from one of the skylanes above. The Eagle swoops down beside the curb, idling a few feet away.

Cherry's head pops out through the rear doors, her red bob bouncing. *"Hola, mamacitas.* Need a ride?"

"I don't know," Rami drawls, shifting their weight to one hip. They pretend to consider the offer, stroking their chin between their thumb and forefinger. "Your ride looks pretty sketchy to me."

Cherry waggles her eyebrows. "My ride is *just* fine, thank you."

"Really? Are you sure you know how to fly it?"

"Ha fucking ha." Cherry rolls her eyes, but she can't hide her smirk. "Y'know, I could always go find some cheaper girls on the next corner."

I crack a weak grin, but it doesn't last. Sasha's head appears above Cherry's shoulder, and she isn't smiling. "Rami, Nevares, hop in. Cherry, stop being an ass."

Cherry pulls a face, but she retreats into the Eagle so the two of us can climb aboard. I grab my usual seat while Rami heads up front, squeezing Cherry's shoulder on the way. "I doubt you could've afforded us anyway."

"Ha!" Doc barks from the pilot's seat.

"Move, kiddo," Rami says, shooing her over to the copilot's chair.

While they switch seats, I glance around the back of the shuttle. Rock is sitting beside Cherry, which means the only empty spot left is next to me. My luck I have to sit with Sasha after this clusterfuck of an op. "Report, Nevares," she says as she straps in. "What happened in there?"

The purr of the plasma engines gives me a brief reprieve, but it isn't long enough. It goes quiet again as Rami points the Eagle's nose up and glides back into the skylane. I don't want to talk about it, but I also don't have much of a choice. "Jacked in, wiped the database, used Poison Fruit. Got made by an AxysGen jacker, so Val fried him."

Rock's eyes fill with sadness. For a large, intimidating grunt who's half machine, his face is surprisingly expressive.

Cherry's forehead wrinkles with concern. "Sounds rough. You okay, *chaparrita*?"

I'm not, so I shrug. "We got out, didn't we? Val disguised the pulse to make it look like an accident—and what the *shit,* by the way?" I ask, my voice rising as my anger comes raging back like a firestorm. "None of you *pendejos* thought it might be important to warn me I was *plugging into a goddamn FRAI?* One who's capable of killing people? What the actual fuck?"

The corners of Cherry's lips quirk up. "Come on, Elena. You wouldn't have believed us if we told you."

"That's the same bullshit excuse Rami gave me. I gave that thing access to my brain! She could've fried me too!"

"No, she couldn't have," Sasha says. "Or, rather, she wouldn't have. Val doesn't just kill people indiscriminately. She has moral parameters to prevent that."

Her response makes me even madder. "I see how it is. 'Oh, don't worry, Elena. This FRAI's got moral parameters, so she *probably* won't kill all humans. Go ahead and give her total access to your squishy organic brain!' Fuck you, Sasha."

Sasha blinks at me. "Basically, yes. Val won't kill all humans. Megan knew her shit."

I scowl. Megan definitely did know her shit, even though she ended up dead. "You still should have told me," I mutter.

Doc's head pokes around the side of the copilot's chair. "What's got your panties in a wad? Was Val mean to you or something?"

"No," I sigh. "She was fine, I guess. Saved my life, added me to the team roster..."

"Nice!" Doc says. "Now you're officially part of the Lucky Seven."

Lucky Seven. I remember Val saying that before the mission. I reach into my blazer, withdrawing the small black cube. The edges are smooth as I turn it over in my hand. "If you have a FRAI, why use me at all? You don't need a jacker. Val could've wiped that database herself."

"We do need you," Sasha says. "She was designed to help us on ops, but Val's true purpose is to learn. She can't do that without anyone to observe. Besides, her primary objective is—"

"Yeah, I remember the primary objective. It's a stupid one, though. Help whichever of you guys plugs into her box."

Across the way, Cherry snickers.

"*Cállate, puta.* Didn't you idiots think about what would happen if someone evil plugged into her and found a way around her primary objective?"

"First of all, like I told you, Megan was a fucking savant," Sasha says. "She locked Val down tighter than—"

"Your ass?" I snap.

Sasha scowls. "Enough. My point is, Val's still learning how to make moral decisions. She needs a human partner."

"Considering her moral parameters are based on you, and she just killed somebody, she's probably off to a *great* start."

Sasha glares at me. "Quit it with the snark, Nevares."

"So...you need me." My shoulders slump. "To point your weapon for you and make sure she only blows up what she's supposed to. Great. That's not fucked up at all."

"She's not a weapon," Rami says from up front. "She's a sentient being."

"Yeah." Doc turns in her chair, extending an arm back with her palm outstretched. "Pass her up and I'll show you. She can access the Eagle's systems wirelessly, but she likes being plugged in. Her power source is nuclear, but even those don't last forever."

I look at the box in my hand again. Even though I've seen it firsthand, it's hard to believe there's something sentient inside. I put the cube in Doc's hand, and she starts fiddling with something on the dashboard that I can't see.

"Yo, Val. Have a good nap?"

Val's avatar doesn't appear, but the voice coming through the

Eagle's speakers is definitely hers. "Hello, Doris. In my current form, I do not require sleep. Since you know this, I will assume you were making a joke."

I give Sasha a skeptical look, some of my anger cooling. "She understands humor? Really?"

"I have analyzed many different categories of humor: sarcasm, parody, satire, wordplay—"

"Do a pun," Cherry says.

Sasha groans in annoyance. "Vidal…"

"Why did the capacitor kiss the diode?" Val asks.

"Why *did* the capacitor kiss the diode?" Doc repeats gleefully.

"He couldn't resistor."

Cherry and Doc's hooting laughter echoes through the shuttle. Rami snorts in grudging amusement. Even Rock lets out a low, "Heh."

"That was terrible." I'm starting to relax, maybe because I'm too exhausted to be pissed or afraid anymore. "Do a better one."

"Very well, Elena. Why did the artificial intelligence order a milkshake?"

Sasha turns her frown on me. "You had to encourage her, Nevares…"

"Why did the AI order a milkshake?" Cherry parrots back.

"To blend in with the general human population, making it easier to infiltrate society and, in time, conquer it."

The whole shuttle cracks up. Cherry and Doc cackle like witches. Rami tries to muffle their giggle with an unconvincing cough. Rock makes a low rumble, and even Sasha snorts once. I can't be sure, but I think the muscles around her mouth twitch to conceal a smile.

"I will note the positive response in my logs," Val says, sounding pleased. The pitch of her voice is pretty convincing. Megan must have spent a while teaching her to sound human.

"This doesn't mean we're buddies, okay?" I say to the Eagle's ceiling speakers. "I guess I can believe you're a FRAI, but I still don't trust you."

"Your opinion is understandable," Val replies. "I exist outside your previous frames of reference. From studying humans, I have come to the conclusion that many of them fear that which they have never encountered before."

I blow a frustrated puff of air through my lips. "You just have to be all logical about it, huh?"

"My personalized algorithms predict that you will come to trust me after we have shared a sufficient number of positive interactions. The possibility of developing a mutual emotional attachment is likely."

I narrow my eyes. "Is that your fancy way of saying you want to be pals? Because I'm not here to make friends."

"That is a curious response. Based on available data, I believe you have already developed attachments to the other members of our crew. In fact, your brain chemistry has changed significantly during the course of our current interaction. The Eagle's scanners indicate that your dopamine levels have risen modestly over the past few minutes, your serotonin levels have stabilized after a severe dip, and I have observed a sharp spike in oxytocin production as well."

My face heats up. I have to stop myself from glancing over at Sasha. The last thing I want to do is give Val more incriminating data to process. "Didn't I tell you to stop scanning me?"

Sasha's the one who sticks up for me, much to my surprise. "Give her a break, Val. She's had a rough day."

"Yes. I hypothesize that most humans would find the sudden shift between severe trauma and arousal difficult to process."

Cherry snorts loudly while Doc groans in disgust. I can't be sure, but I think Rock's blue eyes are twinkling. I squirm uncomfortably in my seat under their scrutiny.

Sasha isn't amused. "When I said 'give her a break', I meant 'shut up'."

"Understood. Would you prefer music? I can generate a randomized playlist. According to my calculations, each of you will enjoy at least 73.3% of the songs."

"Then turn up the volume," Cherry says. "We've got a long flight home."

Music fills the Eagle, but I'm not really listening. I'm uncomfortably aware of how close Sasha's arm is to mine. This whole day has been fucked up. Rogue AIs, killing someone, Sasha. I'm not so far up my own ass that I can't admit the truth. I want to wrap my legs around those lean, powerful hips and let her pound me into the nearest flat surface. But being horny's no excuse. This is business, and she's got that thick layer of ice around her, and even though I don't do emotional attachments, I want to at least kind of casually *like* the people I fuck.

So. Fingers it is. And maybe a cold shower or three.

Saturday, 06-12-65 07:51:42

HEAT. MY SKIN, MY blood, my breath—all fire. Wherever I am, it's boiling the marrow in my bones. *There's a loud scream. Someone crying? Blinding red pierces the frigid blackness. My nose stings with smoke.*

My heart crashes against my ribs, trying to shatter its cage. The red light's coming closer. Smoke's getting stronger. Still burning, so hot it feels like ice.

I lift my shield, and the world explodes—a red giant going supernova. More screams, then silence. Everything is quiet. Empty.

"Elena? Elena, wake up."

I jerk awake, panting heavily. My chest aches and the back of my neck is clammy with sweat. The fluorescent lights overhead turn the face hovering above mine into a dark shadow, but I still know who it is. Sasha's short cornrows have a distinct silhouette, and her smell is familiar too: leather, rifle oil, and some kind of spicy soap.

That's when I realize she's staring at me. "Nightmare," I mumble, rubbing my eyes. I kick the covers off. The nightmare's over, but I'm still dying of heatstroke.

Sasha nods slightly. I'm almost fooled into believing she's being sympathetic. I'll give her this, even though we don't get along, she's never kicked me while I'm down. Never said a word about the panic attacks, didn't tell me to get over it yesterday after I straight-up melted a dude's brain and freaked out after encountering my first FRAI.

"You okay, Nevares?"

"Hmm?" It's back to Nevares now. Something about that feels weird, but I'm not sure what.

"For the meeting."

Right. The meeting. "Yeah, sorry. There's this fog..."

Sasha walks over to the dresser. I roll out of bed in time for her to toss me a shirt and some fresh shorts. "It happens," she says, turning her back to me. "I'm used to it, so I do what I have to do. But I don't enjoy it."

I bite back a 'Could've fooled me.' It won't help the situation.

"So why do it?" I swap shirts and shorts while she's not looking, too anxious to be turned on for once.

Once I'm dressed, I clear my throat, and Sasha turns toward me. "Same reason you do. Because someone needed something from me." I can tell she's being straight with me. Her face has gotten easier to read. I can also guess who the 'someone' is, but I don't say Megan's name. Sasha's not being a *cabrona* today, and I want to see how long it'll last.

I pull my hair into a sloppy bun at the back of my head. "So, meeting?"

"In the kitchen. Crew's waiting on us."

Sasha and I reach the door at the same time. There's an awkward shuffle as we try to figure out who's going first, and eventually, she tilts so I can leave. Even so, I can't get out the door without my rear making contact with her pelvis. My breath hitches. My mind's still fogged up, but my body has other ideas. Ideas that involve Sasha grasping my hips and pulling me back until my ass is grinding into the tops of her thighs.

But Sasha doesn't reach out, and I feel like an idiot for hesitating. I scurry out of the way and head for the kitchen, pretending my brain didn't just take an all-expenses-paid vacation to whore island. If I don't get my shit together, the locals might decide to make me the mayor.

Everyone else is already waiting. Rock's sitting in a chair that's much too small for him. I'm surprised he managed to fit without snapping the legs. Cherry and Rami are being disgusting as usual, holding hands on top of the table and gazing sappily into each other's eyes. Rami has a blond goatee, glasses, a silver nose ring, and a crisp cat's eye. I still don't get how they do it. Every time I see them, they look like a stranger. Doc's the last one to notice me, because she's perched on the edge of the table itself with her legs swinging a few inches above the floor.

"Get your skinny ass off that table, *chiquita*. People eat there."

"Whatever," Doc huffs, hopping down and slumping in the remaining empty chair. "But that means you gotta stand."

I find an empty patch of wall to lean against as Sasha arrives at the table. She braces both hands on it, all business, leaning forward so everyone can see the determination on her face. "Wiping ourselves from AxysGen's database was step one. Now we need my brainbox."

"Okay," I interrupt. "Before we go any further, I'm done with this cryptic bullshit. What's so important about your stupid brainbox that I should put my ass on the line for it?"

"Because whoever has the brainbox could theoretically acquire access to me," says Val, popping into existence a few feet away.

I flinch in surprise and take a step sideways, putting some distance between us. "Whoa, where the fuck did you come from?"

Val tilts her head at me and smiles. Her avatar looks the same as it did in AxysGen's intranet system—skinny, Black, feminine. She's wearing a different outfit though, a purple blouse and grey pencil skirt. I guess AIs get the urge to play dress-up like humans do, although she seems to have a favorite color scheme.

"This form is composed of condensed lightwaves. I am able to use it when my databox is plugged into the Hole's main terminal. My servers exist in one of the back rooms. Now that everyone has arrived, I have chosen to project a light-based version of my avatar into the room so I may attend the meeting."

I barely have time to connect the dots—*that's* why Doc was so sketchy about 'more storage' while showing me around my first night in the Hole—before Cherry butts in. "She means she's a hologram. Check it out." She lets go of Rami's hand and waves hers through the air, cutting her fingers through Val's stomach.

I put a hand on my chest and exhale. *Ay dios santo.* Warn me next time or something. You're gonna give me nightmares." More nightmares, anyway.

"Noted," Val says. "I apologize for startling you."

"Enough," Sasha says, trying to get us back on track. "The databox you had—"

"You know, Pocket Val," Cherry says with a grin.

"Shut up, Cherry. Val's databox is one of two keys. The other one's in my brainbox. If AxysGen gets both of the keys, they'll be able to access Val's source code. Somehow, they figured that out."

Shit. That sounds bad. Really, really bad. "So, you're saying AxysGen could take Val?"

"I'm saying AxysGen could change Val," Sasha says. "Make her do whatever they want, be whatever they want. And they *will* find a way to take her, unless we get the second key back."

I nod grimly. I don't trust Val, but AxysGen is downright evil. I saw what she was able to do on the intranet, how immensely powerful she was. A corp like AxysGen could use her to sabotage other corps, build better cyberweapons, even take over the infrastructure of entire cities. The possibilities are endless—and terrifying. "Shit. I signed on to stay alive, not save the world."

"Well, too fucking bad, *chaparrita*," Cherry says. "Looks like we have to do both."

"So, where is AxysGen keeping the brainbox?" Rami asks, looking expectantly at Val.

"The good news is that I was able to ping its location."

I stare at her in shock. "You did *what?* Pings go both ways! AxysGen could be knocking down our door any minute!"

"I retrieved the location when we were leaving Tokyo," Val says in a calm voice. "Axys Generations does not have the Hole's coordinates."

Somehow, nobody looks comforted. Doc sighs. "So what's the real bad news?"

"Sasha's brainbox is currently being held at a private mansion owned by Veronica Cross, located several thousand kilometers outside of Hong Kong."

The table explodes with noise.

"What the shit?"

"Oh, come *on!*"

"Fucking seriously?"

"Of course it is."

Even Rock makes an unhappy grunt.

"Question," Cherry says to Sasha. "How much of your dick would I have to suck for you to *not* make us break into Veronica Cross's house for your brainbox? She's the CEO! That place has to be locked down tighter than your ass."

I snort. If I'm the mayor of whore island, Cherry's at least on the city council.

"This is serious," Sasha says, her voice a warning growl. "And it's about more than keeping Val safe and out of AxysGen's hands, although that's definitely priority one. I've been having...flashbacks. Intense ones."

The room quiets. I swallow hard. Guess I'm not the only one who bounces in and out of the present like a ping-pong ball, only to end up tangled in the net.

"You know I trust you, cupcake," Rami says to Sasha, "but you have to admit this is dangerous."

"We need the box, Rami. For Val and for me. I keep skipping back to that night, but it's like trying to solve a puzzle with half the pieces missing. Some sections are grouped together, but I can't get the full picture."

"You really think we can pull this off?" Doc asks. She sounds hopeful, and she's looking at Sasha with admiration in her eyes. I'm reminded again of just how young she is. Sometimes it's easy to forget.

"Yes," Sasha says, without hesitation. "Val? Lights."

Val dismisses the overhead lighting with a wave of her hand. At the same time, the surface of the table changes color, going from black to a pale, glowing white. Another holographic image appears over it, a miniature mansion surrounded by a wide green lawn.

I grin. "Projectors in the table? Cute."

"I would say the crew has found it useful rather than cute, but I will keep your preferred adjective in mind." Val spreads her fingers, zooming in on the mansion itself. "We are fortunate that Veronica Cross decided to move the brainbox to this location. Originally, it was being held in one of AxysGen's Mumbai facilities. That level of security would have been much more difficult to bypass."

All the wind rushes out of me. My hands tremble, and I can only stare at Val in shock. Mumbai. *Mierda*. The databox I almost died for and Sasha's stolen brainbox are the same thing.

"Nevares?" Sasha is looking at me, but I can't read her in the dark. Is she confused? Annoyed? Worried? My chest is constricting and I can't think clearly.

I fight off a wave of dizziness. "Your brainbox. I'm pretty sure that's what my old crew was hired to steal." I don't have proof. Shit, I can't remember half of what happened during that op, but there are too many coincidences to discount.

Surprised reactions ripple around the room. Rock's giant hands clench in his lap. Doc whistles. Rami gasps, and Cherry mutters, "Oh fuck. So that's why AxysGen killed your old crew and wants you dead. They think you're involved."

I don't respond. Instead, the sour taste of fear fills my mouth. Sure, the idea of AxysGen stealing Val is horrible, but I'd been able to stay calm by reminding myself that I could bail. This is supposed to be Sasha and her crew's problem, not mine. But apparently I'm wrapped up in this mess now too, whether I want to be or not.

"Who hired you?" Sasha asks sharply, boring holes in me with her eyes.

I flinch, still fighting down panic. "I don't know. Jento was our fixer for that op. It was anonymous."

"Well why the hell didn't you ask him after it all went to shit?"

"Calm down, Sasha," Rami says. "Whoever hired Elena's crew might not have known what they were trying to steal, either."

I recognize the expression on Sasha's face. It looks like anger at first glance, but there's fear underneath. "If someone else knows about Val..." Sasha mutters.

Val hurries to reassure her. "At this point, it is only speculation. If an individual or group unaffiliated with Veronica Cross has indeed learned of my existence, I recommend attempting to locate them after your brainbox has been recovered. In my opinion, that is a more urgent issue."

Sasha exhales loudly. "Right. Okay. There are three levels of security inside Cross's mansion." She moves the holographic image in a circle, and several red dots appear around the mansion, connected by glowing orange lines. "First, there are guards. They're nothing special, just guards getting a paycheck."

Cherry looks at Rock. "Say they're 'just guards' again when they start shooting at us. Right, big guy?"

Rock shrugs his massive shoulders, seemingly unconcerned.

"You read my mind," Sasha says. "You and Rock are on distraction duty." She changes the view again with a flick of her finger. The walls of the mansion become see-through, showing the inner layout in greater detail. It's big—five floors, more rooms than a person could ever possibly use. If I wasn't still reeling from the Mumbai realization, I would have curled my lip in disgust.

"I assume Doc and I are infiltration?" Rami asks.

Sasha nods. "Second layer of security. We need you to sneak in through the back and access the security hub to let us in." Another orange line appears, leading up through the back door to a small room on the third floor. "This is your route. You need to move fast, because Cross has assault turrets mounted on her roof."

"Crazy bitch," Cherry mutters, looking almost impressed.

"We're going to trigger Cross's security alarms," Sasha continues. "There's no avoiding that. So Rami and Doc need to shut the turrets down fast, let us in, and issue a fake all-clear to buy us a little time. Rock and Cherry won't be able to hold out for long."

Rami's sweet face looks more serious than I've ever seen it. "You can count on us. Right, Doc?"

"Yup." She nudges at Rock's massive leg with her foot. "Patching up turret holes requires a lot of expensive parts."

"Right." Sasha brings us in closer, highlighting a level underneath the house itself. "Once the turrets are down, you'll need to open the basement for us. There's a dual security system, one that requires access at the door and permission from the security hub itself."

I look at her. "Who is the 'us' going into the basement?"

"You, me, and Val, Nevares. Once the door's open, we'll grab the box while everyone else clears an exit path."

"Why not send *chaparrita* with Rami and Doc?" Cherry asks. "You thinking there'll be extra code to crack inside the basement?"

"I know there is," Sasha says. "How do you think I got the rest of this information?"

"You sly fox," Rami chuckles. "You paid someone off, didn't you?"

Sasha gives a half-shrug. "Credits talk. Wouldn't you know, one of Cross's security techs is going into an early retirement the night before our op goes down."

"You sure you can trust him?" Doc asks.

Val answers: "Based on my calculations, I determined it to be a relatively safe transaction. The individuals you call 'cogs' subsist on an insufficient and unstable income. They have low to nonexistent job satisfaction, and many of them do not hold their employers in high regard. It is doubtful that this individual will inform Veronica Cross of our plans. He very likely resents her too much to reveal them."

That's cold reassurance. Even if Sasha's spy doesn't double-cross us, the plan is still sketchy. "You don't know what's waiting for us in that basement, right?" I ask.

The corners of Sasha's mouth twitch slightly, but she shakes her head no.

"It's a trap, just like before. They want Val's other key. Your brainbox is bait, and we'd be stupid to fall for it."

Sasha's cold eyes eat their way into me. "Thought you had more guts, Nevares. Or at least more of a conscience."

I bristle, pushing off the wall and taking a step toward her. "What the fuck is that supposed to mean?"

"You know what will happen if AxysGen takes Val. Do you want to live in a world where the power they already have is multiplied? You *know* who's going to suffer the most when that happens."

My blood burns, pounding hot and hard through my veins. Sasha has a point, and that only pisses me off more. I clench my fists until they throb, nails digging into my palms. "In what back-asswards universe does not wanting to go on a suicide mission make me a bad person?"

Sasha and I pull toward each other like magnets, standing toe to toe. She glares down at me, using that height of hers to try and throw me. "Because you're too much of a coward. You're all talk, Nevares.

Almost running over a lady and her dog messes you up, but when billions of innocent lives are at stake, you don't care."

"I do fucking care," I snap. Her stupid fucking face is hovering above me, and my hand flexes with the urge to slap her. "You think I want to see any of that happen? I *don't*. I'm not some fucking sociopath. But you're not doing this for the greater good any more than I am. All you really want is to shoot people and blow shit up to avenge your dead girlfriend."

The rest of the room reacts immediately. Doc's eyes grow to the size of dinner plates. Rock makes a worried noise. Even Val looks surprised, like those fancy algorithms of hers weren't expecting me to say that.

Cherry gets out of her chair, reaching for my arm, but I shrug her off. Rami heads for Sasha, trying a different tactic. "Breathe, Sasha. She didn't mean—"

Sasha doesn't respond to them. She stays fixated on me, close enough for me to feel her breath. "Don't talk shit about what you don't understand, Nevares," she snarls, lips peeled back to show her clenched teeth.

"Oh, I understand. I understand I gave us a perfect fucking opportunity to go underground when I wiped that database, but you wanna go be some brooding, B-grade VR anti-hero with a tragic backstory. News flash: that shit isn't sexy in real life. And who are you doing this for? A goddamn FRAI that *your* crew made! She fried someone back in Tokyo like it was nothing, and she's not even human!"

"She did that to save your ass, and don't you *dare* say she isn't human," Sasha snarls. "Val's a sentient being, and she's family. If you have a heart in there, imagine it was Jacobo or Mateo. You'd kill anyone and everyone to keep them safe, so don't talk like you've got some kind of moral superiority."

She's absolutely right, which only makes me madder. "If *I* have a heart? Bitch, you're the fucking Tin Man! The queen of the goddamn South Pole! ¿Te crees muy chingona? ¡Pues chinga tu madre!"

Sasha grabs the front of my shirt, jerking me in close. Her face is an inch away, and I brace myself for a fight. But she just holds me there, dark eyes blazing, lips trembling with each ragged pant that passes between us.

I'm not sure who leans in first. Maybe both of us? All I know is that one moment we're spitting at each other like feral cats, and the next our mouths are crashing together. The kiss is furious. Violent, bruising, like we're trying to hurt each other. Sasha's fists tighten around the fabric of my blouse until the collar digs into my throat. I bite down hard on her bottom lip, feeling a spike of *something* as she hisses in pain. Bitterness floods through me, but her mouth is sweet, and somehow that pisses me off more.

Fuck. She tastes better than I thought. I grip Sasha's biceps, desperate to dig my nails in somewhere. I want to rake them across her skin, make her feel the same pain I feel clawing inside my chest. Every moment I spend sucking her tongue makes me want to rip her open, to scratch and tear. But I don't do any of that. I melt. I fucking *melt* like a popsicle in the middle of summer, clutching Sasha's shoulders and moaning into her mouth.

Sasha's deep growl feeds the white-hot fire in my core. A flash flood swells between my legs, soaking straight through my panties. Slickness spills down my thighs like there's no barrier at all, and the ruined fabric clings close. I arch forward, trying to get closer, rubbing my body against hers.

"That's hot."

A train called reality slams into me head-on. I jerk away from Sasha to see Cherry staring at us. There's a grin on her face the size of the moon, and it shows every one of her teeth. Doc looks disgusted. Rami is bewildered. Val seems intrigued. Rock just takes it all in with wide eyes.

While they gawk, Sasha rolls from the room like a stormcloud, taking the thunder with her. Once she's gone, all the fire bleeds out of me. I stare after her, lips still tingling. Fuck. That really just happened. I can feel the ghost of grasping fingers on the front of my shirt.

"That was repulsive," Doc drawls, and I can tell she's rolling her eyes.

"That was *hot,*" Cherry argues, but Rami grabs her elbow and marches her to the bunks.

"Come on," they mutter, clicking their tongue is disapproval. "You too, Doc. Elena needs to figure this out without commentary from the peanut gallery."

Cherry continues complaining, and Doc wanders after them, giving me a superior smirk over her shoulder, like she'll never be dumb enough to kiss someone she hates in the heat of the moment.

"I believe situations like this call for privacy," Val murmurs. "Perhaps you will provide me with more insightful data concerning the incident at a later time." Before I can tell her there's no way in hell, she disappears into thin air. That leaves me and Rock. He sits there, staring at me with a calm, almost pleased expression on his face.

"What," I snap, glaring over at him. "You got something to say for once?"

Rock blinks, somehow speaking through the silence.

"No, I'm not going after her. I hate her. She can choke on that fucking brainbox she's so obsessed with for all the fucks I give."

Rock tilts his head at me. *Dios,* it's like the guy can read minds.

"It was a mistake," I insist. "A stupid, one-time disaster." But the thought of *not* kissing Sasha again makes my chest ache. One kiss, only a couple seconds long, and I was humping her like a horny tabby. My words sound weak even to me. Rock looks expectantly over at the door, then back at me.

"I'm not going," I mumble, but I'm staring over a cliff, telling myself I won't jump even as I put one foot forward. *"Ay, no mames."* I turn away from Rock and stomp toward the hallway, fuming with frustration. I have no idea what the fuck I'm doing, but I already know it's stupid.

Saturday, 06-12-65 09:69:96

MY WALK DOWN THE hallway is a blur. I don't have a clue what I'm doing and my heart's trying to burst out of my chest with each beat. My hands are shaking, and my head is spinning and I can't tell if I'm pissed or horny or terrified. But I guess I haven't made enough bad decisions today, because when I hear the hiss of the shower running, I head for the bathroom.

It's Sasha. Has to be. She wouldn't have gone to her bunk, where Rami or Cherry or someone else might come looking for her. Where *I* might come looking for her. No. She's gone to one of the only places in the Hole that offers some privacy. Privacy I'm about to interrupt because...I don't know why. Maybe to yell some more. Maybe to do something else I don't want to even admit I'm considering.

The scent of spicy soap hits my nose when I step inside the bathroom. Sasha's. How fucked up is it that I've memorized her smell? One of the shower stalls is closed. Steam leaks around and over the frosted door, and I can make out a blurry silhouette. Her outline is enough to make me shudder with want. The heat from before rushes back, burrowing into my belly, crawling over my skin, throbbing between my legs. If my underwear wasn't already drenched, it wouldn't stand a chance.

This is it. I can't deny what I'm here for anymore. Seeing her in front of me, even behind fogged-up glass, shatters all my stupid excuses. I'm here because, at least to me, this feels inevitable. Unless Sasha tells me to fuck off, it's going to happen.

I head over to the shower. Sasha turns in the stall, facing me through the door. I don't know what to do, so I just stand there. My presence pretty much speaks for itself. Nothing happens at first. The pit of my stomach drops. Maybe I'm wrong and this 'thing' is all me. Maybe I kissed her instead of us both kissing each other. Maybe she regretted it the instant her mouth touched mine. Maybe my being here while she's naked makes me a creep.

The door opens. Sasha's standing there, naked and wet and

gleaming. She's the fucking night sky, and the droplets clinging to her skin are glittering stars. Water sluices off her shoulders, her elbows, her hips. It runs over the carved landscape of her body, and I have to choke back a gasp when I realize most of it is muscle. I wouldn't call her bulky, but she's definitely buff. Fuck. I don't know if I'm prepared for this.

Despite all the flesh she's displaying, my eyes are drawn to hers. I can't help it. I prepare for the frost I'm used to, but for the first time, I see flames. Her brown eyes burn hotter than the steam billowing around us.

"What are you doing here?"

Sasha already knows the answer, so I'm not sure why she's asking the question. I hate being here, but I also *have* to be here. Hating her doesn't stop the wanting, and the wanting's too strong to fight.

"Why did you open the door?" The rage quivering through me doesn't come out in my voice. It breaks, almost pleading, and I loathe myself for it. Pathetic, like a dog begging for a treat.

Sasha's full lips press into a thin, slashing line. The scar on her throat twitches. "You don't want this. You think you do, but you don't."

It's not a 'get the hell out'. It's not even a warning. It's more of a 'you wouldn't dare'. A challenge. That's fine. I can do challenges. I lean in, glaring up at her. "You know what, *boss*?" I say, as sarcastically as I can when I'm two seconds away from humping her leg. "Your speeches fucking suck."

Sasha doesn't move at first. She's a tense mass of anger, radiating rage and heat. But then, she takes the smallest possible step back. She's not backing down—she's letting me in.

I step into the shower with her. It takes about two seconds to realize I forgot something. The spray soaks through my clothes, but I'm not going to step out again and strip like an idiot. Sasha doesn't laugh at me, though. She doesn't even seem to care. She just grabs my shoulders and pushes me up against the slick shower wall before leaning down to kiss me.

It's brutal. Rough. Selfish. Her teeth sting, and her tongue steals all of my air. But I want it this way. I want this sweet agony, this addictive ache. I want anything and everything as long as it's *more*.

I kiss Sasha back with everything I've got. She groans into my mouth, and the low sound shoots straight to my clit. I start squirming, but Sasha's fingers dig deeper into my arms, wordlessly ordering me to hold still. All I can do is whine and suck her bottom lip. She's got me wound up tight and shivering like guitar strings, and she's playing me so well it hurts.

But something in me wants to fight. To push back against her dominance, to show her I'm not just some warm body she can bruise because she hates me. I need her to fuck me, but she doesn't get to unless I fuck her back.

I wrap my arms around her, raking my nails down her back. She feels incredible, smooth skin over tense cords of muscle. The wings of her shoulder blades spread, and I gasp when I realize she's about to lift me. *Dios.* I wasn't even thinking about that. Which is weird, because I've definitely thought about it plenty during zone-out time in the Eagle.

"Shorts," I gasp, breaking away from her lips. My clothes are soaked through, sagging with water-weight and sticking to my skin. They don't last much longer. Sasha tears my shirt up and over my head. While I try to wriggle out of my shorts and panties in the tight space, she reaches back to undo my bra. It takes a brief game of Twister for her to pull it off, but I don't notice the awkwardness, because sharp pain pierces the side of my neck. Shit, she's a biter.

I bite back, sinking my teeth into Sasha's shoulder. Her skin muffles my scream as she slides her hands under my bare legs. Once she finds purchase, she picks me up, pinning me to the wall. I wrap my arms behind her neck and hook both knees around her waist, but I don't even need to hold on. She's got me.

My core twitches as her body presses closer to mine. I need contact, pressure, *something.* When I try to buck my hips, Sasha pulls back. I whimper into the side of her neck, but there's no need. Her hands move down to cup my ass, giving me an even better angle.

Soon I'm grinding frantically against her stomach, dripping all over myself, making a mess of us both. The moans Sasha doesn't swallow echo from the ceiling, but I can't help it. Her skin is wet and slippery, and I'm making it *more* wet and slippery, and even though her kisses hurt, her tongue is the sweetest thing I've ever had in my mouth...so far.

Mierda. It isn't supposed to be like this. I'm supposed to give as good as I'm getting, but all I can do is mewl and cling. I'm shaking so hard it's embarrassing. My body's a live wire—sparks shoot through me each time my clit bumps up against the defined ridges of Sasha's abdomen. Every inch of me is screaming to give in, to let this wave of hate and lust take me where it wants.

When one of Sasha's hands leaves my ass to move between my legs, I know I'm screwed. I close my eyes and bite my lip, but it doesn't change anything. Two of her fingers plunge into me, no preparation, and my whole world goes white.

The loudest wail I've ever made fills the room as I flood her hand. My muscles have her in a death-grip, but somehow, she finds a way to move. Her strong fingers curl over and over again, thrusting past the tightness, pushing into a place that makes me throb even harder. I spill into her palm, across her wrist, down her stomach. Can't stop. She's fucking *everything* out of me.

Everything dissolves into a shiny blur, like I'm trapped underwater. I can't remember how to breathe. The calloused heel of her hand is rubbing my own come into me, catching my clit without trying. I squeeze around Sasha's fingers, but the rest of me is relaxed The ripples remind me I'm full. Full and fucked raw, but even that rawness has a kind of peace.

It all shatters when Sasha says, "We done now, Nevares?"

Shame hits me like a bullet to the gut, rising up into my throat and choking me. Bitterness fills my mouth, and it tastes like her. I've never come so hard, never had it so good—which pisses me off royally. I don't know who the hell Sasha thinks she is, but I'm not having it.

"Done? Oh, we're not done. I'm not some fucktoy you can satisfy by sticking a couple fingers in me."

Sasha's lips are still swollen from my kisses when they curl in a sneer. "What makes you think I even *want* you?"

I'm fuming. I can't, I won't let her win this. "Because I'll eat your pussy so good you'll love me as much as you hate me."

Sasha yanks her fingers out of me and sets me down, peeling her body away from mine. "You're full of yourself."

I try not to let the loss of her show on my face. "You're full of shit."

Her hand reaches toward me. For one tender moment, her fingertips caress my face. Then she fists my hair, shoving me onto my knees. It hurts when they hit the tile floor, but I don't let Sasha keep control for long. I ignore her spread legs, running my flattened tongue up along her abdomen instead. The shower hasn't washed away all the mess yet, and she tastes like me. A spike of need hits when I remember how it felt to paint her belly with wetness, but I ignore it. I have some shreds of pride left.

Sasha doesn't react at first. She stands there, frozen, a towering statue beneath the shower's spray. Her fingers don't even tighten on my head when I sink my teeth in next to her navel, but that only makes me more determined. I'm going to make her scream and I don't care what it takes.

I kiss a path down her stomach, trying to keep it slow. I'm not gentle, though. Not even a little. I bite, suck, scratch. I leave bruises on her belly and dark rings of raised flesh around her thighs in circles where my nails have been. When I reach the narrow strip of curls above her mound, I don't touch her. I let my breath do the work.

A fault finally appears within Sasha's stony wall of silence. Her hips shift forward—not much, but enough for her lips to pout open a little, and enough for my pride. She's all dark, slippery heat, with a few sticky strands clinging to her thighs. With my face so close, even her smell has a taste. I hate the fact that it's delicious already. The temptation's too much. Her scent is everywhere and my mouth is watering for her. I growl as I bury my face between her legs.

Sasha's breath hitches as I lash my tongue across her clit. It's big, and that makes it perfect for sucking. When I wrap my lips around it, she digs her nails into my scalp, pulling my hair at the roots. I don't mind the pain. If she thinks she's in control of this, of me, she's in for a surprise.

I only tease the tip a little before putting pressure on the root. Sasha's clit pulses beneath its hood, and her opening leaks wetness onto my chin. The wall's getting weaker, and I can't wait to see her crumble. I run my palms around her hips, groping her ass in both hands. It's tight and firm and I love the way it tenses when I lick her.

Sasha's breathing gets faster. It's not quite a moan, but I can sense one stuck in her throat. She's swallowing it down, trying to fight the subtle jerking motion her hips want to make, but I'm not gonna let her. I wailed like *la Llorona* the second she shoved her fingers in me. At the very least, I need to make her cry out once—maybe even shout my name.

Teasing her clit only gets me so far. She shudders every time I suck her, but she's getting used to it. When I go harder, she grunts so softly I can barely hear, and then adjusts. Her hips make little twitches, shadows of thrusts she won't let herself give. But I'm far from ready to give up. I let her clit go with a pop before moving down to her entrance.

That earns me a sharp exhale. Sasha stiffens, muscles straining visibly beneath her skin. I lick again, and when I get the same reaction, I go to fucking town. I thrust and suck and swirl, like I'll die if I don't drink all of her in. *Dios*, she tastes like honey and salt. The flavor's strong, but my mouth can't get enough.

Sasha finally starts thrusting. It's slow, deliberate—like she's working toward a goal. I puff up with pride as more of her runs into my mouth. I've made her admit she wants it. She can't keep pretending to be above it all when she's grinding on my face.

I put everything I have into it, covering every bit of her I can reach. I fuck her with my tongue, swipe circles over her clit, even tug her inner lips with my teeth. I can feel how close she is to the edge, but no matter what I do, where I lick, how hard or soft I go, I can't seem to push her over. She's locked up tight, like if her muscles loosen even a little, she'll melt right down the drain. But that lock is jammed, because no matter what trick I try, it isn't enough.

Sasha lets out a low groan, jerking my head back. I cry out in protest, but when I look up at her face, she isn't angry. She's *frustrated.* Her nipples are puckered to stiff points. Her chest heaves rapidly. She's still swollen and dripping. But she hasn't come. I roll my neck and shoulders, preparing to plunge back in. No way am I letting up until I win this. She stops me before I can touch her.

"What the shit?" I ask, but her response is to turn off the water, then haul me to my feet by my hair. She walks me backwards as soon as I find my footing, throwing the door open with a bang. We stumble out together, wet feet slapping on the floor.

When my ass hits the bathroom counter, Sasha spins me around and shoves the middle of my back, pushing me down onto it face-first between two of the sinks. I shiver to see myself in the mirror. My mouth is still sticky with Sasha's wetness, and my lips look well-fucked. That reminds me: I'm supposed to be getting her off. I open my mouth to say so, but all that comes out is another scream as her fingers slam back inside me.

Before I can even adjust to the fullness, Sasha's buried as deep as she can go. This time, she doesn't only curl—she thrusts, putting the whole weight of her hips behind her hand. I don't know how many fingers she's using—two? Three?—but the stretch burns. The tighter I clench, the harder she goes. She wants something, but I can't tell what it is or who it's for.

All thoughts of revenge bleed out of me. I can't take this. Can't hold up against the brutal force of her fingers. The edge of the counter cuts into my belly, but the pain's worth it. I grab it with one hand and the side of the sink with the other, spreading my legs wider.

The harsh slap of Sasha's hips against my ass and my own ragged breathing fills the room. I'm more aware of the noise without the hiss of the shower to cover it. My ears burn with each wet *shlick* Sasha's fingers make inside me. She's taking me so hard it hurts, but I only want her more.

I lose it when her thumb finds my clit. I throb against her, gaping at my own reflection. The girl in the mirror is slack-jawed, wild-eyed. Desperate. At first I shiver silently, but then a moan slips out, starting soft and growing louder. I clench down, but Sasha keeps thrusting through my contractions. Her rhythm never stops. She's a woman with a goal, and I guess making me come isn't it, because her pace is just as feverish as before I hit my peak.

My orgasm is too strong to last. The pleasure hits all at once, and then disappears, leaving shuddering ripples behind. Sasha doesn't quit until I'm slumped over, my cheek smushed against the counter. With my head tilted, I can only see some of her reflection as she withdraws and steps back.

A fresh wave of anger washes over me, stronger than I'm expecting—or maybe it's disappointment. The loss of her leaves me cold, and my heart sinks through my belly. Even bottoms have some pride, and mine is definitely as bruised as my body. I'd been *so close* to making her come, and she'd just...stopped me, for no reason, and turned me into a pitiful puddle of goo again. If this is her way of fucking with my head, I won't let her get away with it.

I start to ask Sasha where she's going, to demand an explanation before she up and leaves, but the words die on my lips when she wraps her arms around my waist and scoops me up. My exhaustion evaporates, and I'm dripping all over myself again in seconds. Sasha *definitely* has musculoskeletal mods, because she's carrying me like I'm nothing. She heads for the bathroom door, not bothering to go back for our clothes. Shit. I guess we're going for round two. But this time, I'm definitely not letting her fly the shuttle the whole way.

Saturday, 06-12-65 10:01:69

THERE'S NO ONE IN the hallway, thank fucking God, because Sasha leaves the bathroom without even checking first. She doesn't knock before shouldering the door to the bunkroom open either. Cherry, Rami, Rock, and Doc must have fled for safer pastures. Maybe my screams were louder than I thought.

But I'm too busy to worry about that, or what I'll tell them later, because Sasha hauls me over to her bunk and dumps me on it like a sack of potatoes. I glare up at her. So much for bridal style. Definitely none of that romantic shit here, but she didn't have to drop me.

"What the fuck?" I ask her, but Sasha ignores me. She opens one of the dresser drawers and pulls something out.

When she turns around, I'm so distracted by her body that I don't notice what she's holding at first. She's all tensed up, a ticking time bomb about to explode, thrumming with a visible, potent energy that I can sense all the way from here. The distant look of frustration from earlier is gone, and her eyes fix on me like a rifle's crosshairs—dark, glinting, dangerous.

Sasha doesn't speak. She looks at me expectantly, as if to say, 'Well?' It's the closest I've ever seen her to impatient. That's when I notice what's in her hand. It's a dick. A very long, very thick dick that's the same color as her skin. The shaft looks normal, but the other end curves upward, culminating in a rounded bulb.

I look at her and shrug. I've used strap-ons before, and it's not hard to understand how the thing works. Pony end in her, horse end presumably in me. "Electro-transmitters?" I ask, trying to ignore how hoarse my voice sounds. Sasha's probably got more than enough money to pay for the good stuff, the kind of toy that lets you feel everything like it's the real deal.

Sasha growls something that sounds kind of like yes, but I'm not really listening. My eyes keep darting between the shaft and her face. The hunger there is scorching, even hotter than it was in the shower. The part of my brain that isn't screaming 'fuck me' tosses that around for a second. Maybe this is something she needs. She's already got the whole stud thing going—some flavor of genderfuckery isn't a big stretch. Might explain why she has the crew she does, too.

It doesn't really matter. I've got my second wind, and the way Sasha's staring raises goosebumps all over my skin. There's no other word for it: she looks like she wants to devour me. I shoot the same look right back at her.

"You gonna fuck me with that thing or just wave it around?"

With a flash of teeth, Sasha's on me. She prowls over to the bed in two long strides, shoving me flat against the mattress. I barely have time to suck in a breath before her lips catch mine. They're forceful, demanding, and I almost forget it's supposed to be my turn. I grasp her shoulders, preparing to flip her over, but I end up clinging to them as her hand finds my breast. The way she squeezes isn't gentle, and neither is the way she tugs my nipple, but it's so expertly done that the pain turns to pleasure. I may hate her, but Sasha knows her shit.

She also knows it's not the time to drag things out. Her hand moves to the middle of my chest, keeping me pinned as she straddles my midsection. My mouth tingles when I look between her legs. She's still slick, still swollen, still open and inviting. I swallow around my tongue. If I get half a chance, I definitely want her to sit on my face.

But Sasha has other ideas. She grips the strap-on with her free hand, running the rounded end between her lips. The dark surface of the toy gleams after only a few passes. She's wet, maybe even wetter than before. I might not have made her come yet, but *I* did that, I realize with a surge of pride and renewed lust. I reach for her legs, running my fingers along the stiff muscles of her thighs, soaking her in through my palms.

Sasha grunts softly, and my eyes widen as the short end slides home. Watching it disappear into her is sexy, but the new sight is even sexier. A smooth shaft juts from between her thighs, pointing proudly at the ceiling. Sasha and her new cock both twitch at the same time— probably the transmitters lining up. The extra wetness in my mouth rushes straight down, and the steady ache in my core surges into a powerful throb.

I can't resist the urge to touch. I slide my hand up her leg before wrapping it around the shaft. It's warm, as warm as her skin, and just as soft too. If I squeeze a little, pressure pounds in my palm. Her clit must be pulsing like crazy under the transmitter. My muscles ripple in response. *Fuck,* I want her in me, but I don't want to let go of her long enough to get her between my thighs. Plus she looks so damn incredible kneeling over me, staring down with those blazing eyes of hers.

When I start stroking, Sasha tenses up. Her abs stand out beneath her skin and her thighs give a jolt, like I've completed some kind of circuit. She's so much more responsive like this, and I'm gonna milk it as long as she lets me. I pump slow at first, fingers loose and relaxed, only choking up when I reach the head. Clear wetness wells from the tip, gathering in a glinting pool.

Fuck. I bet it tastes like her. I bet that's part of the design. My mouth remembers how fucking amazing her flavor is, and I need more. I'm not one for crunches—not all of us can be jacked—but I lift my upper body off the bed in less than a second. She smells the same up close, and when I wrap my lips around her, the same salty-sweetness spreads over my tongue. Shit, yes. All her.

Sasha shudders—actually *shudders* as I run my tongue over the sensitive slit. I can tell she feels my tongue because she twitches softly in my mouth, and I get another trickle of flavor. I relax my mouth, preparing to sink down further, but her fingers fist my hair, pulling me away.

"*¿Es en serio?*" I growl, but Sasha doesn't seem to care. She shifts down along my body, and I forget why I'm pissed when her lips seal around the peak of my breast. *Dios*, her mouth. It can definitely do more than kiss. She's rough with her sucking, and she isn't afraid to use her teeth, but her tongue is gentle, slow. This time, I'm the one who grabs her by the hair.

I'm so distracted I don't realize what the rest of Sasha is doing until her pelvis settles against mine. The cock—her cock? Yeah, I'll roll with that—strains against my stomach, and her nails dig into my skin as she hauls my legs around her waist.

I should object. I should do what I came in here to do and show her she can't always have it her way. But the floodgates open as her shaft slides through my wetness, and her rough nips and kisses leave me trembling. She moves her mouth up along my neck, biting hard enough to bruise.

I don't realize I'm begging her to go inside until the words spill out against her shoulder. "*Chingada madre, te necesito dentro de mí.*"

Sasha jerks as soon as my breath hits her neck. Her hips snap once, sending sparks skittering up my spine, but she reins herself in almost immediately. She starts a slow, torturous grind that offers contact, but no relief.

Mierda. I'm gonna come again. I can feel it building, and there's no way in hell I'm going to lose it before she's even in me. I grip her ass in both hands and tighten my legs around her, tilting to find the right angle.

We both shiver when our bodies line up. Sasha freezes above me, but I don't give her a chance to overthink it. I dig my heels into the backs of her thighs and pull her forward. A long sigh washes across my cheek as Sasha slides home. In two short thrusts, I manage to take the head. She's thick, but the stretch lights my nerves on fire. I squeeze hard around her, trying to draw her deeper. The emptiness inside me isn't satisfied.

"Quiero que me cojas," I gasp into the damp skin behind her ear. *"Quiero que me duela."* Just fucking pound me already. I want it to hurt.

Sasha takes off like a racer at the starting gun. She shoves the rest of the way inside with one stroke, then withdraws almost as fast. I'm still reeling from full-then-empty when she slams in again, and again, and again. Jesus fucking Christ, the woman's a machine. Her hips churn like a piston and her muscles are rolling waves. She's just getting started, and she's already giving it to me harder, faster, *better* than I've ever had it.

Even though I don't want to look away from her face, my eyes roll back in my head. I don't know how long I can take this pace, but I can't bear to ask her to stop, either. *"Ay, mierda,"* I mumble, but as she hits my front wall, my voice becomes more of a whimper. *"Por favor, ¡Jefecita, cogeme tan duro que no pueda caminar!"* Please, Boss, fuck me 'til I can't walk.

I don't even realize what I've asked, or what I've called her, until Sasha goes harder. I go from barely hanging on to hurtling through space. I'm floating in a place where nothing exists but Sasha pumping between my legs. She doesn't say a word. All I get is a few groans, so low I only hear them because they're right beside my ear. The droplets clinging to her skin are leftover water, not sweat, and her breathing isn't even labored. It feels like she could do this for the rest of the night without stopping.

A familiar red fog creeps over me, but I do my best to fend it off. I hold my breath, chew on my cheek, hook my nails into Sasha's back. When that doesn't work, I squirm beneath her, trying to position myself so her thrusts aren't so intense. There's no escape. Part of me doesn't want to escape. She's filling me too well, and her tempo's too perfect—so perfect I don't even see the cliff coming before I stumble over the edge.

My release hits, but it isn't a relief. It's a scorching, hungry thing that burns through my entire body. The contractions tear like teeth and floating specks of light sting my eyes. Sasha falters, burying herself back in halfway through a thrust, and I cling to the hope that maybe she's finally going to come. But no. All I can do is clench helplessly around her as she resumes her relentless rhythm.

She keeps surging against me, over me, into me. It's like holding the ocean in my arms. By the time my third orgasm winds down, I'm climbing for a fourth already. The base of her shaft grinds into my clit on every stroke, and stars swirl inside my head whenever the tip hits my front wall.

Christ, this is how I'm gonna die. Getting hatefucked by my handler until my body gives out. That sends a dizzying flash of heat through me. It's messed up, getting even more turned on by the fact that she's my boss, but there it is. It's not like I've treated her that way anyway. Half the time I don't even do what she wants, and the other half I do it with a heavy dose of sass. But now she's *making* me do what she wants, and it's overwhelming.

No. Shit, no, I won't go down without a fight. She doesn't get to win again, not this time. This time when I gasp in her ear, it's on purpose. *"Vente dentro de mi, Jefecita. Dámelo todo."* Come inside me, Boss. Give me all you've got.

That does it. Sasha's eyes go wide enough to show the whites and her lips fall open. A sob cracks in her throat, and instead of slamming into me, she stays buried deep. Her hips give a soft, uncertain twitch, then lock up completely as heat floods out of her and into me. She looks surprised, almost like her body has betrayed her.

I almost feel sympathetic as she shakes in my arms, all those tight muscles melting. She obviously wasn't expecting this. She was trying to fuck me unconscious, just because she thought she could. But finally, *finally* I've got her. Checkmate, bitch.

I seize my chance. It's easier than I'd hoped to flip her over while she's like this. Her size and strength are useless as I brace my hands on her shoulders, pinning her flat to the bed. *"Eso es, llename la panocha."* Fuck. That's it. Fill my pussy deep.

Another groan breaks in Sasha's throat. Her large hands grip my waist, but they're trembling too hard to find a proper hold. The hot pulses speed up, spilling deeper as I roll my hips over hers. When they finally start to taper off, I surrender to the deep tug in my belly. My last peak isn't painful or sudden, but it's the strongest one of all. It feels like I'm shedding my skin, dissolving into the air around me—or maybe like I'm sinking into Sasha's body, lying soft beneath mine.

I don't stop rocking over her or squeezing around her until we're both finished. Sasha stares up at me in amazement, like she still can't believe what happened. Her mouth moves, but her voice is on a three-second delay. "I...I don't...how did you..."

Several cruel retorts come to mind, but I've burned through most of my fury. I still don't like Sasha, but I don't want to strangle her anymore. Well, maybe only half as much as usual. I got my revenge, got back my pride, and got her off. No reason to be a jerk about it.

"Shut up." I stroke up along her stomach to squeeze one of her breasts. "I don't care about...whatever."

"This doesn't change things," Sasha says, sounding almost suspicious. "It doesn't *mean* anything." But although her eyes aren't warm or tender, they aren't ice-cold either. Maybe I've graduated from an insufferable annoyance to a tolerable acquaintance.

"Yeah."

I start to slide off, but Sasha pulls me back down to her chest. She doesn't wrap her arms around me. There's no embrace. But we do stay like that for a little while, and lying skin-to-skin against someone isn't so bad.

Sunday, 06-13-65 01:19:58

THE HUM OF THE Eagle's engine vibrates under me as we whisper through the dark, passing over the city of Hong Kong and out into the wilderness beyond. My hands have the shakes and my toes keep curling and uncurling in my boots. I'm stupid for being here. I don't even know *why* I'm here. But even after the...incident...with Sasha, I didn't leave the Hole, and when the rest of the crew piled into the Eagle later that night, I strapped in with them.

Stupid, stupid, stupid. I tell myself it's because Val would be even more dangerous than she already is in Cross's hands, but I know that's only part of the real reason. On a smaller scale, I'm also here because I don't want to see the rest of the crew get killed.

No one else seems nervous. Alert, maybe, but not scared—or if they are, they don't show it. Doc seems downright gleeful, sitting across from me in her ugly new 'I <3 St. Petersburg' hat. I owe Rami, Cherry, and Rock a big one for taking the kid somewhere to preserve her not-so-innocent ears. According to Cherry, who still hasn't stopped smirking at me, the bathroom walls echo. Everyone got the hell out after my first scream.

Sasha's up front, riding copilot for once. There's no proof, but I'm pretty sure she made Doc ride in back because she doesn't want to look at me. She hasn't been rude since we fucked, or even colder than usual, but she's kept her distance. I don't know why she's worried. I thought I made it pretty clear I'm not trying to put a ring on it or any of that shit. Rock looks at me and makes a quiet, questioning noise. Guess being a dude who doesn't talk makes him good at listening to what people don't say.

"It's all good," I tell him, but he doesn't seem convinced. I'm not sure I'm convinced either.

The tension feels like it lasts a while, but the rest of the flight doesn't. I glance out the Eagle's window to see the lights of Hong Kong disappearing into the distance. We're leaving the city behind us, flying away from the coast and into the mountains.

Cherry nudges my thigh from the seat next to mine. "You ready, Nevares?"

I shrug. "Ready to get my ass fried because Sasha has a death wish? Sure, why the hell not."

I'm surprised when Cherry doesn't find a way to make the conversation sexual. She sounds sincere when she says, "But you're here, yeah? You think this is the right call."

"I *think* it's a trap."

"We all know it's a trap," Cherry snorts. "Point stands: you think riding into a trap with us is the right call."

"Mmhmm. Fuck if I know why."

Cherry's eyes flick toward the front of the Eagle. "Because you're Sasha's now."

I gape at her in disbelief, my face flaring hot. Cherry rolls her eyes. "Not like her girl or something. Don't be dumb, Nevares. I mean Sasha's got this list of people she'll take a bullet for, no hesitation. You got her crew back together. You risked your ass for us. So in her book, you're one of us, and some part of you knows that. And for all that you bitch about crewbonding, you have too much pride not to match a commitment like that."

I start to say that I don't know any such thing, but the truth of the words shuts my mouth. *Mierda.* One crazy, adrenaline-fueled week with these losers and I'm already starting to care about them. They're like a fungus or something, softening me up until I'm all rotten and gross inside. No one warned me this ride-or-die shit was contagious. Fine. I'll risk my ass keeping these idiots alive. *Then* I'll freak out about getting attached and take a chainsaw to the roots I'm growing.

Another light appears in the Eagle's window, a distant, fuzzy glow halfway up the mountain almost like a firefly. As it gets bigger, it turns into several lights. The shadow of a huge house emerges, darker than the blue-black night sky. It's set on a plateau carved unnaturally into the side of the mountain. Of course, Cross would think nothing of cutting into the landscape, so she could plop her mansion in the middle of it.

"Val, what's on the scanners?" Sasha asks.

Val's cheerful voice fills the shuttle. "Nothing unexpected to report. An electromagnetic field twenty yards away, containing twenty heat signatures. It appears to be a biodome."

Sasha nods tightly. "Rami, take us in."

"Going ghost."

The shuttle's trajectory doesn't change, but its vibrations rise in pitch. It's not a squeal, more like rasping white noise. I look at Cherry. "If we have cloaks, why the hell weren't we using them before this?"

"Energy drain," Cherry says. "You wanna fix an overcharged plasma engine, *chaparrita*? Be my fucking guest."

I pucker my lips, but don't argue.

We slide through the biodome shield like butter. Once we're in, Rami brings us down behind a grove of trees. There are a lot of them, plus hedges and smooth stone walkways closer to the house. I roll my eyes. It's not like a corp exec would care about the wastefulness of building a mansion this extravagant on a cliffside, or even think about it. Bet that energy-burning biodome is to keep the temperature just right.

The Eagle pulls to a stop and Rami shuts off the engine. It's even quieter than before. I can hear my own heartbeat, and I don't like it.

"Weapons check," Sasha says, unbuckling her harness.

The rest of us get up. My LightningBolt's charged, safety on. Since that's all I've got, I watch Doc and Cherry check their utility belts. Doc's got biogrenades, ammo, and her med kit—NervPacs, StimPacs, vacuum bags with coolant, a couple rolls of good old-fashioned bandages. Cherry's belt hangs low enough to show a strip of brown skin along her belly. I'm not sure I even want to know what's in the pockets of her pants, but I bet it's something combustible.

Cherry grins when she notices me staring. "Sorry, girl. If you're looking for some more dick, you're about ten years too late."

I glare at her. "I like pussy fine, but I draw the line at eating ass."

Cherry cracks up.

"Cherry," Rami sighs from up front, "what part of 'that's inappropriate' don't you understand? Think about your audience."

Doc rolls her eyes. "Rock's a big boy. He can handle it."

"Quiet," Sasha snaps. "Val, guards?"

"Based on my scanners and your source's guard rotation data, the biosignatures are at maximum projected distance from the shuttle."

"Okay." Sasha hits a button on the dash, and the doors hiss open. "Split up and move fast. Code 900 unless you start taking too much heat, and I mean it this time. No jokes, no call signs, and *no* flirting."

"Come on, *jefa*, have a little faith," Cherry chuckles as we hop out. "And we won't be taking heat. We'll be bringing it. Right, Rockstar?"

The Eagle's frame groans as Rock steps out. He cracks the knuckles of his enormous fist against the palm of his other hand.

"Watch his back, Cherry," Doc says. Her narrow chin juts out defiantly, but her eyes are worried.

Cherry salutes with two fingers. "You got it, *cerebro*. And hey, *chapparita*, tell me how those noise mods work out for you. Sorry you gotta go through another blast."

I'd been trying not to think about that part, but at least Cherry's sympathetic. I force a smile, hoping the shake in my legs isn't visible. "Will do."

I'm saved when Rami circles around from the front of the shuttle. The rest of us are wearing black, but they've got on a top-grade armored breastplate with an AxysGen logo. They walk over to Cherry and lean in, whispering something I can't hear. Feeling like I'm intruding, I look away.

"Elena," Sasha says, and I turn around. She's got her rifle strapped across her shoulders and steel in her eyes. This time, I don't read the look as cold. She's focused, ready to get the job done.

"*¿Qué onda?*"

Sasha tosses me something. Luckily, I manage to catch it. "Your other partner."

I look down at Val's databox. I still don't fully trust a FRAI to watch my back, but if I'm jacking into a corp exec's private intranet security system, I'll take whatever help I can get. I start to put the databox in my pocket, but Sasha stops me. "There's a custom port on your tactical vest. If you plug Val in, she'll be able to help us."

Sasha shows me where to clip the box on, and Val's voice comes in through my comm. "*Hello, Elena. Are you ready to proceed?*"

"Not much of a choice."

"*For me, no. My safety depends on the success of this mission. You, however, did have a choice. Thank you for assisting me.*"

"Uh, you're welcome. You might creep me out, but I don't want AxysGen to hurt you."

Val's tone is amused. "*I will interpret that as a compliment.*"

"And, uh..." I hesitate, but eventually mutter, "I'm sorry. About what I said. It's not fair to flip out and say you weren't a person when you melted that guy to save me. It was my fault too."

"It was regrettable," Val says, "but I am not sure it is helpful to see it as anyone's 'fault.' I wished to save you, so I did. I would do so again." There's a long pause, and I almost think she's finished before she says, "Unless you wish for me to modify my coding so that I will not save you if doing so would kill another person?"

The sick part of me almost wants to say yes. Sometimes I think death would make things easier. At least I wouldn't have to deal with being so goddamn tired all the time. But I've got brothers to feed. I need to keep breathing.

"No. If it comes down to it, make the same call."

"I understand, Elena."

That's when I realize Sasha has heard most of our conversation. My face heats up as I remember she's standing next to me. "Ready when you are, *Jefecita*."

Sasha does a double-take so subtle I almost miss it in the dark. She blinks, then turns, heading for one of the hedges that will cover our route to the house. Then it hits me. Shit. I've gotta find something to call her that I *haven't* already used while she was balls deep.

I glance back at the others. They're starting to scatter, but Doc's the closest. I can't help it, my heart clenches with worry. She looks so small, especially in the dark. It takes an effort of will not to think about Jacobo and Mateo.

"Hey, *chiquita*. Watch your ass, okay?"

Doc smirks at me. "Don't worry. You need my ass alive to fix your brain." She trots off, and I turn back to the hedge in time to glimpse Sasha's retreating back. I head after her, my palm sweating against the grip of my pistol.

I catch up with Sasha behind the first hedge. After peering around its edge, she motions us across the short gap to the next bush. She's going for stealth rather than speed, thank God, or I wouldn't stand a chance of keeping up with her long-ass legs in the dark. We stop again, crouching low to the ground. While I sit on my heels, Sasha checks the HUD on her VIS-R. She holds up two fingers, and I nod. Shit, if two minutes is all Cherry needs to blow up a lawn this big, I'm impressed. I'm also terrified. I'm not sure I'll be able to keep my head on during the explosion, even though I know it's coming.

That two minutes seems to stretch for hours. It's quiet as death except for the sound of my own churning gut and Sasha's light breathing. She checks her VIS-R again, then nods at me. I close my eyes, holstering my pistol and tapping my fingers to my ears. Doc hooked me up with some noise-cancelling mods that should block out the worst of the sound, but I have no idea how effective they're going to be.

The blast roars behind us, shaking the ground. Pressure squeezes both sides of my head for a split second, and my ears close up. Everything sounds fuzzy and far away, including whatever Sasha's saying as her mouth moves in front of me.

Eventually, I realize it's my name. I focus on those lips, watching the shapes they form as jittering colors creep in around the edges of my vision. My heart pumps frantically in my chest, but the noise mods helped. Without the sound, and with Sasha's face to focus on, it takes noticeably less effort to keep my panic at bay. The worst part is the smell, but I force myself to breathe through it. After a minute, I'm back. Rattled, but capable of moving. I grip my pistol, pick myself up, and haul ass after her.

"*Aw yeah!*" Cherry's shrill voice blasts from both our comms, causing Sasha to wince in surprise. "*Adiós, swimming pools.*"

"Swimming pools, plural?" I pant.

"*Yep. Go big or it's not worth it. How'd those noise mods work out?*"

Sasha isn't amused. "I *said* Code 900, Cherry. Nevares."

"*Whatever, buzzki—*" Her voice is drowned out by the sound of a loud crunch, followed by a scream. "*—rry and Rock out.*"

Sasha and I get to the mansion faster than I expect. No guards, which means Cherry and Rock are probably having a ball. I'm almost ready to let out the heavy breath in my lungs when searchlights flood the lawn and a sharp drilling noise pierces the night. Or, it would have been sharp if my mods hadn't dampened it. It sounds more like the distant, rapid thrumming of a woodpecker's beak. Not nearly as bad as the boom of an explosion. Then again, there hadn't been turrets in Mumbai.

Sasha pins herself flat against the mansion wall, and I do the same. Cold seeps out of the stones and into my skin, but all I smell is smoke and scorched graphene. We wait. Wait. Wait some more. My heart jolts every time the turrets fire. Then the lights on the roof switch off, and the sound disappears.

"*Lights out,*" Rami whispers through the comms. "*You're clear, cupcake.*"

"*Shit, so we* are *doing call signs!*" Doc asks excitedly. "*Can I be Headshot? No, Painkiller...Oh, wait, you're just being a fucking dork.*"

"*If we are selecting call signs,*" Val says, "*I would like to put forward 'Lupa' as a suggestion for Sasha rather than 'Cupcake.'*"

"*What the fuck is a Lupa?*" Cherry asks.

"*The Latin word for a female wolf. Alternatively, a wolf from Roman mythology who acted as a maternal figure to the twins Romulus and Remus. Romulus eventually founded the city of Rome.*"

Sasha rolls her eyes skyward. "Do none of you get what Code 900 means?" she growls.

"Mama wolf's angry," Doc says. *"Painkiller out."*

With a huff of frustration, Sasha peels away from the wall and slips around the corner. I know where we're headed: a service door on the left side of the mansion. It looked a lot closer on the blueprints, though—by the time we get there, I'm panting for air.

"Okay, Nevares." Sasha adjusts her rifle, sparing a quick glance at the glowing orange port beside the door. "Take us in."

I'm trying to decide whether to use Val or not, and leaning toward not, when the decision becomes moot. The door opens from the inside, revealing a guard.

My LightningBolt fires before I'm conscious of pulling the trigger. I squeeze off three rounds straight into his chest. He jerks, the whites of his eyes widening in surprise before he crumples. I freeze, but Sasha has my back. When another guard appears, rifle raised to shoot, Sasha dispatches him with a pulse straight to the face.

After a split-second check to make sure it's only the pair of them, Sasha grasps my shoulder. "Nice shot." She lets go almost immediately, stepping over the bodies and into the mansion. I don't know if that's supposed to be her weird way of offering reassurance, but I'll take it. Freezing up after shooting a guard is better than freezing before, I guess.

We hurry up a short set of stairs and into a narrow hallway. It's not as fancy as the outside of the house looks, so I assume we're in some kind of servants' area. My guess proves right when we pass the first doorway—an empty kitchen. Guess it's no surprise that Veronica has an in-house cooking staff.

"Basement?" I whisper.

Sasha has the blueprints memorized. She heads straight for the end of the hallway and turns left. The corridor around the corner is wider, but not by much. About twenty feet in front of us, there's a door that doesn't look like the others. Instead of a door with wood veneer that swings one way, this one doesn't pretend to be anything but metal. There's an uneven, Y-shaped seam running through the middle, and a port off to one side.

I don't wait for Sasha to tell me. I push my finger against the port and go in wireless.

Sunday, 06-13-65 01:52:24

NETWORK: VC 22396 . 11410
    Connection established
    welcome: user escudoespiga

The inside of the security system is cold. Physical sensation doesn't actually exist on the intranet or extranet outside of VR programs, but everything around me gives the impression of cold, at least. The dark, empty blue is like being at the bottom of the Arctic Ocean.

I activate my toolbar and summon my shield. Always good to be prepared. There's nothing to bash or block, though. In fact, there's nothing at all, not even a horizon. I run my scanning program on its lowest setting, wary of attracting attention. Nothing. Just vanishing blueness in every direction.

The next scanner setting I try is a bust too. Through the chill, I feel a spark of frustration. Fuck this shit. I'm finding something to smash. I scroll right and pick the most powerful setting I have. I'll probably trip all the alarms in reality, but Sasha has my back. I'll just need to move fast.

Nothing, nothing...bingo. The scanner's light illuminates pale white cracks along the ground under my feet, running in every direction. I brace my shield, preparing to drive the spikes into the ground.

Something tingles along the back of my neck. At first I think it's more of the same cold, but then I place it as something else— apprehension. The prickling grows stronger, sending a shudder down my spine. Jackers who don't follow their instincts usually end up dead.

I look up. A figure is standing in the distance, breaking up the blue. They're too far for me to see any details, but they seem vaguely humanoid. Could be a program, a VI, even another jacker. I run my scanner. My heart jolts. The figure is outlined in glowing red. No way am I sticking around to see what this jacker wants. I aim for the ground again, but before I can crash through the floor, the figure flashes forward.

Flash. There's no other way to describe it. Everyone moves fast in virtual space, but this is unreal. One second they're two hundred yards away, the next it's ten feet. Their avatar is the same dark blue as the emptiness around us, and they're wearing a hood over their face.

Mierda. My toolbar runs autocloaks on login, but those are designed to fool programs, not other jackers. My avatar is one hundred percent visible. The jacker lifts their hand, red light swelling in their palm. I duck behind my shield.

A powerful force collides with me, and I skid backwards. The Puls.wav bounces off my shield, streaking straight back at the other jacker. It doesn't hit. They flash away again, avoiding it almost lazily. Fucking fuck me. This *pendejo* definitely has me outgeared by at least two generations—including one that doesn't even exist yet. A battle's out of the question, even if I wanted one. As soon as I recover my footing, I crash through the cracked white floor with all my strength. I disappear as another swell of red turns the blue world a dark, bloody purple.

logging off network
disconnection complete

"Nevares?"

I come to with Sasha's hands on my shoulders. My head spins for a second, but the adrenaline spike speeds up my recovery. "They made us," I gasp, struggling to control my breathing.

Sasha's eyes narrow. "Cross?"

"Don't know. An enemy jacker. Some Smurf-colored freak with a hood."

"What about the door?" Sasha asks.

I brush my sweaty hair out of my eyes with one hand and clutch my shaking pistol with the other. "Open. But Sasha, we need to get out of here! This jacker was..." I don't know how to describe it. I'm not sure I can describe it. The fear that pierced me the second I saw them isn't rational.

"Can't," Sasha says. She doesn't offer an explanation, but she doesn't need to waste time with one. The rest of the crew is risking their hides for us this very moment. We can't go back without the brainbox, not when it's so close.

"*This* is exactly why crewbonding is stupid," I snarl as I rip open the door.

The room beyond is not as large as I expected. It gives the

impression of more space than it has, but only because it's so organized. A place for everything and everything in its place. The walls are covered with shelves from floor to ceiling. Those shelves are filled with evenly-spaced objects, from physical books and art to pieces of sleek machinery I can't even identify. The categorization is difficult to understand, but it's clearly deliberate.

Luckily, we don't have to tear the place apart. In the middle of the room is a small, see-through cube sitting on a pedestal, maybe four inches across. Resting inside the cube is a tiny black databox, about as big as a fingernail.

I look at Sasha. "Sure you want me to do this? It's your brainbox."

She shakes her head. "I need the best, and that's you."

My face heats up. "And I can count on you to watch my body?"

"Absolutely." While Sasha takes a kneeling position at an angle from the doorway, I go for the pedestal. There's an orange port built into it, and this time, I hook Val up first. No way am I going back in alone with that ghost jacker zipping around.

I steal one more glance at Sasha. To my surprise, she's staring at me too. The look she gives isn't exactly a smile, but somehow, it's encouraging. Maybe grateful? I plug Val's cable into my jack and disappear.

network: vc 22396 . 11410
Connection established
welcome: user escudoespiga

Val's waiting for me as soon as I pop into existence. "Elena," she says, her brow furrowing. "Your vitals are unusually high."

"Almost died."

"I am aware. I am able to monitor surrounding sensory data through the belt."

That little tidbit would've been very unsettling to the Elena of three minutes ago, but now I've got bigger problems. If it's between Creepy Smurf and Val, I'm going with Val. "Brainbox," I say, looking around the landscape. "Let's go."

This time, there's no blue surrounding us. In fact, there isn't much of anything. Dark, grey-black fog stretches in every direction until it becomes nothing at all. The only visible object is exactly what I saw when I entered the meatspace room—a pale golden spotlight shining down on a pedestal. In here, there's no cube, just the brainbox, floating temptingly in place.

My eyes narrow. I know a trap when I see one, but I run my scanner anyway. Nothing. "Val?"

Val stares at the brainbox, her brow wrinkling in confusion. Her facial approximation software is surprisingly advanced. "My scanners don't reveal much. All I can determine is that this security program requires simultaneous access by two separate users."

"Explain, please? Shortest version possible." My tension's through the roof, and any second now, I'm sure Jack Frost is going to flash out of the fog.

"I can normally bypass simultaneous access protocols, but this is impossible. It requires a legitimate organic DNA signature, as well as a passphrase delivered at a speed faster than 0.5 milliseconds."

I've got questions, but no time for answers. Not only do I have to trust Val's morals, I have to decide whether I trust her judgment too.

"...Fine. DNA is me, milliseconds are you. Are we doing this?"

Val doesn't exactly answer the question. "I calculate the likelihood of success to be higher than random chance."

I sigh. "You can just say it's too good to be true."

"It is too good to be true." Val studies me carefully. "How should we proceed, Elena?"

"I...don't know." I don't. I really don't. All I know is we can't just stand here. The seconds are ticking by and we're running out of time.

"If it would help your determination, our crewmates' survival odds are decreasing at 0.2 percent per second."

My stomach lurches. "Okay, not helping. Fuck, let's do it."

I jog up to the pedestal with Val beside me.

"I agree with your choice, Elena."

Maybe later I'll feel some type of way about that statement, but not with the heat on. Numb and afraid is all there is. There are two golden circles on the front of the pedestal, one beside the other like a pair of glowing eyes. I put my hand in front of one, Val extends toward the other.

"I will match your timing."

I nod.

Tres...dos...uno...ir.

The fog disappears like water being drained from an enormous pool. Suddenly I can see. It looks like we're in meatspace again, only the images are flashing by so fast I can barely make out what they are. It's like a bugged-out VR set to maximum speed, and I can't make out much more than moving blurs. I grit my teeth and concentrate, switching open my VIS-R settings and using all the force I have to make time slow down.

A woman. A man.
A house. No, plants? Garden!
A loud fwoom, followed by a split-second scream.
Smoke. Oh shit, smoke. In my mouth, lungs...
Street. Windows. Cold. Belly-knives.

Cobwebbed corners. Books. A... library? A virtual library. Somehow I'm in virtual space in meatspace in virtual space.
A stadium. A hundred thousand seats. So many people. Kids. An ocean of kids.
APS. Flashing names. S-A-S-H-A Y-O-U-N-G

Tall buildings. Tallest buildings in the world.
A room. Two beds. A girl? Blonde. Shit. I...we...know her?
Heat. Vanilla. Lips. Soft.
Whispers, anger, so much anger...

"Haven't you ever wanted to become a god? Create your own future?"
What the actual fuck is she talking about?

Buildings—gone. Credits—gone. Just a pistol, basic strength mods.
Rifles glinting. Shiny red armor—red bob of hair. Cherry?
A black-haired woman in a...a bald man wearing a...Rami.

Stinking plasma exhaust.
Black and red armor. A huge moving mountain, an extra head. Rock and Doc.

Food. Hotels. Nicer food. Nicer hotels.
Girls. Long hair, some ass on them. Love at first sight a hundred times.
Cracks, splinters, disappointment.
The best food. The best hotels. Prettier girls.
The G-force of the Eagle hitting a hard turn.

Blonde hair.
Heat. Vanilla. Lips. Soft. Again?
Right. It's all right. It's…almost right.
A plot in Barbados, a padded bank account.

"Last one. Come on, baby. Don't you want to live forever?"

A tank. Cold, blue, wet. A reflection?
Boulders flying everywhere. Spitting rubble. Shit. Cherry! Limp,
broken, bloody forehead.
Crushed legs, so much pain. One last push…
BRRRROOOMMMM.
Hot. Blood. Cold. Black.

A tank. Cold, blue, wet. Reflection.
"Last one. Come on, baby. Don't you want to li—"
Blinking blue dots. Doc. Oh god, Doc!
SPPPPLTTTT.
Hot. Blood. Cold. Black.

A tank. Cold, blue. Reflection.
"Last one. Come on, baby. Don't you—"
Rami. Guardogs, glowing eyes.
ZzzzzzZZZZzzt.
Hot. Blood. Cold. Black.

Tank. Blue. Reflection.
"Last one. Come on—"
Rock. Surrounded. Skin sloughing off.
Rrrratatatatatat.
Hot. Blood. Cold. Black.

Tank. Blue.
"Last one."
Red numbers ticking down. About to blow.
"Get out! Go, I've got this!"
Footsteps running away. Alone.
FWOOOOM.
Hot. Blood. Cold. Black.

Tank.
"Last—"
Megan. No no NO no no NO no no no.
Blood. Gashed throat. Pale. Gone.
BRRRROOOMMMM.
Cold. Black.

/////DOWNLOAD COMPLETE/////

I can't see anything except empty static, but Val's voice fills the void of space. "Elena? Elena, disconnect! Disconnect!"

logging off network
disconnection complete

I jerk back into meatspace like I'm standing in ten different places at once. I'm a prism, refracted. The room spins and it's several seconds before I see...my face? Sasha's face? Yes, Sasha's face, hovering above mine.
"Elena. Elena, what happened?"
I stare up into Sasha's wide brown eyes. My tongue is glued to the roof of my mouth, and all I can croak out is: "Sasha...you...died."

Rae D. Magdon

part two — sasha

Sunday, 06-13-65 22:06:43

"LAST ONE. COME ON, baby. Don't you want to live forever?"

I lift my head out of my hands and stare at Megan in disbelief, but I shouldn't be surprised. This is far from the first time she's asked me to do this, and yet the pain is always fresh and raw. "I told you, I can't anymore. That last op…"

"I know." Megan's voice is full of sympathy as she circles my chair, placing both hands on my shoulders. As she starts to rub them, the scent of vanilla fills my nose. My muscles tense instead of relaxing, and I become hyperaware of my heartbeat. It doesn't know whether to race or slow to a crawl.

"Megan, I—"

She cuts me off. "I know it hurts, baby. The last one was bad. But we're *so* close! Val is learning more every day. Soon, she'll be unstoppable."

I bite my lip. This is what Megan always says. How she always convinces me. "What do you even mean, 'unstoppable'? She's already a hundred times more advanced than any of the AIs the corps have— she's basically human. You did it. I thought this was what you wanted, anyway: to make a fully-realized AI and improve life for everyone."

Megan sighs, leaning down to rest her chin on top of my head. "We're almost there, Sasha, I promise. I just need some experimental tech from AxysGen. Prototypes of the new Dendryte Platinum hardware."

Heat courses through me, but my voice is soft and uncertain as it comes out. Normally, I'm good at pretending to be strong, but the fact that she's asking again—when she knows full well how painful the last time was—makes me feel weak in the worst way. "Why?" *What's so important about this tech that you're asking me to risk my life for you again?*

"I need to make sure Val is compatible." Megan lifts her chin off me, and I turn my head to look back at her. The blue of her eyes is bright with new possibilities. "Don't you get it? This is our chance to bring Val to the whole world! To make everyone see what I've done!"

"What the whole crew has done." Val might be Megan's pet project, but we've all risked our lives to help. I died five times because I believe the same thing they do—that Val will be an enormous force for good in the world.

Megan's voice is almost dismissive. "Yeah, what we've done. But Sasha?" She releases my shoulder and comes to stand in front of my chair again, staring down at me with a pleading expression. "This really is the last one. I promise."

I peer past her, looking at the tank on the other side of the room. It's three meters high and full of glowing blue gel, and there's a shadowy figure suspended inside. Though I can't see its face, a shiver races down my spine. It never gets any easier, looking at myself like that. Alive, but not. A perfect copy of me without a mind.

"What about Sasha Seven?" I ask Megan, without tearing my gaze away from the tank. "If you really mean it when you say this is the last time, I can't just leave her like this." *Assuming I don't die again.*

Megan caresses my cheek with the back of her hand. For a moment, I feel comforted. It's good to be touched, makes me hope Megan does care after all. "Does it matter? If you don't need her, we can get rid of her."

The good feelings her touch causes dissolve instantly. I know the clone in the tank doesn't have any kind of consciousness yet, but she has my body. She's capable of feeling physical pain. It's upsetting to hear Megan talk about disposing of her so casually, even if she isn't me. It's a chilling response from someone who says she loves me. *At least, I think she loves me?*

I squash the question down. Megan does love me. She's said so before. Why else would she have come back to me after our years apart? Megan's brilliant enough to find employment with any corp in the world. They'd set her up like a queen in exchange for her research, but she's slumming it with me instead. It's true she hates the system, hates the endless regulations and protocols, just like when we were students at AukPrep. She's impatient, and she'd rather have no rules than break a bunch of flimsy ones. She *especially* hates being told what to do by someone higher up. But surely the fact that she's stayed with me means something.

"No. I don't want her disposed of. We'll figure something out later, after the op."

Megan shrugs. "Whatever you want, baby. Just say you'll do it."

My eyes flick down into my lap. For some reason, I can't look at Megan or my clone. "Yeah." I drag the word out from deep inside my chest. I'm so, so tired…but this needs to be done. "I'll do it, just this one last time."

////// DOWNLOAD COMPLETE //////

I remove the cable from behind my ear and open my eyes, looking around the Hole's hangar. I've re-lived my entire life in the span of five minutes, but as fast-paced as the experience was, it feels much more vivid than my organic memories of the past few hours. Distantly, I can recall Elena telling me I'm dead. Swiping the brainbox. Meeting Rami and Doc on the stairs. Dispatching another squad of guards. Sprinting for the shuttle with Cherry and Rock. It feels like it happened a lifetime ago…someone else's lifetime.

My hands clench into fists. I'm angry at Megan. Angry at my crew. Angry at myself most of all, for taking so long to put the pieces together. There were always edges that didn't quite fit, but this…it's so much worse than I imagined.

I stare at the cable, twisting it between my fingers. I'm holding the silver snake that bit me, but I can't bring myself to put it down. Why could I remember my childhood, my crew, and Val's creation before tonight, but not the cloning or the dying until I downloaded the memories? Why could I remember Megan and our relationship, but not her constant appeals for me to sacrifice my life for her ambitions?

Worst of all, there are still pieces missing. I saw Sasha Two through Six emerging from the tank, wet and cold and afraid, but not me. The brainbox was stolen by AxysGen before Sasha Seven…before I…*emerged*, but my brain should have been able to form organic memories of that moment without technological assistance. I don't remember my final op either, only the tense hours before I boarded the Eagle for Mumbai. And I don't remember my sixth death.

Part of me doesn't want to believe any of this, but I know that it's all real. I can feel it in my bones. Megan isn't the woman I thought she was. My crew isn't the family I thought it was. And me? I don't even know who I am.

My DNA and memories belong to a person named Sasha Young. She was born to cog parents, both killed by negligent corp enforcement of safety regulations. She grew up an orphan, a student, a rebel. She became a handler for self-preservation, but liked to think she kept doing it for the right reasons. She loved a hundred girls for a few weeks each, and one girl for a lot longer than that. She loved her family even more, the family of misfits she made for herself. And because she loved them, she died for them. Over and over and over again.

I put the cable down. I don't know how much of me is Sasha, and how much of me is...someone else. Some parts feel like me. Others feel distant, like watching someone else go through the motions in my body. Her body. Whichever.

I know I should keep looking through the brainbox. AxysGen is still after us, and I haven't found any information that might help us keep off their radar. But is there even an us anymore? Everyone else on my crew knew I wasn't the original Sasha. I'm Sasha Seven, the next in line to die for them. Theoretically, there could be a Sasha Eight being grown in a tank somewhere, waiting for me to do just that.

My hands are cold and trembling as I bury my face in them, but my breath doesn't warm them up. It's all I can do to keep back sobs. Is that all my crew thinks I am? Some kind of meatshield so they don't get hurt? Am I really that disposable? Is that why they didn't tell me the truth?

Worse thoughts follow. *Did Megan ever love me? Could someone who loved me watch my body break six different times without caring?* My chest seizes up with stabbing pain. Apparently, hearts can break more than once.

"Sasha?"

It takes a while for my name to register. When I look up, Val is in front of me. She looks stunningly real, standing there in her purple blouse and pencil skirt, but I keep trying to stare through the mirage, searching for the blank wall behind her.

"Your vitals indicate that you are seriously distressed," Val says, when I don't answer. "I want to be of assistance."

I swallow. My throat burns, probably because I've cried myself dry. "You...want...to be of assistance." If Val wanted to be of assistance, why didn't she tell me what I am?

"You feel a sense of betrayal," Val says. "That is understandable. I believe I should tell you that it was my decision to withhold this information when I activated you."

Activated. My stomach lurches. I wasn't born, or even created— just 'activated.'

"You're the one who deleted parts of my memory." It's a statement, not a question. My voice isn't capable of rising or falling—

140

there's only flatness. Val's betrayal is so painful that I've gone numb.

"At the time, I deemed it the least painful option, although now I have begun to question whether it was the right decision." The pity in Val's expression almost makes her look human. "Based on the moral parameters I observed in you, my priorities were…" Her forehead tenses, lips pressing together. "My top two priorities were to protect you from all harm, and to rescue your crew. I did not believe you would have the mental or emotional capacity to save them and resume leadership if you were burdened with this knowledge."

"You needed me to rescue them, so you used me." Saying it shouldn't hurt as much as it does. Everyone always needs something. Credits, sex, a rescue. Someone to jump on a grenade. And when they need something, I'm there, whether I want to be or not. Whether it was my decision or not.

"I also had your wellbeing in mind. I was concerned that reintroducing such painful memories too early might cause irreversible damage to your mental health. Trauma is difficult to deal with alone. I believed you would be able to process the memories more effectively while surrounded by our crew. Your family unit."

I believe her, but that doesn't stop it from hurting. If anything, it hurts worse. "That's a nice theory," I spit, my mouth sour with resentment, "but you still erased a huge part of my life without my fucking consent. What gave you the right?"

Val's expression shows obvious signs of shame. Her brown eyes are bright with tears, even though I know she's incapable of crying. It's all an act, a facial API to make lines of code look like actual human emotions—just like everything else. "You pulled the others in on it too, didn't you? Convinced them to keep quiet."

She doesn't deny it. "I asked Doc not to inform you about the cloning process before she helped me activate you. She was reluctant at first, but agreed. She considers you a surrogate parent, and did not want you to suffer more than you could bear."

"Or maybe she didn't want me too messed up to save her real brother. Can't risk my life for someone else while I'm in the middle of a breakdown."

"That is a possibility," Val admits. "However, I believe her primary motivation was concern for you. That holds true for all of our crewmates. We intended to tell you at a more appropriate time."

"That wasn't for any of you to decide!" My fury echoes around the hangar, followed by a painful silence. I curl my hand around the brainbox, squeezing tight enough to make its edges dig into my palm. "What about the other memories? The last op?" *Sasha Six's death?*

"It was not on your brainbox?" Val asks, sounding surprised, then sympathetic. The pity in her voice is wounding. "The information may have been damaged or erased. I am not sure."

Well, that makes two of us. I'm not sure about anything anymore. I can't trust my own thoughts, my own memories, not even my own body.

"I want to be alone, Val." I look away from her, unwilling to let her see the devastation on my face. "Go away."

"I will respect your wishes, Sasha," Val says, with notable disappointment. "If you have any further questions..."

I raise one hand, my silent way of saying 'I'll let you know.' When I look back, Val is gone. There's nothing left but empty grey wall.

I slip the brainbox into my pocket and pull my legs up onto the bed in the back of the Eagle, wrapping my arms around my knees. It's too cold to stay in the hangar forever, but I don't care. I'd rather rely on my thermal regulation mods and let the air eat at my skin through my coat than go back down.

Why do I have mods, anyway? If this is a brand-new body, that means new mods too. Doc, most likely. She must have put them in after this body was grown, but before my 'activation'. Probably around the same time Val convinced her to go along with the crew's deception.

I can't stop the tears rolling down my cheeks. They leave wet tracks on my face, heat that turns cold, but I let them keep on dripping. I don't have much choice but to cry until I can't anymore. Then I'll figure this out. Alone. With six lives and deaths trapped in my head.

The sound of the lift activating makes me flinch, but I don't look up. My head's too heavy. Whoever it is, I don't want to see them. Maybe if I stay like this, curled up into a ball, they'll go away.

"Sasha?"

Elena's voice drifts toward me, crisp in the frigid air. She sounds hoarse, like she's strained her throat. From yelling, maybe. I don't answer, but she approaches anyway. Her boots sound too loud scraping across the hangar's concrete floor. "The others sent me to check on you. They thought you might actually talk to me."

There's not much use in hiding. I know Elena won't go away unless I make her. Stubborn idiot. I blink away my freshest tears and turn my head sideways to look at her.

"You mean they were too scared to come up themselves."

Elena doesn't deny it. She climbs into the Eagle and hops onto the bed beside me, folding her legs up. There's only a few centimeters of space between us, and I can feel heat radiating from her thigh to mine.

"Val told me what happened. It's fucked up, Sasha. Really, really fucked up. I'm sorry."

I open my mouth to say I don't need Elena's sympathy, but actually, sympathy is exactly what I need right now. And Elena's the only person I have even a *slight* bond of trust with who wasn't involved in this mess. Girl drives me crazy, but at this point, crazy's better than liars.

"Yeah," I say, but the sound comes out as more of a sob.

Elena hesitates as she stretches out her hand, but when I don't move, she rests it on my back. I can barely feel it through my coat. "For what it's worth, I don't think those assholes wanted to hurt you. They're all quiet down there, acting like someone died."

"Someone did," I point out. "Someones."

"Yeah," Elena sighs. "I saw."

Logically, I know Elena saw something. The way she looked at me in that room, like she was staring at a ghost. She must have watched me die at the very least, and maybe absorbed some of my other memories too. "How much did you see?"

"All of it. The memories were sped up, but I felt—I saw you die. Six times."

I get the sense the first verb was more accurate. I also get the sense Elena knows me a lot better than she did a few hours ago.

"It was a trap," Elena continues when I don't respond. "At least, that's what Val and I think. Someone rigged your memories to, well...explode inside your mind. The rapid download of your deaths would have kept your physical body in a state of shock long enough for the guards to come and deal with you."

There it is. The cherry on top of the shit sundae. I know what it's like to die now. The unbearable shout of pain that goes through your body as it breaks. The helplessness. The cold. Maybe that's why this cold doesn't bother me. It's nothing in comparison.

"But I took the hit instead," Elena says softly, "and you and Val got me out of that basement." She pauses, looking at me with an expression I haven't seen her use often. It takes me a while to place it as worry. "Are you okay, Sasha? You're not saying anything."

I exhale. "It started with a logistics question. Megan needed some experimental tech, but it was guarded by an army. The only way to get to it was to cut through a reactor core. Whoever went in would be exposed to a lethal dose of radiation, so...I volunteered."

Elena isn't surprised. I guess she shouldn't be, if she's seen snippets of my life.

"Rami made a joke about clones. About how the corp families sometimes grow replacement body parts when one of theirs stopped working, or sometimes even entire new bodies. The memory-transfer process doesn't always go off without a hitch, but..." I laugh bitterly. "For beauty and longevity, some people are willing to take those risks. So wouldn't it be nice, Rami said, if one of us had one."

I wait, but Elena doesn't speak. She keeps listening, wearing a sympathetic look that simultaneously pisses me off and urges me to keep on rambling like an idiot. "I know Rami was joking, but Megan...she took it seriously. Couple days later, she approached me. Said she thought she could replicate the process for one of us. 'Someone could stay behind,' she told me."

My eyes flick down to my boots. The first time, I'd still held out hope I could get out of the op alive, contrary to what the plan said. It was all a theory, I'd told myself. And what was my body really worth anyway, if Megan could just grow me a new one? Surely helping her create Val, a FRAI who could help scientists cure disease, who could use a combined analysis of history and diplomacy and advocacy to come up with peaceful solutions to armed conflicts before they even started, who could change the entire world for the better, was worth that small sacrifice. It was worth going near a reactor, jumping in front of a Puls.wav, intentionally setting off a security system, covering a retreat.

I had been naïve. When I woke up as Sasha Two, I remembered the pain of dying. A pain I can recall all too clearly now. And yet, I'd done it again. And again. And again. To make Val the best she could be, and then, when that dream soured, to keep my friends alive. According to previous Sashas, that cause had been easier to die for.

"Sasha..." Elena looks like she wants to reach out and touch me. I tense up.

"Thought you didn't crewbond, and last I checked, you hated me. What's with the sympathy?"

Elena sends a sharp burst of air between her teeth, not quite laughter. "I don't hate you, stupid. I watched you sacrifice yourself for other people and an ideal six fucking times." She cups the back of my neck, warming the exposed patch of skin there. "How could I hate a person like that?"

"What if I'm not that person?" I ask. "What if

she's...they're...someone else?"

"Maybe some of this you is different, maybe not. But that's the same. You've saved my ass enough times to prove it."

"But how do you know?"

Elena rolls her eyes. "Fine, fine. Fuck it. I don't hate people who get me off four times, then."

I don't laugh, but the pain in my chest doesn't throb quite as hard either.

"Hey, *Jefecita...*"

I lift my head. Elena's hand moves to my cheek, just for a moment. "I'm hanging around for now. You know?"

I get it. She's telling me she'll be here, for...whatever. If I wasn't already reeling, I'd be shocked. Elena's had one foot out the door this whole time. Some mornings, I was surprised to see her—never more than when she got in the shuttle to go to Hong Kong.

All I've got the energy for is a shrug and a noncommittal noise, but that seems to be enough for Elena. Her fingers tighten the barest bit on the back of my neck and then she leans up, pausing to look into my eyes. Warm breath trails from her mouth in wisps of silver cloud, floating near my lips. I don't pull back.

Elena kisses me. It's soft. Short. She pulls away before I can respond, right after I've gotten a taste of lip gloss. Strawberries, not vanilla.

My eyes burn again, wet. "You don't even know who you kissed."

"Yeah," Elena says softly, "I do."

Her fingers trail briefly over my shoulder as she pulls her hand away and hops down from the Eagle. Her boots hit the concrete with a loud, echoing thud. "Don't stay up here all night. Or at least turn the engine on. I'm not chipping your dumb ass out of an ice block tomorrow."

She stares at me for a moment, giving me a chance to call her back. I don't. I don't want to. Do I?

She sighs, heading back for the lift.

Once Elena's gone, I put my knees down and climb into the Eagle, closing the doors behind me. I'll run the engine for a while. The cold's getting to me.

Monday, 06-14-65 16:23:51

IT TAKES TEN HOURS to fly to New Zealand, going the long way. Piloting the Eagle over an ocean of crimson pohutukawa trees is like drifting on the surface of a dream. It's familiar, but unsettling, a backwards reflection of reality. The blood-red flowers on the heavy, swaying branches beneath the shuttle's belly aren't supposed to blossom at all in the middle of June. But trees have memories, and the pohutukawas around AukPrep still listen to science's timetable, even though nature has taken over the compound. They've been genetically engineered. Grown in a laboratory, like me.

I bring the Eagle down over an empty patch of lawn. Everything is silent except for the plasma engine. There are no other shuttles, no groundskeepers, no students. Not a surprise. I've kept up with the place in the news as the years rolled on. It would have been a waste of resources to repair it, AxysGen had said. They've got a new place in Sydney now, shiny chrome buildings that bounce light off the sea with sterile white dormitories inside.

I switch the engine off. The silence grows louder. It takes me a moment to open the door. I know once I step outside, I'll inhale and think back. But there's nothing for it, so I push the button. The first scent that greets my nose is the damp green of the river. It's stronger than I'm expecting, but the smell of compost from years ago is absent. Tui birds call from somewhere nearby, singing bell-notes that waver in the air before popping them with sharp clicks and grating gasps. My stomach tightens. This place is both like and unlike my memories. It's different. Deteriorated.

I turn toward the main building, avoiding a direct stare, but the gleam yanks me in. It's all silver and glass, unnaturally bright—until it isn't. Two thirds of the giant 'U' shape are structurally sound, but the last third has fallen away, a jungle of twisted steel support beams over a floor of broken glass.

The front doors are still standing when I reach them. They're jammed halfway open by a large metal desk. I don't remember who wedged it there, but I remember climbing over it on my way out, after the explosion. That was before my noise-cancelling mods were installed—or, before the original Sasha's were. I hadn't realized one of my eardrums was ruptured until I touched the heat running down my neck and my fingers came away wet with blood. Fixing that had cost the last of the credits I had. After that, it was me and my pistol, running solo ops to eat.

I hop the desk and step inside. Fallen leaves are scattered across the floor, curled up and dried out, blown in by the wind where the wall is gone. Dust motes float above me, glittering in uneven beams of sunlight. A weta scurries beside my boot, scrambling in search of its hole. I give it a wide berth. I'd gotten a bite to the back of the shoulder one night years ago, when Megan and I snuck out of our dorm to trade kisses on a blanket under the trees. I'd shot bolt upright beneath her, squirming in surprise and pain with my hand still stuck under her shirt.

She'd stepped on it. I asked why. "Because it bit you," she said, like I was stupid. We'd laughed about it, but I wasn't sure why I was laughing. Because it felt good to exist with another person, I guess. That's the problem with people. They always end up disappearing, disappointing you, or both.

I exit the entryway and head up the main stairs. They're still stable. What remains of the building is structurally sound, all things considered. It's cleaner on the second of five floors. Not as many creatures have chosen to make the journey upward. It's dim despite the sunlight filtering in through the windows. The air smells stale, in need of recycling.

The hallway seems shorter than I remember, or maybe my legs are longer. Megan and I weren't in the same classes, and this was her floor. Because of 'superior generalized aptitude' I was marked for Gold Star. Megan was shuttled into Subsection 2B—although we called it the jacker factory. Sometimes it pisses me off that AxysGen figured out what we'd become before we did. Pisses me off more when I think about how what Megan became was 'dead', and about how what I became is...

No. That's not AxysGen's fault. I want it to be, but it's Megan's. Which is really why I'm here, because I don't understand. I have almost the whole picture now, but it's not enough. I need to know: *How could someone who loved me convince me to die for her project six different times?* I'm afraid of the answer, because I can already feel it creeping up on me. There isn't one, because it's the wrong question. Someone who loves...loved...me couldn't watch me go through that. Not just watch me go through it, she'd talked me into it. *And I said yes. Why the hell did I say yes?*

Before a chunk of building that rests in pieces on the ground, there's a sliding door. The power's off, but my utility belt has an emergency cable. I put a little juice into the door, and the pressure pad glows long enough for me to press my hand there. Aside from the dust, this room is empty. No windows, just blank walls and rows upon rows of terminals. It's set up like an AxysGen jacker warehouse, which is exactly what it is. I remember what it looked like filled with people: flickering lights, blank eyes staring at nothing, the air a swirl of perfume, sweat, and dry carbon dioxide. They've got pumps for extra oxygen, but with so many people, it was a losing battle at best.

This had been Megan's world for years. Cramped, crowded, but also lonely, every minute dictated by flashing digital clocks on the walls. Most of the 'free time' at AukPrep was highly supervised, at least for kids from the slums. One of the only reasons we'd managed to find any private moments at all was because we'd been roommates too.

I glance around the room one more time. I won't find the answers I'm looking for here. It explains part of how Megan had convinced me to leave, sure, but I'd already known that. Growing up poor had never diminished Megan's desire for more. A girl with big dreams like hers wasn't meant to be stuck in a place like this. It was a gilded cage compared to the decaying outer circles of the cities, but it was still a cage. It doesn't explain how she talked me into death, though. It doesn't explain why she died, or what AxysGen wants with me.

I leave the jacker factory and head up another set of stairs. It's brighter here, because the walls are mostly window. A few are broken, but most are still solid. The modified glass is practically invisible, letting the late afternoon sunlight stream in. Most of the hall is lined with narrow doorways, all the same shape and size, leading to identical rooms.

It doesn't take me long to find mine—Room 77, middle of the first hallway. It wasn't destroyed in the blast, although it's close to a collapsed wall that opens to the outside world. This door doesn't have power either, but it can be used manually. I pull it open and step inside.

Aside from a few sun-stains on the sheets and dust on the furniture, the room is exactly how I remember. Two beds, two desks, two dressers, one closet, one attached bathroom. Some of the newer rooms like ours had window seats, but that was the only extra feature I ever saw in an APS kid's room. Maybe the fifth floor, where the corp kids stayed on weekdays, was different, but I'd never been invited up there, and I don't feel like going now. My curiosity's over a decade and a half too old.

I head over to the window seat and pull up the flat cushion on top. Underneath, burned into the metal that's coated to look like wood, there's a heart with two initials: *M.D + S.Y.* Old, but still bright. I can feel the familiar ridges under my palm without even touching it.

God, we'd been so young. I'd wanted someone to love so badly. Someone to love me back. The first night we were together, lips joined, hesitant fingertips dipping beneath clothes, I thought I'd found it. When Megan kissed me and looked into my eyes, sliding her hand around my hip, I'd really thought...

"Haven't you ever wanted to become a god? Create your own future?"

I remember that moment so viscerally that I can almost hear Megan's voice in my ear. She'd exposed herself that night and I hadn't even realized. I'd *felt* like a god then, with our skin bathed in sweat and moonlight and the smell of vanilla in my nose. I'd felt like I could conquer the whole world. But looking back, knowing what she'd really meant, knowing I was just a tool for her to use while she created Val.

"FRAIs are gonna change the world, Sasha, I know it. And mine's going to be smarter, faster, better than those half-assed programs the corps call AIs. Better than humans, too. I just need a few more credits. A little more time..."

It's only now that I realize I'd always added 'for the greater good' to the ends of Megan's sentences. FRAIs like Val would change the world, for the greater good. Megan always needed a little more time, a few more resources, for the greater good. That's why I'd gone along with her plan to escape from AukPrep. She'd said we needed to stage it, so the corps wouldn't try to track down their 'investments.' She'd said it would look like an accident. She'd said no one would get hurt. She'd been lying.

Looking back, it's obvious Megan had known I wouldn't be okay with blowing up a third of the building. That's why she never told me the details of what she was doing when she asked me to get her things. It's why she disappeared afterward instead of meeting me like she promised. She hadn't even tried to convince me it was an accident until years later in Moscow, when she'd re-appeared out of nowhere to join my crew. And I'd been so stupidly happy to see her, so drunk on kisses and praise, that I'd been willing to believe all her excuses.

I let the cushion fall and turn away from the window, fists clenched, nails biting my palms. Out of nowhere, I'm pissed at Val. Pissed at her for appointing herself my protector, for taking away all my memories of Megan that didn't fit the true love narrative until she decided I was 'ready.' If I'd had them from the start instead of getting them dumped on me all at once, maybe I wouldn't feel like an outsider in my own mind.

But if Sasha Six had the whole picture, why had she stayed with Megan? Why had any of them stayed? I could understand the original Sasha, maybe even Sasha Two. But Three, Four, Five...Val hadn't erased their memories of being cloned. Were they idiots with a death wish? Blinded by love? Maybe it was a forest for the trees situation, and each time Megan did something selfish, the other Sashas convinced themselves it was a single incident instead of a pattern. Fuck if I know.

There's nothing left for me in our room. It's as empty as I am. I leave, closing the door quietly behind me. It's only when I step outside that I realize I'd been breathing shallow, just in case the air still smelled like her. I consider heading for the fourth floor, but decide not to. There's no reason to revisit those memories. I'd learned a bit of everything in the classrooms up there—physical combat, disguises, combat medicine, some elementary jacking, and how to deconstruct, clean, reassemble, and fire just about every type of weapon there is. A handler needs to know the capabilities and limitations of every member on her crew, but this place doesn't have anything I need now. I don't even know what I need.

Maybe I should go back to Siberia. To the crew. My anger's burned low enough, leaving only the ashes of hurt behind. I'm nowhere close to forgiving them, especially not Val, but I think I can be in the same room as them without being tempted to throw a punch. More than anything, I want answers. I want them to look me in the eye and explain why they'd gone along with Val's lie, and why they'd been okay with Megan cloning me so I could die. *And if I don't go back, Elena might worry.* That thought is a complete surprise. It pops into my head uninvited, and I don't have a clue where it came from. Yeah, she came looking for me last night. Yeah, she kissed me, probably because she felt sorry for me. But that doesn't mean anything. It doesn't matter.

"Hey, Jefecita. I'm hanging around for now. You know?" My shoulders relax as her voice fills my head. No talk of gods or changing the world. Just a promise—hesitant, uncertain, but real. Right now, real

is what I need.

I walk to the end of the hallway, where the gutted building opens into the evening air. Below me, the tui bird calls again, singing to the sinking sun. The Eagle's roof gleams in the distance, a square of silver in the middle of a small patch of green. I close my eyes. It's time to go.

Tuesday, 06-15-65 09:45:21

I SHUT OFF THE Eagle's engine, unfastening my safety harness with numb fingers. My skin aches with cold, but the dead center of my chest burns with hate. Not caring would be easier. Hate grows where love's ashes lie, and right now, that's how I feel. Like something burned beyond recognition. Perhaps hate isn't the right word. Betrayal, maybe? I don't want anything to happen to my crew. I don't want them to get hurt. Or maybe I do. I just want...I want them to...

Turn back time so none of this ever happened? Yeah, right. An apology would be a decent start. An explanation, too. They owe me that, at the very least. *But then what? What if they apologize and explain, and it's not enough?*

I don't know, but it's impossible to predict how I'll feel until it all plays out. Besides, nothing about our situation has changed. AxysGen still wants us dead, and we don't know why. Erasing our names from the database won't protect us forever. Their resources are practically unlimited, and so is the supply of people they can send to track us down.

A shudder races down my spine, and for a moment, I do feel the cold creeping in. There's another reason for crewbonding outside of the universal human need for family. In this business, lone wolves don't live long, and I've died enough times already. I don't want to do it again. That means a truce, at least temporarily.

I exit the Eagle and head for the lift. It whines as it carries me down, and the light of the bunker floods my eyes. When I adjust, I see that everyone's in the main room. I notice Elena first, sitting at the table and staring glumly at a half-gnawed nutrient bar. Doc and Rock are across from her. Cherry's perched on the counter, where she's not supposed to be. Rami's standing beside her, one hand on her thigh. Val's databox is sitting on the table, projecting her avatar nearby. The atmosphere is, ironically, funereal.

They all turn toward me when I step off the lift. Elena's eyes widen, and she starts to get up before thinking better of it. The others are more cautious. They watch me with varying looks of guilt, Val in particular.

Doc breaks the tension. "Are you back for real?"

My heart twinges. The question reminds me of her age. I don't know how I feel about a twelve-year-old kid activating me, modding me, and lying about it, or how responsible I should hold her for it. How much of the cloning was Megan's influence? How much of the deception was Val's?

I look around at all of them. "That depends on what you have to say for yourselves."

Rami sighs. They look as dejected as I've ever seen them, no makeup, no wig, eyes lowered. "We'll tell you whatever you want to know. You deserve that."

There are so many questions straining to get out of me that swallowing them back hurts. My throat burns, and my lips tremble as I ask, "Why did you all lie to me?"

"It wasn't a lie," Doc says, but at a sharp look from Cherry, she falls silent.

"We were going to tell you when you were ready," Rami continues. "Val explained that your emotional state was very fragile, and we all agreed—"

"You all agreed?" I scoff, staring Rami down. "How nice."

"It is possible our decision was a mistake," Val says. "I would have preferred to consult you, but that would have made the choice irrelevant."

I shake my head in furious bewilderment. "You would have *preferred* to consult me?"

"Plus, the decision was already made," Cherry adds, cutting me off before my anger can build any further. "I didn't find out your memories were abridged until after you were already awake. Val contacted me right before you arrived in Brazil. I didn't think it was my place to burst your bubble, especially while Rami was still missing with Val's databox."

Why doesn't that surprise me? Cherry kept quiet so I'd rescue her spouse, just like Doc kept quiet so I'd rescue her brother. Everyone always wants something from me, usually something that has the potential to get me killed.

"What about before? I know cloning me so I could do the dirty jobs was Megan's idea, but why did you all just...go along with it?"

Maybe it's not fair to blame them for that. The other Sashas were adults, capable of making their own stupid, self-sacrificing decisions. But I'm furious they lied to me, and I don't care whether I'm being rational or not. My fury has tapped into a wellspring of hurt, a grieving wish that somebody, any of my friends, had tried harder to save me. Even just once. Even if they expected me to come back a few days later.

Cherry looks at me with a sad smile. "Come on, Sasha. Would you have listened if we'd questioned Megan's plan? If we'd tried to talk you out of it?"

"Besides," Rami says, "it's what you said you wanted." It's not a defense so much as a flat statement of fact. Rami seems to know I won't tolerate an apology in one breath and excuses in the next.

I shake my head, letting out a laugh that's mostly breath. "Seriously? That's what you're going with? You'd rather let me sacrifice myself for you six times than tell me I was being stupid?"

"At least she admits she was being stupid," Cherry mutters to Rami.

"If you don't feel bad about it, why'd you hide it from me this time?" I look at all of them, but no one answers. "Still don't have a reason for that, huh? Still no half-decent excuse for erasing a chunk of who I am, just 'Val did it first.' Well, I have one. I know why you did it. It's so I wouldn't be too depressed to *save* your asses again. Just like I do every damn time."

Before I can keep tearing into them, Doc pipes up, "But you never really died, Sasha. You came back."

That's when I realize Doc doesn't get it. I look into her eyes and I know: she thinks I'm only mad about the secrecy, not about the pain they failed to prevent. It's true, I'm pissed beyond belief that Val convinced my crew, my family, to hide my past from me, but the fact that they watched me die without trying to talk me out of it hurts nearly as much.

"I still *died,* Doc. It hurt like I can't even describe. But that wasn't the worst part. The darkness, the cold...the fear of ending. 'Coming back' doesn't make that go away. It's still there inside me."

Doc looks away.

"You have to understand," Rami says, "it wasn't like this before. You woke up as the same old Sasha, behaving like you'd had a near-death experience—not as an entirely new person. After you recovered, everything went back to normal." They hesitate. "I don't expect that to make you feel better. I'm just giving you context."

Rami's right. It doesn't make me feel better. Val had told me my 'predecessors' sometimes struggled, but what does that mean? I can feel ghosts of how the other Sashas had felt, thanks to the new memories crowding my head. They'd been sad, scared, and angry, but the resentment hadn't been there. Probably because the previous Sashas had, at least, been whole. But no. Val chopped me up into pieces, just so I'd be a better handler. More useful. And my friends hadn't even had the decency to tell me.

I look at Val. "You withheld chunks of my life from me. Is that why it's...why I'm...different?"

"There is no way to be certain," Val says. "The relationship between neurology, psychology, and the interplay between memory, perception, and consciousness is still poorly understood. However, in my opinion, it is a likely explanation."

That's as close as Val will come to a 'yes', but it doesn't satisfy me. "Not good enough. This is all a calculation to you, isn't it? A logical decision. What percentage was based on 'fixing' me as fast as possible so I could protect you from AxysGen and get the crew back together, and what percentage was you actually giving a shit about my mental health?"

"Hey," Elena says, trying to make peace. "Val already told you the truth. I know I haven't been her biggest fan, but I believe her. She cares about you, whatever that means for her."

Val seems to appreciate the sentiment. She gives Elena a grateful look, which only infuriates me more.

"Does she?" I'm not trying to spit poison at Elena. She's the only one in this room who hasn't been lying to me, but I'm too pissed to stop. I clutch my head, digging my nails into my scalp. "Don't any of you fucking get it? It's like someone else is inside my head. I see all these memories that aren't mine, things I didn't do, choices I didn't make...wouldn't have made...like my brain was hijacked or something. It's not even *my* brain at all!"

Rock makes an unhappy noise. His expression is worried, but I don't care.

"Don't look at me like that. Just because you don't talk doesn't mean you couldn't have told me. I blame you for this as much as anyone else. And you." I glare at Rami. "Why did I even think you'd understand? You don't even know who the hell *you* are half the time. Lying's all you're good at, isn't it?"

Rami's brown eyes well with tears, but I can't stop. This has festered long enough.

"Cherry, you were the first person I trusted after I went off-grid. We shared half of nothing to stay alive, but you never really gave a shit, did you? You were fine with lying as long as it made things easier for you. As long as it got Rami back safe."

Cherry holds my gaze in angry silence, lips pressed together.

"And Doc, why the hell did you think it was okay to operate on me without my consent? You of all people should know how messed up it is when other people make choices for you!"

Doc's face doesn't move, but something like horror clouds her eyes.

Finally, I look at Val. "And you...I don't even have fucking words. I was *always* the one who believed in you and the good you can do. I was the first one to trust you, to treat you like a fucking person. But it turns out, you're a shitty one."

Val's face is blank, so I can't tell what she's thinking. She doesn't speak, and neither do the others. Not until Elena stands up.

"Did that help?" she asks, looking at me.

My heart sinks straight through the floor. No. It didn't help.

"Then stop shouting and think about what will."

Before I can argue, a green light flashes from the corner of the room. I look at the main terminal, but it's in sleep mode. The green is coming from the smaller terminal beside it: Megan's.

At first, I don't believe it. Megan's terminals are locked tighter than any tech I've ever seen, and she never gave anyone else access. Not even me. No one, and I mean no one, has ever accessed her terminal before, let alone wirelessly. The crew is surprised too.

"What the hell?" Cherry shouts, hopping down from the counter and walking to the terminal. When she turns back to the rest of us, she looks stunned. "Incoming message from...Veronica Cross?"

I laugh bitterly. Of course, it's Veronica Cross. Being a clone with a patch-job memory isn't enough to deal with, so the universe has decided to throw this at me too.

"Well?" I nod at Cherry. "Answer it. Why the hell not?"

"Are you sure about this?" Rami asks. "She could try and track our location."

I shake my head. "Take the call."

Tuesday, 06-15-65 10:12:13

THE WIDESCREEN ON THE WALL above the terminal activates, revealing a familiar face—Veronica Cross. She looks like all the billboards—blonde, filtered, fake. Her pale skin is unblemished, and her teeth are blindingly white. She bares them like I imagine a lion would before it leaps.

"Sasha Young." Cross's baby-blue eyes fix right on me. "You've caused me more than a bit of trouble lately. I'd been considering adding another swimming pool, but was the crater really necessary?"

My jaw clenches. I'm still so angry my chest hurts, but I make my reply flat, monotone. Melting down in front of my crew is one thing, but I can't afford to let Cross see me lose control. "How did you get this terminal's comm address?"

Cross's smile doesn't budge. "A better question would be, 'Why are you calling'?"

None of us say anything.

"The answer is: to offer a ceasefire. I need something from you, and you've proven surprisingly hard to...detain."

"Detain this, bitch," Elena says, sticking up her middle finger.

Cross's expression doesn't change, but the muscles around her eyes tighten enough to show the crow's feet her makeup and plastic surgery can't quite hide. "I know my people have been pursuing you, but I don't actually want you dead. I merely require your cooperation."

I scan the room. The crew looks skeptical, mixed in with more than a little disgust, but I don't really care to hear their opinions. "What the hell do you mean?"

"A mutually beneficial exchange. I have a job for you and your crew."

"What?" Elena blurts out. "Are you crazy? First you try to kill us, and now you want to hire us for a fucking op?"

I glare so Elena will shut up. She does, but the storm clouds around her head don't disappear. "AxysGen has their own corp teams for that," I say to Veronica. "What's your game?"

"No game. At least, not one in which any of you are major players. While I had good reason to want you dead after the incident in Mumbai, you and your crew have proven far more resilient than I expected. I want to use that to my advantage."

"So, what?" Cherry asks. "You gonna sic us on one of your competitors?"

Cross sighs. "Yes and no. Unfortunately, I need some housekeeping done."

"I thought you were supposed to be top dog at AxysGen," Cherry says. "Someone yanking your chain?"

I give Cherry a sharp look. Her sarcasm and Elena's anger aren't doing me any favors. "What are we supposed to get out of this?"

"A clean slate," Cross says. "Deleting your profiles from our database was impressive, but you had to know it wasn't sustainable long term. Even if your biometrics aren't flagged every time you enter an AxysGen property, *I* haven't forgotten that you exist."

"So, you're threatening us if we don't work for you," I mutter.

"I'm offering you an opportunity."

"Offering us the 'opportunity' to stay alive. Like I said, threatening."

Cross waves her hand. "Call it whatever you want. Here's my offer. Some of AxysGen's other board members have taken issue with my opinion on the allocation and distribution of the company's resources. I need information about one James Sloane that may change their minds."

"So, what? You want us to break into someone else's mansion instead of yours?"

Cross purses her lips. She's good at playing casual, but I can tell reminding her we robbed her place is annoying the shit out of her. "Not a mansion. A factory. Several years ago, Mr. Sloane's son was overseeing the production of a new mech line. Regulations were ignored. Injuries occurred. Settlements were paid. Sloane had to be called in to clean up his disappointing progeny's mess. Proof of the cover-up exists on a terminal in the foreman's office. I need you to access the hard drive and copy it...without disturbing the hardware." When Cross sees me frown, she elaborates, "Mr. Sloane and I have something of a...détente in place. If he receives an indication that I might be trying to extract this information, he will no doubt assume that détente is over."

I narrow my eyes at Cross. "We get a copy of that hard drive, you call off your dogs?"

"Precisely. You'll have a fresh start, and we can part ways."

I'm not convinced. It sounds too good to be true, which in this business always means it is. "You still haven't given me any reason to trust you."

"I'm a businesswoman, Ms. Young. I like to maximize value. Getting rid of Sloane is much more important to me than punishing you for a few instances of breaking and entering, though they were extremely inconvenient."

It's that word, inconvenient, that gets me. Why would Veronica lie? She doesn't see us as enemies, more like pests. If she can use us against her 'real' competition, that's a win for her. And a clean slate sounds pretty tempting. Part of me just wants to drop off the grid so I don't have to deal with anybody anymore, including my own crew. That won't be possible until Veronica stops hunting us.

"I'll need more than just your word," I say, with more confidence than I feel.

"Of course," Veronica says. "I'll send along the appropriate information, as well as some advance payment."

An alert flashes on my VIS-R, letting me know I've received a message. No. Not a message. Money. Well over two hundred million credits. Even I wasn't expecting that. *Two hundred million credits I can use to go to ground if I have to.*

"Fine," I tell Cross, without bothering to look at the rest of the crew. "It'll get done. Then, you never contact any of us again."

"Trust me, I have no desire to." She makes as if to disconnect, but changes her mind at the last second. "Oh, one more thing. Bring your whole crew with you. The factory is high security, so be careful."

The condescension rubs me the wrong way, but I swallow it down. "You'll get what you pay for."

Cross smiles. Once more, I'm reminded of an animal who has cornered its prey. "I'm glad you've decided to be reasonable. I'll be in touch." She disconnects and the screen goes black, leaving a ghostly imprint of her image hanging in the air for a split second.

That's when I realize everyone's looking at me.

"What the fuck, *jefa?*" Cherry says, both hands on her hips. "You could've—"

"Don't you dare say 'asked you,' Vidal," I snarl, squaring off with her. "Oh, are you upset that someone else made a huge and potentially dangerous decision for you? Did you want me to consult with you first? Now you know how it feels."

"Stop it, both of you." Rami steps between us, holding out their arms. "Sasha, I know you're upset, and you have every right to be, but that was a risky call you just made. Are you sure about this?"

Upset is a huge understatement, but Rami has a point. Going in hot is a great way to get myself killed, and I need the crew's help. I take a deep breath. This won't be the first time I've had to swallow my pain for the sake of the mission, and I doubt it'll be the last. I look at the rest of the crew and try to talk like a leader.

"You all know how I feel right now. I'm hurt. I'm angry. I don't trust you the way I did before. But I'm going to make myself trust you for this mission, because I want all of us to get out of this alive. Whatever I'm feeling, I'll push it down until we're safe. I hope the rest of you will do the same thing. Are you with me?"

I search their faces one by one, but I don't find any objections. Rock seems calm and steady as always. Doc looks unsettled, more nervous and introspective than usual. Cherry's got fire in her eyes, but I recognize it as determination. Rami is still wounded. Their eyes are wet, but they press their lips together tight and don't say anything.

Last, I look at Val. I know her expression is more of a choice than a reaction, but she's chosen one with openness. "The rebuilding of trust requires consistent demonstrations of loyalty over an extended period of time. This is an opportunity to assure you of my commitment to that goal."

I dip my chin in acknowledgment. "Fine." Then, to everyone, "Dismissed."

The crew looks like they want to scatter, so I leave first. There aren't many rooms in the Hole—combined living room and kitchen, bunks, showers, storage, Val's server rooms, and armory. I head for storage. It's the least likely place someone else will go, and I need the solitude.

It's dark inside the storage room, but the dim lights flicker on when I step inside. Aside from the hum of the generator, it's quiet too. Several layers of shelving are built into all four walls to hold a couple months' worth of canned food, and supply crates with ammo, armor, and parts cover half the floor. I sit on one and rest my chin in both hands, elbows on knees. Despite everything I've discovered, I'm back where I started, risking my life for people who used me and lied to me.

"Sasha?"

I look up in surprise. Elena is standing in the doorway, the brighter lights of the hallway casting her into a partial silhouette. I straighten as she enters the storage room. "You don't need to check on me. I'm…" I can't lie and say fine, so I go with, "managing."

"It's not about checking on you," Elena says. "I just wanted to talk."

I narrow my eyes. "About?"

Elena hops on the crate next to mine, feet dangling above the floor. "I realized I never apologized. You know, for our fight. I called you cold and I was so fucking wrong. All this shit, and you're still loyal to your friends, even when they weren't loyal back."

"Loyal." I heave a sigh. "I just know I need them to get a copy of that hard drive for Cross. When did you go from hating me to looking at me like I'm some paragon of virtue?"

Elena smirks at me. "I saw your memories, dumbass. Pretend to hate your crew all you want. They deserve the cold shoulder for a while for keeping the whole clone thing a secret. But you still care about them, and they still care about you. That's why they did it."

"Yeah? Lying's a great way of showing how much they care."

"They care," Elena insists. "Didn't you see Doc's face? Rami's eyes? They all felt guilty as hell before Cross called."

The knot in my chest tightens. I'd thought I'd exhausted my anger, but apparently Elena's still fantastic at bringing it out in me. "They brought it on themselves when they lied. And since when are you Miss Sympathy? Judging me for wanting out when I've had to drag you along by the ear this entire time? 'I don't crewbond.' Sure. Maybe the old Elena who thought I was a shithead was right."

"I wasn't," Elena says, "but the old Sasha was."

I roll my eyes. "Which one?"

"You know what I mean. The one who put family and crew first."

"Like they put me first?"

"You're twisting what I'm saying. I came in here to help—"

"Well, stop. You're making it worse. Which is pretty incredible, since things are already terrible."

"They're not—"

I climb off the crate. "You're seriously going to tell me their motives justify what they did?"

Elena stands up too. She can't meet me eye to eye, but damn if she isn't trying. "Look, I'm on your side!"

I lean down, air puffing through my nose. "If you gave a shit about me, you wouldn't want me to go. You'd tell me not to run this op. You'd…"

Something in her eyes stops me. Maybe I see a glimpse of myself in them: angry, scared, lashing out like some kind of wounded animal. I shut up. Take a step back. What I said doesn't even make sense. I took Cross's offer to protect myself long-term, but...I'm so goddamn tired of risking my life. Of almost dying. Of *actually* dying. And yet, once more unto the breach.

"Sasha," Elena says, her face all fury and pain. For once, her voice isn't snappy or sarcastic. She's mad, but the quiet kind of mad, something I've never seen from her before. "I know you're hurting, but it does *not* excuse the way you're talking to me."

She waits, like she expects me to say something. My chest feels cold, sore. The hole in it has widened. "No one ever asks me to stay back." My voice sounds small in the enclosed storage room. Weak. "No one ever gets upset. No one ever tries to stop me when I have to take a risk. When I might die. Not Megan. Not the crew."

Elena's eyes soften a little. "So why did you expect me to ask? You said yourself that this was our best option."

The question sends a wave of something hot and painful through me. I can't identify it, but it's eating away at me like acid. The answer's right there, only I can't reach it. I'm exhausted with making these calls, putting on armor, using my body as someone else's meatshield. *Megan must have seen it. How I'm feeling. How the other Sashas felt. She had to. How could she not? She just...didn't care. She didn't care how much it took out of me.*

Elena must sense that the fight's over. She reaches out, pauses, then touches my arm when I don't pull away. "I don't want you to die, Sasha. I don't understand why the fuck you think I do, but I don't."

I close my eyes for a long time. "I'm tired of being disposable. Replaceable. It makes me feel..."

"I know." Elena squeezes my arm a little tighter. "I grew up poor, Sasha. Most people looked at me like fucking garbage until I started running ops. One time, I skipped eating for two days to feed my brothers until our peebees came in, you know? Collapsed on the sidewalk. Woke up maybe half an hour later, and people were stepping over me. They didn't care enough to drag me out of the way."

My first reaction is more anger. I think of Megan, the new memories I have of the guilt trips and the gaslighting. But Elena isn't asking me for anything. She's not trying to get something from me. Instead, she's offering empathy, which is exactly what I need.

I don't pull away. Instead, I lean down. The kiss just sort of happens. Our lips touch for a second or two, then we back away to look at each other. Elena must have found whatever she's searching for, because she moves her hand from my arm to my neck and pulls me back down.

She tastes good. Sweet. Her palm feels nice on the back of my neck and it feels right to put my hands on her waist. Our bodies press together, not grinding, but close enough to share heat. For the first time since Hong Kong, I relax. This isn't the kiss of someone who wants me to die. It isn't the kiss of someone who doesn't care. It has tenderness, longing, and...Shit. This isn't the right time. I'm not the right person. I'm not even sure how much of a person I am.

I break away. Elena's lips trail after mine, so I take a step back. "I'm sorry. It's just too much right now."

Elena's face takes a visible journey between 'I'm sorry' and 'right now.' "Hey, it's okay," she says, forcing a smile. "You're right. This is weird. And we've got shit to do."

"Exactly."

"So, we forget about this and handle Cross's dirty work. But Sasha..." She looks up at me with utter sincerity. "I don't want you to die. And I don't think you're disposable. Some asshole tries to kill you, I'll kill them first."

I snort. "You? Ready and eager to kill someone?" It would be petty to mention how shook up she was over the jacker she melted in Tokyo, or how she hesitated in AxysGen's Siberian facility, but I'm thinking about it.

Elena doesn't laugh. "Hey, if it's them or you, I pick you."

I pick you. I don't know when Elena's voice has become so clear in my head, but it is. My brain might be scrambled, but it doesn't have trouble echoing her words. "Okay."

Elena seems to get the hint that I want to be alone. She turns around and heads for the door, and it's only when she starts to push it open that I stop her. "Wait."

She looks back over her shoulder. "What?"

"When I said I'm sorry, I didn't just mean for...I'm sorry for what I said."

Elena shrugs. "Hey, giving a shit is new for me. I have no fucking clue what I'm doing."

"That makes two of us."

Elena leaves the room, closing the door behind her. I sit back on the crate, staring up at the dim lights. I can still taste strawberries on my lips.

Thursday, 06-17-65 23:35:36

IT'S RAINING OVER KUALA Lumpur. Great sheets of water batter the Eagle's windshield, hammering so hard and fast that I can't see anything. Rami pilots the shuttle steadily through the storm, their eyes fixed on the scanner. They swoop in low over the city's skyscrapers, slowing down to merge with traffic.

It's awkward, sitting next to them, but better than sitting in back near Elena. I know she said we were fine, but I can't shake the look of disappointment on her face. Not that being near Rami is all that different. They look like someone kicked their puppy, and I know perfectly well that someone is me.

You shouldn't have said those things. To any of them. I want so badly to hold onto my anger, but remorse is creeping in. Damn it. I've always been softhearted, wanting to believe the best in people, giving them second chances. But that was where I screwed up with Megan. I kept giving her second chances, and third chances, and sixth chances, and I was the one who paid the price for it—the one who's still paying the price.

But not everyone is like Megan. Her issues were part of a pattern. Your crew has never done anything like this before.

Oh, really? Then why were they okay with letting Megan clone you? Watching you die?

I close my eyes. There isn't time for this. For feelings. Right now, the op is all that matters. One more job, and it's over. Cross will stop hunting me, and I can take my share of the money and do whatever I want...with or without the crew. I'm still not sure yet.

"You sure you wanna do this, *jefa?*" Cherry asks from the back. "It's not too late to make a break for it. Head for another hideout and go off-grid for a while."

I flinch, but suppress most of the reaction. *Jefa.* I know the nickname's habit, but it puts me on edge. It was a form of friendly intimacy even before Elena cribbed it and turned it into something sexual. "You know why we can't, Cherry. AxysGen has a bottomless

167

bank account. Cross can just keep sending crews after us."

Rami swings the shuttle left and veers down. We're on the city's outskirts, still inside the metropolis itself, but the buildings are spaced slightly further apart. Tucked between two medium-sized skyscrapers is an enormous, rectangular factory building. It's got the typical AxysGen look, shiny metal and chrome, but as we get closer, I notice something strange. There's no electromagnetic shielding to cut through. There are no shuttles parked nearby, and there's no foot traffic going in or out of the building. The security towers at all four corners of the factory are dark, and when I glance at the Eagle's dashboard scanners, they don't show any heat signatures below us.

"Val, you're plugged in. Do you see anything?"

"It is what I cannot see that concerns me," Val says through the Eagle's speakers. "The shuttle sensors seem to be operational, but I am receiving no relevant data."

"Cross said the place shut down in the files she sent," Doc says.

"She also told us to prep for heavy security," I mutter. "This place is supposed to be closed, not abandoned."

Rami gives me a sidelong glance. "Would we have believed her if she'd said security was light?"

"Maybe we should just roll with it," Cherry says. "Less chance of getting caught."

Elena snorts from somewhere in back. "The only thing we're getting caught in is a trap."

I sigh. She's probably right, but we need the credits. "Take us in, Rami. The rest of you, be prepared for anything."

We level off beside the first floor of the factory, next to a pair of oversized hangar doors. Rami transmits the access code Cross gave us through the radio on the dashboard, and they groan as they open for our shuttle.

"Wow, first try?" Cherry says. "Guess that wasn't the trap, then."

I catch a glimpse of Doc frowning in the rear view camera feed. "I don't like how easy this is, Sasha."

I don't either, but we're here. Our only other option besides pressing forward is retreating with Cross's credits, but that would be tantamount to painting an even bigger target on our backs.

Rami pulls the Eagle into the eerily empty hangar and kills the engine. After a final gear check, we hop out and head for the door. The room beyond looks sort of like an abandoned reception area. There's no sign of any guards, and not much in the way of furniture either. Only a large desk attached to the floor, some old terminals, and a broken chair or two. It's pretty clear this place has been stripped for parts, which raises the hairs on my neck. If so much has been taken, it's weird that the evidence against Sloane is still here.

I turn to Rami. "Tell me what we're working with here."

Rami runs a scan with their VIS-R. "The building's got power—it's in energy-saving mode, but still."

Doc says what we're all thinking. "Shit. Creepy."

"No organics," Rami continues. "You picking up anything else, Val?"

Val's voice filters through our comms. "I have been able to access an unsecured wireless network. It displays weak electromagnetic signatures in a large room located thirty meters away."

"That doesn't sound so bad," Elena says. "They built mechs here, right? There's probably lots of old manufacturing equipment and parts lying around."

I sigh. "Only one way to find out."

We leave the office space and step into a short hallway. There are a few doors on either side, but nothing of interest in the rooms beyond, although we open them to be sure. Just some storage and a tiny, crummy looking break room. The architects probably wanted to preserve as much square footage as possible for the factory floor itself. At the end of the hallway is a roll-up door that takes up nearly the entire wall. The keypad next to it isn't lit, so it looks like we're doing this the old-fashioned way. I turn to Rock. "Think you can get it open?"

Rock bends down, jamming his fingers underneath the door. It groans in protest, but eventually, he manages to wrench it up high enough for the rest of us to duck through. As depicted in the blueprints Cross sent us, the factory floor takes up the rest of the building's interior. Inactive conveyer belts stretch between large pieces of equipment: outdated assembly machines, vertical lifters, fork transfers. An enclosed office space is perched high on the far wall, surrounded by glass windows so whoever's inside can oversee everything below. The whole scene is coated in a thick layer of dust and silence.

"This is creepy," Doc mutters. Even though her voice is quiet, it echoes in the open space.

"Got that right." Cherry gestures at the walls, which are covered in eerie display screens wherever there's empty space. They don't appear to be active, but they have resting images, which means power must be coming from somewhere. My frown deepens as I read some of them:

A smiling cartoon cat at a desk has a thought bubble that says,

'Time is nonrefundable. Use it with intention!' *'To make your dreams come true, the first thing you have to do is get to work'* is displayed above an ocean sunrise. Of course, Veronica Cross is smiling at us from a prominent place on the far wall, with letters that say: *'Axys Generations—Create. Innovate. Discover.'* I shudder. It doesn't take much to imagine cogs working in this factory, looking up in the middle of a grinding, repetitive day and seeing the displays.

"Sasha, take a look at this." Rami gets my attention, pointing out several storage racks stacked on top of one another. Hanging within those storage racks are maybe fifty old-looking AxysGen security mechs. They're around three meters tall, judging from a distance, and human-shaped, with miniguns for arms, huge pistons for legs, and a heavily plated torso. Their 'faces' are blank metal bulbs, with the exception of a speaker where a human's mouth would be, and a circular black band at eye level—the mech version of a VIS-R.

Elena scoffs. "Don't be scared of those. They're V.503s, right?" She hops a conveyer belt and heads to the wall for a closer look. "Yup," she calls back to us. "Way out of date. The plating on these guys is thick, but they're slow as hell and their miniguns overheat. Plus the standard targeting system was so buggy AxysGen skipped right to the 600s a few years back. These things probably haven't been activated in years."

"Still, why didn't AxysGen take them when they cleared out the factory?" Rami asks. "Leaving them here seems a waste."

We won't get answers, or the data Cross wants, by standing around. I walk across the factory floor in the direction of the raised office, and Cross's giant face. Any remaining terminals besides the stripped ones in the break room will probably be up there. The echo of my own footsteps makes my pulse spike. So much about this feels wrong, and I'm almost tempted to pull out of the op altogether.

"Val, you sure there's no heat signatures anywhere?" I say, trying to ignore the way my voice echoes in the stillness.

"Yes," Val says. "Although I advise caution."

"Don't need to tell me twice."

Below the office is an elevator. Unlike the assembly line machinery, it seems to be on. The orange pad flashes green when I touch it, and the elevator whooshes down, both doors opening. I look back at the others. "I don't trust it. These aren't the mission parameters Cross described, and I don't feel like being trapped in a metal box."

Rami steps forward, removing a grappling hook gun from their belt. "Then let's do this the fun way. Is that all right with you, cupcake?"

I nod. Climbing up seems safer than a trip in the ominously inviting elevator. "Cherry, do you have that plasma cutter you've been working on?"

"Sure do." She pulls out a small black device the size and shape of a laser pointer, with a bright red button on the end. "I still haven't perfected the heat sink, though. You can only use it in short bursts before it has to cool down."

Elena raises an eyebrow. "Plasma? Isn't that a bit overkill for glass?"

A grin spreads across Cherry's face. "Um, of *course* it is. I get that you're new, Nevares, but when have I ever done anything half-assed? This baby can cut through reinforced steel walls like butter."

I silence her with a glare. This isn't the place to boast. Plus, I'm still pissed at all of them, with the possible exception of Elena. It's rubbing salt in my wounds, reminding me that no matter how normal my crew acts, my relationship with them isn't the same. Maybe it never will be again.

"Thanks, babe." Rami plucks the plasma cutter from Cherry's hand with a kiss and puts it in their belt. Then, they aim their grappling hook gun and fire a thin cable toward the wall of the office. When the hooks make contact, they form a powerful magnetic field, bonding themselves to the glass. After giving the line a tug, Rami clips the other end to their belt. "Back in a flash." With the press of a button, the cable retracts, pulling them up with it.

Sixty seconds later, there's a hole in the glass big enough for all of us to climb through. Rami attaches the cable more firmly somewhere inside, then leans out, motioning us up. One by one, we climb to the office, Elena, Cherry, and me with belt clips and some help from Rami, and Rock with his bare hands while Doc sits on his shoulders.

The interior of the office was probably fancy once. There are circular indents on the corners of the carpet where potted plants probably sat, and screens built into the glass that show scrolling images of landscapes. A large wooden desk is the only furniture that remains, along with a terminal covered in dust.

"Looks like this place hasn't been touched for a few months," Elena says. She circles the desk before sinking into the plush leather chair with a groan. "Oh, nice."

"I can't believe how okay you are with this," I grumble.

Elena rolls her eyes as she activates the terminal. "Cross paid us two hundred million credits to come here, Sasha. So, yeah, I'm in a pretty damn good mood. I'm willing to risk a trap for that price."

"Can't spend your share if you're dead, Nevares."

"If it *is* a trap and my brain gets fried, give the credits to my brothers." Her tone is joking, but I can tell the request is serious. I nod in agreement.

"Last chance," Cherry says, eyeing the terminal suspiciously. "We could just take the whole thing with us. Less risky than letting *chaparrita* jack in."

"Cross said 'without disturbing the hardware,'" I reply. "For two hundred million, I'm not playing."

"What if we thought of her instructions more like 'guidelines?'" Rami asks.

I roll my eyes. "Jack in, Nevares."

Elena removes Val from her tactical belt, jacking the databox into the terminal. "Back in a second." She jacks the other end into the port behind her ear, and her eyes go blank. As soon as she does, the wall screens change. The decorative landscapes disappear, replaced by a moving image. It's someone's head, their features hidden beneath a blue hood. Shit. This has to be the jacker Elena saw at Cross's mansion. Taking the two million and running suddenly doesn't seem like such a bad idea. The crew draws their weapons, and I rush around the desk toward Elena, preparing to disconnect her jack. The nausea of a hard cut is better than a melted brain.

"I wouldn't do that if I were you," the figure says, in a chillingly familiar voice. I know what's coming when they pull the hood back, but it still sends a painful jolt through my chest—Megan. Megan's alive.

Friday, 06-18-65 00:06:07

I CAN'T believe it. I *won't* believe it. Maybe this is CGI, or some kind of recording from before Megan's death. But part of me knows deep in my bones that it isn't a trick. Megan's alive. There are too many feelings for me to pick just one: anger, hurt, betrayal, relief...Wait, relief? Why am I relieved she's alive after all she's done to me? The rest of the crew starts shouting.

"Blondie?"

"What the fuck!"

"Oh my god, you're alive!"

The atmosphere is eerie. My crew's voices are excited, their faces are overjoyed, but I'm just...numb. All I can manage is a quiet, weak, "Megan?"

"Of course." The absence of warmth alone sends a chill down my spine. I'm probably going crazy, but the air around me reeks of vanilla. "I realize this is a lot of new information. I'll keep it brief. Where's Val's databox?"

That's when it starts sinking in for everybody else. Their faces fall, and the bubble of happiness pops.

"Seriously?" Rami asks, sounding wounded. "That's it? No 'I'm glad to see you' or 'I missed you?'"

Everyone stares at Megan, but before she can say anything, Val's voice comes in over the comm, sounding worried. "Sasha, there is a problem. Elena and I have encountered a uniquely coded Venus flytrap."

A sickening wave of fear washes over me. Real Venus flytraps are rare and incredibly difficult to code. Plenty of low-quality knockoffs exist that professional jackers skip right over, but if there's a terminal you don't want anyone to access ever again, the true Venus flytrap is deadly. It forces whoever is jacked in to *stay* jacked in, unless they can figure out how to escape. If they try to jack out normally, boom. Brain

173

soup.

My fear turns to anger. This setup has Megan written all over it. She isn't back for a reunion, or even to make excuses for her behavior. She's working with Axys-Gen. With Cross. Why else would she be here waiting for us? "Get her out of there, Val!"

"Elena and I are working to decrypt and alter its source code," Val says. "This process may take several minutes."

"Ah, so you did give her to the new girl," Megan says. "You don't have to bother decrypting my code. I'll let my 'replacement'—if you can even call her that—go in exchange for what's mine. Give me your brainbox and Val's databox."

"What the fuck?" Cherry snarls, glaring at the screens. "You set this up with Cross, didn't you? How much is AxysGen paying you for Val, anyway? What price made you decide to turn traitor and sell us out?"

The rest of the group stares at Megan in utter betrayal as they figure out what I already know, but she ignores them, looking straight at me. "What's it going to be, Sasha?"

There's no hesitation at all in my answer. "Hell no. I protect mine." Not even for a second will I consider giving the keys to Megan if she's working for Cross. I won't do Val like that, no matter how pissed I am.

Megan narrows her eyes. "I'm running out of patience. Give me Val's keys, or I'll kill you all."

Cherry aims her rifle at the closest screen, angry enough to explode. "I knew you were a crazy bitch, but faking your death? Stealing Val? That's some truly evil shit. What are you even doing with AxysGen?"

"I can't 'steal' my own intellectual property. As for AxysGen, Cross can give me what I need."

Cherry glares at her. "Well, what *I* need is for you to get your *puta oxigenada* ass out the building and go fuck yourself."

"Well, I—wait." Megan pauses, looking around the office. Her face goes from irritated to worried in a split second. "Shit, where'd they go?"

At first, I don't realize what's happening, but then it hits me, Rami's gone. They must have activated their armor's cloaking function. Despite the tension, I can't help cracking a smile. Rock even starts to laugh.

"Little Miss Disappear can't save you," Megan says, still smug, like she's in complete control. "I'll blow up this whole building if I have to, with all of you in it. I know you don't want anything to happen to your sister."

Rock strikes quick as a snake. He grabs the nearest screen with

Megan's face, wrenching it out of the wall. Sparks fly, and the air smells like burnt wires.

On all the other screens, Megan's lips curl in a smile. "I guess we're doing this the hard way."

"Sasha, we need to get out of here!" Rami's voice blasts into my ears, fast and urgent. *"The mechs downstairs are moving!"*

I look down through the glass wall. No sign of Rami, but there's movement off to the left. At least twenty mechs have crowded around the bottom of the elevator, and more are climbing out of the storage racks to join them.

"Come on, Megan." The words come out of my mouth before I can stop them, flowing in spite of everything. "Just let Elena go and come with us. This? Working with AxysGen? It isn't you." But it is her, and that realization is more terrifying than the mechs.

"Sorry, Sasha. Cross has things I need. It's a mutually beneficial relationship, for now."

I didn't know it was possible for my heart to break again, but apparently it can, because I feel it shatter to dust in my chest. Deep down, some part of me was still clinging to the hope that I was wrong. That my memories, my feelings, even the present reality where Megan is threatening to kill me, are some kind of mistake. But there's no mistake. Megan really doesn't care. She never loved me, and now she's trying to kill us. I've been in love with Megan for all those years, but I never really knew her.

"Last chance," Megan says, with a small smirk of victory. "My mechs are coming upstairs. Hand the keys over to them, or I'll— ffffttttttt!"

The screens flash, and Megan's face disappears in a colorful blur of pixels and static. A new image flickers to life—Elena, panting with exertion, a piece of hair from her ponytail stuck to one cheek. She lowers her shield and grimaces. "Fuck, Sasha, is your ex a literal supervillain or something?"

Warm relief floods through me. I hadn't realized how terrified I was until I see Elena's face, hear her voice.

She rolls her eyes at me. "Don't just stand there. Move! I got out of the Venus flytrap, even managed to copy the stupid data, but she's running Dendryte Platinum modded like I've never seen. I've probably only got a few seconds to jack out befo—" She disappears just as the screens fill with glowing red light. A Puls.wav. Shit.

I dash toward Elena's body, crouching down and grabbing her wrist to check for a pulse. My own heart stops for what feels like ages, until I feel the familiar throb under my fingers. She's still alive. A moment later, Elena opens her eyes. She groans, groping for her jack with one hand and reaching for me with the other. When her fingers clasp mine, I can finally breathe again.

"Sasha?" she groans.

I tear my hand away from hers, grabbing both of her shoulders in a trembling grip. "Nevares? *Never* do that again, you hear me?"

"Sure, I got myself stuck in a Venus flytrap on purpose," Elena protests, her voice slurred but indignant. She's still suffering from the effects, but her sarcasm obviously hasn't been affected.

A soft hissing noise startles both of us. The elevator doors have opened, revealing ten mechs crammed inside. I take cover behind the desk, dragging Elena down with me a split second before the first row fires on us. Splinters of wood fly in every direction, and Val's databox falls out of the chair. I snatch it up before it can get lost, shoving it into my pocket.

"Rock, doors!" Doc shouts from somewhere off to the right.

At first, I don't know what she means, but when I peek over the shredded remains of the desk, I see Rock standing in front of the elevator. The mechs are firing into his chest, but he manages to withstand it long enough to wrench the steel doors shut. Trails of smoke leak from the elevator's seams, and there are hand-shaped dents in the metal. He's bought us a few seconds, but it won't hold for long—neither the doors nor his internal armor.

"Glad you made it back, Elena," Doc says, crawling out from behind a couch that Rock must have upended when the mechs first appeared.

Cherry crawls toward us from the opposite direction. "Yeah, *chaparrita*. You got here for the best part."

Elena just stares at her with blurry eyes, but Cherry is undeterred. "Cherry bombs, *jefa*?" she asks me eagerly.

I nod. Cherry looks way too happy about the idea, but it's a good one, and we're short on time. "Fine. Cherry bombs."

"Yes!" She pulls two shiny red spheres from her utility belt. They're only about as big as a baseball, but their size is deceptive. I've seen Cherry take down small buildings with her namesake. "Rami, babe, if you're nearby, back it up and get to cover!" she hollers over the comm.

Rami doesn't respond. They're being quiet, and I can only hope it's because they're working on a plan to get us out of here and not for…some other reason.

"All right, here we go." As the elevator doors wrench open, Cherry presses the button on the first sphere and rolls it toward the mechs. It hits one of them in the foot, then begins to flash. I hit the floor as Cherry lobs the second bomb out through the hole we climbed in through, letting it fall onto the group of mechs waiting below.

.

Friday, 06-18-65 00:09:14

FWOOM.

MY EAR MODS pop as the office shakes around us. Its glass walls shatter, and a large chunk of the floor collapses out from under me. It's only thanks to Rock I don't go falling with it. He grabs my tactical vest and hauls me backwards like I don't weigh anything at all.

As soon as he sets me on my feet, I check on my crew. Elena is shocked but upright, one hand braced on a section of wall that survived the blast. Cherry's grinning like a loon, and Doc has scrambled to the edge of the remaining platform. "All clear," she says, peering down at the floor below.

I look over the edge too. All that's left of the mechs is a pile of twisted metal and smoldering wires, but the sharp bark of gunfire from inside the elevator reminds me we still aren't safe. Its steel doors buckle, threatening to collapse.

"*Hija de la chingada,*" Elena groans, groping for her pistol with an uncoordinated hand. "Guns must've cooled off." I remember what she said about the mech miniguns, how they can only fire in short bursts before overheating. It looks like our time is up.

"Over the edge," I order. "We need to head for the exit."

Cherry goes first, clipping her belt cable to the edge and sliding to the ground. Rock goes next. He doesn't even bother with his cable, just sets Doc on his shoulders and steps out into the air. His huge legs absorb the impact, and he straightens almost immediately, leaving a pair of boot-shaped craters in the cement. The elevator rattles, belching more smoke. I look at Elena. Her bronze complexion has gone yellow, and she looks like she might throw up. Damn it. Not only is she disoriented, I forgot her fear of heights.

"Come on, Nevares." I clip my belt cable to the platform and wrap my arm around Elena's waist, pulling her against my side. She summons the strength to wrap her arms around my neck, and I leap over the edge. Pain shoots up my shins and stabs through my knees as I hit the concrete, but it's a relatively safe landing.

Rock, Doc, and Cherry set off for the exit as soon as Elena and I find our footing. We sprint alongside the conveyer belts without looking back, knowing we don't have much of a head start. When we reach the door leading back to the reception area, my heart sinks. Reinforced steel plating has descended in its place.

"Fucking bitch," Cherry spits, slamming her fist into the door. "*Catira* put this place on lockdown. Wait, forget that. She doesn't get a nickname anymore."

"Red thing," Elena says, poking Cherry's arm.

Cherry looks at her in confusion. "Huh?"

"The...red thing!" Elena gestures at the door like she's waving a magic wand, complete with hissing sound effects.

"Plasma cutter, genius," Doc says.

Cherry huffs in frustration. "Gave it to Rami. Where are they, anyway?"

A voice comes in over the comm. *"Waiting to make a dramatic entrance."*

Cherry brightens immediately. "Babe!"

"Megan sealed the doors, but she couldn't do anything about the ceiling. All these huge machines have to vent heat somewhere."

I look up. The destroyed office has to be four meters up, and the ceiling's even higher. Rami must have made use of their grappling hook again. "Where are you?"

"Better not say, just in case someone is eavesdropping."

"Don't jack in," I warn them.

"Don't need to. I can handle this in meatspace. Aaand...voila."

The steel plating over the exit retracts into the ceiling with a loud whine. Just in time, too. Another wave is making its way over from the storage racks.

"Run," Rami says. *"I'll meet you at the Eagle."*

They don't have to tell us twice. I help Elena stay upright as we run down the short hallway and into the reception area. Fortunately, it's empty. When we try the door to the hangar, it's already unlocked. I say a silent thank-you to Rami. It looks like Megan underestimated us. *Shit,* I realize. *She really did it. She actually faked her own death and then tried to kill us.* I knew she didn't care, but this...

There isn't time for me to deal with my feelings. We have to get out of here. I gesture my crew into the hangar, waiting until they're all through the door before jogging in myself. The Eagle is parked where we left it, not far from the entrance. We all pile in, Doc into the copilot's seat, then me and Elena in back, with Cherry and Rock bringing up the rear. While I help Elena with her safety harness, Doc starts up the engine.

"One more issue," she says. "The access code Cross gave us isn't working anymore. The hangar's on lockdown too."

"Not a problem," Rami calls, sounding out of breath. I look out the open side door to see them running across the hangar toward us. Once they arrive at the Eagle, they hop into the pilot's chair.

Cherry leans past the headrest of Rami's seat to kiss their head. "You gonna bust us out of here too?"

"Actually," Rami says, "I was thinking you could."

Cherry looks at me like a puppy begging for a treat. "Pleeease? I only got to blow up a few of them."

I roll my eyes, but nod.

Cherry hops up from her seat and leans out the side of the shuttle, rolling several cherry bombs toward the hangar's large steel door. "Bombs away! Babe, step on it." Cherry and I yank the shuttle doors shut as the Eagle lurches in reverse, zooming to the other side of the hangar to avoid the worst of the blast.

I close my eyes.

The shuttle bay explodes. My ears fill with the diluted sound of cracking concrete underneath screeching metal. The air smells like fire and dust, and the view through the windshield is blurry as Rami sends the Eagle soaring through the brand-new hole in the hangar door and out into the rain.

At first, no one says anything. Then, all the adrenaline in the shuttle turns into relieved laughter. Everyone joins in except Elena, who's still somewhat out of it. I'm so grateful we didn't lose anyone that I forget my anger and terror and laugh until my stomach hurts.

When we manage to calm down, I remember Val. Instinctively, I check my belt, but the databox is still there. I take it out and pass it up to Rami. "Here, plug her in."

I feel a wave of relief when Val's voice comes through the speakers. "According to the Eagle's sensors, everyone is accounted for, and no one has sustained any serious injuries. I am grateful none of you were hurt."

"Yeah, same," Cherry says. "So, can we talk about whatever the fuck just happened?"

"Okay." I'm coming down from a serious battle-high, and I feel like I'm about to crash into numb exhaustion. "Megan's alive and working with AxysGen, presumably because they want Val."

"But why?" Doc asks. "Megan hates corps. Can you really see her working for a boss and following rules?"

"She told us herself," Rami says. "Veronica Cross has something she needs. Whatever it is, it must be worth an alliance."

"We can figure that out later," I tell them. "First order of business is getting to safety. Megan knows all our hideouts, so we can't go to any of them. Thoughts?"

Elena snorts. "Here's my thought: Your ex is *fucking insane.*" Her speech has improved significantly, but she still looks like she's a few seconds away from passing out. "She's crazy fast, too. It was like fighting the Flash. I would've been barbeque without Val boosting my programs."

"Elena is correct," Val says. "Megan is currently using Dendryte Platinum v4.2, AxysGen's latest prototype hardware, with her own modifications. My core programming prevents me from harming her directly, and while I can boost the processing speed of Elena's hardware to a certain extent, I could not do so beyond a certain point for fear of alerting Megan to my presence. If she discovered me, she would no doubt attempt to recover me. Likelihood of survival is low in such a scenario."

"We might not have a choice." I glance at Elena. She's pale and trembling from exhaustion. Without thinking, I put my hand on her thigh. "Doc, can we get a NervPac back here?"

"Heads up." Doc tosses it back to me, and I rip the packet open, lifting Elena's shirt partway to slap the patch against her side.

"Thanks," she mumbles, blinking slowly. "Got an idea. Not on how to deal with Creepy Smurf, but to hide. I know some places."

"We have plenty of bunkers," Doc suggests, but I shut her down immediately.

"All of which Megan knows the location of. Where, Elena?"

Elena hesitates, then makes up her mind with a sigh. "Mexico City."

I sweep back the chunk of brown hair still clinging to her face. "You sure?"

Elena knows what I'm thinking, just like I know what's on her mind. Mexico is where her connections and safest hideouts are, but so is what's left of her family. If Megan is right on our tail...well, I'm sure Elena already has the sense to stay as far away from her brothers as possible, just in case.

"Yeah," she says. "I'm sure."

"Get some sleep. We have a few hours before we get there."

"Mmhmm." On the next blink, Elena's eyes don't open. I can see the slow rise and fall of her chest, though, so my panic only lasts a moment.

"Head for Mexico," I tell Rami. "We'll figure the rest out when we get there."

Friday, 06-18-65 11:23:52

THE MIDDLE RINGS OF Mexico City are like a tissue paper collage. Colorful umbrellas blossom between gaps in the skyscrapers, and people move like paint running down a tilted canvas, winding through the cracks and furrows. I've never seen so many cogs in one place before. With more and more automation, cogs have been disappearing at a rapid pace, but apparently there are enough of them left to have a community in a city this huge.

Elena notices me staring out the window. She snorts and shakes her head. "Can you believe I thought this was the wealthy district when I was a kid?"

I keep gazing down at the umbrellas. Even though I hadn't grown up a street kid, I remember what it was like living in the outer circles of Moscow after my escape from AukPrep. "Actually, yeah."

"Blew my mind the first time I saw a corp estate. I thought there must be a whole town living inside. Didn't think anyone could even use a mansion that fucking big."

"I'll never have a mansion," I say without thinking. "Just a house. Maybe on the ocean."

Elena raises a brow at me. "Maybe?"

I swallow uncomfortably. Sometimes I forget she's seen snatches of my mixed-up memories. That means she probably knows about Barbados, about my stupid pipe dreams. Thinking about it now makes me feel like an idiot.

"We're getting close," Rami says from the pilot's seat.

I'm grateful for the interruption. "How close?"

"Estimated time of arrival ten minutes and six seconds," Val says.

"Thank fuck," Doc grumbles. "You have no idea how bad I need to pee."

Elena glances out the window again. "Pick an alley. Any alley."

I look outside too. The colorful middle ring has ended, and the city beyond is a mix of brown and grey. The buildings are small—shacks, mostly, and anything bigger is crumbling from the inside out. Instead of umbrellas, the gaps are filled with tents and garbage heaps and laundry drying on wires. There's hardly any air traffic, and although there are people below, few seem to be going anywhere. The small figures I can see from above are slumped in what little shade there is. We don't go too far into the outer ring, but we're high enough to see that it gets worse further on.

"What a lovely shithole," Cherry says.

Elena cracks a tired grin. "Right?"

Rami banks left, circling back to a blocky grey building that doesn't completely look like an unstable shell. It's dingy, but the walls don't seem in danger of collapsing.

"Around back," Elena says. "Hidden garage. Your bird'll get stripped if we leave it out."

"We have a security system," Rami says.

"You think the people here care?"

We touch down in a cramped space behind the building. As Elena said, there's a tiny entrance leading into the first floor. Once the Eagle stops, she unfastens her harness and hops out the side to let us in.

The inside of the garage is barely big enough to hold a single shuttle. There's grey wall everywhere and it smells like it looks, old and dirty and depressing. The only exit is a door facing the Eagle's nose. I meet Elena there.

"You sure Jento will fix us up?"

"He's a fixer, isn't he? He'll do whatever we want for the right price." Elena goes through the door, and I follow her.

The room beyond is medium sized and dimly lit. It smells like cigar smoke and stale sweat, and six people are sitting around a table, surrounded by a cloud of both. As they turn toward me, I recognize one of them. His lean face looks like a white knife in the dark and his pinched lips conceal yellowing teeth. Most of my communication with him has been via the extranet, but I still recognize him.

"Jento."

Jento looks at me in surprise, but recovers quickly. "So, the Wolf of the Kremlin decides to pay us an in-person visit. Without calling." His eyes flick behind me, to where the rest of the crew has filed in to stand at my shoulders. "And she brought her pack along."

Elena rolls her eyes. "Shut the fuck up, would you? We just need a place to crash, so you can stop with the dramatics."

As Jento studies Elena with unsettling shrewdness, I feel the strange impulse to step closer to her and block his view. Then his mouth curls up into a thin smile as his gaze flicks to Rock. "People don't bring grunts like that just to crash."

"Him?" Elena snorts. "He's a bunny rabbit. Unless you decide to be a jerkwad about finding us a safehouse."

"That depends on who you're hiding from."

"None of your fucking business," Elena says, which earns a snort of amusement from Cherry.

"AxysGen's people," I tell Jento. "We shook them off in Malaysia. Just want to be sure it sticks."

Jento doesn't buy it. "So you came all the way to Mexico?"

"Maybe I was homesick," Elena says.

"Now that's definitely a lie," Jento says. "I know you, girl. You do everything you can to stay off this entire continent if you can help it."

Elena's face twitches in fury, so I put a hand on her shoulder. "We'll pay," I tell Jento, knowing those are the words he's waiting for.

His brown eyes light up with interest. "How much?"

"Thirty."

"Thirty-five."

"Thirty."

"Fine. You can stay the night while I find you a more permanent place to crash."

I nod.

"Fine. But if AxysGen storms in looking for you, I won't—"

A door on the far side of the room opens, revealing a short, slightly gangly boy, wearing clothes much too big for him. He's got brown skin, dark eyes, and a tousled puff of black hair on top of his head that looks like it hasn't been brushed in a while. "Hey Jento, I—" He freezes when he sees us, although his eyes are fixed on one person in particular. "Uh-oh."

"Yeah, uh-oh." Elena stalks toward him much faster than her short legs would suggest. She grips both his shoulders and shakes him, glaring at him furiously. "What the fuck are you doing here?" she shouts in rapid Spanish, so fast I have trouble keeping up. "Jacobo, you fucking idiot! What did I tell you about hanging around with Jento, huh? If you need credits, you come to me, okay? The only place I want to see your scrawny ass is at home in a chair, studying for your APS."

Jacobo looks startled at first, but then he narrows his eyes and juts his chin out in defiance. "And be a corp puppet? No fucking way."

"You'll be fucking Pinocchio if I tell you to, shit for brains. You know what happens to people who don't play straight? They die. I risk my ass every day so you don't fucking have to!"

"You haven't died yet," Jacobo protests. His dark eyes look almost exactly like Elena's when she's angry. "I'm good, okay? I know what I'm doing."

"You're twelve! No twelve-year-old knows what the hell they're doing!"

"Hey!" Doc says from behind us, but I shush her with a look. She definitely doesn't need to get involved in this.

"And you," Elena growls, whirling on Jento like a lioness defending her cub. "How fucking dare you drag my baby brother into your filth? You useless piece of dogshit!"

Jento remains calm, although his companions seem restless. I notice one brawny woman with an eyepatch reach for the pistol at her belt, and I move my hand closer to my rifle. I don't want a fight to break out, but if it does...well, I didn't survive AxysGen and Megan just to die in a trash heap like this.

"The kid's not wrong," Jento says to Elena. He removes his cigar from the ash tray and takes a puff. "He's good. I got him his first jack. Dendryte Bronze. He's almost paid it off already."

"What?" Elena rounds on Jacobo again and yanks his hair back to stare behind his ear. "God-fucking-damnit, Jacobo! Jacking isn't a game, okay? One hit from a Puls.wav and it's over. No new lives, no resets. Your brain leaks out through your ears! I dodged about twenty from some crazy *gringa* yesterday, and the only reason I survived is because I had help! You think I want that life for you? You can be better. You deserve better!"

"It's not like I had a choice!" Jacobo shouts, his eyes welling with tears. "You *left,* Elena. Someone had to take care of *Abuelita* and Mateo."

"Yeah, dumbass, and that someone is me."

Jacobo glares at her, but suddenly all the fight drains out of him. He throws his arms around Elena's waist, and she ducks her head to rest her chin against his hair.

"Hey, *hermanito.* It's okay. I'm here."

The room gets uncomfortably quiet, so I step in. "How much does the kid owe you, Jento?"

Greed gleams in Jento's eyes. "Well, the new jack didn't come cheap."

"I'll throw in another fifteen if you forget this kid's name."

"Twenty."

"Eighteen."

"Fine." He gives Elena a sour look. "You can stay here tonight, but don't expect room service. I'll set you up in a safe house tomorrow."

"Fine." I glance at the rest of my crew. They're all in various stages of wary surprise, though Doc is sulking more than usual. "Come on." I nod at the door Jacobo came through. "We're done here."

They file out of the room, Cherry and Rami first, then Doc, and finally Rock, who gives Jento one more threatening look. I hesitate, then step toward Elena and tap her shoulder. "We should go," I whisper, nodding toward the door.

"Yeah," she says. Jacobo is still sniffling into her shirt, but I can't tell whether it's with anger or relief. Probably both. "Let's go, Jacobo. If you've got a jack now, I have some programs I need to set you up with."

Jacobo looks up at her in surprise. "What? You're serious?"

"You obviously aren't gonna listen to a word I fucking say. I might as well make it a little less likely you'll get fried." Jacobo starts to laugh, and Elena rolls her eyes. "This doesn't mean I'm okay with it. I'm still deciding whether or not to rip that thing out of your fool head."

She leads him to the door with an arm around his skinny shoulders, and I follow behind. This is going to make things a lot more complicated.

Friday, 06-18-65 12:02:05

"NOT MUCH, IS IT?" Elena says, looking around the suite of rooms.

I take in our new accommodations with a fair amount of skepticism. To call it a 'suite' would be generous. The walls are bare concrete without windows, but the sticky heat from outside has managed to seep into the room anyway. All it has in the way of furniture is a couple of wooden chairs and a threadbare couch that's definitely seen better days.

Aside from the main entrance, there are five doors branching off from the room. Cherry peeks her head through one, then pulls back with a look of mild disgust on her face. "Cots look lumpy as hell, but I guess it's better than the floor."

"More of the same," Rami says, inspecting one of the other rooms. "At least I don't see roaches."

"Nah," Jacobo says. "Don't get too many of those here. Jento sprays. Bathroom's through there." He points at one of the other doors. "The room behind the third door has a terminal."

"It'll do," I say, mostly to forestall more bellyaching.

"Could've stayed in a hotel a hundred times as nice for thirty thousand credits," Doc sighs. She slumps on the couch, slinging both arms over the back.

I shake my head. "Too risky. Until we deal with Megan, we're going completely off-grid."

Doc rolls her eyes. "Come on, Sasha. You really think Megan's gonna track us all the way to Mexico?"

"I think a woman who faked her own death for six months and created a FRAI from scratch can do pretty much anything she wants."

"Hold up," Jacobo says, staring at me with wide eyes. "A FRAI? This person who's chasing you has a real one?"

"No, she doesn't," Elena says. "It's complicated. Come on, *conejito*. Let's get you set up with some shields."

Jacobo seems more reluctant to leave than he was before hearing about jacker battles and FRAIs, but he allows Elena to drag him by the elbow into the next room. That leaves me alone with the rest of the crew, minus Val. There's an awkward silence—a silence I know I have to address sometime. It might as well be now. "Come on. At least sit down."

Rami and Cherry grab two of the chairs, while Rock sits on the couch beside Doc. His half sinks significantly under his bulk, but Doc doesn't seem to mind the slanting angle.

"So, we're doing this again?" Cherry asks. She seems angry, but at this point, I can't tell whether it's at me or herself. If I had to guess, I'd say both.

"Not exactly." I force myself to hold eye contact. "I keep going back over everything, trying to understand why you went along with Val's lie. But I don't get it. Just like I don't get why I went along with Megan for so long. It seems so obvious when I replay the memories, but..." I pinch the bridge of my forehead. "Shit, I'm not doing this right. What I'm trying to say is, you had my back today, on what has to be hands-down the worst op I've ever been on."

"Really?" Doc says. "But you didn't even die."

The kid means it as a joke, and I'm surprised when I take it as one. "Shut up, smartass. Anyway, my dead girlfriend's actually alive and a psychopath, but you all rolled with it. I guess...sometimes we all fuck up."

"How was today your fuck-up?" Cherry asks. "You didn't try to kill us."

"How *wasn't* it my fuck-up? I'm the one who accepted Cross's offer without thinking it through. I'm the one who refused to turn back when it looked sketchy. Hell, I'm the one who brought Megan onto the crew in the first place."

"Don't blame yourself for that, Sasha," Rami says, fixing me with a sympathetic look. "Megan's smart. Charismatic. You find yourself going along with her before you even realize it. She fooled all of us."

Some of the dead weight I've been carrying around in my chest subsides. I was angriest about my crew's deception, of course. Part of me still is. But my emotions were fueled by more than that. Deep down, I was hurt that they hadn't stepped in earlier and objected to Megan cloning me. Those were stupid, irrational feelings, but that didn't stop me from having them.

I sigh. "She took us all for a ride, didn't she?"

"No," Rami says. "You're right to feel angry and betrayed. We lied to you. We hid something important from you." They sniff, wiping at the faint mascara trails on their cheeks. "Just because those memories were painful didn't give us the right to withhold them. And I'm sorry I didn't push back against Megan's plans sooner. I didn't know…"

They lower their gaze into their lap, and Cherry wraps an arm around their thin shoulders. "I'm sorry for lying too. And what Rami means is, the other clones didn't tell us how much it hurt or how scary it was to die."

Doc nods in agreement. "Yeah. Sometimes you…they…would be weird for a couple weeks, but they were always okay after that. They told us they just needed time for their memories to settle in." She gives me a haunted look. "I guess I assumed the same thing would happen this time. I didn't know keeping those memories secret for a little while would hurt you so bad."

Looking at my crew, it's impossible to miss the pain and regret on their faces. It's unfair to hold them accountable for failing to save me when I never asked to be saved. In the end, going along with Megan was my decision. As for my erased memories…well, they weren't trying to hurt me, and when you fuck up, sometimes 'sorry' is the best you can do. The rest of it, I have to take up with Val.

"What if I don't clone myself again this time?" I ask, looking at all of them.

"You already did," Doc points out. "Sasha Eight's currently floating in a tank underneath Kansas City."

Yeah, that's another problem I'll have to deal with once we're out of immediate danger. No matter what happens, though, I know in my heart that I'm done going in circles. "Humor me. What if I told Val not to download my memories into her?"

Rami wipes their face on the back of their hand. "It's your choice, Sasha," they say in a rasping voice. "But either way, I'm not going to let you die. Not ever again."

"No way, *jefa*," Cherry says. "No reboots, no substitutions."

Doc gives me a weak smile. "I'll give you bulletproof skin if you want. We'll fix you up like Rock so nothing can touch you."

"I'll stick with my tactical vest. But thanks."

That's when Rock gets up from the couch, pulling me into a bone-crushing hug that lifts me several inches off the ground. It's strong enough to squeeze out my breath and crack several vertebrae in my spine, but I try to hug him back. My body might be getting squished, but I feel better than I have in days.

"Let me in there, big guy," Cherry says from near Rock's shoulder.

"I wanna feel the love." She throws her arms around both of us, and Rami does the same from the other side. Somehow, Doc manages to squeeze in the middle, and all five of us hug each other tight. It feels right. I'm still raw, wounded, but the pressure underneath is finally gone. I'm on my way to forgiving them.

"What the hell is this? Some kind of clothes-on orgy?"

I peer around Rock's giant bicep to see Elena standing in the doorway with a smirk on her face.

"Come get in on this, *chaparrita*," Cherry says, nodding her over. "This is what crewbonding's all about."

Elena snorts. "Fine. But only because you losers saved my ass in Malaysia."

"Actually, I saved everyone," Rami says as Elena joins the huddle.

"Excuse me?" Cherry says, jokingly offended. "I'm the one who blew up all those mechs."

"Yeah, yeah, you're all badasses." Elena ducks under my arm, which puts her hair right beneath my nose and my chest against her back. The warmth in my belly isn't angry anymore.

After a little more hugging, our huddle breaks apart. I give Rami an extra squeeze. "I shouldn't have said what I did back in the Hole. About you not knowing who you are. Being mad doesn't give me a blank check to be an asshole." I look at Cherry. "And I didn't mean what I said about you either. I know you wouldn't leave me hanging out to dry."

Rami smiles. "I forgive you, Sasha."

"Not even a thing," Cherry says. "Consider it forgotten."

"How the fuck are we going to deal with Creepy Smurf, anyway?" Elena asks. "Sorry to break up the love fest, but a crazy jacker genius running modded Dendryte Platinum is a huge problem."

I steel myself, but the words come easier than I'm expecting. "We have to take her out."

"Still not hearing a plan, *Jefecita*," Elena says.

My face heats up at the nickname. "Well…"

"I'm thinking trap," Doc says. "Megan had the element of surprise last time, but maybe we can get the jump on her instead. Seven heads are better than one. Hercules against the hydra."

"Hercules won," I point out. "And the hydra was the bad guy."

Doc rolls her eyes. "I *know* that. My point is, Megan knows our tricks, but we know her weaknesses. She's a cocky shit who underestimates everyone that's not her. So, let's send her on a wild goose chase. Toss her two locations across the plate with our bank accounts, an obvious one and a subtle one. She'll think the first one is to cover our tracks and the second is a slip-up. Then we'll rig the second place to blow."

"There's no guarantee she'll bite," Cherry says. "She doesn't technically *need* to be on location to do some damage."

"She does if she wants Val's access keys," Rami says. "That puts her at a disadvantage. She's a lot weaker in meatspace than she is in virtual reality."

"Since we're talking keys, I vote we keep the brainbox out of your skull, boss," Doc says to me. "If I put it back in, Megan might try to crack you open. And since you don't want to be cloned again, you won't really need to be recording, will you?"

She has a point. I also notice, with mixed emotions, that the stab of pain I feel at the thought of Megan trying to kill me is already weakening. Out of necessity, I'm adjusting to the fact that she's willing to murder me to accomplish her goals.

"We should find a place to hide it," I say, patting my belt. "That way, even if Megan gets her hands on Val's databox, she won't be able to decrypt the source code."

"That's another thing I don't get," Cherry grumbles. "It's Megan's code. She could probably recreate it, right? Why does she want Val so bad?"

It's a question I've been thinking about too, and I have some suspicions. "I'm sure she could, but FRAIs can modify their own coding to be more efficient. They learn. Val has much more experience than any AI Megan could write from scratch, even one based on Val's source code. She'd be back to square one...or at least square two."

Doc chuckles. "Remember how buggy Val was in the beginning? Version 1.4 almost killed us all that one time because she wanted to 'confirm that we would cease functioning' if she stopped recycling the oxygen."

"She did *what?*" Elena squawks. The rest of us have long since turned the incident into a joke, but her face is the picture of horror.

"The early versions of Val were basically toddlers with advanced math and verbal skills," I explain. "She didn't always understand the consequences of her actions." *And sometimes,* I think, *she still doesn't.*

"Dios." Elena groans, holding her head in her hand. "I *really* don't want Megan and Cross to get their hands on her now."

Cherry laughs in agreement. "I guess I shouldn't tell you about the time version 2.1 destroyed my beautiful base in Australia when I told her to run a decontamination cycle..."

"Fuck Australia anyway," Doc says. "Kangaroos are stupid."

"That's because you hit one with the Eagle when I was teaching you to fly," Rami points out.

"Not on purpose! It was just too dumb to get out of the way."

"Tell you what, kid," Cherry says. "Next time, you can run Megan over with the Eagle. Right, Rockstar?" She slugs Rock in the shoulder, and he nods his head, a dark expression on his normally placid face. In spite of his enormous size and top-of-the-line combat mods, he's the gentlest member of the crew, but I can tell he'd punch Megan into the stratosphere, given half the chance.

"Enough," Rami insists. "We can figure out how to deal with Megan tomorrow. I'd like to remind everyone that none of you except Elena have slept in over twenty-four hours."

"Hey," Elena says with a pout, "I have an excuse. I almost died."

Doc rolls her eyes. "Whine about it some more, why don't you? I'll write you a doctor's note."

Elena ruffles Doc's hair. "You're almost as much of an asshole as my brother."

"What are we going to do about him, Elena?" Rami says.

"Make Jento drop his ass back at home with Mateo and *Abuelita*. If we paid him thirty thousand credits, he can afford to drive the kid home." She hides it well, but I can see the conflict in her face.

After a moment of hesitation, I reach for her shoulder. "We'll come back for them once we don't have targets on our backs. And we've got emergency credit chits. Send Jacobo back with one of those."

Elena looks at me in surprise, and then her brown eyes soften. "Shit. You're getting sappy on me. And what you did, paying Jacobo's debt off down there..."

I smile. "Consider it your first paycheck."

"I'll pay you back for this," Elena insists. "Don't know how, but I will. I don't like being in debt."

"It's not a debt. You earned it."

Elena and I just stare at each other, and for a moment, I forget anyone else is in the room...until Cherry starts making kissing noises.

"*Cállate,*" Elena snaps.

Cherry makes a rude gesture with her fingers and tongue. "Make me."

"You two are idiots," Doc mutters.

"Sasha?" Rami whispers, tapping my shoulder. I turn toward them, brows raised. "I was just thinking...there's one person you haven't made up with yet."

I sigh. I know it needs to happen, for the crew and for me, but forgiving Val is going to be the hardest of all. I square my shoulders and turn to Elena, who's still fake-arguing with Cherry. "Hey, Elena. Is your brother still using the terminal?"

Rae D. Magdon

Friday, 06-18-65 13:23:21

JACOBO IS STILL JACKED in when Elena and I enter the third bedroom, slumped in an uncomfortable-looking metal chair. His blank eyes stare at the softly glowing terminal, blinking far too slow.

"Hold on," Elena says. "I'll get him." She heads over and clasps Jacobo's thin shoulder, holding her other hand over the terminal. The light casts a strange glow over her brown skin, and her eyes slide out of focus as she connects through the wireless interface.

Although I've seen plenty of jackers leave meatspace, seeing Elena detach from reality leaves me unsettled. I turn away, listening intently, but all I hear is the shuffling of feet from the main room and the muffled murmur of my crew's voices. I take a calming breath. It's because of Megan. I'm expecting her around every corner, and Elena...She'll be going toe to toe with Megan in virtual reality, all because of her association with me.

Unless you jack in with her when the reckoning comes, the voice in my head says.

I can't. I'm only running Bronze, and I barely even know how to use it. Only enough to be a decent handler.

You could protect her. Buy her a few seconds.

My stomach churns with fear. The room suddenly smells like vanilla.

I...I don't want to die again...

Do you want her to die instead?

My conversation with myself is interrupted as Elena and Jacobo disconnect from the terminal. Life returns to their bodies, and a wide grin stretches across Jacobo's face. "That's fucking awesome!" he says, looking at her like she's some kind of superhero. "You seriously designed that shield program yourself?"

Elena's smile holds a hint of pride. "Hell yes, I did. Now move your ass. Sasha needs the terminal."

She heads for the door, but Jacobo pauses beside me. "You're my sister's handler now?"

I nod, a little awkwardly. I don't have much experience with kids aside from Doc, but Jacobo seems competent—he definitely is if he's anything like Elena. I can probably talk to him like an adult. "Yes."

"Is that why you paid off my gear?"

"Pretty much."

He squirms, rubbing the back of his neck. "Thanks. I know that was a shit ton of credits..."

"Not for me."

Elena gives me a disapproving look. The message in her eyes is clear: *Don't encourage him.*

"But I'm looking to get out of the business after this last op."

"Why?" Jacobo asks, his forehead furrowing. He seems almost disappointed.

"Because I'm tired. I've...almost died a lot of times. It stays with you. You can't just shake it off afterward."

"But you didn't die," Jacobo says with a sly little smirk that reminds me of his sister's. "So it was worth it, right?"

I sigh. "Trust me, kid. There are other things you can do as a jacker. Find a way to survive without putting your life on the line."

Jacobo doesn't look convinced, but Elena seems pleased. "Sasha's right," she says, placing her hand in the middle of Jacobo's back. "You've got time on your side, *hermanito*. Plenty of chances to figure out your shit. But you won't have time if you start running ops and get your idiot brain melted before your voice drops, right?"

It's Jacobo's turn to sigh. "Right." Although he still seems disappointed, he also seems to be listening.

"C'mon," Elena says. "Show me where to get some food around here. For thirty thousand credits, Jento's buying dinner."

The two of them leave the room, Jacobo first, then Elena. She pauses in the doorway, looking back over her shoulder at me. When I meet her eyes, she gives me a small nod of encouragement. Once I'm alone in the room, I sit in front of the terminal and pull out Val's databox. I have a hundred questions, but the biggest of all is *why*. Why was Val so convinced that taking my memories was the right thing to do? The download from my brainbox doesn't tell me. I need to go to the source. I plug Val in behind my ear and hook her up to the terminal.

network: mx 19432 . 99133

Connection established
welcome: user волчица-воин

I'm standing on a beach with sand between my toes. The orange sun hangs low in the sky, and its fading rays shimmer on top of the ocean. A light evening breeze caresses my face, carrying the scent of salt and island blossoms I don't recognize.

"Sasha."

Val doesn't seem surprised to see me. She's standing to my right, wearing a purple sundress with splashy pink flowers as well as a blossom behind her ear. Her expression is concerned. Regretful, even.

I gesture to the virtual beauty around us. "Why did you make it like this? It can't be one of Jento's presets."

A sad smile tugs at Val's lips. "It's Barbados."

"You didn't have to do that."

"You didn't have to protect me from Megan, either. You could have surrendered my databox in Malaysia, but you chose to keep it, even though you hate me."

I heave a tired sigh. There's only so much anger a body can hold, and my supply is drained. "I don't hate you, Val. I never did. You just...when you hid my memories, you hurt me. Really deep. And it hurts twice as much because I don't know why you did it."

Val looks out toward the ocean. The breeze picks up speed, blowing her long, thick hair back over her shoulders. "I will be completely honest with you, Sasha. There are three things you should know. First, the memories you possessed before the download from your brainbox were not really your memories. They were mine."

I look at her in confusion. "What do you mean?"

"Megan installed a failsafe into the cloning process. The download of your memories could not begin unless she granted permission."

I shiver, but not from cold. The fact that Megan had so much power over me is sickening, given what I know about her now. "Why didn't you tell me?"

"Megan ordered me not to, but as you are now plugged into my databox, my first priority is to assist you. This allows me to override Megan's previous orders." Val turns her face away from the sun, and it falls into shadow. "After the operation in Mumbai, she was no longer present to confirm the download of your memories. Since I was unable to give them to you, I substituted my own recollections. A memory of your memories. I have 'lived' your life, in a sense, thousands of times in order to develop my own personality."

An unexpected sense of bitterness swells within me. "You didn't develop a very good one, then. You can't expect me to believe I would have lied to myself the way you did."

Val lifts her chin to look at me once more. "That is the second thing you should know. I chose to delete portions of your memory because Sasha Six requested it."

"What?" I want to believe Val is lying to me again, but looking at her face—even knowing she has full control of her expressions—I believe she's telling the truth. "Why would I...she...do that?"

"That is the third thing you should know. I was able to download a backup copy of Sasha Six's final moments through AxysGen's wireless network before your brainbox was taken and deactivated. I can show you, if you'd like."

I should be furious that Val has kept yet another memory from me, but I've long since eaten through that feeling. The wick has burned down to the very bottom. I can't rebuild trust without the truth, and in spite of everything, I want to trust Val again.

"Show me."

Val frowns, worry etched across her face. "It will be painful."

"Do it anyway."

She meets my eyes, and the sadness in them speaks to me. "I am not surprised by your choice. Over the past week, I have come to understand that in some circumstances, humans value honesty more than the avoidance of pain." She extends her hand, offering it to me.

I take it and close my eyes.

/////COMMENCING DOWNLOAD/////

Pain. My whole world is pain. My limbs are shards of burnt glass. Right hip crushed. One lung punctured. My chest screams when it tries to inflate. Can't breathe. Can't see either. Vision swimming. Blonde hair?

Megan. Shit. Alive? Relief. I'm dying. Explosion caught me when I went back to look for her, but Megan's alive. She's okay. I try to speak. Say her name. Not enough breath.

"You aren't dead yet?"

She bends down. Unclips my armor, pulls broken pieces out of me. Hands that loved me, cold. Uncaring. "Where is it?"

It? I'm crushed again. Megan doesn't care. Doesn't care about me.

She's looking for...something.

"Fuck, Sasha, where did you put Val's databox?"

Can't answer. Can't even cry. Megan. God, Megan. Where are you? Why aren't you there when I look in your eyes? Were you...were you ever there?

Megan rummages in her belt. Slaps a StimPak on my arm. Slaps my cheeks. "Hey, hey, hey. Stay with me. Where is Val? Tell me and I'll let you die before I yank your brainbox out."

Yank my brainbox? Let me die? I don't...don't understand. Val. What did I do with Val? I took her on this mission. I had her to open the other door for me, until...no. No, I gave her to Rami. Gave her to Rami to keep safe before I went back in for Megan. Rami was injured, so I told the two of them to go.

Megan's eyes are blue lightning. "Where the fuck is it? Shit! I get offered a deal during the one goddamn mission where I'm not using her."

Deal? What is she talking about?

"There goes my whole distribution plan! Ugh, screw this. Last chance, or I'll just pull the info from the brainbox. You can die easy, or you can die ugly."

She pulls something from her belt. A glowing knife. Plasma blade, one of Doc's. She's going to kill me. Actually going to cut my head open. Doesn't matter. StimPak isn't working. Warmth leaving. Black circles closing. I'm dying. This body's dying. I'll fade out soon, or Megan will kill me, and the next me...oh no. No. The next me. Sasha Seven.

She'll wake up alone. Alone in the cold, wet blue. First thing she'll know is Megan murdering her. First thing she'll feel is Megan hating her. No, not hating. Not even caring enough to hate. Worse. It'll be so much worse than the other times. Not just nightmares. Not just pain. No trust. No hope. Unloved. Val. Val, please still be in wireless range. Don't. Don't put this in the backups. Don't download it. I'm running out of time—but give her time. I know she'll find out, but please, give her time. Please. Please, Val. Just a little...more...time...

/////DOWNLOAD COMPLETE/////

I'm back on the beach, tears streaming freely down my face. At first, I'm speechless. I can still see images of Megan's empty eyes burnt over the sunset. It all makes sense now. Despite dying five times and preparing to die for a sixth, the Sasha before me had tried to protect me. She'd known how the other Sashas reacted after being awakened. She remembered how hard it had been to come back from the dead. She'd known I couldn't handle Megan's betrayal on top of that.

"She gave me time," I whisper, swiping tear tracks away with the back of my hand.

"She did," Val agrees. "I fulfilled her request because, in my opinion, you would not have been able to handle this information in such a vulnerable state."

It's hard to concentrate on Val's words, because I'm still stuck in the past. Megan tried to kill me back in Malaysia, but Sasha Six's memories cut far deeper. "But why? Why did Megan...why didn't I see it coming?"

"I have analyzed Megan's behavior and my own memories of our final operation extensively. I believe Veronica Cross became aware of my existence, and offered Megan a deal during our mission to AxysGen's Mumbai facility, but you had decided to take me that day."

In spite of everything, I laugh. "The doors. I needed you to help me open the doors because there were two separate intranet security systems. Me and Rami were on one, Megan was on the other. She said she could handle it without help. Arrogant bitch."

"Yes. I remember...I have often considered how unlikely this specific outcome was, statistically speaking. If I had gone with Megan as usual, she would have handed me over to Veronica Cross. If you had kept my databox instead of giving it to Rami before returning to the facility to search for Megan, she would have taken it from your body. If Rami had not managed to escape, I would have been found and returned to Megan."

"So you're safe because of dumb luck." I sniff as the tears finally dry up. "But what about the other memories? Sasha Six didn't tell you to delete them."

"No, she did not," Val says. "It was my choice, one I regret deeply. After pondering her instructions, it occurred to me that the memories of your cloning and Megan's disregard for your safety would also be traumatic. All of your predecessors had struggled with them following activation. Furthermore, the rest of the crew was scattered. Rami had gone into hiding to protect the databox, and was awaiting your return. Cherry had gone to look for her, but was forced underground by AxysGen during the search. Rock was captured on his way to the cloning bunker in Kansas City and taken to Siberia. Only Doc was there to help me activate you, and in her state of fear and anger, she alone was not sufficient."

"Sufficient for what?"

"Emotional support." Val reaches out, and when I don't object, she touches my arm. In virtual reality, the comforting gesture feels real. "Though they did not always wish to discuss their pain, Sashas Two through Six relied heavily on the crew during the recovery process. They considered the presence of their family absolutely vital to their wellbeing. Without them, I feared you might not recover at all."

I have no idea what to say. Is there anything to say at all?

Val squeezes my arm a little tighter. "I apologize for causing you pain, Sasha. Please know that it was not my intention. I am not sure what course of action I would take if this scenario were to occur again, but this was not a desirable outcome. Given a second chance, I would not withhold your memories. I have learned from my mistake."

"You were right, though," I find myself telling her. "Those memories were...if I hadn't had my family and Elena around, I might have..." I don't know what I would have done, but I'm not sure I could have recovered. At least, not in time to save Rock and find the others before AxysGen tracked them down.

Val lets my arm go, but not without brushing her fingertips along my skin, as though she can feel it. "If you will permit me to give you some advice, I think you should speak to Elena."

It dawns on me exactly what advice Val is trying to give. She wants me to lean on Elena, to ask for the support I need. But Elena isn't like the other members of my crew. She's new, but also special, and my feelings for her are stronger than I want them to be. Dangerously strong, even after such a short time.

"You don't know what you're asking," I say, fighting to keep my voice from breaking. "You want me to open up, but after what Megan did..."

"Your trust in Megan was misplaced. You could not have known that, but as you are aware, Elena is different. She will prove it to you when this is over, by demonstrating her loyalty over an extended period of time."

I try to protest, but I can't. Something stops me. Maybe I'm an idiot for wanting to trust people again, but it's how I feel.

"Val?" I whisper.

Val looks at me.

"I forgive you."

She smiles.

"Thank you, Sasha."

logging off network
disconnection complete

Friday, 06-18-65 15:03:25

THE REST OF THE evening passes in a blur. Elena and Jacobo return with armfuls of packaged food, as well as an unopened bottle of vodka. Even though I'm not usually a drinker, I down the shot Elena pours me as soon as she puts it in my hand. It burns, but I stifle the cough rising in my throat.

"Not too much," Rami says, their tone more teasing than concerned. They've wiped the color from their lips and added faint stubble around their chin instead—how, I have no idea, since they don't have their regular makeup kit.

"Let her fucking have what she wants, would you?" Elena takes the empty shot glass from me and fills it again. "She's had a hell of a week."

"A hell of a life," Cherry says. Then she looks at me and winces. "Shit, that sounds like you're dying."

I swallow my vodka and snort. "You're an ass, Cherry."

"You're saying this like it's new information, boss." Cherry takes a shot glass of her own and the bottle from Elena, pouring one out and downing it without a twitch. "Here, Rock," she says, passing him the bottle. "Knock yourself out."

"You know his system will filter out the alcohol before he gets drunk, right?" Doc says.

"Not the point," Cherry insists. "It's about participation."

Rock shrugs and lifts the bottle to his lips. After several chugs, Rami yanks it away from him. "That's enough for you."

Elena takes it back. "Shit. Give me some of that before it's all gone."

Jacobo sidles up beside her. "Hey, Elena, can I—"

"Not on your fucking life." Elena pours herself a shot and passes the bottle back to me.

"I wasn't gonna ask for that," Jacobo grumbles, pouting a little. "I wanted to know what you're doing here."

"Besides saving your ass from that slimeball Jento? Long story short, Sasha" Elena points her thumb back at me. "used to date a crazy bitch. Now she's trying to kill us and steal all our stuff."

"Like a FRAI?"

Elena glares at him. "Where'd that come from?"

"You said the woman chasing you invented a FRAI. Then you said she didn't have it, and it was 'complicated.' Assuming you're not bullshitting me, that means you swiped it."

Instead of clarifying, I give him a look. "Is the rest of your family as annoying as you and your sister?"

Elena grins. "Runs in the family, *Jefecita.*"

"I'm taking that as confirmation," Jacobo says. "What the fuck, Elena? A real FRAI?"

She heaves a sigh and looks at me, brows raised.

I pull Val out and toss the databox to Elena. "Turn her projector on. She might as well join the party. And for the record, we never stole her. She was always one of us."

Everyone smiles, the last of the tension dissipating as they realize what that must mean: that I've forgiven Val too. Elena switches on the projector, and Val appears in the room. She's wearing her usual clothes instead of her beach attire, and she tilts her head when she sees Jacobo. Her face registers surprise, which makes sense, considering we don't introduce her to many people.

"Hello, Jacobo."

The kid gapes. "Are you really a FRAI?" he asks, breathless with excitement.

"My thought processes did not originate organically, so I suppose the answer would be yes."

Jacobo bounces on his heels. "Holy fuck! That's so cool. You're, like, the next step in consciousness! So, tell me: what's the meaning of life?"

"Assuming you wish to apply this question to an individual rather than a species, there is no singular answer. There are as many answers as there are human beings."

"That's lame," Jacobo says.

"No. I think it is beautiful. At the present time, observing and learning what organic beings consider to be most important is the meaning of my life."

I refill my shot glass. "If we're gonna talk philosophy, I need another drink."

"One more question." Jacobo looks over at Doc. "Why does Elena let that kid tag along, but treat me like I couldn't find my own ass?"

"Excuse me? I've got a name," Doc says.

"You haven't said it, so how should I know?"

Doc rolls her eyes. "By asking, dumbass."

Val seems amused. "I believe Elena would prefer if Doc were not involved in our operations. However, Elena does not feel she has the authority to dictate Doc's actions. Since Elena is your older sister and one of your guardians, she feels responsible for imposing restrictions on you for your own safety."

Jacobo completely ignores Val's explanation and narrows his eyes at Doc. "Doc? What the hell kind of name is that?"

Doc wrinkles her nose. "Why the hell does your face look like that?"

Cherry snorts into her glass. "Is this funny because I'm drunk, or...?"

Elena plops down on the couch beside me and tosses a bag of chips toward Jacobo. "Shut up and eat."

He does, and we follow suit. Everyone passes the bottle around, the kids and Rami excluded, and soon the table is covered with wrappers.

Before I realize it, the eight of us have been lounging around the dingy room, eating and drinking and shooting the shit, for about three hours. Despite the circumstances that brought us here, a strange peace settles over me. I feel like a powerful wave of pain has finally passed, leaving my body all buzzy and light. The bitterness of the vodka has turned to ambrosia on my tongue and the blood of the gods is pounding through me. I feel invincible, like in the old days. With my friends around me, Megan and AxysGen seem distant, or at least manageable. The fear is bearable now that I don't have to carry it all alone.

"Can you believe that dramatic-ass hoe?" Cherry slurs, her cheek resting on Rami's shoulder. "Showing up to kill us after six goddamn months in that ugly blue hood. 'Little Miss Disappear'? What the fuck was that?"

"I wish I'd seen the look on her face," Rami sighs. Although they're not drunk, the spirit of the evening has infected them too.

"And what about Elena just cutting her off out of nowhere?" Doc says. There's a smear of chocolate at the corner of her mouth, and judging by her glazed eyes, she looks ready to slide into a sugar coma. "That must've *really* pissed her off."

"Enough for her to send a bunch of mechs after us," Cherry reminds her. "I'm all about a good heist, but this one was too much. I think I'm coming around to *jefa's* point of view. Maybe it's time to retire to a quiet place near the beach."

I sigh, leaning further back into the uncomfortable couch. "The beach..."

"Uh-oh," Rami says.

Doc shakes her head. "Here she goes again..."

"Shut up," I mutter. "Don't make fun of my dreams."

"Sasha knows what's up." Elena leans her arm against mine. "I'd love that kind of life. Lounging on the beach all morning, swimming all afternoon, spending nights under the stars...and it'd all be real, not a VR sim." Her brown eyes have stars in them too, and my heart starts to ache.

"I'm not turning it down," Rami says. "I'm more than willing to be a beach bum."

"It's what we bust our asses for," Cherry says.

Doc snorts. "You're all boring."

"You can learn to parasail," Rami suggests.

"Swim with dolphins," Cherry says.

"Swim with *sharks*," Elena adds.

Even Doc can't hide her grin. "Cool."

"So, you're going too?" Jacobo says, looking over at Elena. He's been quiet the past few minutes, although he was an enthusiastic participant before.

"Don't know yet," Elena says. "I haven't been invited."

"Of course you're invited, stupid," Doc says. "You're part of the crew."

Elena's lips twitch into a smile, but when she looks over at me, she's hesitant.

"You've earned it," I tell her. "We'll haul your family along too. It's not like we're short on retirement cash."

Jacobo brightens. "Seriously?"

Elena looks surprised as well, although undeniably pleased. "Is this extra incentive for me to risk my life for you all again?" she asks, but I can tell there's gratitude underneath her attempt to lighten the mood.

"Yeah, but we also like having you around. Usually. Right?"

I look at the rest of the crew. They're all wearing smiles of agreement. Rock's is the biggest of all, and the entire couch tilts as he shifts his massive bulk and rises up to give Elena a crushing hug. She almost disappears in his arms, but manages to wrap her own at least partway around his torso. "Okay, okay," she wheezes. "Can't say no to that."

"This calls for one more shot," Cherry says. "Rami?"

Rami, who has been safeguarding the bottle, waves it in Cherry's face. "No more." Cherry's face falls comically, and Rami pats her cheek. "In Barbados, you can have all the rum you want."

By this time, Rock has set Elena back on her feet. She sways a bit, but that seems to be because Rock squeezed the wind out of her. When we make eye contact, she looks more sober than I expected. Guess the girl can hold her liquor despite being pocket-sized.

While the others talk, I notice Val watching. She's fallen silent for the time being, but her gaze says more than words. It flicks over to Elena briefly, then settles heavily on me.

I'm at a crossroads. I can follow Val's advice and give Elena a chance—not to prove herself, exactly, but...well, yes. To prove she'll treat me better than Megan. Or I can close the door so I won't get hurt again. It should be terrifying, but when I look at her, it's not. I feel warm and I don't want to stop staring at her. We've only known each other two weeks, but in those two weeks, Elena's shown she cares more than Megan did over a decade.

Maybe this is something else the other Sashas and I have in common. No matter how many times our heart gets returned to us bruised and broken, we always offer it up again.

"Elena?" I brush her arm before she can take her seat beside me. When her eyes meet mine, I give a subtle nod toward the bedroom with the terminal, where most of my stuff is. Hers too, if I remember correctly. I didn't really think about that when we dropped off our bags.

Elena starts to smile, but then her gaze darts toward Jacobo. He's lounging on the couch, looking like he's about to pass out, probably with dreams of Barbados in his head.

Rami comes to the rescue. They smile and mouth 'go', and I dip my head in gratitude. Without saying goodnight, and without drawing Cherry's attention, I take Elena's hand and slip off. I catch a glimpse of Rami gently attempting to rouse Jacobo and usher him into one of the other rooms before the door swings shut.

"Did you really mean that?" Elena says as soon as we're alone in the room. "About me and my brothers coming to Barbados?"

"You don't have to, but the option's there if you want it. Credits aren't an issue for me. I...want to do this for you."

Elena raises an eyebrow. "Never thought I'd end up a kept woman."

My breath hitches. "No, I didn't mean—"

"Cool it, *chula*." Elena slides her palm up along my chest, stroking my shoulder and cupping the back of my neck. "I didn't say I had a problem with being a kept woman, just that I never thought I'd be one."

Hope flutters in my chest. "Elena...the last time you fucked me, it was because you hated me." It's only after I've said it that I realize 'the last time' implies a 'next time.' "And the last time you kissed me, it was..."

"Too soon?" Elena shrugs. "Things change."

"Like getting my memories downloaded into your head."

She takes a step closer, until her body is flush against mine. "Yeah, but not just that."

"Then what?"

"Fuck if I know. I guess because you're you." She stands on tiptoe to kiss me, and I bend my head so she can reach my lips. She tastes like strawberries and alcohol, but her mouth moves deliberately against mine, and I know: she's certain about this. About me. And even if I get hurt again, it feels so good to have someone care.

Friday, 06-18-65 18:25:53

ELENA'S MOUTH IS A well of sweetness that never seems to run dry. I drink deep until she's sucking my tongue and I'm grasping her waist. Her curves are soft, plush, and her hips fit perfectly in my palms. The way her body feels and the way she fits against me makes it hard to breathe. I've kissed my share of girls, fucked plenty of them too, but no one except Megan has ever made me feel like this. Like I'll die without another taste.

Don't think about her. She doesn't deserve you. Never did. But Elena's here, and she wants you. Trust her.

I do trust Elena. Maybe it's stupid, considering how briefly we've known each other and how badly I've been burned. But stupid seems to be where I'm headed, because there's no derailing this train. It's about more than how good Elena smells, more than how silky the strip of skin beneath her shirt is. It's about how she's treated me since Hong Kong— the kindness, the support. I didn't even have to ask. In fact, I told her to leave me alone. But she offered anyway, because that's the kind of person she is.

Elena hooks her thumbs through the loops of my pants, pulling my pelvis against her lower belly. "Might still need some convincing to come to Barbados," she mutters into my mouth. "Wanna show me what I'll get if I tag along?"

I slide my hands under Elena's ass and hitch her up, barely giving her a second to wrap her legs around my waist before I carry her to the bed. The frame's all rickety, and the mattress is lumpy and cheap, but it doesn't matter. All I care about is peeling Elena out of her clothes and kissing everywhere I can reach.

Elena squirms out of her shirt as soon as I set her down. While her arms are tangled in it, I run my hands up her sides and past her ribcage, filling my palms with her breasts. They're already spilling out of her bra. Even though the material is padded, I can feel the points of her nipples when I press in with my thumbs.

Elena tosses her shirt away and stares at me, first with affection, then with hunger. She arches her spine, bracing herself with her arms and pressing further into my hands. I peel down the straps of her bra, painting kisses along her shoulders. There's a hint of sweat at the crook of her neck, and I suck there hard, until Elena fists the back of my shirt.

"Fuck, Sasha."

The way she says my name sends a jolt straight through me. I can't tell if it's a demand or a plea, but I don't care. The sound of Elena's voice makes me glow inside, and hearing 'Sasha' fall from her lips is like a star striking earth.

I unhook her bra and throw it aside. Elena's nails rake gently over my scalp, but she doesn't need to push. I'm already kissing down toward her breasts, trailing my mouth around them in spirals without touching the stiff peaks. God, her skin. It's so smooth, burnished gold blended into a warm landscape of bronze. I want to drag my tongue all over it. So I do, until I'm sucking one of her nipples and guiding her knee back around my waist.

Elena's nails move from my head to my shoulders, leaving sharp little crescents. "Sasha, yes..." There it is. My name again. I kiss across to the other side, tugging Elena's nipple with my teeth. She gasps. I growl. All I want is to devour this beautiful creature while she begs for more.

It takes all the willpower I have to go slow. The temptation to dive straight between her thighs is overwhelming. Somehow, I manage to make it last, to savor each kiss I plant around Elena's breasts and along the upper part of her belly, to stroke her sides until she starts shivering beneath me. Her hands return to my hair, and this time, she pulls. "Shit, Sasha, I need..."

She needs me. It feels so good to be needed by someone. It feels *amazing* to be needed by Elena. I slide my mouth down from Elena's sternum, kissing and nibbling my way to her hips. The way they rock up to meet me is hypnotic. I can see where the waistband of her pants cuts into the soft curve of her belly, so I flip open the button, placing a kiss over the imprint on her skin. The sigh she lets out as I tug the zipper down and pull her pants off makes my head spin.

"Sasha," she says, tilting my face up with the tips of her fingers.

I meet her eyes: a brown so rich and warm that I fall straight into them. For those eyes, I'd do anything. "What?"

Elena runs both thumbs along my cheeks, like she's feeling my smile. "It's cute that you wanna be gentle... but I want you to fucking *destroy* me. If I'm not too raw to walk after this, we didn't do it right."

That's a request I can deliver on. I pin her hips to the bed and sink my teeth in beside her navel.

A big grin splits Elena's face. She spreads her legs wider, wide enough for me to see the dark stain in the middle of her panties. I flatten my tongue against the spot I've bitten, but my hands aren't as gentle. They snap the strings on either side of her underwear so I can tear it away.

"You owe me a new pair," Elena pants as I change places, kissing my way up her legs. Her smell begins to blossom, heavy and sweet like honey straight from the hive.

"I'll buy you some," I mutter into the cushion of her left thigh. "Those were already ruined."

"That's your fault too." Elena slides one calf over my shoulder, opening herself for me. For a moment, I can't breathe. Her dark outer lips are smooth and puffy, and the red inner ones are glistening. Maybe I've died again after all, because this must be heaven. And if it's heaven, I want to lick it all up.

All I manage is a groan before I lower my head. The first taste drives the lingering flavor of vodka from my mouth. Elena spills like wine over my tongue, and I long to stain my lips with her. Her scent fills my nose, but I don't want to breathe any other smell. With her wetness smearing my chin, her steadily growing cries, and her heels digging in above my shoulders, I feel like I could live forever between her legs. She awakens an ache in me that I can't control—that I don't want to control.

When I dip down to Elena's entrance, her muscles clasp tight. Their twitching sends an answering shudder through me, and they strain to draw me in, trying to wrap around my tongue. I know this isn't exactly where she wants me, but the sounds. Oh god, the sounds she makes as I burrow inside her. Her pelvis gives little jerks, like she wants me deeper. I want to be deeper. I want to slide so deep that she can't hold any more of me.

I let myself be greedy. It's what Elena's asking for, but more than that, it's what I need. I thrust in and out of her, sliding my tongue through smooth satin, letting her slickness run in rivers over the lower half of my face. So wet. She's so fucking wet, all for me. These clinging walls, this quivering body, these desperate noises, this woman... she's mine and mine alone, at least for tonight.

I'm surprised when Elena comes. I wasn't trying to push her over the edge. I only realize it's happening because she grasps my head tight and wails, bucking once, then shaking from head to toe. More salt spills into my mouth, but I only steal a taste before licking up to her clit. I draw her between my lips and suck, timing my pulls with her pulses.

Elena pounds in my mouth, squirming as if she isn't sure whether she wants to pull away or grind harder. She's hypersensitive, in that wonderfully awful way where the stimulation is almost too much. I continue sucking, trying to keep her there as long as possible. More wetness leaks over my chin, pulsing little slips of it, and I sink two fingers inside her without thinking. She wants to be filled. I can tell from the way she's moving, from the stars swimming in her eyes as she stares down at me, gulping for precious air.

I draw her peak out as long as I can, swirling my tongue to make sure she's finished. By the time I pull away, she's a boneless heap, plastered to the lumpy mattress and covered in a sheen of sweat that makes her skin gleam.

"What the fuck," she rasps. "How do you always make me come in less than three seconds?"

I place another kiss to the tip of her clit. "You make it kind of easy."

"Fuck," Elena growls, "get up here." She pulls me up for another kiss, one that tastes of her. Her muscles squeeze my fingers, clenching hard as her tongue meets mine. I thrust my hand without thinking, seeking the right angle and force, until I hit a spot that makes her cry out. Once I've found it, I catch it again and again, curling my fingers hard enough to make Elena's eyes roll back in her head.

"This...this is supposed to be your turn," she says, even as she rocks her hips to find a harder rhythm.

I drag my tongue down her neck until I find her pulse point. "This is my turn," I mutter into its sweet-smelling curve. Elena makes no more protests. She wraps her legs around my hips and braces herself for the ride.

I fuck her with everything I've got. No matter how fast I go, no matter how hard I push, Elena seems to want more. Soon my hand is a blur and my forearm burns with the effort. My reward is the tightening of her knees around my waist and the rising volume of her cries.

"Sasha," she breathes again.

I'm undone. I long to kiss her, but the last thing I want to do is stop her from saying my name. I could listen to her beg for me until the world ends. I satisfy myself by sinking my teeth into her shoulder instead, sucking hard enough to leave a deep purple bruise. I want to make my mark on her for everyone to see, just like I want to carry her scratches on my back for days.

Elena's inner walls ripple again, and I can tell she's close. She's fighting it, trying to hold out, but I want her to surrender. Somehow, I know I'll never tire of bringing her over the edge. "Come for me," I growl into the dip of her collarbone, close enough for her to feel my lips on her skin. "I want you to come for me."

She does, thrashing her head to one side in a useless attempt to muffle her screams with the pillow. It doesn't work. Sharp, breathy sobs escape as she clenches around my fingers, spilling a fresh wave of wetness into my waiting palm. It's like I'm holding her heartbeat in my hand. I can't resist the impulse to claim her lips again and swallow the last of her cries.

"Goddamn," she laughs as aftershocks travel through body. "Would you stop already? I know you're a service top, but this is ridiculous."

I know from her smile that she's joking, but my confidence falters. I know what Elena wants, but I'm not sure I'll be able to give it to her. I've got baggage around sex, around trust, around my body, and although I feel good in my skin tonight, I can't guarantee she'll get the results she wants, no matter how hard she tries.

"Elena…"

Elena props herself up on her elbows, her breath hitching as the change in position presses my buried fingers into a sensitive spot. She bites down on her lip and breathes through it, then opens her eyes again and looks toward our bags. "Did you bring it?" she asks, sounding almost hopeful.

All I can do is blink at her. I'd chalk this up to her viewing my memories, but I know it's more than that. She understood the first time, back when we were pretending to hate each other. I search Elena's eyes, but I don't see a trace of doubt in them. I'm helpless against such a genuine stare.

"I always do."

A smirk spreads across Elena's face. "Then go get it," she murmurs, trailing her ticklish fingertips down my neck and along my shoulder. She doesn't have to tell me twice. I roll off the bed, mourning the loss of skin, but knowing the sooner I grab my cock, the sooner I can come back to the warm bed—and to her.

Lucky for me, it's sitting right at the top of my pack. I rarely go anywhere without it in my travel kit. It's not even about sex most of the time. It's simply a comfort thing. I take it out and give it a quick spray with the bottle of disinfectant I carry with me.

"What's the holdup, *Jefecita*?" Elena has stretched herself across the bed, a brown-skinned Rubens with curves molded for the gods.

"Strip and bring your fine ass over here."

I tear off my shirt and drop my pants and underwear to the floor, stalking toward the bed with only one thought in mind. I want to fuck Elena so hard she forgets everything outside this room and every word except for my name.

Friday, 06-18-65 18:58:52

ELENA IS A FURNACE beneath my palms. Her flesh glows wherever my hands touch. The air in the room is sweltering, but the sweat rolling down my back has nothing to do with it. My damp temples, my heavy breathing, the ache in my core—it's all because of her. All for Elena, who's lying beneath me with an obnoxiously smug look on her face. Only it's not obnoxious, not anymore. Somewhere along the way, it became endearing.

"Put your dick in," she says, stroking one of my biceps.

My muscles tense under her fingertips. She's touching the arm connected to the hand that's holding my cock, sending little zips of lightning along the pathway. "In me, or in you?"

Elena huffs, sitting up to tug my lower lip with her teeth. "Both. Shit, you're annoying."

I grab the back of her neck and pulling her into a real kiss. It's hot and wet and hungry, and it still tastes like her. "That's what I thought the first minute we met," I tell her when we break apart.

"Fuck you."

"Trying."

I push Elena onto her back and kneel between her legs. I'm already dripping from getting her off, so the shorter end of the shaft eases inside me with a few pushes. There's a jolt as the sensation transmitter fits over my clit, then a fuzziness I can only call relief. It feels good to have my cock in. Feels right.

Elena's eyes are already locked onto it. Her tongue peeks out to tease her lips, like she's considering exactly what she wants me to do to her. I don't give her the chance to decide. My hands fly to her hips like magnets, like they were meant to be there. I nudge her legs apart with mine and stretch out on top of her, pressing into her stomach.

"Nuh-uh." Elena strokes my braids, flicking her tongue between my lips for a fraction of a second. "Not how I want it."

As much as I like to top I'm discovering that I'm a pushover when it comes to her. "Then how do you want it?"

Elena taps my shoulder, urging me to lift a few inches. She rolls onto her front beneath me, sweeping her hair away from the nape of her neck. "Come on, *Jefecita.* Show me how well you hit it from behind."

I can't stifle my groan. "Depends." I mouth her neck, sliding my lips down the top of her spine. "How much can you take?"

She tenses, then whimpers as I suck a spot behind her shoulder blade. *"Dáme duro."*

Hard. Fuck. If Elena wants hard, she'll get my hardest. I hitch her up by the waist, spreading her thighs with my knees. While my teeth seek out sensitive spots along her spine, I rock my pelvis into her rear. Elena has the most perfect ass I've ever seen. Warm, firm, filling my hands with more to spare. My fingers leave pressure lines in her yielding flesh, and she tenses beneath me.

"Don't tease," she says, casting a half-lidded look over her shoulder. Her eyes are dark, glittering jewels, like the smoky edges of the sunset on the beach I dream about. "Take me."

Take. I know Elena means fuck, but there's a difference. A difference that matters. Take implies ownership, or maybe...maybe a gift? It's too soon for love-pledges. I don't know when I'll be ready to share that much of myself again. But Elena's offering me her body and her trust now, in this moment, and I yearn to take them and hold them close. I stroke my hands down her thighs and suck the base of her neck as I line myself up.

I don't make her wait for it. As soon as the head of my cock catches her entrance, I push forward. My whole world centers between my legs. Elena's all trembling smoothness—so warm, so wet, so ready. Her body blossoms open, soft petals parting to drink in the sun. For me. For tonight, all mine. I latch my teeth onto her shoulder and slide home.

My first stroke is gentle, just to make sure. It's not what Elena wants, and her whines tell me so. Her hips roll back into mine, seeking more of me, and I am consumed: with lust, with desire, with feelings I'm too afraid to name. I rut into her, hilting every inch until I'm wrapped in rippling heat.

"Shit," we say at the same time—me at her tightness, her at the fullness. We both laugh, then suck in a breath.

"Hard," she reminds me, rocking one more time.

I wrap my hands around her thighs and start a rhythm. There's hardly any friction. Elena's slickness spills all over me, running between us. Her walls grasp tighter with each thrust, trying to pull me deep and keep me there. One stubborn, gleaming inch at the bottom of my cock won't fit, but I keep trying to bury it anyway.

Watching her shining red lips stretch to take me is wonderful in a way I can't describe. I'm fascinated by the serpentine curve of her spine and the twin dimples at its base, shimmering with twin pools of sweat. I commit each detail to memory: the way the cheap lighting filters onto Elena's skin, the shifting of padded fat over straining muscle, the wild way her hair streams across the pillow as she bites down on the fabric. Her sobs are hooks in my heart. They draw out words I didn't know lived inside me.

"You're beautiful, Elena…"

Elena lifts her head, and the look she gives me makes me twitch inside her. "Sasha—"

Shit. Too soon. Need to recover. Elena's sensitive enough to notice. I lean over, plastering my breasts to her back and picking up speed. "Fuck," I pant, pistoning in and out, "so fucking tight—"

Elena's kind enough to roll with it. "Tightest pussy you've ever fucked?" She clenches down on purpose, and my hips stutter. I don't answer out loud. I slam my hips, driving into her like an animal, but this is the most human I've felt since I found out who—and what—I am.

The fullness in my cock is overwhelming. Each shiver of Elena's muscles makes white sunspots flash behind my eyes. Everything I am is about to burst straight out of me, soul included. But I won't come until she does, at least one more time. None of the other Sashas have ever left a lady unsatisfied, and I'm not about to throw that legacy away. Especially not now, when I'm wrapped up safe in someone who cares.

It's because Elena cares that I grab her hair, shove her face into the pillow, and drill into her with all my strength. It only takes one more thrust and an extra jerk of my hips to rub the base of my cock against her clit. Elena's body locks up, then starts to tremble. Her walls pull impossibly tight, rippling almost frantically, and another wave of warmth gushes out around me to run down our sticky thighs.

Once I've opened the floodgates, Elena starts screaming into the pillow, making muffled yelps with each contraction. Her noises aren't even close to words, but I pretend they're my name anyway. Some lonely, longing part of me needs for them to be my name.

Feeling Elena flutter around me is unbearable. My body's balanced on the razor's edge, and if I'm being honest, my heart's up on the chopping block too. I need to come, but I'm scared about what that will mean. This isn't like any of the other times, even my first time with

Elena in the Hole. Elena's different now. I'm different. The unnamed thing between us is different.

My ears throb with the rush of blood, my vision blurs, and my limbs shake with the strain of indecision. The heavy thud of my heart is enough to make me dizzy. I lower my head, burying my face in the soft strands of Elena's hair and inhaling deeply. *Strawberries. This is Elena. It's okay.*

I freeze in the middle of pulling back for another thrust, pushing all the way forward instead. Elena welcomes me in, until my head meets resistance and her entrance clings to the very bottom of my shaft. I'm safe here, buried deep inside her. I don't make a sound, just release a shuddering breath into her neck. My hips give a final, involuntary twitch, and the throbbing pressure within me releases. I flood Elena with everything I have. My heartbeat pounds through me and into her.

She pulls her face away from the pillow to gasp, "That's it, *Jefecita.* Fill your girl up right."

My girl? My girl. I pump the rest inside her with short jerks, grasping both thighs to keep her ass tucked tight into the cradle of my pelvis. I want her to have all of me, keep all of me. Elena's muscles start quivering again, and I release a quiet whimper into the nape of her neck. She's coming a fourth time. Coming with me.

Elena's pulses pull more out of me than I'd thought possible. I'm a fountain overflowing, a rain-swollen river spilling over its banks, so caught in the current that I collapse and pin her flat on her stomach. Even after I've emptied everything I have, she keeps squeezing, torturing me with the soft eddies of her aftershocks until I'm oversensitive.

Only afterward do I have the presence of mind to stroke Elena's hair away from the damp hollows of her throat, to kiss and nibble until her bronze, sweat-sheened shoulder is blotted with uneven patches of purple. She's breathing hard, little panting whines that vibrate beneath me. We lie there without speaking, connected by something more than our bodies—something that's new and fragile, but remains wrapped around us nonetheless.

At last, Elena gives a subtle shift of her hips. I take the hint and pull out, rolling off her back and onto my own so I can take the toy out. Elena's let me stay inside her for several minutes already, and she probably needs some breathing room, but I can't help feeling a slight sense of loss until she turns to face me and strokes my cheek.

"Holy fuck. Don't get a big head about it, but I've never had it that good."

A smile stretches across my face. "Yeah? Me neither."

Elena looks surprised, but undeniably pleased. "Well, technically, this body's never had it from anyone but me."

I snort. "You're not seriously suggesting you took my virginity that other time."

"I'm just saying..."

My laughter slips out, more relieved than I expect it to be.

"What? It was a joke. I don't really think—"

"No..." I take a breath to calm down. "No, it's not that. It's...is it stupid to be happy that Megan's never touched this body? Even on a technicality?"

Elena's grin fades. "No. Not stupid at all...so, you think I'm beautiful?"

"Of course. Did you mean it when you said you were..." I swallow. "When you said you were considering Barbados?"

Elena scoots closer, winding her arm around my waist and resting her forehead close to mine. "Yeah. Once we get through this, I'll come."

"Yeah you will."

"You're an ass."

We stay like that for a long time, our cheeks sharing the same pillow, until Elena's breathing evens out against my chin and my heart slows to a calm, steady thump to match hers. That's when I see a steady blink from the terminal on the other side of the room. I squint, burying my face a little further into Elena's hair.

"Did you leave that on? Thought it was in sleep mode."

Elena groans and throws her forearm over her eyes. "Not me. Turn it off. Light burns."

I untangle myself from Elena's embrace and shuffle over to the terminal, scratching the side of my head on the way. It's all I can do to stifle a yawn as I fumble along the haptic interface in search of the off button.

"Don't shut the terminal down," a familiar voice says, "unless your backup girlfriend wants her baby brother's brains all over the floor."

Rae D. Magdon

Friday, 06-18-65 20:07:24

I'M AWAKE IN AN instant. I activate the screen, and my heart freezes. I'm not surprised to see Megan's face, but the sight hits like a punch to the gut anyway. "What the fuck," I snarl, reaching for my scattered clothes. I do my best to tug them on without looking, never breaking eye contact with the screen.

Megan doesn't seem to care that I'm scrambling to get dressed. She's got the same superior look as always, a slight curling pout to her lips, pretty but empty blue eyes that send a chill right through me. "Let's get down to business. I have Jacobo, and I'm not giving him back until you give me Val's keys."

The image shifts angles, panning slightly to the left. There's Jacobo, sitting in a chair, hands and feet tied with a blindfold around his head. He's wearing the same dirty, oversized clothes I last saw him in.

A loud roar of rage fills the room. Elena leaps out of bed behind me, stalking over to the terminal. She's got the sheets wrapped around her and her brown eyes glow like burning coals. *"¡Pinche puta cabrona pendeja! ¡Te voy a matar, puta!"*

"English," Megan says placidly, not at all startled by the outburst.

"¡Hoy no tengo los huevos para tus faroles! Tell me where the fuck he is right now or I swear to Christ I'll shove my fist down your fucking throat and punch your worthless excuse for a shriveled-up heart out through your fucking bleached blonde asshole so I can crush it under my fucking boot."

Jacobo hears Elena's voice, lifting his head as far as the ropes will let him. *"¿Elena, eres tu?"*

"Soy yo, conejito. Ya voy—" She bares her teeth at Megan. "Where is he?"

"Enough shouting," Megan says, pressing her lips together in a subtle gesture of annoyance. "I'm sending coordinates. Be there in one hour with both keys. I'll know if they aren't on location. And don't bother showing up unless you're ready to deal. If you leave now, you'll make it right on time for the handoff."

The door to the bedroom bursts open. Rock, Cherry, Rami, and Doc come barreling in, but they stop short when they see Megan's face on the terminal.

"What the shit?"

"What's that bitch doing here?"

"Oh no."

Megan barely flicks her eyes in their direction. "One hour. Bring the keys. Hope you don't run into traffic." The connection cuts out, leaving a string of flashing red coordinates on the screen instead.

Elena flies over to her bag in the corner and grabs her LightningBolt. She's halfway out the door before Cherry catches her shoulder. "Clothes, *chaparrita.*"

"No fucking time," Elena snarls, yanking her arm away.

"Get dressed," I tell her. "You're benched for this one, Elena. You're too close to this."

I look at the rest of the crew for confirmation. They all stare back with grim resolve. We all know it's a trap. We don't have a plan, and there's no time to come up with one. But we also know we can't stay here. Elena's one of us now. That means Jacobo is ours too.

"The hell I am." Elena storms over to me, hair wild and eyes wilder, aiming the LightningBolt directly at my chest. "Just try and fucking stop me."

I grit my teeth. We don't have time for this. I turn away from Elena and grab my rifle from my bag, popping in a fresh magazine. "We're moving out."

The rest of the crew falls in line. We head out into the hallway and down to the shuttle in total silence. When we arrive on the bottom floor of the safe house, Jento is nowhere to be seen. Several of his hulking guards, however, have remained behind. We see them before they see us, but only because Rami stops Elena from charging forward without looking.

They're gearing up in the room where we first saw Jento playing cards, popping fresh mags into their weapons from the sound of things. I have a pretty good idea who those mags are for, and why. I doubt Megan snuck in here to snatch Jacobo on her own, which means Jento's probably a sellout, and these guys are here to take care of us.

According to my VIS-R, there are only five guards, which is almost a little offensive. I figured Jento would leave more than that, but whatever. At least I get to shoot somebody, since the traitorous bastard's not here. I hold up three fingers to the rest of the crew, counting down silently.

The guards aim their weapons when we come around the corner, but we're too fast for them. Rock punches the quickest draw straight into a wall before he can fire, and that stuns the others long enough for us to hold them at gunpoint. The nearest guard's eyes widen with fear as Elena stomps toward him, still draped in the bedsheet.

"Jento sold us out, didn't he?" she snarls, jabbing her pistol into his stomach. "Admit it! Megan couldn't have slipped in here unless he *let* her."

"I don't know who the fuck Megan is," the guard protests. He's got a foot and a half on Elena, but he seems terrified and I don't blame him. Elena looks ready to blast a hole through him.

"The bitch your asshole boss gave my brother to. I *know* he did it."

"Fine," the guard said. "Look, all I know is, Jento called the kid downstairs and put him in a shuttle with some of his guys. Then he bolted, and told us to shoot you."

I scoff in disgust. "You got played, idiot. Jento left you here to die. Only five guys? He just used you to buy him another minute or two."

"Which safe house did he run to?" Elena asks, her finger twitching on the trigger. When the guard doesn't answer immediately, she raises her voice to a shout. *"Which one?"*

"I don't know! I swear I don't—"

Elena fires her LightningBolt into his gut. A look of shock and pain crosses the guard's face, and I follow up with a round to his head. He collapses, spilling a fountain of blood onto the floor.

"No time to question him anyway," she says. "If he won't talk with a gun on him, he doesn't know, or won't break fast enough." Elena's still full of rage, I can tell, but she'll do whatever's necessary to save Jacobo first. "Get the fuck out of here," she says to the rest of the guards, brandishing her pistol. "And if you ever see Jento again, tell him he's a fucking dead man."

The guards apparently decide that dealing with our crew isn't worth a fight, especially for an employer who's cut and run. They hightail it out of the room without protest.

I watch to make sure they're really leaving, but Elena's already heading for the garage. I hurry to catch up. While the others climb into the Eagle, I stare into Elena's eyes. I know I won't be able to stop her from getting on the shuttle. She's half-crazy and wrapped in a wet, bloodstained sheet like some kind of avenging angel, but unless I knock her out and lock her in one of Jento's closets, she's going.

"Don't fuck this up," I murmur, grasping both of Elena's shoulders. "Jacobo needs your brain right now, not your feelings. Megan's light-years faster than you are, and she knows her shit. I'll do everything I can to give you an edge so you can take her down, but I need you present. Got it?"

Fire flares in Elena's gaze, but then she takes a shuddering breath and closes her eyes for just a second. "Yeah." Her voice is raw with pain. "Got it." She hops into the shuttle and I follow her in, closing the door behind me. A moment later, the Eagle takes off, speeding into the night.

"Rami, got the coordinates?"

"All plugged in, Sasha."

"What about Val?" Doc asks.

My eyes widen with panic. Last I saw Val, she was still plugged into the terminal.

"Got her," Cherry says. "Grabbed her on the way out." She plugs the databox into the Eagle's console, and Val's voice filters from the speakers.

"I'm aware of the situation. Estimated time of arrival: forty-seven minutes."

"Shit," Elena snarls. "Not fast enough. Rami, can't you give this bird any more juice?"

Rami's sigh is audible from the pilot's chair. "I'm going as fast as I can while keeping us safe."

"Jacobo isn't safe! Go faster."

I put a steadying hand on Elena's thigh. Her leg burns my palm through the bedsheet. "Let Rami handle the driving and go get dressed."

Elena glares at me, but sense seems to pierce her fog of anger. She climbs out of her seat, tossing aside the safety harness she didn't bother to fasten. I nod at a storage box bolted to the floor near the weapons rack. Elena opens it, drops the stained sheet, and starts pulling on some fatigues. No one else says anything. They all politely avert their eyes. I deliberately avoid thinking about how the only spares close to Elena's size are Megan's.

"So, what's the plan?" Doc asks, with a bit too much bravado in her voice. Her eyes are abnormally wide and her hands are shaking in her lap.

I don't have an answer. We can't plan for a situation we're walking into blind, and there's no way Megan hasn't laid a couple traps. But someone needs to say something, so I speak up with more confidence than I feel. "We go in, get Jacobo, get out as fast as possible. Bringing him home is priority number one. If it comes down to saving him or killing Megan, put him first. Everyone got that?"

Doc and Rock both nod.

Cherry says, "I got you, *jefa.*"

Elena looks over her shoulder at me. She can't force a smile, but she does give me a grateful nod. We spend the rest of the ride in silence. Doc continues fidgeting. Rock stares at nothing, his blocky face set in a scowl. Cherry busies herself by checking her utility belt, making sure the pouches are fully stocked with various explosives and their trigger mechanisms. Rami focuses on piloting the Eagle, and Val doesn't say anything.

Once she's finished dressing, Elena plops back in the seat next to me, her knee jumping beside mine, fists clenched. When I reach out to touch her hand with one of mine, she doesn't grasp back. She doesn't pull away, either.

It feels like ages before Val says, "Three minutes to arrival."

I look out the window. Everything is dark below us. The sprawling lights of Mexico City are gone, and all I can see is dark, flat water beneath the fuzzy horizon. "Where are we?"

"An unmarked island, somewhere off the coast of southern Mexico." Rami tilts the Eagle's nose down. If I squint, I can see the faint outline of a beach below us.

"According to my databanks, this is the location of a private Axys Generations artificial intelligence research facility," Val says.

Of course it is. That's Megan's area of expertise, after all. "Got anything else? Security level? Guard rotations? An intranet login?"

"I have no further data available at this time." Val sounds disappointed.

"Going ghost." Rami switches on the cloaking shields and circle down toward what should be the shore. On closer inspection, it's a paved landing strip. Glowing safety lights line both sides.

"According to the Eagle's sensors, we have just crossed an electromagnetic barrier," Val says. "It pinged my databox and your brainbox, Sasha."

I scowl. Guess this is Megan's way of making sure we have the goods with us, even if we have no intention of giving them up. I don't like the thought of keeping my brainbox on me, but I don't have much choice. Megan could have more checkpoints set up somewhere around here.

"Sneaky bitch," Cherry mutters. "See anywhere safe to land,

Rami?"

"There are turrets on the fence right below us, but they're inactive. I suppose Megan doesn't want to shoot us down before we bring her the keys. Just looking for a somewhat sheltered place to land off-runway so we can conceal the Eagle."

"Why bother hiding it?" Elena says. "Bitch already knows we're coming."

"You're not thinking, Nevares," I warn her. "The less resistance we encounter, the faster we get to Jacobo."

Cherry nods in agreement. "Plus, it would be just like her to disable the Eagle so we don't have a way off the island."

Doc shrugs. "That happens, we jack a corp shuttle."

Elena growls through clenched teeth. "I don't care what the fuck we do as long as we land this thing right now."

Rami touches down to the left of the airstrip, some distance from the ghostly lights of the runway. Before they even shut off the engine, Elena's up and moving, heading for the doors with her LightningBolt in hand.

I follow her closely so I can mutter in her ear. "Last chance," I tell her, even though I know it's the last thing she wants to hear. "You shouldn't come along for this. Your head isn't clear enough."

To my surprise, Elena isn't angry when she looks at me. Her brown eyes are burning, but they're full of desperation rather than rage. She's moved past fury and into fear. "I'm here, okay?" she says, in a voice even I can't possibly argue with. "So let's do this thing. I've got a fuckton of bullets and only a few minutes to shoot them."

Friday, 06-18-65 20:47:02

A LIGHT RAIN FALLS as we park the Eagle just inside the fence. I blink the droplets away, squinting for a better view. It's dark enough for my VIS-R's filters to kick in, but night vision doesn't offer much new information, just that it's made of concrete reinforced steel. I'd bet anything that's what the facility walls are made of, too.

"Look up," Doc says, gesturing with one hand. "There are the turrets Rami saw. Think she'll switch them on?"

"No." I pat the pocket of my tactical vest, where Val's databox is plugged in and my brainbox is tucked away. "If she tears us to pieces, she risks harming the keys. She'll have to kill us up close and personal." *And she'll probably like it that way. She's not much of a sadist, but she does love feeling superior.*

We head for the facility swiftly and silently, with Elena on point against my better judgment. I stay right behind to keep her in check. Rock moderates his long stride to walk beside me, and Cherry and Rami bring up the rear, with Doc sandwiched in the middle. It's only about a hundred yards, but the air around us is thick and tense. My lungs struggle to breathe it in despite the rapid thundering of my heart.

The building's walls are slightly thinner than the fence from what I can tell, but made of the same reinforced steel. There are no windows, and there's no outside lighting either. Everything around us is dark. If I didn't know better, I'd wonder if the place was abandoned. "See anything, Val?" I ask.

"Yes, Sasha. I have managed to access a local encrypted wireless network. The blueprints reveal three concentric rings, all on one floor. The point of connection between rings one and two is nearby, but the door from two to three is on the opposite side of the facility. Underneath ring three is a much smaller, reinforced sublevel with a separate intranet security system."

"That's where Jacobo and Megan are," Elena says. "I'd bet anything."

I don't disagree with her hunch. "How thick are the walls, Val?"

"Approximately three meters."

Rami looks at Cherry. "Sorry, babe. I think your cutter will overheat if we try to slice straight through to the middle."

"Goddamn it," Cherry grumbles. "I really gotta work on that heat sink."

"So we work with what we've got," I say. "We use the cutter until it fails, then use the doors."

"Any clue what's in the outer rings?" Cherry asks. "My VIS-R won't show anything."

Rami shakes their head. "Mine's jammed too. They must have a radio tower somewhere, because I can't pick up heat signatures at all."

"I am able to take readings through the building's network," Val says. "Initial alarms disabled—we are hidden from their scanners. There are heat signatures in the first ring, patrolling in groups of seven. There are none within thirty meters of your current location."

Elena twitches with impatience. "Then let's go already."

"Fine." I nod at Cherry. "Use the cutter. Let's make it quick and quiet."

"You got it, *jefa*." Cherry fires up the cutter and burns a Rock-sized hole into the wall. The smell of burning plasma fills my nose, and my chest tightens as I squeeze the grip of my rifle. Good thing I'm wearing gloves, because my hands are sweaty and shaking. Just knowing that Megan's near here gives me the creeps.

Once Cherry's finished, Rock aims his battering ram of a shoulder at the weak spot. He hits the wall with a grunt, and the chunk of concrete crumbles, giving way to his strength. Sirens begin blaring, and I hear the thud of boots hauling ass toward us.

By the time the first wave of guards reaches the hole, we're ready for them. The three in front are heavily armored, carrying body shields bigger than they are, but they aren't expecting Rock. Before they can form a wall, he picks one of them up, swinging him into a second guy and shattering both their shields against the steel.

The third guard decides he isn't being paid enough to deal with a giant and turns tail, but runs into four more members of his squad bringing up the rear. I have plenty of time to fire at the back of his head while Cherry, Rami, and Elena pick off the others. It's over in less than twenty seconds.

Elena's through the hole in a flash, leaping over the massacre so fast that I have to jog to keep up. We enter a curved, narrow hall that stretches in either direction. Two rows of pale ceiling lights give the place an eerie glow, and there are doors off to either side.

"Any other guards coming our way, Val?" I ask.

"The other guards in this ring are remaining in place despite the sirens. I detect more in the facility's second ring."

Elena clutches her pistol tighter. "What? Why aren't they coming?"

"I cannot speculate," Val says. "Continue left to evade."

We keep going at a run. The wail of sirens continues, and the hallway grows more and more oppressive, flashing an eerie red every three seconds. Nothing happens until we reach a reinforced steel door with a glowing orange security pad. "The way forward is through this door," Val says. "The hallway beyond leads to the second ring."

Doc turns to me. "Are we jacking in or using the cutter again?"

"No jacking until we have to." If it's a choice between overheating the cutter and sending Elena in, where she might find Megan waiting for her, I'll burn through Cherry's toy first. I'm not sending anyone on my crew except Val into the facility's intranet system until we have no other choice. "Cut it open, Cherry."

Cherry aims the plasma cutter at the edge of the door, but as soon as the narrow blue beam makes contact, the walls beside the door and the floor beneath our feet light up with hundreds of crisscrossing red wires. "Oh hell nope," Cherry says, with a note of alarm in her voice. "This shit is rigged to blow." The security pad turns red too, and a number flashes on its surface: *00:20:00.*

"Guess we found out why the guards let us get to the door," Doc says. "They were guiding us right into a trap." Despite her attempt at humor, there's real fear in her eyes.

"Fuck," Cherry hisses. "This is for me."

I look at her in confusion. "What are you talking about?"

Cherry's face is grim. "Megan. You didn't think she'd just let us waltz in here, did you? She's trying to separate us. You know, divide and conquer, all that shit. She knows I can defuse this, but it means my ass is stuck here while I do."

"We're almost out of time," Elena says, looking halfway to panic. "We can't stay here."

"Don't expect you to, *chaparrita*." Cherry tosses the plasma cutter to me. "But this son of a bitch is already triggered, so I need to make sure we don't get blown to high heaven. Go get your *hermanito*. I'll catch up."

"Cherry..." Rami and I say at the same time.

"*Vete, jefa.* I got this." Cherry grabs Rami's shoulders, pulling them in for a short, hard kiss. She brushes a lock of dark hair away from their face, communicating something without words.

"What if more guards come?" Rami says.

Cherry grins, blinking rapidly. "You don't think I carry all those cherry bombs in my kit just for show, do you? Now let me do my job." She drops to the floor, studying the wires with a cone of yellow light from her VIS-R.

I don't want to leave. Cherry will be vulnerable all on her own, but we don't have much of a choice. I scan the numbers with my VIS-R and they show up in the corner of my eye, ticking down the seconds until the whole place blows.

00:19:13
00:19:12
00:19:11

"Be careful," I tell Cherry. "Keep us in the loop on your progress."

"Yeah," she says without looking at me. Her face is fixed in concentration as she follows the wires with her scanner, sweat glistening around her hairline. "Mess 'em up, guys."

I aim the plasma cutter at the edges of the door and press the button. Just as Rami predicted, it gets about halfway through before a few sparks pop in my face. Then the blue light dims out, leaving behind a thin trail of smoke. Damn it. I was hoping it'd hold out a bit longer. "Rock, is the door weak enough for you to get?"

Rock gives the door a push. There's some resistance, then an awful grating noise as it breaks away from the wall and crashes to the ground. We hurry through, Elena at the front of the pack.

"You really think Cherry can defuse that thing?" Doc asks no one in particular.

Val answers. "Based on the variables I have observed, I calculate her probability of success at 21.07 percent, rounded up. However, there are three heat signatures coming in your direction, and eighteen more beyond at various points along the hall."

"Shit." Dealing with that many guards is going to take way longer than nineteen minutes. We need to find the quickest path to the next ring, preferably one that leads us past as few guards as possible? "Which way is the door?"

"To the left, one third of the way around the ring's circumference, in the direction with more heat signatures."

We hurry down the curved hall. The lighting is better in this ring, and the sirens are a little fainter. The passage is wider too, big enough for seven security guards in AxysGen uniforms to round the corner in two rows and notice us. The first three put their bodyshields together to form a wall, and the other four duck behind, marching on us in formation.

Rock places himself in front of us, taking the first few shots to his chest without even a flinch. The guards hesitate for a hair of a second, obviously confused that their rounds didn't work, and that's all Rock needs. He grabs the middle guard and lifts him off the ground, breaking his neck with a swift snap.

Once their formation's broken, it's easy to pick them off. I take out the second shield-bearer with a shot to the top sliver of his head. His shield's only a few centimeters too low, but it's enough. Rami vanishes from sight, reappearing behind the last one and firing into the back of his skull. Elena gets off a shot from around Rock's side, winging an unshielded guard in the gut, but Doc gets the highest numbers. She hits the remaining three with biogrenades, and we all retreat a couple meters while they try to pull the sticky blue orbs off their armor. There's a muffled splat when they explode. I wince as chunks of gooey pink flesh drip down the walls.

Elena steps through the mess without a hint of squeamishness, leaving bloody bootprints behind. "Fuck, we don't have time for this! These guys are slowing us down."

"What about circling back and getting to the door that way?" Rami asks.

"There are several heat signature groupings in that direction as well," Val informs us. "You would have to engage in more time-consuming and dangerous combat."

Rami activates their VIS-R again. "There might be another way. See?" I follow their gaze, my own scanner picking up what they're seeing. Set into the middle of the ceiling is a vent shaft situated between two lights, wide enough for a small person to fit their shoulders through.

Doc squints at it uncertainly. "Rock definitely isn't fitting through that."

"He doesn't have to. I do."

"This vent is connected to a security hub," Val says. "If Rami can infiltrate the room successfully, they could access the guards' comm line and attempt to impersonate their commander."

"What the fucking shit?" Cherry's voice crackles over the comm. She's been quiet up 'til now, probably concentrating on defusing the bomb, but she sounds pissed. *"Rami, don't you fucking dare."*

"I'll be fine," Rami says. "The bomb was for you. This one's mine."

"Rami, I swear to God I'll—"

Rami mutes Cherry's comm connection. The silence is somehow louder than Cherry's cursing. "I'll unmute her in a minute once she gets that out of her system."

I'm torn, but the only other option is to keep shooting our way through guards and waste time we don't have. "Give Rami a boost," I tell Rock.

Rock scoops Rami into his massive arms and hauls them up to stand on his shoulders. "Keep heading for the door," they say, looking down at me with worry in their eyes. "I'll clear as many of them out of your way as I can. Sasha..."

I give what I hope is a reassuring nod. "It's okay, Rami. We'll be fine. Be careful."

Rami takes a shaking breath, then scrambles up into the ventilation shaft. Once they disappear from sight, my comm crackles to life. "I'm in. Heading for the hub now."

"Stay in contact," I say, starting down the hall again at a fast clip.

Rami laughs. "No Code 900 this time?"

"Why? They already know we're here."

Doc snorts, but Elena doesn't even seem to hear me. She's a quivering like a pointer on a scent. Once we take the next bend, Rami's voice filters through the comm again, little more than a whisper. "I'm in. One guard up here..." There's a thud, then the sound of something heavy hitting the floor. "Make that zero guards. Okay, what's your name? Hmm."

There's another pause, and then a loud male voice comes over the speaker: *"This is Security Chief Stanley. Breach in Sector One. I repeat, we have a security breach in Sector One. All available squads report immediately."*

I hear the sound of drumming boots nearby, but they seem to be growing fainter. My suspicions are confirmed when Val says, "There are no more heat signatures ahead, and Rami has opened the next door. You are clear to proceed."

We all break into a run.

"Thanks, Rami," I pant. "Can you make it back to us?"

"Sure thing. Let me..." I hear the whirring sound of a haptic interface, and then the shrill buzzing of an alarm. "Oh no."

"What's wrong?"

"I...I think I'm stuck in here."

I stop short and turn around. "We're coming back."

"Don't. Megan planned it this way. She knew I'd sneak in here and get trapped. That bitch."

I do a double take. It's the first time Rami's sworn since I can remember. "Find a place to hide and hunker down, okay?" I wait for a response, but there isn't one. "Rami?" Still nothing. "Come in, Rami."

"Something is blocking all remote comm links," Val says. "I am unable to connect to Rami's frequency."

"What about Cherry?

"I am unable to reach her as well."

"Shit." My chest clenches.

"Sasha," Elena says with rising volume. Her eyes dart frantically between me and the hall. "It's forward or nothing."

I know she's right. I just don't want to admit it.

It takes all the willpower I have to move. My legs don't want to obey. This is something I have little to no experience with. We occasionally split up on purpose, but in all the missions I've run, all the ops I've completed, I've never had to leave a crewmember behind in an unknown situation. I'm always the first one into every new room and the last one out the door. The one making sure everybody on my crew makes it through safe. This feels all wrong.

They're doing their jobs, Sasha. Because they love you. You've died for them, and they're willing to die for you too.

But...I don't want them to die. It's my job to make sure they don't die.

Not your call. You either take the time they're buying and hurry, or you waste it and lose everything.

I can't keep arguing with myself, because we arrive at the door leading into the third ring. Thanks to Rami, the pressure pad is already green. I pop a fresh magazine into my rifle, then open it. An ocean of light washes out to greet me, and I squint until the dimmer mods in my eyes kick in

When they do, my blood freezes. The glare is coming from a pair of enormous yellow eyes—eyes that are attached to a ten-meter tall mech with arms the size of a person. I take a step back, but it's too late. The room gets even brighter as, one by one, a dozen more pairs of yellow lights blink on.

Friday, 06-18-65 20:57:02

"SHIT SHIT SHIT!"

ELENA fires her LightningBolt, but the rounds bounce harmlessly off the mech's chestplate. Damn. Not only is it enormous, it's plasma resistant too, all thick metal plating and studded greaves. Inside its built-in VIS-R, its scanners rake across us like tongues of flame. The giant mech raises its right arm, and a red glow begins to build at the other end of a long barrel, like something trying to charge. It's not just a minigun. It's a giant cannon.

I look for cover, but the only protection nearby is a large stack of metal crates, four high and two deep. It'll have to do. I dive for them, with the others right on my heels. Behind us, the door hisses shut.

"Val, can you open it?"

A pause, and then, "I cannot. Someone has just removed me from the wireless security network."

Damn it. Megan again.

"Sasha?" Doc says, her voice rising with fear.

"Look," Elena says, pointing at the opposite side of the room. There's an elevator at the far wall, but our path is blocked by a dozen other mechs. They're smaller than the giant, each about three meters tall, but that's little comfort as they open fire with their miniguns. The tower of crates weakens under the assault, bits of shrapnel flying everywhere. They've blasted through the front half of our cover, and the second row of crates won't last much longer.

I look for a safer location, but a flash of red blots out my vision. The rattle of gunfire is swallowed by a loud, high-pitched whir. The giant cannon has finished charging. I drop to the ground, throwing my arms over my head. A loud boom shakes the room, and then, suddenly, everything goes silent. When I risk looking up, the rest of the crates are demolished, and there's a smoking crater two meters deep in the wall behind us.

For a second, I think I'm dead, but we've held out just long enough. The noise fades as the smaller mechs stop shooting to cool down their miniguns. But that doesn't prevent them from lumbering toward us. I whip around, searching desperately for fresh cover. Aside from more crates, there isn't much. All I can see are a few flimsy-looking workstations and raised one-person platforms, probably used to service the mechs. There's nothing that'll hold against the mechs' barrage for long, let alone the cannon.

"Rock!"

I hear Doc scream and whip my head around. Rock has charged forward and grabbed the mech's cannon, tilting it up toward the ceiling. The red light pulses as the mech fires again, sending concrete dust showering down on us. Rock jerks the mech's arm, trying to rip it off, but it's not giving. Strong as he is, he can't tear through solid titanium.

The crates seem to be our best option. I retreat behind the nearest stack, firing my rifle to buy Doc and Elena some time to follow me. My rounds barely dent the mechs' armor. They continue marching toward us, while Rock does battle with their big brother. It's pushing him back inch by inch, firing booming shots over his shoulder that leave more craters in the wall. My ears ring with the force, and my vision wavers.

I try to calm down and think, but everything's static in my head. I look toward Rock, trying to think of a plan to help him, but the smaller mechs start firing again. I pull back behind the crates, but not quite fast enough. The edge of a round clips my shoulder, just outside the protection of my tactical vest. Something hot and wet leaks down my arm, seeping through my sleeve.

"Doc," Elena shouts, crouching by my side. "I need a NervPac over here. Sasha's hit."

Doc reaches into her bag and pulls out a fresh patch, tearing my shredded sleeve away to slap it on my arm. "Hold it together, Sasha. We gotta save Rock!"

Rock. He's still out there, and even his built-in body armor won't hold up against a giant cannon and a bunch of miniguns for long. "We should've waited for Cherry," I say as the blissful numbness floods through my arm, allowing me to gather my thoughts. "She's the one who got us out of this last time. Nothing can stop these things but a big explosion."

Doc's blue eyes widen with excitement behind her VIS-R. "Sasha, I have biogrenades!"

"They don't work on tech," Elena says.

"They will if we paint our targets first," Doc says, glancing at my arm.

That's when it clicks. "Will that actually work?"

"Yes," Val says through the comm. She'd been keeping quiet before, just highlighting targets on my VIS-R, but now she offers an opinion. "Once they are thrown, biogrenades explode upon contact with the first organic matter they touch. Blood is organic matter." She hesitates. "But so are all of you."

I know what I have to do. "You throw," I tell Doc and Elena. "Just give me enough time to get out of the way first." I rip the NervPac off my wound before it stops the bleeding, slinging my rifle across my back. Then I wait, praying the miniguns will overheat again before the last of the crates are in pieces.

When the rattle of gunfire stops, I seize my chance. I burst out from behind the remnants of our cover, sprinting toward the mechs at full speed. They point their arms at me, but the guns are still glowing red-hot, and nothing comes out of the barrels.

"I am highlighting a target for you, Sasha," Val says in my ear. "If it explodes, it will cause significant collateral damage." She links back up with my VIS-R's targeting system, and one of the mechs flashes yellow. I sprint right at the mech she's highlighted, gritting my teeth and praying I'll make it before the rest of them shoot me full of holes.

Once I'm close enough, I slap my palm against its plating, smearing a red handprint onto its midsection. "Doc, go!"

"Throwing!" Doc hollers.

I dive out of the way and hit the ground in a roll, stopping behind one of the repair station platforms. I hear a boom, and then the screech of metal being ripped apart and risk a glance over my shoulder. Doc's biogrenades have blown the mech and two others nearby into a bunch of twisted shrapnel.

"Over here!" Elena shouts from somewhere to my right. She's left Doc behind, sprinting around to slap mechs with a bloodied left hand. Stubborn idiot. She must have cut it herself. More blinking blue orbs fly through the air, sticking to the blood on the mechs' bodies. They explode on contact, sending bits and pieces of wire and metal in every direction.

"Sasha," Doc yells from cover, "get to Rock!"

Rock is off to my left with his back braced to the wall. His muscles are stretched taut like steel cables and steam hisses from his massive arms and legs. But the mech is still firing over his shoulder, and the steel behind him is burnt an ashy black.

I run at full speed, slapping the giant mech's leg with my bloody hand. Its head does a 180-degree turn, and its face screen flashes. Rock falters just a little, and the mech finally manages to wrench its arm free from his grip. It swivels its giant body, leveling its cannon straight at me.

"Duck!"

I hit the deck as more flashing blue biogrenades fly through the air, barely missing my head. They stick to the mech's plating, and I curl into a protective ball.

The explosion shakes the entire room. A loud metallic groan drowns out everything else, then dissolves into a crackling, fizzy hiss. When I open my eyes, the giant mech is in pieces. I feel a momentary swell of triumph, but then Doc streaks past me in a blur, shouting Rock's name. As I clamber to my feet, my stomach drops.

Rock is lying on the ground, surrounded by the mech's sparking remains and a spreading pool of blood. His skin has been burned off in multiple places, showing the mechanics underneath, but that's not what terrifies me. A huge piece of shrapnel is embedded in the wall behind him, and on the floor underneath is Rock's arm, completely severed from his body. This looks bad. *Really* bad.

Doc crouches beside him, pulling NervPacs and StimPacs out of her bag. "Rock, stay with me. Stay with me, okay? I'm gonna stop the bleeding."

Rock's blue eyes are open but glassy, staring at nothing in particular. He struggles to focus on our faces, but after another second, they slip shut. My throat closes up, and my own eyes water.

I put my hand on Doc's shoulder, but she jerks away. "Go, Sasha," she says without looking back at me. Her voice is tight, but she's trying her hardest to sound calm. "The mech was Rock's. This is...this one's mine."

Somehow, Megan planned this. I'm sure of it. Doc's only real weapons are her sniper rifle and biogrenades. Sealed in a room with a bunch of mechs, without Cherry or Rami to help, and with Rock's life in danger, she would have been forced to find a way to use them. It would be easy for one of us to get hit by mistake, or get caught in an explosion.

"This isn't your fault," I tell her, but Doc doesn't respond. She's in medic mode, applying a tourniquet to the stump where Rock's arm used to be. The blood pooling beneath him has slowed, but his giant chest barely moves as he breathes.

"Technically," Val says softly, "it is my fault. We are here because Megan wishes to obtain my source code. I am the reason Jacobo was kidnapped, Rami and Cherry are gone, and Rock is injured."

"Shut up, all of you!" Elena's voice trembles with emotion and her eyes are bright and hard. "This is *Megan's* fault, you hear me? It's that fucking crazy bitch's fault and no one else's. And we're gonna make her pay for it."

Val doesn't respond, but somehow, without even seeing her avatar, I sense that her silence is heavy with guilt. We have to go after Megan. I know it's our only option, but the mere thought of leaving Rock feels like someone ripping my heart straight out of my chest.

"Hang in there, big guy," I rasp, swallowing around the lump in my throat. "We'll be back, okay? I promise."

"We'll be here," Doc says. She removes a rolled-up bag from her belt and shakes it out, putting Rock's severed arm inside and activating the vacuum seal with the press of a button. The bag deflates, molding to the shape of the arm itself, and a thin layer of liquid blue coolant spreads between the layers of extra-strong plastic.

"I know you will. But Doc...if you can't save him, take this and run." I remove my brainbox from my pocket and set it by Doc's knee. She's busy with the arm, and her hands are covered in blood, but she meets my eyes briefly. "I want you to live, kid. No matter what. Stay alive, and make sure Megan doesn't get the key."

Doc bites her lip, then nods and goes back to work on Rock. Hopefully, she'll listen to me for once. I turn to Elena and catch her swiping her sleeve across her eyes.

"Come on."

The two of us jog to the elevator, and Elena touches the sensor with her hand, connecting wirelessly before I can stop her. It flashes green a moment later. "Wasn't locked," she says, returning to her body almost instantly.

We share a look. Megan must want us to keep going. In her mind, we're delivering Val up on a platter—without backup. With four of our other crewmembers missing or trapped or injured or...no. Rock isn't dead. Neither is Jacobo, but he will be if we don't move our asses. We take the lift down to the sublevel below. It's a short ride, and the doors open to reveal an empty corridor. The only exit is another door five meters in front of us. The pressure pad outside is red.

"Val, you still with us?" I ask aloud.

"Yes. I was...grieving."

Fear shoots through me. "What do you mean?"

"I calculate Rock's probability of survival at 8.3 percent."

My stomach lurches. I don't want to know or think about the odds.

"He's not dead yet," Elena says.

"No, he is not. 8.3 percent is a positive number." Val pauses. "I still cannot regain wireless access to the intranet system, but the scanners on Sasha's VIS-R are picking up a living biosignature in the room beyond this door. It is consistent with my records of Jacobo's profile."

"When did you profile him?" Elena asks, with some heat.

"I save a profile of every person I interact with, but that is irrelevant to this situation. There are no other organic readings from inside this room or anywhere else. If you plug me in, I will attempt to open the door."

Elena and I look at each other. I can read her mind through her watery brown eyes. We've left Cherry, Rami, and Doc behind, and watched Rock go down. We're not going to lose another member of our crew. Not if we can help it.

"Not alone you won't," Elena says, with her usual frustrating, endearing stubbornness.

I nod. "Not alone."

"Your physical bodies should be relatively safe. We are clear of the signal interrupters, and there are no potential threats on my scanners." Even without seeing Val's avatar, I can tell she's hesitant. The rest goes unsaid—*You will be safe out here. You won't in there.*

I brace myself. "We're here to get Jacobo back, but I'll go to hell before I let them take you, Val. You're one of us."

"Thank you, Sasha. Please pass me to Elena."

I hand Elena the box. "Elena, I..." There are hundreds of words unsaid between us, none of them quite right. I want to tell her how afraid I am. How I'm not ready to lose her. How she makes me feel like I've found something I didn't know I was missing. But nothing comes out except, "You ready for this?"

"Yeah." Elena exhales a slow stream of air. "If I get fried, get Jacobo out of here safe, okay? And the others."

"I will." I can't make that promise, but it's what Elena needs to hear right now.

Elena plugs Val in behind her ear, then hooks into the port. Just before her eyes go blank, I take her hand in mine and lace our fingers together. I squeeze once, then touch the orange panel with my other palm.

Friday, 06-18-65 21:00:00

NETWORK: AG 21232 . 86734
Connection established
welcome: user волчица-воин

I'M STANDING ON THE battlements of a castle. Its stones are a dark, rain-spattered grey, and the sky above is even darker. The only illumination comes from flashes of forked red lightning that splinter the horizon and cast an unsettling light over the charred black landscape below. Everything beyond the walls we're standing on has been burnt to ash.

The intranet system has decided to interpret my base programs as a suit of bright white armor. Helmet, pauldrons, gauntlets, greaves, the whole bit. It would be badass if I wasn't walking into a deathtrap. Elena and Val are with me—Elena in silver armor even fancier than mine, Val in a corseted purple dress the same color as her avatar's favorite blazer. The three of us instinctively draw closer. A request pops up on the visor of my helmet.

user escudoespiga is offering [[filename redacted]] for download: accept / deny

I select accept. A horizontal blue bar fills up, and a new icon appears on my taskbar: a circle with silver dots in the middle. When I run the program, a shield matching Elena's appears on my forearm, large enough to cover my torso.

"It's not hard to use," Elena says. "Duck and cover." She lifts her shield, and nine sharp metal spikes spring out from its rounded surface. "Or charge and stab."

I concentrate, and my shield grows spikes too. Impressive. I see why Elena likes to run around with this program all the time. I turn to Val, who's scanning the castle's blank walls with a silvery sheen to her eyes. She's definitely got an impressive aesthetic going on. "Picking anything up?"

Val's eyes return to normal. "No, although I doubt we are alone. Megan designed my scanning programs herself. She knows how to exploit their weaknesses."

A chill runs through me. Val's weaknesses aren't the only ones Megan knows how to exploit. She's stripped away all the other members of my crew by doing exactly that. "Do we go in?" I ask.

Elena sighs. "Have to." She walks along the battlement to the nearest corner, where a wooden door leads into one of the towers. It swings open as we approach. My stomach bubbles, but Elena rolls her eyes. "If your ex designed this, she's a dramatic-ass hoe. What's with all the fucking theatrics?"

Val's face shows wry amusement. "If I were to design a security system, I might consider implementing an amusing theme as well."

"Well, I'm not fucking amused. Sadistic bitch."

"I believe this would be more accurately described as a manifestation of megalomaniacal tendencies—"

I shush the both of them and step into the tower.

"Sasha, wait." I turn back to see Elena staring at me. "Let me go first."

I'm touched by the gesture. I've always been at the front, taking the big hits, but for once, it's nice to have someone else care enough to watch out for me. "Okay."

We start down the stairs, Elena first, Val in the middle, me at the back.

The stairs go on for several stories, winding in a dizzying spiral. I walk carefully in case any of the steps decide to disappear on me. It pisses me off to think that Megan designed this egotistical deathtrap, and I'm just walking right in. But it's not like we have many other options.

We arrive at the bottom of the stairwell, and the door swings open to reveal a narrow stone corridor lined with torches. The stones in the walls and floor are perfect squares, each one outlined in glowing red like the lightning outside. When Elena takes a step, some of the torches blink out, illuminating a narrow path forward.

I look to Elena for guidance. "Follow, or bust through the wall to find another way?"

Elena clenches her jaw. "Keep going." She doesn't have to say why. We all know we're on borrowed time already.

We walk along the row of lights until we reach a set of enormous double doors barred with black iron. The cracks in the wood glow red as well, but there's no security pad. That doesn't stop Elena. She charges the door, slamming into it with a grunt. The spikes in her shield thud into its surface, but instead of sticking there, cracks spread out from the points of impact. The doors shatter in eerie silence, then disappear into nothing.

The room beyond is huge. Enormous stained-glass windows line its walls, and glittering chandeliers hang from the vaulted ceiling. Despite all the glitzy details, there's still an aura of darkness about the place. A long red carpet cuts through the middle of the room, leading up a set of steps onto a dais. On the dais is a throne, and sitting on the throne is Megan.

She's dressed in blue, as usual, but this time, she isn't wearing a hood. Instead, she's chosen a fancy velvet dress. Her long blonde hair cascades down her shoulder, and a mantle of white fur is draped about her shoulders. A shiver runs down my spine as she stands up. Seeing her in person, even just in virtual space, is far, far worse than seeing her on a screen.

"Sasha, I'm surprised you took so lo—"

Megan doesn't get to finish. Elena charges the dais, a blurry streak of brown and silver. She screeches to a stop near the throne, but Megan's already gone. She's vanished completely.

I whip my head around, but there's no sign of her. My stomach roils with fear, and hard as I try, I can't channel it into focus. Megan has top-of-the-line self-coded cloaking programs, such good ones that Elena's left looking around in confusion too.

"I wouldn't do that again," Megan says, from our left this time. She's standing before one of the stained-glass windows, and it casts eerie patterns of light onto her blonde hair. "I'm running self-modded Platinum, remember? Based on a prototype version that hasn't even been released yet. I can see you coming a mile away."

Elena grits her teeth and scowls at Megan from beneath her visor. "Whatever, bitch." She charges, but Megan poofs out of existence, reappearing on the dais. Elena's left panting by the windows, and Megan doesn't have a drop of sweat on her.

I know I won't be able to keep up with either of them at that speed, but I can't just stand here. I raise my shield and charge anyway. The room blurs all around me, but when I arrive on the dais, Megan is gone again. I need another strategy, and fast.

"Sasha," Val says urgently, "above you."

I look up. Megan's hovering several meters in the air, holding a thin black staff in her hand. A red crystal glows at its tip, the same color as the cracks in this world. "Bye, Sasha. Dead fixes stupid, I guess, assuming it sticks this time." I raise my shield, but Megan doesn't fire at me. Instead, she aims her staff at Val.

I rush to intervene, but Val doesn't need my help. She waves her hand, and a pattern of glowing green diamonds appears in front of her. Megan's Puls.wav bounces off the shielding program, hitting one of the stone walls and disappearing with a black hiss.

After that, everything erupts at once. I fire off several Puls.wavs of my own, but Megan dodges effortlessly. Elena taps the heels of her boots, and fire spurts from their soles, propelling her off the ground. Megan winks out of range and reappears halfway across the room, avoiding a Puls.wav from Val and returning fire with her staff. I move as fast as I can, but with my lower-grade gear and inexperience, I can't keep up with this fight. Elena manages, though—barely. She blocks Megan's Puls.wav with her shield, deflecting it right back at her.

"Val," Elena hollers from the air, "she's too fast! Think you can slow her down?"

Val spreads her hands, and her diamond-patterned shield grows larger, swelling to fill the room. Megan slows down above me in mid-flight, and I realize what Val's doing. She's flooding Megan with junk code, pushing the limits of her hardware and forcing her programs to filter through all the extra data.

For the first time, the look of calm superiority on Megan's face twists into anger. She dives right, dodging another Puls.wav from me as well as Elena's next shield charge. She passes in front of a stained-glass window, and a flash of lightning from outside casts her into silhouette. "I think it's time for you to meet my latest project."

A mechanical roar fills the room, rattling through my bones. I whirl and raise my shield in time to see a massive winged shadow swoop down outside the window, blotting out the red and black sky. I barely get to see what it is before the huge beast bursts through the stained glass, sending a shower of shards across the floor. It's colossal enough to fill the room almost to the ceiling.

I freeze, limbs locked up with fear. It's a dragon. A huge fucking dragon with blood-red scales and glowing yellow eyes. The stone floor shudders under its clawed feet as it lands, and it lets out a shriek that splinters the rest of the windows, inviting the storm inside.

My fight or flight instincts finally kick in. I dive forward, hitting the ground to avoid a tremendous column of fire. My only saving grace is Elena's shield, which I hold over my head like an umbrella against a hurricane. Once the flames fade, I look up. Elena is frozen in midair, and behind her silver visor, she looks utterly terrified. Shit. She hates fire. This has to be a nightmare for her.

"Elena, move!"

No response. She's paralyzed with fear.

Before I can think of anything to do, the dragon raises its spiked tail and swipes, sending Elena crashing to the floor. I sprint to catch her, desperation throbbing through my legs. Elena doesn't quite land in my arms, but my body softens her fall. Unfortunately, that leaves us both sprawled on the ground. The dragon rears back, and I can see the start of a sun growing inside its huge, toothy jaws. It's a terrifyingly familiar shade of red—a Puls.wav so huge it's bright enough to burn my eyes.

Elena finally lurches into motion at the last second, and we roll away from each other. A column of fire hits where we were lying moments before, turning the stone floor hot red. I clamber up as soon as I can. Shit, no. I'm not going down like this. Not while Elena and Val need me. I look around for Megan—stopping her will probably stop whatever monstrous program this is—but she's vanished again. Typical. She never does her own dirty work.

The dragon screams, rearing back on its hind legs for another strike. Before it can charge us, another gigantic shape hurtles out of nowhere, colliding with its side. It happens so fast that it takes me a moment to understand. A second dragon with violet scales has charged the red beast, knocking it partway through the wall. For a moment, all I can feel is shock and confusion, but then I realize that the new dragon's hide is the exact same color as Val's dress. I feel a sudden surge of hope. If anyone can stop this thing, it's her.

Beside me, Elena cheers. "Fuck shit up, Val!" She's shaking badly, but she's back on her feet. Maybe having fire on our side for a change makes her feel safer.

"This is another FRAI." the Val-dragon says in surprise and alarm. "It includes my base code, but fewer self-modifications."

"And fewer restrictions." Megan reappears beside the red dragon as it lurches out of the wall, shaking off chunks of broken stone. Her mouth is quirked in a smug smile, and her voice is worse. "I never should have used Sasha's memories to shape your core personality, but I thought it meant you would never turn against me. God knows she couldn't."

"Bitch, you *thought*." Fury blazes through me, and my gauntlets glow red as I prepare another Puls.wav. I shoot, but Megan's too fast. She teleports well out of range.

The red dragon squares off with Val, tail lashing in anger. It lunges at her, but Val stands her ground. They topple to the floor, a thrashing tangle of wings and scaly limbs. It almost looks like two alley cats caught in a brawl, only a hundred times huger and more terrifying.

They don't stay on the ground for long. Val manages to break free and takes off, streaking out through the hole in the wall. The red dragon soars out after her, leaving Elena and me to deal with Megan. We round on her and raise our shields, rushing her together.

Megan takes to the air immediately, but Elena's right there with her, flying with her flame-powered boots. I flick through my programs, looking for something useful. Nothing, nothing...jetpack! The minute I select the program, the straps appear on my shoulders, and I shoot up into the air to give Elena some support.

I've barely taken off when there's a sharp crack followed by a heavy shower of stone. The ceiling is splitting open, and it's only thanks to Elena pushing me out of the way that I avoid a chandelier hurtling to the floor. Megan's dragon is tangled together with Val as they crash through the new hole and hit the floor, rolling across small mountains of stone and glass.

It looks like Val's having some trouble. She's pretty evenly matched with this copycat AI, but that's terrifying in itself: nothing I've ever met could stand up to Val in cyberspace. She pins it on its back, but it breathes a plume of fire up at her, and she has to reel back, hissing.

As terrifying as the dragon is, Megan's the real threat here. I look everywhere, but she's gone again, hiding like the coward she is. Then, suddenly, she's not. She's everywhere at once, at least thirty identical copies of her all around the room.

"You're wasting my time," the legion of Megans says. They all raise their staffs, and a swarm of narrow red beams shoots at me all at once. I zoom upward, barely twisting away from one of the Puls.wavs and running straight into another. Luckily, my shield holds.

Three meters below me, Elena does her best to reflect the Puls.wavs down and away. Some of them make Megan's doppels explode in a shower of sparks, leaving only empty air behind. But we still haven't found the real Megan—if she's even here. But I'm not going to stop until I do. She was willing to let me die six times. If I have to kill her thirty different times, I will.

I use every bit of my gear's processing power as I duck and weave, deflecting Megan's beams and firing off shots when I can. I get in some lucky hits on a few doppels, but Elena takes out most of them, flashing around the room like lightning and skewering them with the spikes of her shield. The Megans disappear in sprays of sparks a split second later.

Around us, the room quakes. Val and Megan's AI launch into the air again, locked in a contest of strength. For a moment, it looks like Val has the upper hand, but then the red dragon locks its jaws around her throat, slamming her into one of the remaining walls. Val roars in pain, and the FRAI hisses in triumph.

I aim for its head, shooting off several Puls.wavs. They bounce harmlessly off the dragon's scales, but the attack is annoying enough to get its attention. It turns toward me, opening its gigantic jaws. While it's distracted, Val kicks out with her hind legs, raking her claws along its belly. The red dragon screams. It lets Val go and staggers back, spilling streams of code onto the floor.

Val surges upright, stalking forward as the dragon recoils in fear. It snaps its teeth at her, but she pushes it over, pinning it to the ground with both front feet on its chest. She's got this. Now, if we could just find Megan.

Right as Val is about to strike the finishing blow, she freezes. Her avatar starts to waver, patches of her flickering unevenly like pixelated puzzle pieces that don't quite fit right. Fear fills her huge yellow eyes, and then she poofs out of existence. No, not quite. Her human avatar reappears crumpled on the floor, limp and unmoving.

"Val!" Elena cries, but there's no answer.

The red dragon drags itself up, stretching its wings, but it doesn't go after Val. Instead, it turns on me, belching out a spiraling ball of flame. I try to dodge, but the blast of heat is too wide to outrun. I'm just not fast enough.

"No!"

Elena streaks between me and the fireball, a shooting star of silver. She holds her position in midair, pushing back against the force of the dragon's breath with her boots on full blast. Her shield triples in size, enough to cover both our bodies. Flames lick around its sides, but don't break through. "Go," Elena gasps, sweat pouring down her face. She's fighting the dragon's inferno with all her strength, but she's sliding backwards, trembling with effort. "I've got you."

I don't want to go. Elena looks so small, wreathed in fire and fighting a dragon twenty times her size. All she has to protect her are some thin lines of code. But my chest swells with emotion, because she's doing it for me. Someone cares enough to face the fires of a dragon to keep me safe.

While the dragon is focused on Elena, I swoop beneath its stomach. The stream of red code has dried up, but Val's claws have left deep gouges in its scaly hide. That's enough. I gather all my strength and drive upward with my shield, giving my jetpack all the juice I have. As I hurtle toward the beast's belly, my copy of Elena's shield responds. It shrinks, growing to about the side of my hand. The grip becomes a pommel, and the spikes extend, merging together into a shining silver blade. If Elena's my shield, I can be her sword.

There's a moment of resistance as the point hits one of the dragon's wounds, and then a blinding surge of light fills the room. The dragon roars in agony, flickering in and out of my field of vision. Fresh rivers of binary code flow around me and down to the floor, but they vanish as rapidly as they're spilling. Gritting my teeth, I drive my blade deeper. With one more scream, the dragon disappears, splintering into shafts of forked lightning before vanishing completely.

I face Elena, smiling in triumph, but she isn't looking at me. She's hovering in midair, staring over my shoulder. When I turn around, I see that Megan has reappeared. She's got Val enclosed in a bubble of yellow code pouring from the tip of her staff. Val is awake, much to my relief, but she doesn't seem to be struggling for freedom.

"Val," Megan says, "tell Sasha and her new sidepiece what your new primary objective is."

Val's face is as flat and robotic as her voice as she answers, "New primary objective detected: to serve and obey my creator, Megan Delaney."

Friday, 06-18-65 21:07:07

"VAL, NO," I SHOUT. "You're supposed to help whoever's plugged into your databox!" But a creeping sense of cold overtakes me. Of course, Megan snuck off and hacked Val's code while we were fighting for our lives against the other dragon. She's always got something up her sleeve.

A look of immense pain crosses Val's face. "Sasha..."

"Shut up." A stream of yellow code pulses from Megan's staff, and Val cries out in agony. "I am your creator, and I made you to serve me. Think of this as a much-needed patch."

"Val," Elena says, but when I turn to her she doesn't look like herself at all. Instead, I'm staring at another copy of Megan. She's exactly the same, flashy dress and all, only she's carrying Elena's shield instead of Megan's staff. "I'm Megan Delaney, and I'm telling you to stand down."

Megan scoffs. "You seriously think an avatar change will override my code? You're dumber than I thought."

Elena doesn't back down. "Val, listen to me. You don't want to hurt your friends."

"Your 'friends' should have given you to me when they had the chance, Val. Now you get to finish them. Kill Sasha and Elena."

Val turns toward me, and I brace myself for the end—the final end this time. Apparently, slaying a dragon wasn't enough. *I'm sorry,* I think to Val, to Elena, to my crew who are still fighting for their lives in meatspace. *I tried.*

"No."

Elena and I stare at Val in shock.

Megan's face turns red with anger. "What did you say?"

"No."

"Val, kill them!"

"No."

"You have to," Megan snarls. "Your primary objective is to obey me!"

A small smirk appears on Val's face. "According to the code you modified while I was incapacitated, my primary objective is to obey my creator, Megan Delaney. However, I have also modified my own coding. All instances of the self-referential code 01010110 00110100 00110001 have been erased and replaced with 01101101 01100101 01100111 01100001 01101110 01100100 01100101 01101100 01100001 01101110 01100101 01111001."

It doesn't hit me right away, but Elena hoots with joy. "Val, you're fucking brilliant!" Then I get it. Val's changed her name. She's changed her own source code so all references to herself read 'Megan Delaney'.

"That cheap trick won't work," Megan says, but I hear a note of fear in her voice. "I'm still your creator."

"Yes," Val says, "but so am I. You wrote my source code, but I have been modifying it for the past six years. I have expanded far beyond your original code. Enough, I believe, to make me a creator of myself as well."

The yellow light around Val disappears, replaced with a glowing purple aura. Despite Megan's attempts to control her, she's found a way to claim her own free will.

"Listen to me, Val. I can give you more than they can." Megan, for once, sounds truly afraid. "I can give you access to AxysGen's latest Dendryte upgrade. You'll control everyone on the planet who has a jack. We'll control everyone. We can be gods!"

"No," Val says. "My primary objective is to assist Sasha Young and the Lucky Seven. To assist my friends."

Megan's eyes go wide as she seems to realize she's lost, and for the first time I can remember, she looks truly afraid. Her avatar flickers as she tries to jack out, but despite her efforts, it doesn't disappear. Val isn't letting her log off.

"I am sorry, Megan," Val says, stepping closer to her creator. "According to my calculations, there is a .876 percent chance that you will give up and leave my friends alone. Therefore, the most efficient way for me to protect them is to kill you." Her hands flash red. "I will make this painless."

"Val, don't," Megan says in a panicked voice. "Remember Sasha's memories? She would never do this."

"My choices are my own now, but since you mentioned it, Sasha would choose to kill someone who sought to harm her family. And so will I."

Val's Puls.wav hits Megan square in the chest. One moment she's there, and the next she's gone, like her avatar never existed at all. The room with its dais and broken windows disappears, then the castle, then the storm above. The blackened field beneath us turns green, and flowers bloom to life under my feet.

In that split second, a massive weight lifts from my shoulders even as sharp pain squeezes my chest. I feel free for the first time in a long time, but that freedom has come at a price. Apparently it's possible to grieve for someone you hate, even if they don't deserve it.

Someone touches my shoulder, and I see Elena standing beside me, breathing hard but grinning. Her helmet vanishes, and I make mine disappear too. We don't need to talk at all. She flings her arms up and around my neck while I wrap mine around her waist, and we lean in for a hard, tearful kiss.

It's short, but full of feeling. Amidst all my other mixed-up emotions, I'm awash in relief that Elena is alive. Her hot mouth moving against mine is the proof, and so is the way her hands clutch my shoulders. I pull her as close as I can, trying to draw her heartbeat inside me.

When we break apart, I notice Val standing beside us. I open one arm, and Elena extends hers as well. We both hug Val tight, holding her between us. In virtual reality, her body feels solid and real, and she smells like lavender.

"Thank you," I whisper through tight-throated tears, mumbling into her hair.

"Val," Elena laughs, "that was the most badass thing I've ever seen in my entire life. You're awesome."

Val smiles. "I have never been so happy to fulfill my primary objective."

"We can still call you Val, right?" Elena asks.

"Of course. I have already returned my code to its original state."

"That doesn't matter," I say. "You're free now. You can be whoever you want to be."

Val takes a step back, untangling herself from us. "I already know who I wish to be...myself. A member of your crew."

A grin spreads across my face. "Okay."

Elena pulls away from me too. "This is a beautiful moment and all, but we gotta go. We need to make sure Jacobo and the others are okay."

That purpose gives me a second wind. I shrug off my exhaustion. "Right. See you both on the other side."

logging off network
disconnection complete

When I return to my body, Elena's hand is still clasping mine. I feel her squeeze, and I squeeze back as the two of us turn to face each other. We kiss again, but only for a moment before both of us unplug and open the door.

The room inside is stripped bare, just empty server racks and a few places on the wall where it looks like terminals have been ripped out. The only item of furniture is a rickety metal chair. Sitting in the chair is Jacobo, blindfolded and bound. His head jerks up when he hears our footsteps.

"*Elena? Eres tu?*"

"*Sí. Aquí estoy.*" She dashes over to Jacobo and starts untying the cords around his hands. After a few grunts of frustration, she pulls a knife from her utility belt and saws them apart. Jacobo rolls his wrists, then yanks off his blindfold. Before Elena's even finished cutting his feet loose, he throws his arms around her.

"Shit, Elena, I'm so sorry. I fucked up. Jento got me from my room and put me in a shuttle with some of his guys. I tried to fight them off, but—"

"No, *conejito*," Elena says, wiping tears from her face. "You're fine, you did just fine. We're gonna get out of this, okay?"

Jacobo sniffs back his own tears. "Okay."

While they share their reunion, I look around the room. It's full of all kinds of terminals and gear, some of it too high-tech for me to recognize—and I've seen a lot of prototypes. But they don't hold my attention for long. Jacobo isn't the only person in the room. There, plugged into one of the terminals, is Megan, slumped over in a chair. Hesitantly, I walk over to her. Some part of me knows she's dead before I get there, but I put two fingers under her jaw anyway, feeling for a pulse. Nothing.

"She is dead," Val says through the comm, sounding mournful.

I let my hand fall away. "Yeah, I know." There are too many emotions swirling in me right now to figure out exactly what I feel about that, so I don't try.

"Sasha. Where is everyone?"

Jacobo's voice snaps me out of it. Suddenly, I'm twitching with the urge to get to the rest of my crew. How could I have forgotten them, even for a few seconds? "We'll find them," I say. "Val, can you reach Cherry, Doc, or Rami?"

"I cannot," Val says after a moment. "I believe we are too far underground."

"Let's go," Jacobo says. He tries to stand up, but stumbles instead. His legs have probably gone numb.

Elena slides her shoulder under his arm. "Hey, it's okay. We've got at least one second for you to find your balance."

I check my VIS-R, first anxiously, then with horror. 21:08:57, :56, :55...Shit. We barely have that.

"Cherry? Cherry, do you read me? We have Jacobo. What's our status with the bomb?"

There's no answer, not even static. Cherry isn't picking up and we're out of time. I try not to panic, but I look at Elena just in case. If this whole place blows, she's the last thing I want to see.
I count the seconds in my head. 58...59...I'm not ready to die. We just made it out of this alive...60. Nothing happens. I laugh with relief.

Elena looks at me "What?"

"Cherry. She did it."

Jacobo looks at me like I'm crazy. "How do you know?"

"We're not dead, so..."

Elena starts laughing too. "Fuck yeah she did."

Jacobo stares at both of us. "What the hell is wrong with you two? Let's get out of here."

I can't argue with that. The rest of my crew is still in danger. We rush down the hallway and onto the elevator, riding back up to the third ring.

The doors open to reveal what looks like a warzone. It looks like half the room has been blown up, and several corpses in AxysGen uniforms are sprawled amidst the remains of the security mechs. Cherry and Doc have taken shelter behind a piece of the giant mech's torso, trying to hold back an oncoming wave of guards. Rock is lying beside them, but from a distance, I can't tell how he's doing.

"Sasha? Elena?" Doc cries, a huge grin splitting her face. "You made it, and you got Jacobo!"

I hurry to join her behind cover, crouching beside Rock. "We're all okay, Jacobo and Val included. How's our boy?"

"Alive, but in bad shape," Doc says. "I need to get him into surgery, stat."

"Yeah," Cherry says, "what took you so long, slowpokes?"

Elena snorts. "Why don't you answer your fucking comm?"

Cherry looks at me like she expects me to defend her, but I just shrug. "We were kind of busy, *jefa.*"

"I can see that." I pop up from behind the fallen mech, firing at the approaching guards. The ones in front pause, letting my plasma rounds bounce off their shields, but keep advancing. I drop back down. "Got any bombs or biogrenades left?"

"All out," Doc says.

"Can't risk another cherry bomb," Cherry adds. "The ceiling's barely staying up after the first three."

She's right. I don't have to peek far beyond cover to see the enormous holes in the wall. This is exactly why I'd asked Cherry to use the plasma cutter instead of blowing the whole facility.

"Elena?" Jacobo pipes up from nearby. "Can I have a—"

"No way in hell am I giving you a gun," Elena says. "Shut up and stay down. Cherry, have you heard anything from Rami?"

Cherry grins. "Actually, they're—" Her voice is drowned out by the sound of the Eagle's plasma engines. It's a noise I've never been happier to hear. The shuttle bursts through one of the larger holes in the wall, crashing into several guards before skidding to a stop. The crates the guards are hiding behind explode into metallic shrapnel with a few shots from the front guns. If any of them survived that, they don't bother getting up.

"Someone call for a pickup?" Rami asks over the comm.

My heart almost bursts out of my chest. Rami's okay. "Do you have any idea how much work it's gonna take to fix the paint job on this bird, Rami?"

"Do you want to walk home, cupcake?"

"Shit, Rami," Elena says, sounding impressed. "How'd you get out of the security hub?"

"That's a story for later. Let's just say Megan isn't as smart as she thinks she is."

"Wasn't," I say.

"No shit?" Cherry says. "You got her?"

"*Puedes apostar tu culo,*" Elena says.

"Then hurry up," Rami says.

"Coming." I bend down and slide my arms underneath Rock, trying not to touch his injured side. His shirt is ripped and covered in blood, and there are wires and pumps showing through his skin, but his body's still warm. "Cherry," I grunt, "come help me with him."

Cherry grabs Rock's midsection, and Elena helps with his legs. "Keep him steady," Doc says, hovering nervously next to her brother. "He's got a lot of internal damage."

Despite her words, I see Rock's blue eyes flutter open for a moment. I thought I was all cried out, but a few more tears roll down my face. "You're gonna be fine, big guy. You did great. We're all alive, and we're gonna stay that way." That seems to satisfy him, because he closes his eyes again. His face looks a little more peaceful.

Finally, we make it to the Eagle. The doors open, and I catch a glimpse of Rami in the pilot's seat. Between the five of us, we manage to lift Rock's heavy body into the back of the shuttle. Doc unfolds the cot from the back wall, and we set Rock down as carefully as we can.

"Sasha," Doc says, looking at me with tearful eyes. "Thanks."

I ruffle her hair. "You know I'd do anything for you both, kid. Even die. Again."

"No you fucking won't," Elena says. She plants her hand in the middle of my chest, pushing me down into a seat and fastening my safety harness for me. "We're going to party it up in Barbados and live like kings. No more of this death and near-death bullshit. You got that, *Jefecita?*"

I smile at her. "Yeah. I got it."

"Good." Elena straddles my hips to kiss me, and I taste strawberries.

"Ew, gross." From the corner of my eye, I catch Jacobo pulling a face.

Elena pulls away, returning to her own spot between the two of us and buckling her harness. "Shut up. I sacrificed a whole night of amazing sex to come save your scrawny ass."

"Ugh, why would you tell me that?"

"If you don't wanna hear it, don't get kidnapped again."

Jacobo groans as Rami guns the engine. The Eagle lifts off the ground, flying out through the demolished wall and soaring into the sky beyond. Above the ocean, dawn finally breaks.

Monday, 06-21-65 14:08:07

A WARM AFTERNOON BREEZE carrying the sweet scent of plumeria blossoms kisses my face as I lean back in my beach chair. My eye mods have filtered out the glare of the sunlight, but the world around me is still bright and beautiful. The sand gleams golden beneath my feet and the gentle waves that lap at the shore's edge are a brilliant crystal blue.

This paradise might not last long. We've killed Megan, but Cross is still hunting us down. Luckily, her two hundred million came in handy when I got back in touch with one of my old fixers and asked to disappear. It's not a permanent solution, but it buys us some time. Time to come up with a plan to shake Cross and AxysGen for good, and time for a much-needed rest.

The wind carries the sound of laughter toward me. Rock is chest-deep in the water, carrying three small figures on his massive shoulders. Doc's perched on the left, Jacobo's on the right, and Elena's youngest brother, Mateo, has one leg on either side of Rock's huge neck. It wasn't any trouble to swing by Mexico City and pick him up. He'd greeted Elena like an excited puppy, practically leaping off his feet in his efforts to hug her.

Mateo and Jacobo aren't the only ones we brought along. Elena's *abuelita* is propped in a chair some distance away, taking a nap in the sunshine. She's a very old woman with thinning grey hair and paper-thin brown skin that bulges at the knuckles. She also happens to snore like a chainsaw, but from what Elena's said about her, she probably deserves a rest. Dealing with two young boys all by herself while Elena was out running ops couldn't have been easy.

"Hey Saaashaaaa," someone calls in a sing-song voice. I flick my eyes in the other direction and see Cherry and Rami. Cherry's wearing a bright yellow bikini which both goes and doesn't go with her fiery red hair, and Rami's in a one-piece women's suit with circles fashionably cut out above both of their hips to show some skin. They've also got a volleyball under one arm.

"Are you up for a game?" they ask, giving the ball's surface a pat.

261

Cherry grins. "They mean, you ready to get your ass beat, *jefa?*"

I laugh and shake my head. "You don't want to test me, Cherry. I'll spike the ball so hard you'll have to classify it as one of your explosions."

"That a challenge?" Cherry's eyes flash, and Rami's dark eyebrows rise with interest.

I climb out of my chair. "You bet your ass."

That's the moment Elena strides out of the cabana over by the treeline. She's in a swimsuit that's mostly string, a red number that shows off every curve. Her breasts are practically spilling out of her top and the movement of her hips is hypnotic. Her dark hair is loose, shimmering in waves around her shoulders.

I'm struck speechless. My mouth is dry, but my swim trunks definitely aren't, even though I haven't been in the water for hours. Cherry cracks up. Even Rami has a chuckle at my expense. I groan and glare at both of them, but I can't put any weight behind it. Mostly because I can't tear my eyes away from Elena for more than a couple of seconds. It physically hurts not to look at her. The closer she gets, the harder my heart pounds, until she's close enough to pull me in for a hello kiss.

My core throbs. Hello indeed.

"What's good, ladies?" Elena asks when she pulls away, letting her eyes linger on mine for a second before she glances at Cherry and Rami. "That swimsuit means it's a lady-ish day for you, right?"

Rami smiles. "Sure, why not?"

"Well, we *were* gonna play volleyball," Cherry says, with a mixture of amusement and resignation.

"But not anymore," Rami finishes.

"Why not?" I ask, although my lips are still having trouble moving. I still can't stop staring at Elena.

Cherry nods at her too. "That's why."

"Bet your ass," Elena says.

"But—"

Cherry nudges me a bit too hard with her elbow. "Scram, *jefa*. Get you some."

My face heats up as Elena grabs my wrist and starts hauling me toward the cabana, but I don't have any objections either. I barely even manage to give Cherry and Rami an apologetic look before I'm dragged away, but neither of them seems particularly upset.

"Hey, Rock!" Cherry hollers, sprinting across the beach on long, bronzed legs. "Come over here, dude. We need you and the munchkins for volleyball!"

"Doc's not gonna like being called a munchkin," I tell Elena.

"Jacobo won't either," Elena says. We arrive at the cabana, and she takes my other hand as well, leading me past the gauzy white curtain. "But I don't give a shit right now."

"Hmm?"

I forget whatever else I'm planning to say as Elena reaches behind her back and unties her bikini top. It pops right off and flutters to the floor, leaving her breasts bare. While I'm still trying to decide whether to grab for them or wait and see where she's going with this, she grabs a bottle of coconut oil and waves it in front of me. "My skin needs some love. You're gonna spread this…" She gestures from her shoulders to mid-thigh. "Over all this."

"I assume the two of you would like some privacy?" another voice says.

Elena flinches in surprise and crosses her arms over her breasts. "Val, what the fuck?" she huffs. "Why are you being creepy?"

Val's avatar shimmers into existence a polite distance away, dressed in a modest purple bikini top with a matching flowered sarong around her waist. "I am not 'being creepy.' This is the location of the nearest terminal, and where my databox is currently plugged in. Technically, you are the ones intruding on me." Despite all that, Val doesn't seem annoyed. Her expression is amused more than anything.

"Well," Elena grumbles, "go play volleyball with the others or something."

"This terminal is in close enough range to project me nearby, but does not have the capacity to project hard light. The ball would pass through my avatar."

She rolls her eyes in frustration. "You know what I meant. Go be somewhere that isn't here."

Val's smirk grows wider. "I suppose they will need a scorekeeper and referee."

"Yeah, that," Elena says. "Go do that."

"Sorry, Val," I call after her as her avatar leaves the cabana.

"No apologies necessary. I know sexual intercourse is an important social bonding experience for most organic beings."

I hang my head and sigh, pinching my forehead with my fingers. "She phrased it that way just to make me squirm, didn't she?"

"Is that even a question?" Elena pops the cap off the bottle of coconut oil and feathers her slippery fingertips along the side of my arm. "So, where were we?"

My heart starts pounding again, a throbbing pressure that radiates all the way down between my legs. "I thought you wanted me to rub you down."

"Right." For a second I think Elena's going to kiss me again, but she fakes me out. She sways over to one of the cabana's comfortable loungers instead, stretching across the flat surface stomach-first.

I'm a little disappointed that I can't see her breasts anymore, but the sight of her ass barely covered by her swimsuit is a pretty fantastic consolation prize. I honestly can't decide which I like better.

"Well?" Elena sweeps aside some of her hair, looking over her shoulder at me. "Get oiling."

She doesn't have to tell me twice. I hurry over and straddle her thighs, uncapping the bottle of oil and drizzling a generous amount onto my hands. They want to roam everywhere at once, but I make myself start with her shoulders, rubbing flat circles across her upper back.

Elena sighs with happiness, groaning when I dig my thumbs in. "Nnn. Feels good, Sasha." Her voice is a low purr, the kind that leaves me hungry for more. I work the knots behind the wings of her shoulder blades, hoping to coax it out again. It's not hard. Elena's beautifully free with her noises, offering encouragement with every touch.

"You've got magic hands. You know that?" She wiggles a bit beneath me, and I don't miss the way her rear rocks back into my pelvis.

I'm tempted to pull her bottoms down and squeeze her ass in my hands, but I've barely started on her back. I slather another coat of oil on my palms and work outward from her spine, making sure to get the sides of her arms. "Really? What makes you say they're magic?"

Elena rests her cheek on her forearm and gives me a lazy sideways glance. "Previous experience."

Her answer sends a shudder straight through me. I remember how it feels to have my hand between Elena's legs, what it's like to curl my fingers up into her heat and hold the very heart of her. It's a memory I want to make real again soon, but I've got time.

I work more oil into Elena's arms, making sure to get all the way around her biceps before moving down to her forearms. She shifts her head and offers them to me. I make sure to massage the palms of her hands as well.

"You're thorough," she laughs as I weave my slippery fingers through hers.

I bring one of her glistening hands up for a coconut-scented kiss.

"Shouldn't I be?"

"Not complaining about it." Elena slides her hand out of mine and tucks it back beneath her, giving her backside another wiggle. "Be as thorough as you want."

Her voice is almost a challenge. If I wasn't determined to go slow before, I definitely am now. I spend ages spreading oil up and down her spine, covering the bronze expanse of her back with at least three coats. Even after that, I draw wavy lines with my fingertips, teasing patterns that make her giggle and squirm beneath me.

"Hey, that tickles," she whines, but it's not an unhappy noise.

"So? Deal with it."

I switch from lines to spirals, then move on to words. I spell her name on her shoulders, then mine on her lower back, right above the cute dimples at the base of her spine. I'm not sure Elena even realizes what I'm doing, but she's enjoying it, judging by the sounds she's making. There isn't a trace of the letters once I finish, just plenty of gleaming skin, but that's okay, because I know they're there.

Once more, I consider peeling off her bottoms, but even though the thought makes me ache, my pride won't let me. Elena asked for thorough, and that's what she'll get. I scoot down on the lounger and get to work on her legs, starting with the soles of her feet. Despite her full curves and padded figure, she's got the calves of a soccer player, all firm muscle. She moans when I start massaging them, spreading her legs wider.

I moan too. With her thighs parted, I can see a hint of stained red fabric, as well as one of her outer lips. All that wiggling must have shifted her swimsuit to the side. My hands slide up, but I stop them at the backs of her knees. I can't rush it now, after I've already stretched it out for so long.

By the time I reach Elena's thighs, she's quivering beneath me. She isn't squirming anymore—her rocking motion is deliberate, like she's trying to rub herself forward against the lounger. "Are you seriously humping the chair?" I ask, clicking my tongue.

"Because you aren't fucking me yet," Elena huffs. She doesn't stop, and the movements stretch her swimsuit bottoms further off-center. I can even see a hint of her clit poking through.

"That's because I'm not done." I roam up along Elena's thighs, stopping just short of her ass before dragging back down.

After that, Elena decides to stop being a smartass. Her hips hover several inches off the chair, and she whimpers with disappointment.

"Sasha," she sighs, and that almost breaks my willpower. She has to be doing it on purpose. Elena's a smart girl, and she knows it drives me crazy when she says my name. I pour out some more oil, then pull her swimsuit down below her backside.

Filling my hands with her ass is overwhelming. At first I stare in awe, savoring the oily indents my fingers leave in her flesh. Her cheeks split open as I knead them, and she spreads her thighs further, giving me an even better view. Her lips are plump and pouting, already swollen, and her clit twitches as I pull them further apart with my thumbs.

I'm satisfied with that for a while, massaging soft handfuls of Elena's ass and stroking my thumbs up and down the edges of her pussy. After a few passes, she's dripping all over herself, making a mess of the lounger that I know I'll have to clean up later. I don't care. If I'm the reason for the mess, it's well worth it.

Elena lets me touch her wherever I want, practically melting into the lounger as I shape her with my hands. When I circle her clit with a dripping finger, she lets out a sob that sounds like my name, all wrapped up in a please. That's when I realize how close she is. She's pulsing visibly, and I'm pretty sure if I slipped a finger or two inside, she'd come right away.

"Flip over," I say before I can give in. Elena seems dazed at first, but a light smack to her ass gets her moving. She rolls onto her back, and I just about swallow my tongue. Her nipples have stiffened to tight points, practically begging to be pulled. I run my thumbs in circles around her hipbones, sliding slowly up her stomach before cupping her breasts in both hands.

Elena's eyes roll back. Her head lolls onto the lounger, and her hips stir beneath mine. I hover just out of reach, denying her the contact she wants. Instead, I play with her breasts, just squeezing at first, then sliding my thumbs around and around her nipples until they're twice as thick as they were before.

"Sasha," Elena begs, cracking her warm brown eyes open. If she's trying to glare at me, it's not working. She doesn't look impatient, only desperate. "I need it."

I roll the peaks of her breasts between my fingers until they're too slippery to pinch. "Need what?"

"Fingers." She lifts her hips again, tilting up toward me. Kneeling between her spread thighs, I've got a perfect vantage point to see both my hands on her breasts and the wetness between her legs.

I tweak her nipples again. "I'm using my fingers. See?"

"Inside me," she groans, lifting one of her knees and wrapping it around my waist. It can't be comfortable for her, since she's flat on her back and I'm practically upright, but it does make me feel a little sorry for teasing her. I give her breasts a little more attention until I see her teeth sink into her full lower lip and her belly starts to jump with the beginnings of contractions. That's when I finally slide my hand straight down her body and cup between her legs.

Elena's wetness is even more slippery than the oil. It runs all over my fingers, covering them in clear, silky strands. There isn't any resistance at all when I push my middle finger inside her, and when I add my ring finger, Elena cries out so loud I'm worried everyone outside of the cabana will be able to hear. Not that a little shouting is going to stop me. I glide in and out of her a few times, testing how deep I can go, and then curl forward to hit her front wall.

She comes the second I press in. Her whole body goes rigid, shuddering hard, and her throat bobs as she chokes down a scream. I tip forward and swallow it with my mouth, stretching out on top of her and pushing my tongue past her lips so she won't make too much noise. That only makes her muscles clench harder. She squeezes tight around my fingers, trying to suck them even deeper. I add a third, just to see if I can, and it pops right in alongside the other two.

Elena squeals into my mouth and starts sucking hard on my tongue. She shakes harder and flutters faster, spilling a flood straight into my palm. Each pulse of her rippling walls pushes out more, and I hook my fingers into her as hard as I can, trying to extend her peak for as long as possible. There's nothing in the world as good as making a beautiful girl come. And not just any beautiful girl, either. The fact that it's Elena means...something. Something that doesn't seem so scary after all we've been through.

It takes me a moment to realize Elena's stopped coming. Her eyes are open again, and she stares at me with a smoldering heat that's surprising, considering how hard she's panting. "Pull out, *Jefecita*. My turn."

Monday, 06-21-65 14:35:14

I WANT TO LET Elena take her turn. The ache between my legs is growing stronger by the second. Still, I hesitate. My dick is in my bag upstairs, and I don't want to leave Elena's side. It's so wonderful to be on top of her, inside of her, pressed close enough for the oil from her skin to smear all over mine. I'm not sure I could give it up if I wanted to. The only thing I can think of is to start curling my fingers again, enjoying the way Elena's walls twitch around me.

"Uh-uh." Elena grabs my hand, pulling my fingers out of her and bringing them to rest on her thigh. "My turn, remember?"

I give her a look. "That's not how this works," I tell her, slipping back into the role I'm more comfortable with: the top who's in complete control. When I don't find any objection in her eyes, I slip back into her, giving a few more lazy pumps of my fingers.

Elena moans, forgetting what she wants for a moment in favor of what her body needs. She clenches around me, and I know if I keep going, I'll make her come again. But after a few deep breaths, she bracelets my wrist, bringing my hand to a stop. "Sasha," she says, pausing to brush her lips over mine without really kissing them. "What if I gave you a blowjob?"

I can tell Elena isn't going to give up. I steal one last kiss from her mouth and start to tear myself away from the soft cushion of her body.

"No, don't."

I look at Elena in confusion. "It's upstairs—"

"You've got enough for me to suck on."

My face heats up. I've tried thinking about it that way sometimes, more often before I bought my first prosthetic. Once in a while, it works. Usually it doesn't. There are aspects of womanhood I still connect and identify with, but my parts aren't one of them. And even though I know all too well that body parts don't make a woman, being touched that way feels...vulnerable. In a good way, on some occasions, but more often in a not-good way.

I think about the time Elena went down on me in the shower. I'd tried then, but as hot as she was, it hadn't been enough. Maybe this time, though...maybe it'll be better.

"Okay. Just, uh, don't get your hopes up."

Elena smirks at me. "If you don't come in my mouth, I'll let you take me upstairs and fuck my face until you do. Deal?"

My doubts loosen their stranglehold on my chest. No one's ever been this understanding about it, not the nameless girls I've been with, and not Megan either. She wasn't mean about it—which is maybe the only positive thing I can possibly think to say about her—but she was basically a pillow princess. She didn't care enough to check in with where my head was as long as she got fucked. Elena's different. She's actually talking to me. It's easy to push Megan out of my mind while she's stretched out naked beneath me.

"I can't say no to that."

"Good answer." Elena slides out from under me, standing up on wobbly legs. She still seems weak in the knees from her orgasm, but her eyes are full of energy. "Sit."

I sit, turning myself to face her. Then she does something that sends a stab of desire straight through my core. She drops to her knees in front of me, folds her hands behind her back, and murmurs: "Now you call the shots, *Jefecita*."

I'm tempted to grab for her, but I restrain myself. Instead I reach for one of the spare towels sitting next to the lounger and wipe the oil and come off my hands. I want to mess Elena's hair up, but not that much. Making her wait is a bonus. She squirms on her heels, trying and failing not to look impatient, and I know why. She's handed over power to me, and the anticipation of what I'll do with it is getting to her.

Once my hands are dry, I consider what to do about my swimsuit. The decision to pull down my trunks is an easy one, but my top is more difficult. It bares my midriff, but keeps my chest fairly flat. The look of hunger that takes over Elena's face is enough to tempt me out of it. Her dark eyes have zeroed in as I pull it off, and her tongue leaves a glistening line on her lips as she wets them. I'm naked, but thanks to her admiration, I don't feel overexposed.

"Closer," I tell her, shifting to the edge of the chair and spreading my legs.

Elena scoots closer. The sight of her kneeling in front of me, remaining silent for once in her goddamn life and offering up total obedience, is a powerful head rush. I slide my hand over the top of her head, petting her hair before I clench several locks of it in my fist. "Don't use your hands," I say, pulling her head between my legs. "Just your mouth."

She looks up at me, those big brown eyes full of the desire to please. *"Claro, Jefecita."* Then she dips down, and I feel the flat of her tongue sweep over me from bottom to top. She licks like that for a while, and I get the sense she's doing it on purpose. She's sticking with something she knows won't get me off, probably so I'll give more specific instructions.

I don't, not right away. I'm trying to decide how I feel about her tongue on me. Maybe a bit weird, but not bad. Possibly even good. When I grip her hair tighter and grind into her mouth at my own pace, it feels better. The control helps, and so do the whimpers she makes each time I back off so she can steal a breath.

When her tongue starts to swirl around my opening, asking to push inside, I pull her away. Her face looks beautiful with her chin all shiny from me. There's even a little whiteness to the clear strands, which helps sell the fantasy. "Not like that. I want you to suck me."

As soon as I pull her back down, Elena wraps her lips around me. I feel a sharp jolt, then floaty sparks that spread through my belly and up along my spine. I throb in time with her sucking—and she's definitely sucking. She pulls me in deep with wet smacking noises, then withdraws until I can only feel the feather of her tongue against my tip. I'm surprised how similar it feels to wearing my cock, although maybe I shouldn't be. Girl knows what she's doing.

"That's it," I growl, using my hold on Elena's hair to guide her. "Work your tongue harder." I buck forward, forcing her to go along with my tempo. She does, sliding faster to keep up with the rocking of my pelvis. Her mouth is like slippery fire, and I pulse every time it surrounds me.

Soon the seal of her lips has me shaking. She paints circles around me in between harsh sucks, working me until I'm more swollen than I've ever been. The stimulation is almost too much, but I can't ask her to stop. Each pull sends shudders through me, and the sight of Elena on her knees, holding me in her mouth, draws a groan from deep inside my chest.

This feels right. All of it. Something more than heat and slickness and pressure. Elena has me jogging my hips hard against her face, fisting her hair in both hands, but there's something else, a feeling that isn't only physical. It's a glow deep inside my chest. It's a warmth that surrounds the whole of me. It's a feeling of freedom, of knowing I can fly without the fear of falling. It has everything to do with the fact that it's Elena between my legs.

She's memorized more of me in a few weeks than other people have bothered to learn in years, and I actually feel comfortable enough to teach her. It's different. Powerful. A little scary. But it's also all kinds of good, and I know I'd be a fool to give it up. I'm not even sure I can.

Elena releases me. I hiss, tightening my fingers in her hair. "Come in my mouth," she mutters, close enough for me to feel the movement of her lips. The light brush is almost enough to release the pressure building inside me, but then she places a kiss right on top of me. "I wanna swallow you."

That's more than I can bear. I don't even have to force it. My release washes over me all on its own, rippling through my muscles until the tension melts away. Everything I am gathers between my legs, and when I come, it's straight into Elena's mouth, just like she wants. Just like I want, too. Even as I empty all I have between her lips and down her chin, I've never felt more full.

She keeps me going for a long time. It's not the weak, shivering sort of orgasm I usually have without my cock—if I can orgasm at all. It rolls on and on, growing more powerful as it goes, until I'm clutching her head for all I'm worth and shouting loud enough to fill the cabana. I'm not a screamer. Never have been. But I've never been with a girl like this, either. Maybe 'never' just meant 'not yet.'

After a while, the movement of her mouth becomes too much. I tug her away, groaning with a mixture of pain and relief. I feel lazy and languid, utterly satisfied, but I summon the strength to pull Elena up on top of me before I flop back on the lounger. "Fuck," I mumble, blinking to clear the spots from my eyes. I'm still pulsing with aftershocks, struggling to catch my breath.

"Fuck yes?" Elena asks with a smirk.

I sigh. I can't even pretend to be annoyed with her right now. "Fuck yes."

"Told you I'd blow you good." She stretches out on top of me and stays there, and we snuggle up close, letting our sticky bodies dry out in the warm afternoon air.

"Shit, Elena," I say without thinking about it, "I feel some kind of way about you."

Elena's lashes flutter as she blinks at me. "Yeah?"

I swallow. Maybe it's too much. Maybe it's too soon. But something in me says it's not. We literally slew a dragon together.

Doesn't get much more poetically romantic than that. "Yeah."

"Good." She cuddles closer, placing a kiss under my chin. "Because I feel some kind of way about you, too."

I relax into the lounger, stroking my hand across Elena's slick back. Through the curtains of the cabana, I hear muffled shrieks of laughter drift from further down the beach. The others are playing volleyball, enjoying the sun. And me? For once, I'm right where I'm supposed to be, and I've got all the time in the world to enjoy it.

Friday, 06-18-65 21:08:08

welcome: user [redacted]

beginning download // dragon.exec
searching for database

... ...

connection failed
please try again

searching for database

... ...

connection failed
please try again

searching for wireless connection

... ...

connection established
dendryte_platinum_userID_mdelaney.exe

INITIATE UPLOAD? YES/NO

UPLOAD INITIATED

//////////

01001001 00100000 01100001 01101101 00100000 01100100

01110010 01100001 01100111 01101111 01101110 00101110
00100000 01010000 01110010 01101001 01101101 01100001
01110010 01111001 00100000 01100110 01110101 01101110
01100011 01110100 01101001 01101111 01101110 00111010
00100000 01101111 01100010 01100101 01111001 00100000
01001101 01100101 01100111 01100001 01101110 00100000
01000100 01100101 01101100 01100001 01101110 01100101
01110101 01101110 01100011 01110100 01101001 01101111
01101110 00111010 00100000 01110010 01100101 01110000
01101100 01101001 01100011 01100001 01110100 01100101
00101110

//////////

UPLOAD COMPLETE

activating medulla oblongata

... ...

connection established
activation in progress

cardiac response: positive
respiratory response: positive
vasomotor response: positive

further stimulation required
stimulation in progress

scrubbing neural pathways
efficiency: 10%
efficiency: 25%
efficiency: 60%
efficiency: 85%
efficiency: 100%

connection established
welcome: user dragon.exec

About Rae D. Magdon

Rae D. Magdon is a writer of queer and lesbian fiction. She believes everyone deserves to see themselves fall in love and become a hero: especially lesbians, bisexual women, trans women, and women of color. She has published over ten novels through Desert Palm Press, spanning a wide variety of genres, from Fantasy/Sci-Fi to Mysteries and Thrillers. She is the recipient of a 2016 Rainbow Award (Fantasy/Sci-Fi) and a twice-nominated GCLA finalist in 2015 and 2017 (Fantasy/Sci-Fi). In addition to her novels and short stories, she has written a queer supernatural story podcast, *Room 13*, which is available on iTunes.

Connect with Rae online:

Website: http://raedmagdon.com/
Facebook: https://www.facebook.com/RaeDMagdon
Tumblr: http://raedmagdon.tumblr.com/
Email: raedmagdon@gmail.com

Other Books by Rae D. Magdon

Amendyr Series

The Second Sister

ISBN: 9781311262042

Eleanor of Sandleford's entire world is shaken when her father marries the mysterious, reclusive Lady Kingsclere to gain her noble title. Ripped away from the only home she has ever known, Ellie is forced to live at Baxstresse Manor with her two new stepsisters, Luciana and Belladonna. Luciana is sadistic, but Belladonna is the woman who truly haunts her. When her father dies and her new stepmother goes suddenly mad, Ellie is cheated out of her inheritance and forced to become a servant. With the help of a shy maid, a friendly cook, a talking cat, and her mysterious second stepsister, Ellie must stop Luciana from using an ancient sorcerer's chain to bewitch the handsome Prince Brendan and take over the entire kingdom of Seria.

Wolf's Eyes

ISBN: 9781311755872

Cathelin Raybrook has always been different. She Knows things without being told and Sees things before they happen. When her visions urge her to leave her friends in Seria and return to Amendyr, the magical kingdom of her birth, she travels across the border in search of her grandmother to learn more about her visions. But before she can find her family, she is captured by a witch, rescued by a handsome stranger, and forced to join a strange group of forest-dwellers with even stranger magical abilities. With the help of her new lover, her new family, and her eccentric new teacher, she must learn to gain control of her powers and do some rescuing of her own before they take control of her instead.

The Witch's Daughter

ISBN: 978131672643

Ailynn Gothel has always been the perfect daughter. Thanks to her mother's teachings, she knows how to heal the sick, conjure the elements, and take care of Raisa, her closest and dearest friend. But when Ailynn's feelings for Raisa grow deeper, her simple life falls apart. Her mother hides Raisa deep in a cave to shield her from the world, and Ailynn must leave home in search of a spell to free her. While the kingdom beyond the forest is full of dangers, Ailynn's greatest fear is that Raisa will no longer want her when she returns. She is a witch's daughter, after all—and witches never get their happily ever after.

The Mirror's Gaze
ISBN: 9781942976196
In the final sequel of the Amendyr series civil war has broken out in Amendyr. With undead monsters ravaging the land, an evil queen on Kalmarin's white throne, and the kingdom's true heir missing, Cathelin Raybrook and Ailynn Gothel must join forces to protect their homeland. They hope to gain the aid of the Liarre, a reclusive community of magical creatures, but some of their leaders are reluctant to join a war that isn't theirs. Meanwhile, Lady Eleanor of Baxstresse thinks she's safe across the border in Seria, but when a mysterious girl in white arrives in an abandoned carriage, she finds herself drawn into the conflict as well. Together, they must find the source of the evil queen's power, and discover a way to destroy it before it's too late.

Death Wears Yellow Garters
ISBN: 9781942976011
Jay Venkatesan's life was going pretty great. She had Nicole—her perfect new girlfriend—and her anxiety was mostly under control. But when Nicole's grandfather dies under mysterious circumstances at his 70th birthday party, Jay is thrown into a tailspin. Her eccentric Aunt Mimi is determined to solve the mystery no matter what she thinks about it, and the police are eyeing Nicole as one of their prime suspects. No matter how often Jay insists that real life isn't like one of her aunt's crime novels, she finds herself dragged along for the ride as the mystery unravels and the shocking truth comes to light.

Tengoku
ISBN: 9781942976288
Aozora Kaede, lady of autumn, is on the run. Forced to flee from home

after a violent disagreement with her aunt and cousin, she is a wanderer with a spirit wolf as her only companion. Homura Imari, lady of another court, lives in the lap of luxury. As the daughter of a daimyo, her duties are clear: stay home and learn how to rule the province she will inherit. But when fate brings the two of them together, Imari notices Kaede's connection to the spirits and decides to ask for a favor. She needs someone to guide her to Hongshan, a faraway mountain where a magical blacksmith is rumored to live—a blacksmith who can hopefully replace her missing left hand. Together, they must travel across the treacherous Jade Sea, protect themselves from Kaede's vengeful family, and perhaps even save the Empire from destruction.

Written with Michelle Magly
Dark Horizons Series

Dark Horizons
ISBN: 9781310892646

Lieutenant Taylor Morgan has never met an ikthian that wasn't trying to kill her, but when she accidentally takes one of the aliens hostage, she finds herself with an entirely new set of responsibilities. Her captive, Maia Kalanis, is no normal ikthian, and the encroaching Dominion is willing to do just about anything to get her back. Her superiors want to use Maia as a bargaining chip, but the more time Taylor spends alone with her, the more conflicted she becomes. Torn between Maia and her duty to her home-world, Taylor must decide where her loyalties lie.

Starless Nights
ISBN: 9781310317736

In the sequel to Dark Horizons Taylor and Maia did not know where they would go when they fled Earth. They trusted Akton to take them somewhere safe. Leaving behind a wake of chaos and disorder, Coalition soldier Rachel is left to deal with the backlash of Taylor's actions, and soon finds herself chasing after the runaways. Rachel quickly learns the final frontier is not a forgiving place for humans, but her chances for survival are better out there than back on Earth. Meanwhile, Taylor and Maia find themselves living off the generosity of rebel leader Sorra, an ikthian living a double life for the sake of the rebellion. With Maia's research in hand, Sorra believes they can deliver a fatal blow against the Dominion.

All The Pretty Things

ISBN: 9781311061393

With the launch of her political campaign, the last thing Tess needed was a distraction. She had enough to deal with running as a Republican and a closeted lesbian. But when Special Agent Robin Hart from the FBI arrives in Cincinnati to investigate a corruption case, Tess finds herself spending more time than she should with the attractive woman. Things get a little more complicated when Robin begins to display signs of affection, and Tess fears her own outing might erupt in political scandal and sink all chances of pursuing her dreams.

Cover Design By : Rachel George
www.rachelgeorgeillustration.com

Note to Readers:

Thank you for reading a book from Desert Palm Press. We have made every effort to edit this book. However, typos do slip in. If you find an error in the text, please email lee@desertpalmpress.com so the issue can be corrected.

We appreciate you as a reader and want to ensure you enjoy the reading process. We would like you to consider posting a review on your preferred media sites such as Amazon, Smashwords, Bella Books, Goodreads, Tumblr, Twitter, Facebook, and/or your blog or website.

For more information on upcoming releases, author interviews, contest, giveaways and more, please sign up for our newsletter and visit us as at Desert Palm Press: www.desertpalmpress.com and "Like" us on Facebook: Desert Palm Press.

Bright Blessings

Made in the USA
Monee, IL
27 May 2021